BURNERS

BOB MAYER

FIRST FIG

My candle burns at both ends;
It will not last the night.
But ah, my foes, and oh, my friends
It gives a lovely light!
Edna St. Vincent Millay

HUNDREDS OF YEARS IN THE FUTURE, AFTER THE CHAOS

Grace would be dead in thirty-one days, but at least she had thirty days of Heaven to look forward to before she expired.

If she could get back to hive in time.

She forced herself to walk slowly down the wide, tree-cordoned road leading to the Wave. A difficult thing for a burner: slow.

"My candle burns at both ends," she whispered to herself, the words etched into her consciousness from the first days in the womb of hive. A comfort in this most uncomfortable of endeavors.

She halted abruptly as a figure scurried out from under the trees.

"Who are you?" the man asked.

She vaguely recognized him, the Evermore who worked in the Oval, personal assistant to the Person, who ruled the Sound. How he recognized her was another matter. Why he was here, as she was trying to leave Island, a much more worrisome matter.

"I am Millay of the People," Grace said, trying to put as much disdain, command, and dismissiveness into her tone as she could. Mostly failing since all three were foreign to a burner. "How dare you question me?"

"Because you are *not* People. I have been watching you." He stepped farther into the road, the dimmed streetlights of Island pushing back the dark enough to hint at his features. A fringe of white hair around his otherwise wrinkled, bald skull. His face looked folded in on itself, as if the years had piled pressure on his forehead, down toward his chin. His eyes were little beady black spots peering out through folds of flesh. "There is no record of you in Dealer."

Grace slid her left hand under the vest she wore over her white coverall, fingers curling around the leather-wrapped handle of her scraper. She shouldn't have brought it here with her; a sure confirmation of this creature's accusation. With her right hand, she tapped the white card dangling on the gold chain around her neck. "I am People."

"Do you know who I am?" the man demanded.

"Some Evermore who works in the Oval," Grace said, looking past him, down the road leading to the water's edge and the docked Wave. Beyond, across the water, was the City. Its towers and buildings weren't as grand or as clean as here in Island, but were impressive nonetheless, even though it was obvious some had been badly damaged during the Chaos and imperfectly repaired; some even abandoned.

"I am not just *some* Evermore," he said.

Grace pointed to the Wave. "I must be on my way."

"People rarely go to City," he said. "And not at night."

"People go where they want."

He took a step closer and peered up at her.

Grace was tall, just an inch under six feet. Her body was lean, even though she'd bulked up for the switch, trading on the black market for extra 'tein to gain the pounds her sister could never lose, even though Millay was slender too. For a People.

There's a difference.

Her face was all angles, framed by short brown hair. Her sister had cut hers a year ago in preparation for the switch. Apparently burner look was something of a fad in Island.

Indulgence in something of which they knew nothing.

Short hair wasn't just a necessity in hive because of all the machinery; no burner would want to waste time on the maintenance of long hair; it was chopped off, quickly and efficiently with a pair of shears.

Her eyes were ice blue, the same as her sister's and Grace knew others focused on the eyes, missing details, and that had helped in the deception of the switch.

Until now.

"I am Claude," the Evermore said. "Personal assistant to the Person. You have had the discreet attention of the Person for a few weeks. Which means you have had my attention."

He had a green card around his neck, the countdown to his Deathday etched in black on it. He reached out and flicked the white card around her neck, pure white, blank. "This is *not* yours. So who are you?"

"My card says who I am," Grace said, a truth she could muster, although she wasn't wearing *her* card.

"That card you wear—" Claude began, but sputtered, tried to regroup to say the impossible—"it does not exist."

Grace took a step back. " Of course it does." *Of course it did*, she thought. It was Millay's.

Confusion rippled along the lines of Claude's face. "It's real, but it doesn't exist. That can't be. Dealer knows all." Claude lifted his hand and two figures loomed out from underneath the trees, metal feet thumping the ground.

Dealers. Grace froze in mid-breath.

"Why is the Person interested in you?" Claude demanded. He reached out and grabbed her hand, the one not cradling her scraper. "Your skin." His fingers ran over the calluses. Years of scraping the 'tein vats didn't go away in a few weeks. "You work with these hands. You're a burner."

Grace slashed with the scraper, but the Evermore had already started to retreat as the two Dealers approached. He ducked and the tip of the blade drew blood across one cheek.

Grace turned and ran.

Three determined strides.

Then slammed in the back by a Dealer's stunner.

Darkness.

Because she didn't expect to die later that evening, Millay's biggest concern was that she was late, a foreign concept to a person who rarely had deadlines.

Millay was jingle-jangled, a term she'd learned in hive. She whispered a prayer to Dealer for guidance as she gingerly made her way along the old trail. There was no moon and the lights from hive flickered only so far into the bleakness that surrounded the buildings. The night sky was overcast, as it almost always was here at hive. The gray had been almost unbearable these past weeks, one of many unbearable things. She'd always seen the clouds from a distance, across the water, well beyond City and City Edge, hovering over where she'd known hive—and her sister—was, and not paid much attention. It had never occurred to her to wonder what it must be like to live underneath them, day in and day out, rarely seeing the sun.

She came to a gulch and slid down on her butt, holding her card tight against her chest even though it was on a steel chain. She corrected herself; it wasn't her card, it was Grace's card. It was the same size and shape as her own card, but it felt different. Her card was something she'd never really noticed, but Grace's felt heavy, a weight that made it impossible to breath late at night when Millay accepted what the red color and changing black number on it truly meant.

Millay pulled herself up the far side of the gulch. Through the stunted trees, she saw the lights of her sister's hive, which she'd just left. Her sister's home. It looked like a slice off the edge of a sphere;

round base, gentle curve upward to twelve stories high. But the base of each building in this part of hive covered many acres. Similar shaped buildings also housed work, where burners toiled at their various assignments. And there were all the other clusters of hives arcing left and right around City Edge, each with their own particular role in production. It was a necklace of resigned desperation around the eastern edge of the Sound. Despite the late hour, all hives were lit, not just out of the windows, but powerful lights flickering here and there, so that burners could go to work and back. Twelve hours on, twelve hours off, shifts off-set six hours so that someone was always working and there was continuity. Every day.

It wasn't the light though that made had her head throb in pain; it was the noise. Always noise. hive was never quiet; more accurately, burners were never quiet. The music and the Stream vid were always loud and she could hear voices and laughter. Excited manic laughter that had filled her nights for the past four weeks and kept her awake. She thought of the quiet in the place she'd left a month ago and to which she was going back. She briefly wondered how Grace handled the noise, but snuffed the image as quickly as it flickered: burners knew nothing different. But now Grace did know different and Millay wondered, not for the first time since they'd done this foolish thing, whether she had done her sister a disservice by letting her go to Island and be among People. Because now her sister had experienced different also.

But what did it matter, Millay immediately thought? Grace went to Heaven tomorrow and it would all be different for her. Millay imagined Heaven must be very similar to Island, which caused a surge of guilt because Millay had then been in a version of Heaven ever since Dealing Day and Grace would only get thirty days. 'Three zero', she corrected herself automatically which caused her to smile sadly at how much she'd immersed herself into burner. But the smile didn't last long. She had to get to City Edge to meet Grace and swap cards, and then pass through City, and take the Wave home to Island.

Millay heard chanting and recognized the calls of a game of tracers. She paused at the edge of the dead trees and peered out. In the reflected light from a hive, a crowd of several hundred burners were watching two teams, a dozen on each side, scramble, duck and dodge through a field of broken concrete and debris, trying to hit each other with their guns. Their only protection from the tracers the weapons fired were hartgards and eyegards, and those were only provided because burners had to work and beating hearts and intact eyeballs were requirements for that. It was forbidden by Code for a burner to kill another burner, because that meant there was one less set of hands to do the work that Dealer decreed needed to be done.

A life for a life was one of the most basic elements of Code.

Millay wondered if she should move farther south to avoid the game, but City Edge was so far away and, more importantly, she'd made a promise about the time to Grace. It had taken longer than expected to leave hive, mainly because she'd had to say good-bye to Haydn and that had proven much harder than she could have imagined after knowing someone for only a couple of weeks. He'd insisted on coming with her, escorting her, but she'd insisted he not. He was not a man who took 'no' easily and finally she'd had to sneak out under a pretense, promising to be right back so he could go with her.

She was regretting that decision now. Unlike most burners, Haydn was steady and calm, a rock in the middle of a turbulent storm.

She came out of the trees and skirted the rear of the audience, but they didn't see her because their focus was on the game. She hadn't understood it when she first arrived, and still really didn't. Deliberately cause pain to each other? Run around when they worked so hard that rest was such a blessed relief? It made absolutely no sense and she'd never bothered to watch a match.

One of the players screamed and Millay flinched. He'd been too slow and gotten hit. And being close to it for the first time, Millay finally began to grasp the purpose of the game: move slow and you got hurt. The screaming and cursing lasted for half a minute, until the tracer expended its electrical shock into his nervous system and he was back in the game.

Millay kept moving but then halted, a chill slithering up her spine. What was it? Nothing here, but something there, out there. Grace? She tried to focus on it, but the feeling was already gone. *Nerves*, Millay thought. Thirty days in hive would cause any People to be on edge.

Millay looked up at hive, bubbling up from the ground. She tried to determine her sister's plexi and wished she could see clearly enough to know if Haydn was there on the other side, staring out, missing her.

She imagined he was. She wanted to believe he was. He was so different from any man of the People she'd ever been with. So intense, so focused on every single moment, you could tell his mind was never elsewhere. Wherever he was, whoever he was with, he was all there. He'd overwhelmed her with his passion, an unexpected twist to this ploy. And, surprisingly, he took almost nothing seriously, treating each day as if it were some joke Dealer had dealt, to be laughed at and reveled in; another unusual trait in a burner.

Millay scampered up a block of concrete, rather than push through the crowd. She counted floors and then tried to guess which one was her sister's cubby, reversing the dismal view she'd had for the past month. Was Haydn looking out toward City Edge where he knew she was heading? Had he forgiven her for sneaking away? She could not imagine him holding a grudge and—

When the errant tracer hit her chest she was so stunned, she barely felt it, which was odd since it was designed to cause pain. She didn't even cry out, sliding down off the block, both hands on her chest, one still holding the card. The other was over her heart, feeling the metal dart pulsing bolts of electricity into her. She tried to rip it off, but the tiny claws were designed to hold on until the charge was finished; punishment for being too slow.

She fell to her knees, then on her side. The pain was coming now, searing into her heart. She twisted her head, looking up past the gathering burners toward the stars that weren't visible.

Grace came to consciousness with a dark figure looming over her.

"You've got to run," a man's voice insisted, a voice that was vaguely familiar to her. "I can't keep Claude at bay much longer. I'm sure he's already informed Dealer that I kicked him out of here."

Grace blinked and recognized him: the Person, the man in charge of Sound. Of their entire world. She'd seen him in the Stream, making speeches. She sat up. Looking past him, she could see perfectly clear windows and stars indicating she was high up in the Capitol building.

"I am Andrew of the People," he said. He had thick hair with a touch of gray at the temples, worry lines around his eyes. A solid face, not gaunt like a burner's.

Grace was trying to get oriented, trying to understand this sudden change. Her hands fumbled for the white card she'd worn for the past month around her neck, the lie. It was gone.

"Where—" she began, but he hushed her with a finger to her lips.

"Your card, your sister's card, is gone. Claude took it. There isn't time to explain, and, frankly, I can't tell you what I don't know. And that's a good thing, trust me." His fingers wrapped her hand around a small ball, the surface soft. "Once you get out of here, into the open, squeeze this; you'll feel when it's activated. It's a tracker. Hold it in front of you. It will pulse twice when you're going in the right direction. The pulses get closer together as you get closer to the destination until you're there. Follow where it leads. There will be answers then. Don't press it while still inside this building or the tunnels or Dealer will find you. Wait until you're outside." He pulled her to her feet and pointed at a door. "The service shaft. It will take you down to a tunnel that leads to the industrial Wave. But you can't take any Wave without a card. And if you try to hide on one, the Dealers will find you. Turn left on the shore. Activate the tracker. Follow it."

Grace was trying to think, to ask questions, but she was burner, and burners didn't ask questions, especially of a People, most especially not of the Person.

He was pulling her along. As they approached, the doors slid open. He pushed her in the large, dingy gray elevator, pausing in the space where the doors would close. He reached with both hands and gently cupped her face, looking into her eyes. A part of her noted how soft the skin was on his palms.

"You are important, Grace. Your sister is important. The two of you are the Prime. And I don't even know what that is or how you and her can be that. I don't know why you did this switch but it upset the Backdoor. I don't know much, but this was *not* the plan. That could be good though. Dealer calculates, plans logically. A broken plan could confuse it. Keep you a step ahead." The words were babbling out of the Person, jingle-jangling Grace.

He gathered himself. "Go!" He smiled sadly. "What is it you burners say? A life for a life."

And then he stepped back, and the doors slid shut.

The elevator descended.

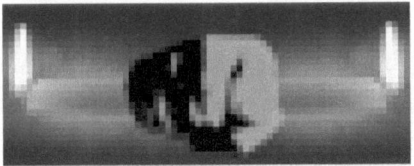

Millay had broken her promise about the time. Grace would be waiting for her, but she wouldn't be there to keep the promise.

The burners were confused, their excitement turning to panic because she wasn't a player, and you got in trouble for hitting a bystander.

"Josh!" a girl cried out. "You'll lose a day of Heaven."

"Floe me!" Someone was cursing and it had to be Josh, decrying his bad luck and his wild shot.

Millay struggled to speak, to tell him it was okay, but she knew it wasn't as the pain rippled out from her heart, vibrating along all her nerves. She wanted to weep for him, a boy she didn't know, but she couldn't stand the mounting pain, and her hand dropped from the tracer, shocking those gathered closest, who now saw where it had hit, into silence, because they all knew what a tracer to the unprotected heart did.

The girl started screaming, incoherent at first, then her words finally made sense. "She's going to die!"

Millay was awash with a feeling of utter stupidity. Wanting to give her sister the quiet. And now there was no quiet. Just the girl screaming, and in the distance, the deep throbbing siren of an approaching Dealer Lift. She was going to die in the midst of noise. She, a Person, guaranteed to live with no Deathday, was going to die because of a wild shot in the midst of a hectic game played by burners.

Because she'd made a promise to her sister on Dealing Day.

She was a fool to have agreed to this crazy plan.

Flashing lights strobed across the burners as the Lift hovered overhead, the engines emitting a deep thrumming noise. A simple design, a rectangular form with engines at each corner that could rotate from parallel to vertical, depending on what was required. Right now, all four were vertical, washing everyone below in the downdraft.

No one ran. There was no running from Dealers. Doors on the side of the Lift slid open, and two Dealers leapt out, landing heavily on their mechanical legs, hydraulics absorbing the impact. The Lift moved to the side, found a clear spot and settled down on skids.

Millay closed her eyes against the intense pain, not caring, trying to block out the noise, the burners, the engines. She went to the last good time and place of family: herself and Grace, six years old, in their best dresses on Dealing Day as the siren called everyone out of their local hives. At Assembly Field there had finally been quiet as all the six-year-olds stood in orderly rows. The cards that had been determined at birth were now pulled from the deck by Dark Angels and dealt. Their mother had cried because her two girls, so sweet, so identical they had the same cowlick, were now so different in an instant, that they were no longer of each other at all and they would leave her: one to go to hive womb, the other to the Island womb.

It should have been a time of great joy for their mother that one of her daughters had been dealt as People. So few were, and it was part of the hope of hive.

Millay, dealt as a Person, had seen her sister's arm reach for her, but had felt utter dismay at the red card that had been looped on its chain over her sister's head by the Dealer, the Deathday countdown appearing on it in black letters. 20/04/09. Twenty years, four months, nine days. Two-zero-slash-zero-four-slash-zero-nine in burner lingo.

Given that they were six, that was more than the median twenty-five years for a burner, a slight piece of good for her sister, Millay now knew, but she hadn't known then.

It is as it is.

"I'll make it right for you, Grace," Millay had whispered fiercely as the Dealers came through the ranks, separating out the mere handful dealt People, Evermores and Middlemores, with their different colored cards, white, green and blue. The lucky families were bidding farewell to the chosen ones, cherishing that they had been blessed with longer lives.

There weren't many to pull out. Roughly one People of every ten thousand, then three Evermores and nine Middlemores.

The rest: burners.

"I don't care what I have to do," Millay had said as two Dealers gently took her. "I'll make it right. I promise. I promise."

There were tears in her sister's eyes, but Millay now knew they had been about the separation, not about Grace's fate. They had all expected red.

She hadn't been a fool.

Memory faded away as Millay opened her eyes and saw a Dealer bending over her. The smooth white face with a black band where the eyes should be gave no tell, no emotion, just a Dealer doing its job. It made no attempt to save her. It was too late for that, as everyone knew that the damage to her heart was already done with the charge from the tracer expended into it. And, after all, she was just burner.

The Dealer straightened and pointed a metal claw at someone and issued the terrible words in the flat voice every Dealer had: "To be judged by a Dark Angel, by order of Dealer, for crime against Code. For expiring another burner."

"A life for a life," several of the burners reverently murmured, but the girl was still sobbing and Josh was screaming.

Millay's heart was slowing and her vision became tiny dots and her last thoughts were of the time and the promise and her sister's card.

She closed her eyes and wished to die faster so that the awful noise coming from the boy, Josh, would disappear.

And then it did.

As the elevator rumbled downward, Grace shivered. An invisible cold hand lightly brushing down her throat and coming to rest over her heart and taking hold with bony fingers. She tried to focus, to understand what she'd just experienced, but it would not come, and as quickly as it touched her, it was gone, leaving her chilled and short of breath.

Millay? she wondered, and then wondered why she wondered. She'd felt like this only once before, just before their cards were dealt. Grace shook her head, trying to clear it of the vague bad, trying to focus on the specific here and now.

She was jingle-jangled: Claude, Dealer stun, Person giving instructions. Nothing was right; nothing made sense.

The elevator came to a halt and the doors ground open, revealing the service tunnel, part of the system that honey-combed underneath

Island, allowing the Evermores to keep things functioning while staying out of sight of the People whom they served.

Grace stepped out of the elevator and the doors slid shut behind her.

And she remained frozen, the small ball from the Person in her hands, uncertain what to do next, but still feeling those cold bones wrapped around her heart.

She had no card. She was no longer part of.

She looked down the long tunnel, no end in sight.

THREE ONE UNTIL
GRACE'S DEATHDAY

"Time to pay for your passage," the Ferryman said just as Ryker snapped into consciousness. "Your card."

The problem was, Ryker wasn't quite sure how he'd gotten in this wooden boat; or where he came from. He did have an idea where he was going, but just a vague thought, nothing clear. It was night, he was on the water, and was being asked for some sort of payment: those were the only certain facts.

"What's wrong with you?" Charon asked.

Ryker looked about, seeing the lights of the City to the south and east and Island to the south and west. "We're only halfway across the water," he said. "It's not wise to pay the Ferryman until we get to the other side."

He wished he knew how he knew that.

"Do you swim?" Charon asked. He had no hair, his bald scalp was wrinkled and liver-spotted. His face was lined with wrinkles. But his body was bulky, muscled from years of rowing, that of a much younger man.

"I don't know," Ryker said.

Charon laughed. "burners can't swim."

Ryker was lean, like all burners. He had a narrow face, with piercing gray eyes. His black hair was shorn tight to his skull, burner fashion. Thick, dark stubble covered his chin.

Charon had his hand out, the oars resting in their locks. "We're past the point of no return." He nodded forward, past Ryker, at a dark shoreline. "Void is out there. You can't go back. Unless you want me to dump you in the deep, you have to pay."

Ryker reached up, then removed the chain from around his neck. He handed the chain and red card to Charon.

The Ferryman looked at it. "Still quite a bit of time for you."

"What good is my card to you?" Ryker asked, more curious than caring.

"I use your credits, max it out, then toss it in the deep," Charon said, pointing toward the dark water all around them. "And this way, Dealer can't find you out there in the Void, not that it cares." He removed the card from the chain. H took out a deck, opened one end, then slid the card in, snapped it shut and put it back in his pocket on his dark coverall. "You are now back in play."

"What does that mean?"

Charon shrugged. "Not ruled by the card."

"Not sure if I ever really was," Ryker muttered.

"What was that?"

Ryker shrugged. "Memories."

"Of what?"

"I feel like I've had a life before this life."

"Your life is ahead of you," Charon said. "What's left of it."

"What color card do you carry?" Ryker asked.

"I carry no card."

"You're not burner."

"Of course not. I'm the Ferryman."

"Over the river Styx. Is that what you call the water?"

Charon blinked in surprise. "How do you know about Styx?"

"Mouth to ear," Ryker said, wondering himself how he knew that. He didn't even remember getting in this boat or why he was folding and going to Void.

"Ah!" Charon was pleased. "You carry the words. So few do now."

"It's not exactly encouraged. But you're still not burner."

"No."

"Evermore?"

"No."

"Middlemore?"

"No. I'm the Ferryman."

"How can you not be of one of the four?"

"You ask too many questions."

"I seek more words."

"Here are some words," Charon said. He pointed to the east. "Mark each new day." He snorted, now pointing to the west. "Or, as most do, mark the end of each day. Now you have no card counting down to your Deathday, but die you still will. And no Heaven."

"Everyone dies."

"Do they?" Charon made it both a question and a statement.

Ryker replied in the same manner. "You've never ferried a People have you?"

"Why would a People fold?"

"Guilt?"

"Why would a People feel guilty?"

"For living when others die so quickly."

"That privilege is to be celebrated," Charon said.

"Not by the dead."

"Besides," Charon added, "a Person could walk to Void, go over the Lone Bridge."

"Do any do that?"

"How would I know?" Charon cocked his head. "Who are you?"

"Just someone who folded. In play, as you say. A gasper as you also say."

"I've ferried over many who folded. Many who were floed. If you know about the river Styx, then you know he ferried those he carried to hell."

"You're taking me to Void," Ryker said.

"Exactly."

Ryker agreed. "Some say it *is* hell there. That there are those out there who eat others."

"Some say many things," Charon said. "You want to live, you get to Delta quickly once I put ashore. You'll be safe in Delta with the others. As safe as one can be in the Void. But watch out for the jokers."

"How do I find this Delta?"

"Usually there is a group from Delta waiting at the landing to do the sorting," Charon said. "But since you insisted on going immediately, out of schedule, there will be no one. There is a path leading you there. It's marked. You'll see."

"And if I don't go to Delta?"

"You won't last long in the Void. If the jokers don't get you, you'll starve. Or become a joker yourself."

"And where is Heaven?" Ryker asked.

Charon didn't answer, but Ryker caught a flicker in his eyes, a quick movement to the north where a distant, dark smudge indicated an island.

Ryker pointed in that direction. "Heaven is there?"

"Oh, no," Charon said. He pointed a single finger up. "Heaven is above us. Where Dealer rules."

"That's what they tell children in the womb of hive," Ryker said. "They tell children many stories. Not all are to be believed."

Charon grabbed his oars. His well-muscled arms began to work, propelling the small wooden boat to the west, where a dark mass indicated a shoreline. It had no lights or signs of civilization.

"No one in hive knows where Heaven really is," Ryker said. "Ever take anyone there?"

Charon laughed. "Not possible. And you can't go there without your card. When it's your time."

Ryker shrugged. "My loss."

"Few give up Heaven."

"Maybe some of us don't believe in Heaven."

That caused Charon to miss a stroke. "I don't think you folded. I think you got floed."

"I don't care what you think," Ryker said.

Charon spat over the side as he continued to row. "You're a fool."

Ryker tapped the side of his skull. "There's something bouncing around in my head, old man. Something I can't pin down but it's driving me. Making me do this. Ever feel that?"

Charon dipped the oars into the water and pulled hard. "This is my driving force."

"Your Prime," Ryker said.

Charon dropped the oars, only their locks keeping them from falling into the water. "What did you say?" He started to reach inside his shirt.

And before he could get what he was going for, Ryker drew one of the two heavy blades he'd had sheathed on the belt around his gray coverall and stabbed Charon in the heart.

Leaving the knife in place, Ryker felt the old man's chest and pulled out a card. Not the white of People, or the green of Evermore, or the blue of Middlemore, or the red of burner. This card was pitch black, with nothing on it. No countdown, like a Person's white card, but blacker than the night around the boat.

"What is this?" Ryker asked Charon, who was staring at the knife in his chest with a mixture of shock and surprise. "You'll live a little longer," he added. "The blade is actually plugging the wound."

And he wished he knew how he knew that, along with knowing he'd never seen a black card.

Charon shook his head. "You fool," he managed to say. "No one is bigger than Dealer."

Ryker reached forward and retrieved the deck from the old man. He opened it and slid the black card in, joining the handful of others, including his own.

Ryker leaned close, mouth to ear, and as he pulled the blade out, he whispered, "No more journeys, old man. You can rest easy and in peace now. It is no longer what it was."

The Centre cannot hold.

Those four words mantra'd through the Person's mind as he took the People elevator upward. His office, the Oval, was several floors above, at the very tip of the tower and it took only seconds to get there.

The door slid open and there was a Dealer hulking there, still as a statue. Almost exactly the same as most other Dealers: black metal body, articulated joints forming arms and legs, flat, white face with a narrow black strip for visual input, no attempt to make them look human at all other than the form of two legs and two arms. One must not make a machine appear human.

It was Code.

But this Dealer, this particular one, was unique from all others because it had a thin band of gold around the top of the head just above the narrow black band.

The Person tried to act normal. "Good evening, Michael."

"Good evening, sir." The voice was flat, emotionless, coming from a speaker somewhere in the machine's head. But then the machine did something Dealers, even Michael, weren't supposed to do to the Person. He asked a personal question. "Is everything all right?"

The Person felt his skin go cold. "Yes. Quite all right. There's work I need to do."

"Of course."

The Person had a desk in the center of the Oval. All around the circumference of the office, images were being projected, each showing a different part of the Stream, mainly that of Island and City.

The Person walked around the Oval slowly, glancing at the projections. Between each display was a window, giving a three-hundred-sixty-degree view of Island, the place of the People. To the east was the water and the City and on clear days, of which there weren't many in that direction, the Wasted Mountains, once known as the Cascades. He'd looked it up. Those mountains had helped save the Sound during the Chaos, Before Dealer (B.D.). They'd been torched, and all passages through blocked. Everything on the other side of those mountains was long dead.

To the north, south and west: Void. Beyond Void, past water and the Broken Bridge, was Deep Void. He sometimes wondered what was out there, since the rumors about Void were bad enough. What could be deeper?

It was all part of Code, the laws drawn up so that the Sound could rise up out of the ruin of the Chaos.

It worked.

Had worked, Andrew amended.

The Centre cannot hold.

Michael stood at the lift, as still as the doors.

"Michael. I wish to be alone."

The Dealer didn't move or respond for at least four seconds. A troublesome record.

Michael turned and went into the elevator. The doors slid shut.

It didn't really matter. Andrew knew it was over for him.

It is what it was supposed to be.

She had to be in the tunnels by now. She needed more time.

He went to his desk and sat down. One piece in motion.

Maybe.

He had to give Grace some time, and he also had to get the other half moving, but he'd hoped for more time.

He'd never worried so much about time.

He turned to a display, recorded a message, set it to send later, after; when things would be confused.

He looked up as the lift doors slid open, but it wasn't Michael returning. Claude was seventy-six and less than a year from his Deathday, two years beyond his median but Evermores and Middle-mores had a much wider variance of median on their Deathdays than burners. His green card rested on his brown coverall, the numbers clicking down each midnight. Claude was already interviewing Evermores to fill his position. As far as Andrew could tell, it did not seem to occur to Claude that this was unfair or even slightly cruel.

Fair didn't enter into it.

It is what it is.

Claude, like almost everyone else in the Now, appeared to have forgotten that there ever was a fair. Perhaps in B.D., before the Chaos, there had been this thing called 'fair' but look how that had turned out?

There was just the Now.

"Where is she, sir?" Claude asked, like Michael's question, impertinent and a dangerous indicator.

Andrew took a deep breath, trying to understand what he felt, and it came to him. Fear. A foreign thing for a People.

"Who gave you the authority to detain a People?" Andrew demanded.

"Dealer."

And the elevator doors slid open once more and Michael walked into the Oval. And behind Michael were three Dark Angels.

The Streams cut off and the Oval, always full of activity, curtained down to complete stillness.

"Where is she?" Claude asked again, dropping any attempt at respect.

"Why do you care?" Andrew was buying time, not sure if it were for Grace or for himself. "What is she to you?"

"Wrong question," Claude said. "Why is she important to *you*?"

"I don't really know," Andrew answered honestly. Almost honestly.

Michael's flat voice cut through. "How can she have had a card but not be in Stream?"

"Dealer knows all," Andrew said, feeling some slight satisfaction, although insulting a machine with no emotions . . .

"Why did you let her go?" Michael asked.

"She's People. Claude had no right to apprehend her."

"We gave him the right," Michael said, speaking for Dealer. "By authority of Code."

Andrew got to his feet.

"Who is she?" Michael asked.

"*The Centre cannot hold,*" Andrew said.

Michael ignored that. "Where did you send her?"

"*The Centre cannot hold.*"

There was silence for a few moments; calculations. Then Michael lifted a metal hand and pointed a single articulated finger at the Person.

At the signal, lap dog Claude shook his head. "I'm sorry, Andrew."

Claude had never used his name before, and he didn't sound sorry at all. The Dark Angels trooped in, their mechanical footfalls heavy on the floor. They triangled him. The tiny metal wings on top of their metal heads made them different from other Dealers. The flat surface of their face was different also, black instead of white, with a white stripe for sensory input. The stunners on their wrists were deployed, ready for action.

Claude stayed clear of the machines, but close to Michael, whose flat voice filled the room. "We regret to inform you, Andrew-four-seven-echo-seven, that you have been found in violation of the Code of Life."

"I'm the Person," Andrew protested. The numbers and letter after his name had been given to him at birth. He hadn't heard them since he was six and dealt his white card, officially brought into the womb of the Island as People. That dealing had not been a great surprise, since both his parents were People.

Red would have been a great surprise.

"No one is above the Code," Claude added, and Andrew saw a gleam in his little piggy eyes that he'd never caught before. Ambition? Revenge?

The three Dark Angels took a step closer, and the two to either side took his upper arms in a grip that was unbreakable for a human. The third one was directly in front. Even Michael or Claude couldn't pronounce sentence. It had to be a Dark Angel. That was Code.

"For violation of Code, Andrew-four-seven-echo-seven will be boxed."

The actual words from the third Dark Angel were almost an afterthought, the former Person thought as they dragged him out.

It had to be this way.

The Centre will not hold.

THREE ONE UNTIL
GRACE'S DEATHDAY

The boat scraped onto the pitted concrete ramp and came to an abrupt halt. Ryker pulled the oars in and placed them inside. He stepped over the side of the boat, onto land. Looking up, he could see stars sparkling high above.

To his left, extending out into the water, was a huge pier, deteriorating. A very large boat was half-submerged next to the pier, rust eating away at it. A concrete pad extended out over the water, leading to the pier. Numerous hunks of metal were on it, cars, long abandoned.

All relics from B.D., Before Dealer. A time that was lost in the Chaos.

Looking past the wreckage, he could see the gentle lights of Island to the south. He didn't look back from where he'd come. That was done. Ahead, all he saw was darkness.

Void.

A large paved area was directly in front of him, crumbling, pierced with scrub and small trees. There were lumps of metal here and there, wheels rotted away, windshields broken.

Was he too early or was he too late? And then wondered: For what?

He shook his head, trying to clear the jingle-jangled images, trying to gain some clarity. But it was as if he were stumbling around in a fog with a blindfold on. There was so much specific he couldn't access, yet so much general he could. Some information of this world was there, but details of his own memories, nothing. There were memories he sensed were there, but couldn't bring up.

What had happened to him? Who was he?

He pulled out Charon's deck. Charon's black card. What was that about? Ryker had never heard of a black card, not even a whisper in his jumbled brain.

Ryker pulled his arm back, ready to throw the deck into the dark water, but then he paused. There could be value in the cards. A hand to be played if necessary. He put the deck back in the pocket of his gray coveralls.

As he looked at the dark line of trees, a saying popped up: *Here there be monsters.*

There were stories in hive of Void. What was fact and what was fiction, no one knew, because no one came back from Void. Once the Ferryman took a person over, they were gone. Which made Ryker wonder where the rumors came from? Charon?

Something glittered, a brief flash in the starlight. Ryker walked forward, weaving through the debris of B.D.. A rear view mirror salvaged from one of the wrecks dangled from a branch at the edge of the woods, spinning lazily in the breeze. Beyond it, a narrow path beckoned.

"*Follow the yellow brick road,*" Ryker said out loud, not sure where that came from. Some mouth to his ear long ago.

Whose mouth?

He glanced back at the boat: *She is ahead and she is behind.*

What the hell was that about? he wondered, frustrated by the lack of answers.

Ryker pulled one of the knives from the sheath inside his belt, noting how evenly balanced it was. He had no idea how he'd gotten the two blades. It was heavy, the blade slightly longer than nine inches and at the hilt an inch and a half. There was a cross-guard which protected his hand. The blade itself was keenly edged on one side. The spine of the blade was straight and flat until about two inches from the point, where it curled down, making the blade double-edged for its first two inches and giving the weapon an extremely sharp point. Ryker hefted it, the feel familiar. The handle was made of some hard, white material attached on either side of the steel haft, and the center of the handle bowed inward, giving his hand a solid grip.

He stuck it back in the sheath. He went to the boat and pulled it higher up on the concrete, judging by the marks and debris that it was now out of the reach of the tide. With great effort, he flipped the heavy wood rowboat. He took the oars and hid them underneath a rusting truck about a hundred feet away. Satisfied, although why he did this he knew not, he went back to the mirror.

And then he passed underneath the trees onto the path.

And in the dark trees, there were eyes watching him.

Grace hadn't moved since getting off the elevator. Bearing Millay's card had been troublesome, guilty; but no card was a debilitating abscence when wearing one was as much a part of as her own flesh and blood for two decades.

It is what it is.

That fallback line of hive twitched Grace. This 'is' was so different, but it was an is. She had to face it. Act.

She began to move, head down the tunnel. Slowly. Trying to gather more courage. Not able to.

Yet.

And the time ticked over to another day.

THREE ZERO UNTIL
GRACE'S DEATHDAY

Millay woke flat on her back to darkness and utter quiet. She was cold, colder than she'd ever been. Was this Heaven for a Person? Nothingness? Maybe this was what they deserved in death after a life of having every need fulfilled?

But she had not had a full life! The unfairness of it caused Millay to try to sit up and she immediately hit her head on something metallic. A low ceiling. She felt around her and was surrounded by steel.

Had she been boxed?

She panicked, flailing about. But she had arms and legs, so she had not been boxed. Only when her hands pressed against the wall on top of her head was there a change, the slightest sliver of light appearing near her feet. She realized she was on a rolling metal tray, inside a metal box. She pressed harder, adrenaline giving her strength, and the tray slid out. She rolled off the slab and fell onto a cold tile floor. The impact stunned her. Then she collected herself, getting to her knees.

She felt her chest, noting the singe marks on her shirt from the tracer. But her heart was beating quickly, too quickly. Millay took a deep breath to try to calm down, but it didn't help. She staggered to her feet.

And she had no card. She spun about and flooded with relief seeing it hanging on the handle of the drawer she'd just been in. She grabbed it and looped it over her head.

A flickering, buzzing, light kept the room from complete darkness. She looked around. There were a dozen tables in the room and there were bodies on half of them. Unable to resist, Millay went to the nearest. A man lay on it.

Millay gasped in horror as she saw that the man was dead. He'd been in a horrible accident; the left side of his torso was crushed, the chest cavity torn open. Millay blinked as she saw that the heart was exposed and shredded. A red card lay on top of the internal organs, discarded since the numbers no longer mattered. She saw that the burner had died with 03/01/06 left. Millay whispered a silent prayer to Dealer for this boy who'd extinguished before his time and who would not get Heaven; a double tragedy.

There was a stack of gray bags containing more bodies near a large bay door on one side of the room. The bags were vacuum-sealed so tight that the outline of the burner inside was clearly visible. The occupants' cards were tagged on one end.

Millay spun about and ran for the other door. She shoved the handle and stumbled into a dingy, gray corridor. Now she heard it. The rumble of hive above her. There was no mistaking it.

And it all came back. It was not a dream.

Millay pressed her hands against her forehead as if the physical action could bring stability to her careening thoughts.

She'd died. She'd been hit by a tracer over the heart. Her heart had stopped.

But she was alive.

Millay nodded.

Of course she was. She was People.

It is what it is.

Grace. She had to get to Grace. Get her card back. See her sister one last time. Give her sister Heaven. Get back to Island and the People!

Millay ran down the hall. She passed a pair of burners dressed in stained black smocks. They paid her not the slightest attention, focused on their work, whatever that might be. Curiosity was not a trait valued in hive.

She found a bank of elevators. Of the six, two were non-functional, as they had been her entire time here. She got in one that worked. The building number, 72, above the buttons for floors, confirmed that this was her, *NO!* she reminded herself, this was *Grace's* hive.

The floors rumbled by. The elevator halted with a grinding of old gears and the doors parted. Millay hurried down the corridor, pushing past burners on their way to work, coming from work, staggering home from a party, rushing out to another party. Bouncing out to play. Trudging in from playing.

hive was never still, something that had overwhelmed her the first week she was here. She reached the outer ring where Grace's cubby was located. She'd been surprised to learn that burners didn't value the view from the scratched and dirty plexi of the outer ring, which Middlemores dictated as a 'reward'. hive, as time passed, shuffled the occupants outward from the center, those freshly of age and straight from Womb, and thus furthest from their Deathdays, beginning in the center in the tiniest slice of cubbys, while those closer to Deathday were shuffled outward, until for their final year they were given the gift of the larger, outer cubbys with plexi windows, for a year, before going to Heaven. The shuffle was an annual event, a measure of time passing and the continuity of hive. The value of the view had diminished over generations of burners, weighed down by what it signified, that one with a hive plexi only counted months and days to Deathday, not years.

Millay had noticed something strange early in her time here, something that the burners didn't seem to see. That there were empty cubby's near the center, while the outer ring was full. That meant there were fewer burners coming of age and shuffling out in hive than for the number for which it had been designed.

As a corollary, there were few young children below Womb age. While burners had sex—there was ample evidence of that just from the noise as one walked down a corridor—fewer women were getting pregnant.

This was not something Millay had seen in reports in Island.

Millay shoved open the door to the cubby, expecting to see her sister waiting for her.

There was no one.

Millay knew she'd missed the rendezvous at City Edge, but she expected Grace to keep coming, to come back to hive. She had to; today she went to Heaven, the ultimate goal of every burner.

Where was she?

Millay sank down on the hard bunk. She'd spent most of the month on it tossing and turning with a pillow over her head, trying to drown out the constant wave of voices trying to be heard, the nonstop music and spontaneous games and endless parties. She'd managed sleep only as the result of utter exhaustion from the unbearable work. She'd planned the entire month since arriving for Grace's homecoming, not realizing her true motivation was longing for her own departure back to Island, her home, her People.

Her desire to have her sister's cubby homey and cute instead of stifling-small had forced her to take extra shifts and Millay wasn't used to working. She was People and they didn't work very much. Mostly they read and talked about esoteric things and they ruled, although there wasn't much of that as the Dealers took care of most of it. The rest was passed on to the Evermores supervising the Middlemores who dealt with the burners, who did the grunt work. Some People 'staffed', as Millay did, taking on positions which needed to be filled and which fit their personalities and desires.

It is as it is.

There was no time to talk about esoteric things in Grace's world. burners worked and when they weren't working, they played and partied and when all that was done they collapsed for a few hours before starting over again. Millay had exhausted herself in just the few weeks at her sister's job, cleaning the 'tein vats. Her hands were soft and she hid the blisters under thick gloves because the softness and the blisters were a glaring tell between the identical twin sisters.

The other members of the work cell had known something was off, there was no doubt of it. They hadn't cared as long as she kept the quota, pushing her body beyond anything she'd ever endured. Grace had warned her that slacking off in a work cell was against a different kind of code, one burners enforced among themselves. A burner was assigned an allotment to be done. That allotment was based on instructions passed on by the Middlemore supervisor who got them from an Evermore who received them from a People staffer who read the calculation from Dealer's Stream. It was supposed to be exactly the right amount of work for the right amount of time. The work to be done wasn't adjustable, but the time was. If any one of the cell slacked off, the rest of the cell had to work longer. Slack off too much and you could get floed: exiled from hive into the Void.

It was an ingenious, self-policing system, and Millay had sometimes wondered as she scraped why none of them saw through it. But then she was beginning to understand there was so much of her own life she had simply accepted because it is as it is. So much she hadn't seen through, but when she approached that rabbit hole, she shied away from diving in.

Millay had worked and saved up credit on Grace's card by doing without and last night the little cubby had shone with candles and smelled of lavender. Now Millay noticed that all the candles had burned to hardened lumps of wax and the flowers, hard to barter for in hive through the black market, were drooping as if they also had also been too exhausted to make it through the night.

She'd even bought some food on the black market, vegetables and spices and other delicacies. A change from the numbing and bland 'tein, processed out of the produce of the poorest quality from the agri and rendering hives.

The knock on the door startled her, but her panic subsided. Grace was back, just in time.

Millay rushed to the door and swung it open, forgetting Grace's warning to always check through the peephole before unlocking the door; that hive wasn't like Island.

Haydn stood there, his face a mask of worry, fear and something

Millay didn't want to see. but was the norm among burners though never before on Haydn: resignation. "Grace?"

Millay threw her arms around Haydn and kissed him. "No, silly. It's me. Millay."

Haydn staggered back, out of her arms. "But you're dead. It's on Stream. You were hit by a tracer. Your heart stopped." Haydn grabbed her hands, almost savagely, and turned them over, looking for Grace's calluses and seeing her scabs. "It *is* you. But how?"

"I'm People," Millay said, the only explanation she'd managed to settle on. "It is as it is."

Haydn regarded her as he would a stranger.

"What's wrong?" Millay asked.

"'What's wrong'?" Haydn shook his head. "What's right? I thought you were dead. You *were* dead. The Stream said a burner, Grace-five-eleven-kilo-one, was killed in an accident during a game of tracers. I know they got it off the card. I know it was you."

"They were wrong."

"Dealer is never wrong."

Millay stepped forward, towering over him, and placed her hand under his chin. She tilted his face up and kissed him hard and deep and slow and he finally knew she was here, she was alive, because no one had ever kissed him slowly before he met her. Haydn was short, even for burner, around five and a half feet, but had the same lean, hungry body all burners had. His blond hair was longer than most burners, roughly cut just enough to keep from falling into his eyes. It was barely combed, usually by running his fingers through it, and gave him an untamed, wild look that had drawn Millay's attention the first time she saw him. He had blond stubble, that had been haphazardly shaved a while ago, but was more fuzz than beard. His nose was crooked, broken a long time ago and badly set, the result of an accident as a child, he'd told her, never specifying the incident. His eyes were a sparkling green, but his forehead was creased with worry.

"This is wrong," Haydn said. "If Dealer says you're dead, and you're not. Then . . ."

"I thought Grace would be here," Millay said.

"So did I."

They were both silent, thinking through the confusion.

"All right," Millay said. "We missed the rendezvous at City Edge. Grace will try again. I know her."

"Her card already turned over," Haydn said. "We'll have to move fast."

Millay held the red card up. The years read zero zero. The months zero zero. The days now three zero. 00/00/30. Except Millay had learned in hive that once you went below one hundred to Death-day, you started counting days, not reciting the number of months and so did the card, flipping from 00/03/10 to 00/00/99. Because there were no more years, and soon there would be no more months. Nine nine days sounded and looked better than months and days at that point.

And now it was thirty days.

But not her thirty, Grace's.

Today, Dealers would come for Grace at hive Assembly.

No! They would come for this card and whoever wore it.

"Three zero days," he said. "You're supposed to be on Assembly Field, waiting for the Dealers by noon." He shook his head, as if trying to dislodge the jingle-jangle. "But if Dealer thinks you're dead . . ."

"We have to meet Grace," Millay said. "She'll—"

Haydn held up a hand as her card buzzed. A black square was projected, no image, but a man's voice trembled out of it; a voice everyone knew: the Person.

"Listen to me, Millay. Listen to me carefully. You have to find your sister. She won't be at City Edge. You need to leave hive. You need to meet her in Void. And Grace will know what to do. Go now. Don't wait. Don't stop no matter what happens. When you—"

And the black square snapped out of existence.

"The Person!" Millay said, shocked.

"We were dammed." Haydn stated the obvious, not as impressed as she with the caller.

"I don't understand," Millay said. "I don't understand any of this.

Why would the Person care? How would he know my name? That Grace and I switched cards?"

"He said we have to meet Grace in the Void," Haydn said, automatically going to the plural, including himself. "Do you understand what the means?"

Grace was still behind him. "We need to meet Grace and make everything right. I'll get my card from her. Go back to Island. Straighten it all out."

"It's not that simple," Haydn said. "Nothing is ever that simple. Void. It means folding."

"People don't fold," Millay said.

But Haydn barely heard her, his mind leaping ahead, his decision made. "We have to go to the landing. Meet the Ferryman on the—" He paused in thought. "The half moon would be the next crossing. That's days away. But first we have to make the journey going around hive along the folding path to the landing."

"What are you talking about?" Millay's voice was shaky. "Let's just call the Dealers. Tell them it's been a big mistake. Just switch back."

Haydn stared at her. "Don't you get it? Grace is running to Void. She must have a reason."

"But I'm People!" Millay protested, an answer that solved all for her. Had solved.

Both their cards vibrated insistently, sounding the special rhythm that indicated Dealer was damming the entire Stream in preparation for an important announcement.

Everything was coming to a halt. It was quiet. For the first time since she'd arrived, there wasn't the torrent of voices, of parties starting or ending, regardless of the time.

"Oh, Dealer, please help us," Millay whispered, fearful of what was coming.

The Stream jazzed out of their cards into the air in front of them, as it did for every People, Evermore, Middlemore and burner.

The flat, emotionless voice of Dealer spoke out of a pure white square: "For crimes against Code, the Person, Andrew-four-seven-echo-seven, has been found guilty and judged by a Dark Angel. He is to be boxed. Sentence to be carried out immediately."

"Oh, Dealer," Millay whispered in prayer. "Please no. Please no. What is happening?"

But it was a one-way transmission, as a Dealer transmission always was. There was no answering of prayers, no change of a course of action.

It is as it is.

"His call to you had to have been on delay," Haydn said. "We have to run, now, Millay. He's trying to gain us time."

But they saw, as everyone else did, the image flicker into view in front of them: a white room, empty except for six red switches on one wall, spaced far enough apart that a person could only reach one of the foot-long levers at one time. Six People entered the room. Each stopped in front of one of the switches.

It had been a while since the last boxing, but Millay remembered it clearly, which was the point. Six People, six switches, only one of them the real switch. Only Dealer knew which so that the People pulling them would not be burdened by the guilt of the boxing. But the key was the humans did it, not Dealers. Dealers were forbidden by Code to harm humans in any permanent way.

But as far as Millay could recall, or had heard, no Person had ever been boxed.

The image shifted once more and there was the Person splayed out on the white table, naked. A large mechanical probe swung into view over him, the tip a glowing crystal. A tube was shunted into him just below the chest and he was muttering something, the words unintelligible. He looked sedated. Pain was not the goal of boxing.

Not initially.

Grace wasn't worried about running into a People in the service tunnels, but Evermores were a different story; this was their domain. An underground system honeycombed the island, which they used to service the People while staying out of the way and out of sight. The floor of the tunnel sloped slightly down to the center, where a grate covered a concrete ditch that collected seepage that managed to get in and let it flow to a pumping center.

As she ran, she heard voices up ahead. Looking about, she remembered something from her time playing tracers: a friend, long gone to Heaven, had told her, 'No one ever looks up.' So Grace looked to the top of the tunnel, where a cluster of pipes and wires and cables were hung, drooped and looped. She jumped, grabbing onto a thick cable and pulled herself up into the dark shadows above the flickering lights. She rolled onto a particularly thick pipe, one that vibrated ever so slightly, carrying who knew what into or out of the Island.

Looking down, she watched two Evermores passing by, but then both came to a complete halt as their cards sounded the alert indicating Dealer was damming the Stream.

Both cards projected the image of the control room. And then the Person splayed out on the table.

"Close your eyes," Haydn whispered. "I have to watch, but you don't."

"I must," Millay said, stopping herself before she added: It's Code. And it was instinct. One always watched the Stream when Dealer dammed it; a habit entrenched so deeply into every child, regardless of what womb they were raised in, that not doing so was unthinkable. "He's being boxed because of me and Grace. I don't understand why, but it has to be." She began to cry at her own mention of Grace and how their Dealing Day promise had turned into this tragedy.

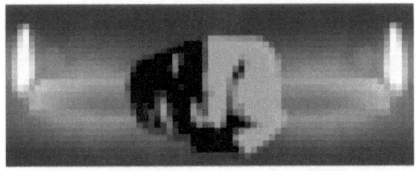

The probe began to move as the crystal glowed red and it halted above the Person's right shoulder.

The Person's eyes flickered wide open. "My name is Andrew," he cried out. "I am a human before being a People and before being the Person. A human like all of us."

Then he began to chant loudly, in a surprisingly clear voice, fragments of the old burner hymn.

> *"My candle burns at both ends;*
> *It will not last the night.*
> *But ah, my foes, and oh, my friends*
> *It gives a lovely light!"*

A red beam lashed out of the end of the probe and with the slightest of hisses the laser went through his arm in a flash, severing it at the shoulder. There was no blood, the heat instantly cauterizing the wound. A grappler appeared and scooped up the dead limb, taking it out of view.

Andrew chanted louder the second time, repeating the stanzas every burner had had sung to them as children in hive womb, four times over as a ritual, as if repetition enforced belief.

"My candle burns at both ends;"

The other arm was separated and disappeared as quickly.

"It will not last the night."

The right leg. Andrew's voice was losing energy as his body lost its parts.

"But ah, my foes, and oh, my friends"

The left leg. His voice down to a whisper.

"It gives a lovely light!"

Andrew's eyes closed and the image shifted so that one could now see the box waiting for what was left of him. The table lifted slightly and he slid into the box. The last image of the Person was his mouth moving silently, trying to repeat the song for the third time.

Then a white slab slid down, sealing the box, just the shunt going in and Andrew within its darkness.

And in hives, across all the land, there was silence, and then, starting like flickers in the dark, a voice here and there would start singing, for the fourth time. The voices were few, but they grew in number as the first line went to the second. And the third. And by the last line, it echoed in hives all around the City Edge.

As *"It gives a lovely light,"* faded out in hives, burners stared at each other, not sure what had come over them, jingle-jangled.

But something was different.

As the voice faded to silence, Haydn grabbed Millay by the shoulders. She was still staring at the air where the Stream had been displayed. "Millay!"

She blinked. "But. The Person. Why would Dealer do that? Not just because of Grace and me? It can't be. Why did he call me? What did we do that was so wrong?"

Haydn dumped burner practicality on People wondering. "It doesn't matter. We don't have time to try to figure it out. We run. We go meet Grace."

"I don't understand," Millay said, but Haydn was pulling her out the door, into the corridor.

In the darkness under Island, Grace waited until the two Evermores continued on their way. She uncurled from her hide spot, lowered herself as far as she could, then let go, landing lightly.

She pulled the ball the Person had given her out of her pocket. It was two inches in diameter. Black. Soft. She held it in one hand. With her other hand, she drew the scraper out of her belt, hefting it, feeling the weight, stretching muscles, well adapted to wielding it hard and fast in either hand. The metal handle was wrapped in worn leather. Scrapers weren't issued with the leather; a burner was taught to wrap the metal handle to save their flesh when they first went into the 'tein vats. From the handle, the metal went out straight for three inches, a haft of steel, then did a ninety-degree curve with a sharp, even edge, perpendicular to the handle, ending at a point. It was effective for scraping 'tein off steel, and the point useful for getting into difficult corners and clearing them. The edges were sharp. She had maintained it well.

She knew how to use it.

"A life for a life."

Grace was no longer part of.

And then she began to run. Not away anymore.

But toward something.

THREE ZERO UNTIL
GRACE'S DEATHDAY

Ryker knew he was being followed. He knew it as he knew he needed to breath air to live. It was instinct.

But it did bother him to not know how exactly he had this instinct.

It was very dark underneath the trees. He kept on the path by sliding one foot forward and then the other, while one hand held a knife and the other was stretched out in front of his face, protection against the odd branch across the path or wandering off course. Slow going. This path led to Delta, given Charon's words. Ryker's plan, such as it was, was to go there and ask for the location of his true destination.

Not much of a plan. But he didn't have much of a memory at the moment, and while it bothered him, it wasn't overwhelming.

It is what it is truly applied here and now.

Ryker paused, head cocked to the side, listening. A slight breeze rustled through the trees. And the smallest of sounds, a footstep on last fall's leaves.

Ryker pulled the other knife out of his belt and whirled, one blade high, one low. And despite the night and the trees overhead, he could see shadows. And two of them were now rushing at him, something long and thick held in their hands.

Ryker dove forward, head tucked in, back of the shoulder taking the impact with the ground, the rolled, coming to his knees, one blade going into the stomach of the person on the right, the other blocking the blow from the person on the left.

Ryker followed his own momentum, going right, using the blade in the man's guts as his pivot point, putting the body between him and the second attacker while ripping open the first man's stomach.

The second attacker's club thudded into the wounded man's head with a solid thud.

Ryker threw his free blade at the center of mass of the second attacker's silhouette. It struck home with a gasp from the man. He dropped his club and both hands went to the hilt of the blade stuck deep in his chest.

Ryker was still moving, dropping the body he'd used as a shield, sliding the blade free of the man's stomach. Ryker slashed at the second man across the throat, spurting arterial blood.

Ryker easily snatched his second blade out of the man's chest and stepped back.

But he wasn't done. He jabbed downward with one blade into the chest of the unconscious, wounded attacker already on the ground, straight into the heart.

He made sure of his kill as the second attacker collapsed to his knees, then did a face plant, a final sigh through the ripped throat.

It was over in less than six seconds.

Ryker stood still, not even out of breath.

"That was interesting," he said out loud, for lack of anyone else to speak to.

Apparently he was trained to use the knives.

He wiped his blades off on the body at his feet. He did a cursory search of the corpse. No card, as expected. Tatters for clothes. A club for weapon. That was it. The second body yielded the same result. He took a moment to feel the body more carefully, working by touch. burner thin; apparently a life of cannibalism wasn't much better than hive. Dirty. He touched several poorly healed scars, indicating a violent life. As he ran his hands over the man's face, a finger slipped into the mouth: the teeth were filed to points.

The better to eat you with, my pretty.

Welcome to Void, Ryker thought, as he stood and set off, once more, down the trail, heading for Delta.

But as he took his second step he paused and cocked his head, as if listening. But this was different than just before. A whisper of the brain:

She was coming.

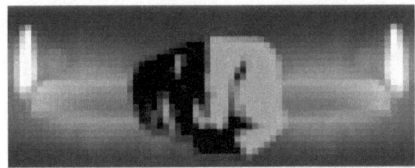

Grace was running hard and fast, a person who didn't know how to pace herself.

Twice more she lifted herself up above the lights to avoid Evermores.

Just when she didn't think she could run any farther, her lungs aching, sweat pouring, the muscles in her legs sore from the unusual activity, she realized the air was different. Not musty and machine-tainted, but with a hint of something else, something she'd only smelled once before when coming out here on the Wave to Island after she and Millay had done the switch: salt water.

Energized, Grace sprinted toward a grayish circle: the end of the tunnel

And ran right into a Dealer that stepped out in front of her.

She hit the machine hard, bouncing back and falling to the concrete floor, the wind knocked out of her.

The Dealer was facing her, as much as it had a face. Grace knew it was scanning for her card.

"Identify yourself."

The voice was always the same; the same voice had announced

Andrew's boxing. It gave the weather each morning in Island. It announced the news. It pronounced sentence. It dealt the cards.

Grace staggered to her feet, trying to catch her breath.

"Identify yourself."

For lack of anything else, Grace settled on the truth. "I'm folding." Even as she said it, she realized she'd never heard of Dealers interfering with someone folding or even getting floed.

Which was odd.

But she'd also never heard of a People folding.

The machine had not moved since their initial contact. Its smooth, white metallic face betrayed nothing.

Then, to her astonishment, it simply stepped aside.

Grace ran past the Dealer onto a concrete pad next to a Wave landing. There were a handful of Evermores unloading a Wave under the harsh brightness of electric lights, so intent on their task they didn't see her. To the east, the sky was beginning to turn gray, heralding another dawn coming over the Wasted Mountains. She could see the lights of City, glistening across water.

Turn left, Andrew had told her.

She turned left, to the north. A pebble-strewn beach beckoned.

And then?

She looked at the ball in her hand. She squeezed and sensed something cracking inside it. She lifted it in front of her. It vibrated, very slightly. Once. Ten second later, another. She turned left, inland, back toward Island.

Nothing.

She made a complete circle and when she was pointing north along the beach, it gave the two vibrations.

Grace stepped off the concrete onto the beach. Waves lapped at the sand and pebbles. There were scattered pieces of driftwood here and there.

As the new day broke, gray and cloudy, Grace began to run once more. This was different than before, not a desperate race to escape. But a measured loping gait, loose and free.

For the first time in her short life, Grace no longer was *part of* and with every stride, it felt as if something were falling off her, some weight dropping like little beads of sweat from her.

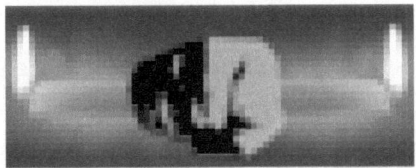

"Come on," Haydn said.

Millay was still trying to process the Person being boxed, so she numbly followed his command.

They were on the first floor of their hive building; his hive building, Millay tried to remind herself. Grace's hive.

"I'm People," she said.

Haydn looked over his shoulder. "What?"

"I'm People."

"So was the Person," Haydn said. He paused as he passed one of the common rooms. A few burners were in it, eating, but what caused him to halt was what sat on one of the tables. A wooden box about a foot tall and six inches to a side. On top was metal spike, and stuck on top of the metal spike was a horizontal candle.

Burning at both ends. None of the burners were looking at it, in fact they were studiously avoiding that, which meant they knew very well it was there.

"Oh," Millay said when she saw it.

Haydn took her hand once more. "Come on."

They went down the corridor. Just before the doors leading outside was a metal locker. He swung the door open. He reached inside and pulled out two tracer guns, extra cartridges, two hartgards and two eyegards.

He handed one set to Millay, while he stuffed the extra cartridges in his backpack. He'd taken all the 'tein in Grace's and his own cubby. He'd emptied three 'chol bottles and filled them with water, wrapping them in extra clothing and adding it to the pack.

Millay took the gun and gards numbly, without really noting what they were.

"Give me your card," Haydn said.

That got through to Millay. "What?"

"Your card." Haydn was pulling his off. He tossed his red card and chain into the locker.

"What are you doing?"

"We're folding," Haydn said with smiled patience. "Dealer will find our cards, but not us. If we're not with them."

It was logical and even Millay understood that. And parting with Grace's card was no great sacrifice. She pulled the chain over her head and handed it to Haydn. He threw it on top of his own, then slammed the locker shut.

"Come on." He emphasized his order by grabbing her hand.

"Where?"

"Have you been listening at all?" Haydn asked. He laid it out. "Millay. We're folding. We're leaving hive. We're going to the ferry. To meet the Ferryman and go to Void. To meet Grace."

Millay nodded. "I understand. But I don't see what will happen. What then? What will we do? Will Grace have my card? She must. But what about her card? You're leaving it here. What about Heaven for her? Void is large. Where will we meet her? How will we find her?"

"Millay." Haydn's voice was like a whip, his normal good humor gone for the moment.

"But Heaven for Grace!" she protested.

"I don't believe in Heaven," Haydn said. "Never did, never will."

"But—" Millay didn't know what more to say to that.

"Believing in Heaven," Haydn amplified, "means believing in Dealer. I know Dealer exists, but I don't have to believe in it as the answer to everything. There is more in the world than Dealer. And we're told Heaven exists, but there is no proof. No one comes back from it. No one has visited it."

"Blasphemy," Millay said, the word spewing forth from years of indoctrination.

"It is what it is," Haydn said, with his usual crooked grin.

"But how do we get to Void? The Wave doesn't go there."

"We walk," Haydn said patiently. "Most of the way at least. To the Sound.

"But where? What direction? How do you know how to get there?"

"Every burner knows how to get to Void if they want to fold."

"What?"

Haydn closed his eyes for a second and recited: "On the outer arc of hive. Turn left. Follow the folding path with Wasteland to the right; hives to left; walk until heading into the setting sun; walk to the water; find rails; turn left; walk on them with water to the right until you reach the old ferry. And then wait for the Ferryman."

"How far is that?" Millay asked. "The water is a long way to walk, even straight through City Edge and City; never mind going around on the edge of hive."

"We'll worry about it when we get to the folding trail," Haydn said. "There's something we have to do first before we run."

"What?"

"Dealer thinks you died. Grace that is. The man who shot you, Josh. They're going to bag him. A life for a life. We have to save him."

Millay was shaking her head. "How? Where is he? Isn't he already dead? Isn't he guarded by Dealers?"

"There's a holding cell near Assembly Field," Haydn said. "They bag prisoners there and take them out on a Lift." He nodded to the north. "It's on the way. We can be there well before formal Assembly and get him out."

Millay was confused.

"He's our responsibility," Haydn said. "He can't be bagged because of us. A life for a life goes two ways." He grabbed the hartgard out of her hand. It was essentially a set of cross belts that went over each shoulder, forming an x in the front and back. Attached to the front and back x were circular, ceramic plates, a foot in diameter, centered over the heart. Haydn slipped it on her.

"What are you doing?" Millay demanded.

Settling the hartgard in place, Haydn suddenly struck Millay hard, right on the gard.

She staggered back a step. "What is wrong with you?"

"Did that hurt?" Haydn demanded.

"Not really."

"Can a tracer get to your heart now?"

"No."

"Can a knife?"

"No."

"Can a Dealer stunner?"

"I don't know."

Haydn smiled. "I don't know either, but it's better than nothing." Haydn wrapped his arms around her. "Just as that protects your heart, I protect you. Stay with me and I will always take care of you."

All Andrew had was sound. There was no light. Nothing except his breathing. There was no pain either, although he knew he was still under the influence of the painkillers they'd pumped into him prior to the boxing. He imagined pain would come once they wore off.

But he had no control over anything other than the breathing and moving his head. No arms, no legs. He'd been licking his lips a lot, savoring the sensation of the slight stubble on his chin. His mouth was parched: the mister in front of him only spritzed occasionally, on a schedule he had not yet mastered. Enough to wet the lips and mouth on the edge of torment. He knew he got his life-sustaining fluid through the tube shunt, but sustenance was far from nourishment.

He was suspended in a harness, kept upright. The mister was in front of his face and the shunt went in just below his chest. The air had to be circulated somehow, but he couldn't feel or hear it. He also wondered what would happen with his excrement and urine. A little detail he'd never thought of before when someone got boxed. It was a punishment reserved for People, Evermores and Middlemores who committed the most grievous of crimes. Such expense would not be wasted on a burner. During his tenure, sixteen had been boxed.

He'd only been in this box less than twelve hours and the future stretched ahead of him with unbearable bleakness. Being a People with no Deathday was now a curse.

"Andrew."

The voice startled him, echoing tinnily out of a small speaker in the box.

"Andrew?"

He recognized Claude.

"You can speak," Claude said.

Andrew, formerly the Person, knew he shouldn't answer. But he also knew he had nothing left. He was boxed.

It was over. Here. Now. But not out there.

"Andrew?" Claude sounded a bit irritated, a tone Andrew had never heard him take before. "I can make your time in that box even more miserable than it's going to be."

A screen in front of Andrew flickered with dim light, but given the previous darkness, it was almost blinding. He could make out a figure standing in front of the box and by the dumpy shape he knew it was Claude.

"And what rough beast, its hour come round at last, slouches toward Bethlehem to be born?" Andrew quoted, his voice cracking from the dryness.

"Ah, you and your poetry." Claude sounded very satisfied. "I am sorry this had to happen." He didn't sound the least bit sorry. "But you went outside the parameters. You broke Code."

"You lie."

"Don't pretend," Claude said. "Dealer is the only thing standing between us and another Chaos. Mankind barely survived that. And now you, and your predecessor, have been trying to change things. Change is not good. Change is against Code."

"Everything has to evolve," Andrew said. "Even Dealer."

"Then Dealer will do so and let its will be known." Claude sighed, the sound echoing in the box. "And you're People! You benefit the most from this system. Why would you go against it?"

"You killed my predecessor," Andrew said. He'd had nothing but time to think for the past twelve hours.

"I didn't kill him," Claude said. "He was violating Code."

"Then he should have been judged by Dark Angels."

"He was on his way to be judged," Claude said, "when he tried to escape. He grabbed the controls of his lift and when a Dealer tried to stop him, there was an accident. Unfortunately, he perished and the Dealer was damaged beyond repair."

Claude sounded more distressed about the machine than the human.

"Do you know the numbers?" Andrew asked. "Point zero one percent People. Point zero three percent Evermore. Point zero nine percent Middlemore. Can you do the math?"

Claude didn't answer. He knew the numbers. It was part of his job. The silence dragged on and Andrew's eyes were beginning to adjust to the glow, more details emerging. Claude's frowning face.

"Which leaves ninety-eight-point-seven percent burner," Andrew continued. "The question is how People manage to live so long? I've only known a few who have died. And they were well past two hundred years. There are even some still alive who went through the Chaos. And those who do die, do it in Hospital, out of sight."

"Genetics," Claude said.

Andrew snorted. "What does that mean? A word we throw around to explain everything. It's on our cards because of what's in our genes. We get dealt our card by Dealer, who has analyzed our genes at birth and done the projection of our life expectancy. How did this come to be? How can we be clustered so tightly around the medians? Twenty-five years for burner. Forty-five for Middlemore. Seventy-five for Evermore."

"The Chaos." Claude gave the approved answer. "Before Dealer, many people were given implants, making them part machine. Some human brains were even placed in machines. And the implants and cyborgs manipulated human DNA. It's why the Chaos happened. The true humans had to defend themselves against the implants and the cyborgs, but in the course of it, all humans were affected by a virus unleashed by the cyborgs."

"That's the story Dealer gives us," Andrew allowed, "but much was lost to the Imp."

"You don't believe Dealer?" Claude asked.

Andrew gave a bitter laugh. "So humans defeated the cyborgs only to submit their will to a machine?"

"Dealer puts our welfare foremost," Claude said. "It's why the Code exists."

"The system is breaking down," Andrew said.

"So you handle that by helping a burner escape Code? A burner pretending to be People?"

"You handle it by boxing me?" Andrew threw back. "You know the data. The drop in the birth rate in hive. Even in City Edge and City. Not in People, of course. Almost all offspring of People are guaranteed to be People come Dealing Day. When was the last time a People was dealt burner on Dealing Day?"

"It's genetics," Claude repeated.

"Yes, yes," Andrew said. "The child gets its genes from its parent. So it makes sense that People give birth to People and burner to burner. There are some exceptions, of course. Aberrations."

"And then there are twins," Claude interjected.

Andrew let the silence drag out for several moments. Andrew could now clearly see Claude standing there. In a bleak room underneath Island where the boxed were stored amongst the service tunnels. He was surprised Michael wasn't behind Claude, a solid mass of metal and computing. Or had a new Person already been chosen and Michael was up in the Oval, at the man's side?

"Seems twins should have the same genetics," Andrew finally said. "I asked the teachers. And I'm sure you queried the Stream once you suspected what I was doing."

"And what did the teachers tell you?" Claude asked.

"You know what they told me," Andrew said. "We don't know how it happened. There haven't been twins since the Chaos, as far as the records show. But I am no fool, Claude. And neither are you. We worked together too long for you to believe that. I didn't help this burner just because she was there. Something bigger is going on. Something beyond you and me."

"You think you can change things? Dealer is everything. You cannot defy Dealer."

Andrew remained silent. His lips were cracked. His mouth dry.

"Your burner," Claude said. "Grace. It seems the previous Person knew about her and her sister from the day they were born but kept it a secret. Where did you send her?"

Andrew felt a surge of adrenaline. So she was gone. Free for now.

Claude continued. "She left here via a service tunnel. We have the image in the Stream security imagery. Where is she going? Trying to take the Wave back to hive? Where was she supposed to meet her sister Millay? City Edge?"

"Track their cards," Andrew said.

"Her card isn't in the Stream," Claude said. "Neither is Millay's. We found Grace's card in a tracer locker in hive."

"According to what Michael said," Andrew noted, "their cards never *were* in the Stream. At least officially."

"There shouldn't be twins," Claude said. "Code says so."

"But there are. And I had nothing to do with that."

"Yes. Indeed. An aberration," Claude said. "I noticed this Grace was different the second day she was here. Probably around the same time you did. I tracked you checking on her and her sister. Do you think after relying on me for so many years you could keep something like that from me? I know you better than you know yourself. So where did you tell her to go?"

Andrew answered with a question of his own. "Who is the new Person?"

Claude laughed. "Ah. Open your eyes, Andrew."

"They are—"

"No. I mean look."

And then Andrew saw it. On Claude's chest was a black card. "I work for Dealer, not the Person. Not People. I work for the system." Claude reached up and slipped the black card inside his tunic, pulling out his usual green one. Claude chuckled, and there was an edge to it, a teetering of sanity. "Your predecessor thought Delta was a solution?"

Andrew felt a chill, even though he knew the air in his box was regulated.

"He thought he could go outside of Dealer and build his own little community; not part of the Sound?" Claude didn't wait for an answer. "And you followed right in his footsteps. Did you two really think Dealer wouldn't know? Dealer knows all. Dealer *allowed* your predecessor to build up Delta. Dealer has factored Delta into the greater good."

"What's going to happen?" Andrew asked.

"We're not ignorant," Claude said. "Evermores that is. Even though you look down on us. Think we're only good for following orders. We have indeed seen the numbers. The drop in birth rate in the hive. Even among Middlemores and Evermores." Claude laughed. "And your predecessor and you handed Dealer a solution. Delta."

And then Andrew understood. He and the previous Person had been played by Dealer.

"Actually," Claude continued, "the Middlemores saw it first. But we talk to them. Unlike you high and mighty big head People. You'd think you'd be more concerned about your future, given that you have one."

"And what of yours?"

"It is what it is. The status quo must be maintained. Code must be followed."

"Don't you want more than just what is?" Andrew asked.

"It is what it is," Claude said in a voice of utter certainty and conviction.

"What are you going to do to Delta? It's in Void. That's forbidden to Dealer by Code."

"There are plans," Claude said, the certainty gone and Andrew knew there were things the Evermore didn't know. Things no one knew, and that was part of the problem and the solution. "Dealer will take care of it."

"What if Dealer is failing?" Andrew asked.

"Where is she going?" Claude demanded.

"Heaven," Andrew said. "She's due."

"Not likely," Claude replied. "Where is she going?"

"Your guess is as good as mine."

"You've been boxed less than half a day," Claude said. "It's bad, but I can make it much worse."

"I didn't send her anywhere," Andrew lied. "She left. On her own. Why are you worried about where she's going? She's just some burner."

"Unlike you," Claude said, "I believe in covering every aspect of a problem."

"I think you're just here to gloat," Andrew said.

There was a moment of silence. "Where is she?"

"I don't know."

And for the first time, Andrew picked up a note of uncertainty in Claude's voice. "We'll find her. Maybe we'll box her so she can spend her last days next to you and you can listen to her last breath."

"Maybe," Andrew said. "Then again. Maybe not. And burners don't get boxed. It's against Code. If Dealer can't find one burner, maybe Dealer isn't so great after all."

THREE ZERO UNTIL
GRACE'S DEATHDAY

Long after dawn broke, with the smudged sun above the clouds indicating midday, Ryker was still walking. The trail had merged with an old B.D. road, which made the going considerably easier. There were other roads along the way, left and right, but a similar mirror was tied to a branch on a tree or post beyond each crossroads, indicating the direction.

He saw a large intersection ahead, with a much wider road crossing perpendicular to his path. He walked into the center of the intersection. It was a gray day, everything damp, but not wet. Much like the weather always was in hive. Ryker had no sense he was being followed or watched, but he was uneasy being so far into the open.

Ryker turned about, looking left, forward, then right, searching for the mirror to indicate the way to Delta. Of course, Delta wasn't where he wanted to go, but he had no knowledge of this area. Rusting signs indicated destinations long defunct: to the left *Bainbridge Island*; straight ahead *Kitsap*; to the right *Port Townsend*.

Each location he read initiated jingle-jangled thoughts, but he couldn't lock them down. He wasn't even sure how he knew how to read. He knew many burners couldn't. Where had all the words floating around in his brain come from? For that matter, he wasn't quite sure where *he* came from.

He closed his eyes, trying to bring calm to his brain and he staggered back as a clear image blossomed: *streaks of green burning through the night air, slamming into bodies, knocking them to the ground, tearing them apart. The people were firing weapons of their own, emitting bolts of red, going in the opposite direction. And they were shooting at—*

The vision was gone as suddenly as it had appeared.

Had he seen it in the Stream sometime in the past?

Ryker opened his eyes. He caught a glint to the right. A mirror hung from a tree on the side of the road, about fifty yards in that direction, indicating the way to Delta. But Ryker looked to his left. *Bainbridge Island.* He felt an urge to go in that direction.

With a sigh, he turned right. He walked a little over a mile and the wide road curved left. Another road passed *over* the road he was one, actually two roads on separate bridges.

And hanging from chains below the closest bridge were bodies. A dozen. Most of the flesh and muscle had been stripped from the corpses, just tattered strips remaining here and there remaining.

Ryker walked up to the bridge, stopping just short. He could see that the teeth in the skull of the nearest body were sharpened.

"They didn't kill themselves," a voice called out. "They're a warning to their kind that this is the Line they cannot cross."

Ryker looked farther up. A man was standing on the bridge, flanked by several others wielding spears and clubs.

"You're fresh off the boat," the man said, which produced laughter from his comrades.

"I am."

"You're out of cycle. Why did Charon bring you over?"

"I asked."

"You asked," the man said. He gestured and Ryker spun about as he heard movement. Five people armed like those on the bridge were behind him, spread in a semi-circle.

"And you walked here from the landing by yourself?"

"Yes."

"Didn't meet anyone?"

"I didn't *meet* anyone," Ryker said. "I was attacked by two of—" he nodded up at the corpses—"them."

"Two. And since you're here, where are they?"

"Dead."

The man was tall and thin, over six feet. His left arm was gone at the shoulder. The empty sleeve of his black shirt was pinned to his chest. He had silver hair, an indicator he was either People, Evermore or a Middlemore near the end of his time.

"Come up," he ordered.

The five circled in tight around Ryker, escorting him to the right and then up a curving ramp onto the bridge. While the man who'd spoken was dressed in brown pants and a black shirt, most of the rest of the group was not so well-fashioned, wearing a collection of worn clothes and animal skins.

They didn't look hungry, even though most were obviously burners. None of them had were cards around their necks.

The man took a few steps toward Ryker, walking with a distinct limp. He stuck his hand out. "I'm Achilles."

"Ryker." He could tell that Achilles had not worked at anything that built up the calluses on his hand. A firm grip, but soft skin.

"You a folder, or did you get floed?" Achilles asked.

"Does it matter?"

"It goes to motivation," Achilles said. "And motivation goes to character."

"Why do you care about character?"

Achilles pulled his hand back. "Listen to me, boy," he said. "You're not in hive anymore. Life out here is harsh. You saw those jokers below us? This is the Line. Anyone not accepted in Delta doesn't pass the Line. You have to pull your weight. That goes to character."

"I'll pull my weight," Ryker said. "I wasn't floed. I folded."

"Why?"

"I folded so I wouldn't have to answer questions."

Achilles ignored that. "You killed two jokers?"

"Yes."

"Jokers come from the ones we don't let into Delta," Achilles said. "Who have bad motivation. Mostly those who were floed. Funny thing is, they get floed because they don't pull their weight in hive. They don't get into Delta because we know they won't pull their weight. Then jokers live the hardest life imaginable out here in the Void and have to pull their weight every day just to survive."

"Irony."

Achilles cocked his head and peered harder at Ryker. "Yes. Irony." He gestured to a comrade. "Doc." An older woman, older being anyone beyond apparent burner Deathday, stepped up. She had short gray hair and a lined, black face. There was a scar running from the edge of her right eye straight down to her jaw. She wore clothes almost as clean as Achilles, loose fitting green pants and a smock. She had a vest over the smock, with lots of pockets, bulging with who knew what. She had a bulky camouflage pack on her back. Tucked into a band around her waist was a hatchet.

"Meet Ryker," Achilles said to her.

"We're not in cycle for a transit by Charon," Doc said. She looked at Ryker. "How did you get here?"

"Charon was gracious enough to give me a ride."

Doc glanced at Achilles, but didn't say anything. Then she turned back to Ryker and stuck out her hand. "Welcome to Delta."

"Thank you." Doc's hand felt like sandpaper.

"I assume Charon got your card?" Doc asked.

"Yes."

She looked at the knives in Ryker's belt. "That what you used on the jokers?"

"Yes."

Doc stepped close to him and looked into his eyes. "Were you trained on the knives? Never heard of that in hive."

"I don't know."

"You don't know," Doc repeated. "Maybe you just got lucky?"

"Maybe." Ryker had the strange feeling she was seeing more in him than he knew of himself. Of course, that wouldn't be much.

Achilles turned abruptly. "Come."

Achilles could move quickly despite his limp and the rest formed a loose formation with him at the point. Ryker was in the middle, not exactly a prisoner, but not part of either. Doc was up ahead, next to Achilles. There was no one behind Ryker and he had a feeling if he turned and ran, no one would chase after him.

What a joke that would be.

"How did you know I was coming?" Ryker called out.

No one answered and Achilles didn't look back or slow down, but Doc glanced over her shoulder at him. They marched in silence for over an hour along the wide road, until a large sign on the right of the road beckoned, the white letters visible despite the streaks of rust: *NAVAL BASE KITSAP*

Achilles turned in the direction of the arrow at the bottom of the sign. Ryker could smell salt water again. A tall wall appeared on either side, overgrown with vines and other vegetation. A small building was in the middle of an opening in the wall, the windows broken out, but a person was inside, spear in hand.

Achilles waved at the sentry and continued. On the left, large bunkers stretched as far as Ryker could see, rectangular mounds covered with grass and even small trees. They were thirty meters apart, each row separated by a road five meters wide, badly overgrown.

Ryker moved up next to Achilles and Doc. "What are those?"

"All of this is B.D.," Achilles said, as if that were an explanation. "Weapons were stored in those."

Then they came to the end of the land. In front of them, projecting out over the water was a massive triangular facility. A bridge right ahead and another over a thousand feet to the right extended out to the base of the triangle, which was a hundred feet from shore. The apex of the triangle was over a thousand feet farther out as two piers extended from the base to it. There were several openings in the triangle that revealed water.

A guard stood at the bridge, underneath an old metal sign which read DELTA PIER. Besides the guard, the only signs of life were trails of smoke, seemingly coming out the concrete itself. The one large building in the middle of the Delta was run down. To the west, across the water, Ryker saw a thickly forested shoreline: Deep Void.

To the right were two more piers projecting out into the water, the closest wedge-shaped, and the farthest a rectangle. Smoke from fires also rose from each and Ryker could make out people, large numbers of people, on each. They looked like insects at this distance.

"What was this place?" Ryker asked.

"In B.D.," Achilles said, "this was a place where platforms for vehicles were serviced. Vehicles that carried weapons from the bunkers which men used to fight each other in the water."

"During the Chaos," Ryker said.

Achilles shrugged, since no one really knew about the Chaos or about B.D.. "The Imp took that information, along with everything other than Dealer."

"Dealer is great," Ryker said automatically, but with a distinct lack of enthusiasm.

"We don't say there here," Achilles said as they walked past the guard.

"Thank Dealer for that," Ryker said with a slight grin. "Going to have to break a lot of bad habits, I suppose."

"You suppose right."

"What kind of vehicles could be stored here?" Ryker wondered. "Lifts?"

"Vessels that traveled under the water," Achilles said.

"In the water?"

"Beyond the water beyond."

"What's beyond?" Ryker asked. "The Ocean?"

Achilles didn't respond, but Doc did.

"As far as we know. Yes. The Ocean."

"No one here ever gone beyond Void?" Ryker asked.

"No," Achilles said.

"The Deep Void," Doc said, "is even more dangerous than Void. As far as I know, no one has ever crossed the mountains to the other side where the Ocean is supposed to be."

"Maybe you can go around them?" Ryker said, but both of them ignored the question.

They reached the base of the pier and now Ryker could see a depressed area, below water level, where a large number of people were living. Achilles led the way to a metal staircase that descended into the dry dock. Ryker estimated there were at least three hundred people, including, surprisingly, quite a few children, but none of them looked quite yet at Dealing age.

"You talk a lot and ask a lot of questions," Achilles said, "for someone who doesn't like being asked questions."

Ryker smiled. "It is what it is."

"We don't say that here," Achilles said, his words echoing off the walls that enclosed them. They were in a long, concrete valley. Walking along a flat floor, three hundred meters long, and fifty meters wide. Vertical walls rose up on either side for twenty meters. Fifty meters of the far end was covered with a rusting metal roof. Various shelters had been erected, from wood huts, to old metal or plastic panels perched as walls and roofs.

"Okay," Ryker said. "Just a habit, you know, like from birth on."

"I know," Achilles said. "Don't do it."

"Whatever you say, boss."

"I'm not your boss," Achilles said. "We're all equal here."

"Whatever you say, equal."

Achilles shot Ryker a sharp glance, but Doc laughed.

"How many people do you have here?" Ryker asked, because many of the shelters were empty. The people were mostly gathered at the far end.

"Over a thousand total here and more on the other two piers," Achilles said. "But most are out. Doing their duties. Gathering food. Wood. Supplies. Guarding the Line from the jokers."

There were a couple of fires ahead, under the metal roof, and voices echoed back along the concrete. Long shadows were cast by the people gathered round the fires.

Achilles whistled and something came galloping down the dry dock from where the fires and voices were, long nails clicking on the concrete. Ryker started as a large, brown and black dog skidded to a halt in front of Achilles, tongue hanging out, panting. It went up to Doc and she reached down and scratched it behind the ears.

"Never seen a dog?" Doc asked.

"Heard of 'em," Ryker said. "Seen them in the Stream."

"They're only in Island," Doc said. "Only People can have them."

"So you're a People then?"

Doc laughed again. "No." Her face looked like it had laughed often. Once upon a time. Like in a story.

Achilles spoke up. "We're all equal here."

"Yeah, you said that. Just wondering how you all got a dog, is all."

Achilles shook his head. "One thing you'll learn is to not get into someone's business here."

"You been getting into my business," Ryker observed.

"I have to," Achilles said. "I'm responsible." He knelt and reached out for the dog. It ducked its head, but didn't move back. Achilles ran his hands through the dog's ruff. "Ace is a King Shepherd. An ancient breed."

"He's . . . large," Ryker managed.

"You can pet him," Doc said, one hand still in Ace's ruff.

Ryker leaned over and placed his callused hands on either side of Ace's head. He was perfectly still and for a moment the dog was too, staring up at him. Ace cocked his head, as if confused, but didn't move back. Ryker removed his hands, and Ace went back to his panting.

"He likes you," Doc said.

Achilles began walking toward the fires, Doc and Ace on one side, Ryker on the other.

"How do you know?" Ryker asked.

"He didn't bite you," Doc said with a smile.

"Does he usually bite newcomers?"

"Sometimes," Doc said. "Mostly he growls. He knows character."

"So I passed?"

Neither Doc nor Achilles responded.

There were over thirty people gathered around three fires, heavy black pots hung over them, containing something cooking. They were all watching Achilles and Ryker, but also keeping their distance as Achilles halted just under the leading edge of the metal roof. To another side, at least fifty children of various ages sat on benches listening to a woman. She was writing on an old blackboard, the sound of the chalk grating, but somehow enticing to Ryker. Words being moved not mouth to ear, but through letters to eyes.

"Welcome to Delta," Achilles said.

"And you're Achilles?" Ryker asked. "Your real name?"

"Another ancient term, from a book."

"I know," Ryker said. "A famous warrior." He nodded at the others in the dry dock. "Are they warriors?"

"The question should be, 'Are we warriors?'," Achilles said. "Since you are now a part of us."

"Are we?"

"No," Doc said. "We're refugees. We fight only to defend ourselves." She cocked her head, curious. "How do you know this stuff? History is not a subject for trashers."

"How do you know that?"

Doc was confused. "History?"

"That I was a trasher?"

She pointed. "Your forearms. Where your armgards rubbed when you lifted the hot bins into the waste processors."

Ryker looked down at his arms. There were calluses on the inside of his forearms.

"Can't use your hands for the bins," Doc said, "because the fingers would, well, crumble eventually. But you know that."

"Okay," Ryker said. So he had been a waste processor. Write that one up on the board.

Achilles pissed on his small moment of personal memory achievement by asking an ironic question. "How do you know so much?"

"I spent my off time pursuing knowledge," Ryker guessed. "Achilles is from one of the oldest poems. Passed down."

"So you're one of those," Doc said.

"One of who?"

"Those who pass the words down, mouth to ear," Doc said.

Ryker nodded toward the waiting people. "How many of them showed up knowing who Achilles was?"

"You have the honor of being the first," Achilles said.

"Is it an honor?"

"It's odd," Achilles said.

"It is what it is," Ryker said, earning a hard look from Achilles.

Achilles gestured at the people. "I don't know why you left hive. Everyone has their own reason for throwing down their cards."

Ryker touched his chest. "I don't miss it."

"But it's still counting down."

"Everyone dies," Ryker said.

"Do they?" Doc said, which elicited a sharp glance from Achilles.

"What about Dealers?" Ryker asked. "They leave you alone?"

"They have more important things to do than worry about a handful of Gaspers," Achilles said.

"Looks like you have a lot more than a handful," Ryker said.

"And Void is off limits to Dealers according to Code," Achilles added.

"And why is that?" Ryker asked.

Achilles shrugged. "It's Code."

"Are there People here?"

Achilles snorted. "Why would a People fold? They've got the winning hand."

"Do they?" Ryker didn't wait for Achilles to respond to that. "So it's pretty tough out here in Void, like they say in hive?" Ryker asked, a semi-question, verging on a statement.

"It's hard enough," Achilles said.

"But you have children here. Do they know their Deathday?"

Achilles smiled. "No. That's the blessing of the Delta."

"None seem of age for Dealing Day, though," Ryker said.

"We haven't been here that long," Doc acknowledged. "And because they were born here, their DNA wasn't scanned by Dealer."

Ryker could feel anger coming off Achilles, like a hot breeze. They were talking into dangerous space. He ignored it for the moment and considered what Doc had said. Not knowing when one was going to die. "So your children are like People, in theory, with no Deathday."

"They have a Deathday," Achilles said. "They just don't know what it is. And they won't either."

Ryker tried to wrap his brain around that. Not knowing every single day exactly when you were going to die. How many less days you were going to have. But every day was still one less day, whether one was aware of exactly how many or not. He glanced at Doc and he could tell she had an idea of what was going through his brain. He also sensed Achilles didn't want to talk about that subject further.

"What *do* you do here?" Ryker asked.

"We have to work to find food," Doc said. "You'll learn how to gather and hunt. We're more than just out of the Stream, we're completely on our own."

"And the Dealers really don't care?"

"Dealers are machines," Achilles said. "They don't care about anything."

"Then the People, the Person," Ryker pressed. "What about them? No one comes looking?"

Achilles snapped: "No." His tone indicated the subject was closed.

Footsteps echoed in the dry dock behind them and they turned. Some people were coming down the center, two men with a deer lashed to a pole they carried on their shoulders along with some others.

Ryker sensed something behind him and turned, hands going for his knives, but he froze as the points of three spears were pressed into him, none too gently. Not breaking skin, but close, very close to doing damage.

A man pulled the daggers out of Ryker's belt and took them to Achilles. He peered at the blades. "These are top-notch. Not made in hive. Good steel. Where did you get them?"

Ryker wished he could tell the man, because it would mean he had a personal memory before coming to awareness in Charon's boat.

Achilles handed them over to one of the guards. Ryker didn't react, letting this hand play out, since he had no idea where it was going.

"Come." Achilles led the way toward an open steel door. Achilles, Doc, Ryker and two guards crowded in, the other two guards taking position outside as the door swung shut. A few candles sputtered, providing dim light and a pungent odor.

"Charon doesn't ferry out of cycle," Achilles said. "Who are you?"

"Told you. Name's Ryker."

"What are you doing out here?" Achilles demanded.

That, at least, was a question to which he had a partial answer. "I have to get to the bridge."

"'Bridge'? What bridge?" Achilles asked.

"Lone Bridge."

"It's guarded by Dealers," Doc said. "Shut since the Chaos. And the bridge to Deep Void is broken. Lone Bridge is deep in joker territory."

"And what are you going to do at the bridge?" Achilles asked, ignoring her.

"I don't know," Ryker lied. Partially.

"Then how do you know you have to go there?" Achilles pressed.

Ryker shrugged. "I just know. Listen, you can keep asking me questions, but most of them are questions I've been asking myself. I'd have answered myself if I could, and seriously, I wish I could."

"What's wrong with you?" Doc asked. "Did you hit your head?"

"I don't know. The first thing I clearly remember is Charon demanding payment for the journey half way across. Before that, nothing of my own life. Just general things."

Achilles stroked his chin as he considered Ryker. "Something's off about you."

Doc spoke up. "Couple different reasons he might not remember. Leave him here with me. I'll check him."

Achilles pursed his lips as he considered the proposal. "Fine. Report to me when you figure it out."

"Right, boss," Doc said.

Achille's face tightened, but he didn't confront her. "Come on," he said to the two guards. "They'll be outside," he added to Doc and Ryker.

He split, but as the two guards were going she grabbed one guard's arm. "Give me the blades."

The guard hesitated, but handed them over. He walked out, slamming the steel door shut behind him.

"Are you speaking truth about your memory?" Doc asked, once they were alone with just Ace. She angled one of the blades in the dim candlelight.

"I remember being on the boat with Charon," Ryker said. "Before that, it's all jingle-jangled."

"Do you remember being trained on these knives? Trained to fight? You must be decent at it to take down two jokers."

"I don't remember."

She jabbed suddenly with the blade toward Ryker's face. He blocked it easily with an upsweep of his right arm, elbow bent, his toughened forearm knocking her thrust upward.

"Muscle memory," Doc said, pulling the blade back.

"What?"

"You don't remember being trained, but your muscles do." She sat down on an old metal stool and considered him, putting the two blades on the shelf next to her. Within easy grasp if he wanted to go for them. A dare or a test. "There's more in your brain. Ready to come out with certain prompts or under the right circumstance. Interesting."

Her hatchet was in her belt, the handle well worn, the steel gleaming.

Ryker folded his arms. "Charon had a card, by the way."

"What color?"

"Black."

Doc was startled. "'Black'?"

Ryker considered pulling the deck out, but he knew, without knowing how he knew, that if he opened the box, all those cards might rejoin the Stream. Probably not something he wanted to do here and now. Unless there was no Stream here.

"What does that mean? A black card?" Ryker asked.

But Doc's mind was elsewhere. "I was wondering why Achilles wanted to walk the Line today. As if he knew you were coming."

"How could he know I was coming?"

"Charon had to have told him somehow," Doc said. "Floe me," she cursed as the implications sunk in. "He floeing knew it." Her bitterness impressed Ryker; the facts more so.

"Then Achilles is in the Stream somehow," Ryker said. "He said he didn't have a card. That no one here has a card."

"He lied."

"You think?" Ryker said.

Doc ignored the dig. "Charon took you over off-cycle?"

"Yes. But I don't remember asking him."

"What happened with Charon?"

Ryker was surprised she could read him so well. "I killed him."

Doc blinked. "Why?"

"What he was doing was wrong."

"How did you know?"

"I just knew." Now he turned things. "Was *I* wrong?"

"I fear not." And suddenly Doc looked very, very old, the creases on her face folding in on themselves, so that the scar looked almost natural, part of the hard life she'd had. "Not if he had a card. Not if Achilles has a card and goes into the Stream somehow. That this has all been a lie. What did you do with Charon's body?"

Ryker made a thumbs-down. "Into the deep. Are you a Person?"

She shook her head. "No. Like you, I'm someone else now."

"What am I?"

"That's not the thing that should concern you right now," Doc said. "What should worry you is that you're a dead man for killing Charon. Achilles will see to that. And I fear it's worse than that for all of us if Dealer decides to act on Delta. The end of all we have known is upon us."

Ryker picked up both blades, then slide them into their sheaths. "Maybe that's not a bad thing."

THREE ZERO UNTIL
GRACE'S DEATHDAY

"Don't hesitate to shoot," Haydn told Millay. "Remember, Dealers are forbidden to kill. At worst, you'll get stunned. Like a game of tracers."

"The last game of tracers killed me," Millay said, holding the tracer gun awkwardly.

"Apparently not," Haydn said. "We don't know what happened, but you most certainly are not dead." And he leaned forward and kissed her, quick and hard, burner style.

Millay gasped as he pulled back. "But what will a tracer do to a Dealer?"

"No clue," Haydn said with a mischievous grin. "Let's hope we don't have to find out."

They were in the shadow of a work hive doorway. In front of them was a large, flat field of brown dirt—Assembly field, hard-packed from generations of burner feet crossing it, standing on it, and also saturated with the tears of the local hive on Dealing Day every year.

And every day, burners gathered daily to be taken up to Heaven.

Noon was a few hours away, but already a cluster had gathered, milling about in a mixture of resignation of impending death tinged with the excitement of Heaven, something almost inhuman about it.

Three arches stood at one end of the field, just short of the landing pads for the Dealer Lifts. They were looped with bright flowers, a rare sight in hive. The flowers were the duty of a handful of burners who brought them in from an agri-hive every few days, keeping them fresh and inviting.

A placard on the top of each arch, above the flowers, proclaimed, left to right:

THE REWARD FOR WORK
HEAVEN LIFE
AFTER LIFE

On the left side of each arch was a digital counter, currently reading 0. Below it, in small print, it read:

MAX 25 EACH LIFT

"Many burners can't read," Millay said, seeing the arches.

"We know numbers, I can assure you of that," Haydn said. "And there are enough who can read that they understand and pass it to the others. We all know each Lift takes twenty-five. It's part of the lore of hive."

"Where do they hold those who've been judged?" Millay asked.

Haydn pointed at a squat, gray building at the side of the field, not far away, with its own Lift platform on the roof. "In there. A Lift lands on top every evening. Those judged get bagged. And they're put into the Lift."

"Where do they get taken?"

Haydn shrugged. "Hell? No one really talks about it." He seemed puzzled. "Where did they take the Person when he was boxed?"

"I don't know."

"So People are like burners. No questions asked."

"It is what it is," Millay said. "But we don't say that in Island. We live it. Because *it* is very good to us."

"And *it* is everything for us," Haydn said. He pointed with the tip of his tracer. "We'll go around to the right. I don't see any Lifts, so I don't think we'll run into any Dealers. But there's sure to be at least one Middlemore. Remember, we have one very big advantage."

"What's that?"

"Everyone else thinks it is what it is." And then Haydn moved off, not pulling Millay as he had been. At least not physically. He slid along the abutment, crouched down. He followed it around the edge of the work hive.

Millay stared after him in surprise for a few seconds, then jolted into action, scurrying after him, more afraid of being alone. They got as close as they could, about ten meters of open ground separating them from a doorway on the side of the holding building.

Haydn glanced over his shoulder at Millay, smiled, winked, and began to leap up onto the field when the thrumming of an approaching Lift reverberated through the air. He abruptly shifted direction and threw himself back behind the abutment.

Three Lifts flew overhead in formation. They settled on the pitted concrete pads on the other side of the arches. The doors on the closest side slid open and metal steps flipped down. Burners filed through, some almost pushing. As each one went under an arch, the top number clicked and when each hit 25, the burners in each line stopped.

"Floe me," Millay said.

"Such language," Haydn said.

"But there were no Dealers. No Middlemores. They just went through on their own and stopped on their own."

"They're burner," Haydn said, as if that explained everything. "They're going to Heaven. And we follow rules. Certainly you've learned that in the last month here in hive."

The three Lifts took off and winged away to the north and west.

"So Heaven lies that way," Millay said.

"Maybe," Haydn said, but he was already poking his head over the abutment and eyeing the door to the holding building. "Let's go."

He jumped out of the low ground and raced across the open space. Millay didn't hesitate this time, following close behind. Haydn pulled open the door, holding it for Millay and then they were both inside.

"You! Halt!"

Haydn fired his tracer at the Middlemore. The round hit the man in the belly and he squealed, hands tearing at his stomach. He fell to the ground, continuing to whine, as Haydn ran up. He looped a piece of cloth around the Middlemore's mouth, squelching his cries of pain, and used another to tie his hands and legs together.

"Hurts, don't it?" Haydn said. He was done before the tracer charge was expended.

The Middlemore flopped about helplessly. Millay looked down at him, uncertain. His kind was two ranks below her, but had been one above for the past few weeks and she was surprised how much his blue card affected her now. She fought the impulse to remove the bonds and hustled after Haydn.

There was only one person in the steel mesh cage. He looked triple-downed on burner: despondent, hopeless, and exhausted.

"You Josh?" Haydn asked.

He barely lifted his head. "Yes."

"Come with us." Haydn opened the cell door, but Josh didn't move. "Come on," Haydn repeated.

Josh jumped up when he saw Millay. "You! You're dead."

"I was just hurt," Millay said.

"Then let's tell the Middlemore," Josh said, his words tumbling over themselves in his excitement. "This has all been a mistake! He can let his Evermore know and then the Person and Dealer."

"No," Haydn said. "The Person has been boxed and—" He paused, trying to figure out how to explain this. "We're folding. You come with us. You were sitting here thinking you were going to be bagged, no more time, no Heaven. At least now, you get time." Haydn glanced at the card on Josh's chest. "Zero four slash zero six slash one eight. Lots of time."

Josh sat down in his cell. "I'm not folding. She's alive. I get Heaven."

Haydn indicated the open door to the cell. "We've given you your life back. Your choice what you do with it." He turned to Millay. "Let's go."

Millay reached out to Josh. "I'm sorry I caused all this. It was an accident."

Haydn put a hand on her shoulder. "Accidents kill all the time. Choices kill. You've given him the opportunity of a life for a life. You duty here is done and the deal is his. Come."

Millay followed, leaving Josh sitting in the cell with the door open.

The beach had been easy moving and the ball kept her moving on it, but it didn't last. High sandy bluffs, overgrown with vegetation, blocked the way, the Sound lapping at their base. She'd gone out in the water, but quickly went up to her neck and, not knowing how to swim, had retreated.

With no other choice, she backtracked and climbed. Grabbing onto branches, vines, whatever, she clambered up to the high bluff, her coverall damp and clinging. At the top, she came upon a path, obviously used often, the undergrowth cut back from it. Like a feral animal, she knelt on the edge of the path, looking left and right, listening, even sniffing.

Nothing.

Grace didn't trust the path. People walked it. And she wasn't People. She'd never been, even when pretending and she couldn't pretend any more.

She used the ball and it vibrated right down the path. While she held it, counting, it vibrated again. Nine seconds.

Closer.

She tried to stay off the path, but moving through the vegetation was virtually impossible, with ferns and vines and fallen logs from old growth blocking the way.

Grace accepted the inevitable and stepped onto the path. It wove through the forest, easily skirting the homes of the People on the left and as close to the water as it could on the high ground, occasionally offering views of the Sound. The buildings were all so well integrated with the environment, it wasn't hard to remain hidden from them. They were designed as if those in the houses didn't want to be seen from anyone on the path. Or vice versa. People valued their privacy; that was one thing she'd learned in her short time here.

She checked the ball and it indicated the same: up the path. And now, eight seconds.

When she heard voices come toward her, Grace scurried off the trail, crawling underneath a thick log, long dead, wood rotting, insects crawling. Two People, women, came down the trail. At their feet was a dog, a small one, scuttling about on short legs. They were discussing something about their hair or the hair of one of their acquaintances or some such big head People unimportance. The dog was running free and headed directly toward Grace's hiding spot. It stopped right in front of her and started yapping. Short, high-pitched sounds that couldn't be credited as barks. It had curly brown hair, a pug nose, and beady little eyes. They reminded her of that creepy Evermore, Claude.

"Tipsy, come back here," one of the women called out.

Tipsy wasn't listening.

Grace stared the nasty little beast in the eye, all her will urging it to run back to its master.

It cared naught for her will.

Then the dog lifted its leg and urinated onto the log, drops splashing Grace. As it finished, some faint genetic coding made it half-ass paw at the ground as if covering its trail from some ancient predator, then it scurried back to the women who continued down the path, out of sight, then out of sound, never once glancing in Grace's direction.

Who were these People? Grace seethed as she lay there. Who were they to walk as if nothing mattered but themselves and their little circle of the world? To be at the top of a larger world they knew so little about?

Grace slithered out from under the log, feeling the dampness of the urine mixed with the water from the Sound. She pulled the scraper from her belt. She remembered wielding it in the hollowing echo of a massive 'tein vat, scraping, as water sprayed down heavily from above every so often, pushing the detritus toward the drain on the bottom, where it disappeared, although Grace had no doubt that it was recycled back into the next batch of cast-off ingredients poured into the vat to make the next batch of 'tein.

Nothing was wasted in hive.

Grace glared down the trail after the women, desiring to go after them, to show them reality. To show them the scraper, her hands, who she was. And use the blade if she had to in order to get them to see.

Grace looked up at the darkening sky. "I am not Millay. I am Grace. Of hive. I am Grace. burner. I am Grace. I was chosen by Andrew, who was the Person. I am all of those and I am Grace. I am Human."

Achilles left the cell holding Doc and Ryker and strode across the dry dock, ignoring the greetings of others, which wasn't unusual. A steel door was set in the concrete and he turned the wheel with his one hand. Well-oiled, the mechanism worked smoothly. He slipped inside. It was complete darkness once he closed the door behind him.

He pulled a headlamp out of his pocket and slipped it over his head, then turned it on.

A concrete stairwell led to the top of the dry dock. He made his way up the stairs, his leg paining him. He pushed open the door.

He walked along the upper edge of the dry dock. The facility reached by the two bridges was shaped like a triangle, with the dry dock being the base. The other two sides connected at the farthest point from land. Achilles walked toward that point. A rusting crane, its boom dipping down into the water, stood at the tip. Achilles climbed up to the operator's cabin, which was thirty feet up.

There was a new electronic lock on the door.

He reached into his pocket and retrieved a black card. He slid it through the reader and the lock clicked. Opening the door, he went inside. In the operator's seat was a Dealer.

Actually, it was only half a Dealer. The upper half. The lower half had been gone for as long as Achilles had been in the Delta and he'd never seen the point of finding out what had happened to it. He assumed that Dealer, in its infinite wisdom, wasted nothing and had seen no point in positioning a completely functioning Dealer out here for a job, half a Dealer could accomplish.

Achilles sat on a console next to the Dealer, took the black card out and slid it through a slot on the side of the Dealer. With a crackle of energy, the Dealer came to 'life,' reaching out, using its own power to search for the Stream on the other side of Void, nearest Island.

"I'd prefer not to be killed," Ryker said. "What's your play going to be?"

"It's getting dark," Doc said.

Ryker waited.

"I always knew it was too good to be true," Doc said. "That Dealer ignored this place and these people. It's too big. When I first got here, five years ago, there were only a handful of us. Barely twenty. Achilles was the one who brought us together. Separated us from the jokers. Made us a community. All the founders of Delta are gone now, their time done. Except for me and Achilles."

"What happens to someone when their Deathday arrives out here?" Ryker asked.

Doc jerked a thumb to the south. "Devils Hole. Not far away. They go there two weeks before. Our own mini-version of Heaven. Achilles makes sure they have plenty of food and water before they trek there."

"Devils Hole is your version of Heaven?" Ryker asked. "Seems like a paradox."

"Fancy word for burner," Doc said. "The name comes from B.D. Just like Delta. It's what the place was called. There's a sign there. The ones before the Chaos had a name for every place it seems."

"And the bodies?" Ryker asked.

"That's another piece of the puzzle," Doc said. "There are no bodies there. They disappear."

"Where to?"

Doc shrugged. "Maybe the water."

"No one has checked?"

"We have our own form of Code out here," Doc said. "We have to, in order to survive. We don't check."

"Dictated by Achilles." Ryker made it a statement.

"Yes."

"So it is what it was?"

"It worked."

"Past tense," Ryker said.

"You don't seem overly concerned about things," Doc said.

"As you noted," Ryker said, "the play is going to be bigger than me, don't you think, if Achilles is in the Stream?"

"How did you know about Achilles?"

"How did you?"

"Too many things that don't add up. It's taken me years to find the questions you've asked in just an hour here."

"Sometimes when you're in it," Ryker said, "you can't see it."

"The Stream doesn't reach out here," Doc said. "So if he can access it, he's doing it some other way than just a card."

"A black card," Ryker said.

"Most likely. Whatever that is. But it still needs access to the Stream."

"So Dealer does care about things out here in the Void."

"Dealer doesn't care about anything," Doc said. "Dealer is a machine. It does what has to be done."

"Why was this place picked?"

"What?" Doc was confused.

"The location. Delta," Ryker said. "And the other two piers?"

"Easily defended against jokers," Doc said. "There's a wall around most of this area and then to get onto the piers, there are only a couple of entrances."

"Which means there are only a couple of exits," Ryker said. "Everyone's back is to the water. And burners can't swim."

Doc pondered that for a few moments. "So it's a trap," Doc finally said. "We have to warn everyone."

Ryker shook his head. "Too late. That's why Achilles left us here. And the Deltans won't believe us and will back Achilles' play." He met her eyes in the flickering candlelight. Ace whined, as if demanding something happen. "Am I right?"

Doc reluctantly agreed. "They'll back him up until the minute the Dealers land, and even then they won't believe he's behind it. Still, it's against Code for Dealers to come into Void."

"Didn't Dealer write the Code?"

"I don't know."

"I don't either," Ryker said. "But I'm willing to bet Dealer can rewrite Code if it sees the need. And I don't see why Dealer can't do whatever it wants here. Why is Void off-limits?"

"No idea," Doc said'

Ryker picked up his backpack then slung it over his shoulder. "You in?"

"How do you know it's too late?" Doc asked.

"Things are happening," Ryker said vaguely. "Can't you feel it?" He looked up, as if he could see through the steel surrounding them, into the evening sky. "Like a dark cloud coming. A storm that will sweep all before it."

"Who are you?"

"I wish I knew." He turned for the door. "You can go quiet," Ryker said, "or you can go trying."

"Trying what?"

"Trying."

Doc opened the metal door. The two guards were still there.

"I have to take him with me," Doc said to them.

The two men exchanged a glance. "Where?" one asked.

"Where Achilles told me to take him," Doc non-answered. But it was good enough, and backed up Ryker's words about which way the play would go if they tried to warn the Deltans. The two guards stood aside.

Ryker followed as Doc climbed the metal stairs.

Ace was right behind both of them, tail wagging.

"Have you been in contact with Charon?" Achilles asked.

Claude's voice sounded tinny, processing through the old Dealer, coming out of the edge of the Stream on a narrow beam. "He's not in Stream."

"What is going on?"

"Is there a problem?" Claude asked. He sounded distracted.

"I've got someone who showed up out of cycle," Achilles said.

"Told me Charon took him because he asked, which is a lie. There's something off about him. Name's Ryker."

"Need more than that to identify him," Claude said. "Do you have his qualifiers?" he asked, referring to the mixture of four numbers and letters after everyone's given name.

"No. What is going on?"

"The Person has been boxed," Claude said. "And if Charon isn't in Stream, it's likely he's out of play."

"You mean dead."

"Charon wouldn't fold," Claude said. "So your Ryker did something to him."

"Why?"

There was a long pause. "How close are your oldest children in Delta to Dealing Day?" Claude asked.

"Zero zero slash zero two slash one four," Achilles said.

"Close enough. Time to close out this group and reboot as planned."

"How do I reboot Delta without Charon?"

"He can be replaced. Anyone can be replaced."

"Why was the Person boxed?" Achilles asked, two conversations mixing in the Stream. "You're holding something back."

"There are a couple of wildcards in play," Claude said.

"Ryker. And who else?"

"I didn't know about this Ryker," Claude said. "Two women. Twins."

"There are no twins."

Claude ignored that. "One is People and one is a burner. They swapped positions for several weeks. And now one of them is down to three zero. And the Person helped her escape the Island, so there's much more going on there. And now she's out of the Stream. A wild card. As is her sister. Left hive and left her sister's card behind."

"Listen, Claude. I've done what Dealer wanted. I've atoned. I want to come back."

"I'm just the messenger," Claude said. "Dealer will decide when you've atoned. Be glad you only lost the arm and weren't completely boxed."

Achilles looked out of the crane's cabin at the darkening sky. On this side, one couldn't see Island, the bulk of Void blocking the view. In the other direction, the Olympic Mountains loomed. The sun was gone behind them, but still sending its last rays over the peaks and clouds. "What does Dealer order we do?"

"We inputted the data," Claude said. "Dealer advises it's time to act."

"Does the new Person concur?"

"I concur," Claude said. "That's all that matters.

"It is what it is," Achilles said, as he rubbed his shoulder where his left arm had been neatly sliced off six years ago.

"Showing the newbie the ropes," Doc said to the guard manning the post where the pier met the land.

The guard'sfocus was on anyone coming toward the Delta, not leaving it. She had a hand-made wood spear in her hand, tipped with a piece of sharp metal. "Will you be back before dawn?" the guard asked.

"Not likely."

The guard looked concerned. "Dangerous out there in the night, even behind the Line."

Doc ignored her. "Come," she said, whistling to Ace.

"What's going on?" the guard asked.

Ryker looked at her. "If I were you, I'd run." And then he turned and walked off down the broken-up road, Doc and Ace at his side, leaving the befuddled guard behind.

"That wasn't nice," Doc said.

"It was true."

"But you didn't explain."

"Dealer doesn't explain," Ryker said as he turned left, off the road and walked into the forest, underneath the old trees. He held a hand up, barely visible in the darkness. "They come."

Doc sighed, shoulders slumping.

"Do you know what they will do with them?" Ryker asked as lights flickered overhead; squadrons of Dealer Lifts flew by, the noise of their engines like an approaching storm.

"No."

"We'll have to find out," Ryker said. "We have to find the truth."

"*Who* are you?" Doc asked.

Ryker rubbed Ace's head. "If I don't know who I was, then I must be what isn't."

THREE ZERO UNTIL
GRACE'S DEATHDAY

Achilles stayed in the crane control room as the Lifts came in to hover. Their searchlights flickered here and there, jingle-jangled rays of light, before fixing on access—and egress—points where the piers met land. Doors slid open and dozens of Dealers leapt out. The thud of them hitting concrete and asphalt echoed in the night air.

Followed by screams.

The Dealers formed cordons at all the entry points to the three piers, sealing them off. A few desperate Deltans jumped into the water, flailing about. Most clambered or were pulled back to 'safety' upon realizing the futility, but a handful disappeared into the dark water, never to rise again.

The rest gave up quickly, except for one of the guards on an entrance to the Delta. She fought with her spear against the closest Dealer, an utterly foolish endeavor against the machines. She was quickly stunned into submission.

Then the roundup began.

Achilles rubbed his shoulder and wondered where Ace was. He missed the dog.

"How did you know about Charon and Achilles?" Doc asked.

"Does it matter how I knew?" Ryker asked. "I was right."

"It does matter," Doc said.

"If I knew, I'd tell you. I just felt it."

They were inside the wall surrounding the entire B.D. base, but well away from Delta and the other piers. The screaming and Lift sirens had faded out. The only indication something was going on were the random lights to the west from Lifts quartering the area, gathering those not caught in the initial sweep. Ryker had his back against one of mounds covered in vegetation. Doc paced back and forth. Ace was on top of the bunker, head swiveling, as if on guard duty.

"So. Middlemore?" Ryker asked. "Evermore? People?"

"People don't fold," Doc said. She sighed. "I was Evermore. Worked in Island half my time. In City the other half."

"So why fold?"

"I didn't fold. But I did lift my head."

Ryker nodded as if he understood. "What did you see?"

"It's all wrong."

"How?"

Doc shrugged. "I was medical. Took care of Evermores and Middlemores."

"But never burners."

"No. But it's the opposite that was strange."

"You never treated a People."

"Exactly. I never got called to take care of People, even though I rotated out to Island, but that was just for emergency work if some-thing happened to an Evermore on duty. It just didn't feel right. And I was good. I was as highly certified as one could get. But never on a

People. I thought they had their own doctors. From among their own."

"But they don't."

"They might," Doc allowed. "But I spent almost a quarter of my time on Island. Never got called to do a thing. Except take care of an Evermore who had an accident. Or was facing—" her voice fell off.

"Evermore's don't get Heaven, do they?"

"They die. They just die. I've seen some collapse while still working, even though they know it's their Deathday. That's how powerful it is."

"What is?" Ryker asked.

"What we believe." Doc paused in thought. "But they have Hospital in Island. People go to it. But no Evermores are allowed in."

"So they do have their own doctors."

"I suppose."

"How did you end up out here?" Ryker asked.

"That's a story for another day."

They both looked up as a string of Lifts thrummed by, heading north and east.

"I wonder if they're going to Heaven," Doc said.

Ryker pointed at the old bunker. "Looks like a good place to spend the night." He got to his feet, then went around to the large metal doors on the front of the bunker. A large, rusting lock secured it. He looked left and right and could see similar mounds as far as he could make out in the darkness. "The ones before the Chaos had a lot of weapons." He continued down the line, past five more until he came to one where the lock had been pried off.

"They did," Doc concurred as Ryker swung up a metal handle. Rust protested, but the metal gave way.

Opening the thick door was more difficult, but it was perfectly balanced on the hinges.

"Safe place to rest for the night," Ryker said, peering into absolute darkness.

"I prefer outside."

Ryker pointed to the west. A Lift was moving slowly, searchlight flickering, here, there, back and forth. "They'll be over this way eventually. Before dawn. We'd best be inside. They don't have time to check this all on the ground."

"All right." Doc stepped into the darkness, Ace following. Ryker swung the door shut.

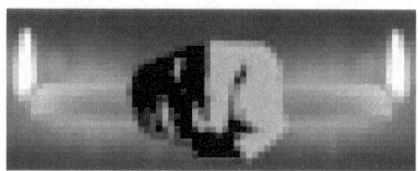

"What is that?" Haydn asked, looking out over the fields to their left in the dying light.

"Corn fields," Millay said.

"What's corn?"

Millay remembered the numbing 'tein she'd eaten in hive for every single meal. "Food."

"For who?" Haydn asked as he led the way down a slight slope toward the field, away from the folding path.

"Middlemores. Evermores. People."

"All but burner." Haydn didn't say it with bitterness. "But burners work these fields, don't they?"

"Agri-hives," Millay said. "Burners get a lot of it, but only after the quota is sent to City Edge. It's part of what's mixed together to make 'tein."

They arrived at the edge of the field.

Haydn put his hand around an ear of corn. "Do burners who work these fields eat it? Or do they get 'tein?"

Millay remembered the reports that had come-gone across her desk, cold numbers, their addition and subtraction all that mattered, the reality something not even considered. "They get it, but indirectly. All burners get only 'tein. It's part corn, part of other food from agri-hives. It's the most efficient way of ..." she fell silent.

"Of course. Efficiency." Haydn started down one of the green rows, now black with the night, heading in the direction they'd taken since leaving Josh behind. North and curving west in the Wasteland toward the edge of hive.

"It's dark." Millay pointed out the obvious. "I've never been outside at night like this."

"I have," Haydn said. "Few burners leave hive, but I've gone out, as far as I can, before having to report back for work. Slept under the clouds. Seen stars some times."

"Why?" Millay asked.

"It was a feeling."

"A feeling of what?"

Haydn paused, glancing up at her, a slender silhouette against the night sky. "Freedom. It wasn't real. Just a feeling. Sometimes I even made it to the Wasteland"

"Weren't you afraid to be outside, all alone? Especially in the Wasteland?"

"No."

"That's so—" Millay began but then she realized Haydn wasn't paying attention. He had the tracer gun out and signaled for her to be quiet. There was a rustling in the stalks to their right and Millay edged closer to Haydn until she was shoulder to shoulder with him. It was only then she thought to pull her own gun out.

A boy, pre-Dealing Day, stepped into their row, barely two feet away. He had a sack looped over one shoulder, stuffed full of ears of corn. He startled. His eyes shifted from Haydn's face to the gun, then back to his face. Then to his chest, and then Millay's chest.

"Dealing from the bottom of the deck?" Haydn said, lowering the gun.

The boy only nodded.

"Corn any good?" Haydn asked.

The boy nodded once more.

"Middlemores don't miss it in the quota?"

The boy licked his lips nervously. "We don't take much."

Millay spoke up. "Is there a safe place my friend and I can sleep around here?"

"You folding?" the boy asked, finally showing more interest than fear. "You got no cards."

"Yes," Haydn said.

The boy pointed. "Outer arc and the folding path is that way." He pointed closer, in roughly the same direction. "Old silo over there. Can sleep inside."

"Thanks," Haydn said. "Be on your way."

The boy hurried off and was instantly lost among the towering stalks.

"He's stealing," Millay said.

"He's dealing from the bottom of the deck," Haydn corrected. "Stop being a People."

Millay flushed, glad he couldn't see it in the darkness.

"Come on," Haydn said, pushing forward.

They walked in the darkness, but Haydn didn't turn off as the silo came up on their left.

"The silo's right there," Millay protested as Haydn continued on.

"And if we sleep in the silo, he'll know we're there. And he might tell someone. And he might deal us off the top of the deck. Dealer might have dammed the Stream again and put out the word to everyone to look for us. We wouldn't know since we don't have our cards."

Millay fell in behind Haydn. He zigzagged through the field, taking a couple rows to the right, then forward, then left, then forward. Every so often he picked off an ear of corn and stuffed it into his pack.

They walked for thirty minutes, then Haydn stopped. They were at the edge of the field.

Haydn pointed ahead. "Wasteland." He nodded at a thin dirt trail at their feet, separating hive from Wasteland. "Folding trail." He looked about. "Come."

He led her toward a rock outcropping three hundred meters deep into Wasteland. "As good a place as any for the night."

Millay sat gingerly on the dirt, with the rock looming over their heads. Haydn sat next to her. Before she could even mention she was cold, he put his arm around her and drew her close, giving her his warmth.

They remained like that as clouds passed by overhead, hiding the stars.

Millay spoke into the darkness. "Are we going to get caught?"

"Possible."

"What's in the Void?"

"Your sister."

"What else?"

"Jokers," Haydn said. "They might just be a rumor, meant to scare burners from folding, so they keep working to avoid getting floed."

"What's out here in the Wasteland? You've been here before."

"Don't they tell you anything in Island?"

"Not about places like the Void or Wasteland."

"Some say there are ghosts out there. I've seen none. Some say everything out there is dead. Some say anything that comes into their fool head. Get some sleep."

Millay fell silent.

But then, words into the darkness once more, a tiny voice: "Are we going to die?"

"Sure," Haydn said. "Some day. But not today."

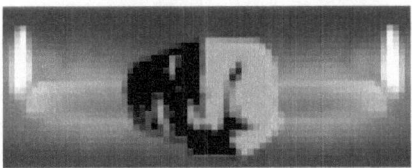

All the Stream feeds were flickering in the Oval but there was no one sitting at the central desk to observe them or issue directives.

No Person.

The elevator doors opened and Claude walked in, the first time he'd been alone in the inner sanctum. He strolled around the edge of the office, glancing at the Streams, looking out the windows at the domain of the People.

Finally, no longer fighting the desire, he turned inward. He stared at the desk. The position he'd served for so many years. The Person before. And then Andrew; who knew so much less about the Sound and the way things functioned than Claude did, even though Andrew was People.

Claude walked to the center, through the opening in the circular desk, to the chair.

He sat just as the elevator opened again.

Claude scrambled to get out of the chair, then realized it was just Michael.

Still, he didn't sit again.

"I talked to Achilles," Claude said, as Michael walked into the room, surprisingly quiet for a heavy machine. No thudding footfalls.

Michael came to a halt on the outside of the desk. Saying nothing. The metal face indicating nothing. That had always irritated Claude. He could get no take on a machine. People were easy to read, as they didn't think they ever had to hide anything from Evermores.

Claude hurried to continue, summarizing the Dealer assault on Delta and his conversation with Achilles.

"He wants to know if he has atoned and can go back to City," Claude finished.

"The name?" Michael said.

Claude was confused. "What name?"

"Repeat the name Achilles gave you. Of the burner who arrived at Delta."

"Oh. Ryker or something like that."

There was a long pause. Then: "Was this burner captured?"

"Uh, well. The Dealers are still processing all the folders rounded up."

There was a shorter silence. "He was not," Michael said. "All data of folders captured so far has been processed. Some have surely escaped."

"Who is he?" Claude asked. "This Ryker?"

"A burner."

Claude waited for amplification, but none was forthcoming. Being alone in the Oval with Michael was not being alone. Yet it was. "I have to go."

Michael said nothing. Claude hurried to the elevator. The last thing he saw was Michael in the same position, motionless next to the Person's desk.

TWO NINE UNTIL
GRACE'S DEATHDAY

Grace watched the first rays of sunlight streak above the clouds covering the Wasted Mountains, counting one day closer to death.

She sat with her back against a tree, facing the water, which was two hundred feet below, gurgling against the base of the high bluff. The sound of the waves had infiltrated her sleep, soothing, so different from the jingle-jangle of hive and the stillness of Island.

More real than either.

Her hand went automatically to her neck and a moment of panic flashed when she realized she didn't have a card. She felt naked and exposed without the chain and card she'd worn ever since she was six. Even Millay's card, while the color had bothered her, had still been comforting.

She took a couple of deep breaths.

She heard a familiar sound, the thrumming of a Dealer Lift approaching. The sound was deep, almost out of hearing range, but it bounced into the bone.

Were they coming for her? Grace wondered, looking up, grateful for the spreading branches and leaves above.

Three Lifts passed by, heading north.

She was hungry. In hive there was 'tein. The daily ration, bland

and the same every day, every meal. In Island, there was more food, in more ways, than any should have. She imagined there was good food in Heaven. That was word in hive. More food than any should have and not 'tein made from the remnants and rejects of the agri and rendering hives

The Lifts disappeared into the clouds. The sound faded.

Grace realized she was still gripping the scraper. Had all night. She got to her feet. The pulled the ball out. Last night, before she stopped, it had vibrated twice in four seconds.

Closer.

She pointed it up the trail and was surprised not to get a shake. She shifted left and was rewarded by one, then two. Four seconds. Slightly off the trail on the landward side.

Grace retraced her steps to the trail. She listened. No People within hearing.

She turned right. Kept moving. Spotted a small stream under a narrow wooden bridge where the path continued. She slid down, knelt between ferns and drank.

The water was better than even that in the Person's quarters.

It was a strange thought to realize something outside could be better than even there.

She was startled to hear footfalls, rapid ones, approaching. Grace crawled underneath the bridge. Someone was running.

From who? What? Grace wondered.

The slap on the dirt thudded onto the bridge as whoever it was ran across. Grace dared a peek. A Person running loosely and confidently, disappearing down the trail.

Grace stayed under the bridge, waiting for whatever or whoever was chasing the Person to come by. After a half hour, nothing, but then the same sound, coming back. The same person, running at the same pace, going back.

Grace didn't understand. One only ran in hive when one was late for work or playing tracers. Running alone, back and forth?

She crawled out from under the bridge and took the path.

Two nine.

Grace pulled the ball out. She directed it up the path. Nothing. Shifted left, got a vibration, waited and two seconds later, another.

Closer.

To what? To who?

She continued on the trail, alert.

Tried the ball again. Two quick shakes.

Very close.

She considered leaving the trail, but the forest was just as thick. She walked slowly forward. She paused when she heard voices to her left front, not on the trail. Children's voices.

She checked the ball. Two vibrations almost on top of each other in the direction of the voices. Against her better judgment, Grace wove her way a short distance through the forest. She came up to a huge log blocking her way. Getting on her knees, she peered over. In a small clearing was a cluster of pre-Womb children seated on the grass. They were facing an old woman on a wooden bench. The old woman wore a wreath of flowers on her head. She had beautiful long white hair, which flowed almost to her waist. Her skin was dark, not black, but deep brown. Instead of the usual white robe or coverall People wore, she had baggy black pants and a colorful smock.

The woman had a book and was reading to the youngsters. A far cry from the life of four and five year olds in hive, where they were responsible for basic cleaning not only of their parents' cubbys, but all the cubbys, scurrying about with rags and mops and buckets, marking time until Dealing Day, when they would graduate to increasingly heavier jobs as burners, except for the tiny handful dealt blue, green, or white.

None of these children would be burner, Grace knew. For it occurred to her for the first time that on Dealing Day, as far as she could recall, she'd never seen a single progeny of People come to the womb of hive. A scattering of Evermore and Middlemore youngsters came, weeping and distraught at their downward fates, but no People children.

Grace couldn't make out the words, but the tone of the old woman's voice was captivating, an accent Grace had never heard before. Grace put her hands together under her chin, hearing the faint rhythm of whatever was being told. But then the woman's voice went up a notch, and words, coherent, reached Grace's ears.

"Once upon a time, children, there was a man who told stories. This was long, long ago, Before Dealer. Before the Chaos." She pointed with one hand at her mouth, and then to her ear. "So long ago before the Chaos, the words were passed mouth to ear before there was even writing, which was a very, very long time ago. And then one day, someone passed the words from ear to paper." She held up the book and wiggled it. "And here are the words, which I will take from the page and pass to you. Word to mouth to ear."

The old woman smiled and looked up, past the children, and Grace started, thinking she'd been spotted, but the old woman looked down and began to tell her story. "Once upon a time, there was a sleeping lion. A tiny little mouse ran by and disturbed the great beast. And the lion snatched out—" the woman startled the children by suddenly thrusting her one hand out at them—"and caught the mouse with his mighty paw. Then he opened his mouth wide in order to swallow the mouse who had bothered him. A tasty little morsel."

She brought the hand up over her head, pretending to hold something. The old woman paused and looked at the children, one by one, ensuring she had their complete attention.

One child dared interrupt. "What is a lion, Mrs. Marash?"

"A ferocious beast," Mrs. Marash responded as she lowered her hand. "Among the animals it was known as the king of them all. With great long claws and huge fangs." And then she put the book down on her lap, raised both hands up, arthritic fingers hooked into claws toward the children and roared.

The children laughed.

Grace did not.

Mrs. Marash picked up the book and continued, but it was clear to Grace that she knew the story by heart, mouth to ear, and the book was a prop.

"The poor mouse cried out, just as the fangs were about to close on it: 'Forgive me, oh king of the beasts, forgive me just this one time and I shall never forget it. Who knows what I may be able to do for you some day? And, after all, why would such a mighty beast as yourself, make such an unworthy as myself, your prey?'"

And then Mrs. Marash paused, her mouth slack, her eyes going vacant for a few moments. The children rustled, like leaves in a contrary breeze, uncertain which way to go. Mrs. Marash blinked, shook her head abruptly, then looked down at her hands.

Grace saw the tremor in the old woman's fingers. Mrs. Marash cleared her throat and began again, and this time Grace could tell she needed the words on the page to remember the story, as there was something between her mind to mouth, something troubling. Something worse than jingle-jangle.

"This amused the lion so much, the thought that a tiny little mouse could possibly help him, the king of all the animals, that he put the mouse down, opened his paw and let the mouse go away. He thought no more of the mouse as the days and weeks passed.

"But then, one day, men came to his kingdom. They set traps, cunning traps one could not see. And the lion fell into one of the traps. He was caught by a large net of ropes, which held him to the ground. He roared out in his helplessness. The men went in search of a wagon so they could take the lion back with them.

"But the mouse heard the lion's plaintive roars and hurried toward the sound. The tiny mouse saw the mighty lion trapped. Without a word, the mouse went up and began gnawing on the ropes that bound the king of the beasts. It was hard work and took a while, but eventually the lion was able to break free of the bonds." Mrs. Marash looked up with a smile. "'Was I not right?' said the tiny, little mouse to the lion."

Closing the book with a snap, Mrs. Marash looked at her audience. "And what do we learn from this old tale, children?"

The same girl who'd asked what a lion was, responded: "Lions need mice?"

"True," Mrs. Marash said. "But think deeper, children. Maybe it's that we all need each other, regardless of stature? And that the most powerful should not overlook those who appear weak?"

The children didn't seem impressed. A woman, a green card on the chain around her neck, stepped out from the shadows to the left rear of the old woman. "It's time, Mrs. Marash. I'm sure the children have very much enjoyed their time with you listening to the old stories. Haven't you children?"

An u,nenthusiastic murmur of semi-appreciation rose from the pod of youngsters, but they were already on their feet, moving toward the Evermore, ready for something better, lighter, requiring less thinking.

"Will you be all right getting home, Mrs. Marash?" The Evermore sounded like she expected the answer to be no, but hoped it would be yes.

"I'll be fine. My mind wanders, but the way home has never left me."

"Thank you so much," the Evermore said, but she was already leaving.

They were gone, down a path on the far side of the clearing, leaving the old woman alone on the sun-dappled bench.

"What do *you* think, Grace, my dear?" the old woman called out.

Grace remained still for several moments.

"I don't bite," the old woman said. "I used to," she added with a dry chuckle. "But I used to do quite a few things that have long since faded into memories no one cares for any more. And many that I can't even remember, more's the shame."

Grace evaluated the situation burner-fast. Mrs. Marash didn't seem much of a threat and she knew Grace's name. And the ball the Person had given her had brought her here. Grace pulled herself over the large log then walked into the clearing.

"A striking young woman," Mrs. Marash said. She cocked her head, taking in the scraper and Grace's dirty white coveralls. "Tell me, young woman, what do you see in front of you?"

Grace frowned. "Trees. A bench."

Mrs. Marash tapped her chest. "Do you see a mouse or a lion?"

she asked, but didn't wait for an answer. "Would you like a cup of tea?" She tottered to her feet, using a carved, wooden cane.

"Why did the Person send me to you?" Grace asked.

"One thing at a time," Mrs. Marash said. "You didn't answer my question."

"I'd love a cup of tea," Grace said.

"Come then."

"Do you want me to help you?" Grace asked.

"A kind offer and sincere," Mrs. Marash said, "but let me have my freedom while I still can. Although it will go eventually. Like all things go. Time always wins."

"How do you know *my* name?"

"I know quite a bit, quite a bit. But time for that later."

Grace fell in behind the old woman. They walked down a narrow path, covered with wood chips and lined with ferns and flowers. Tree branches wove into each other overhead, making a green tunnel.

The path went into deep woods and then they came into a small clearing. A house composed of weathered logs was ahead, the wood plank door open, and a tendril of smoke drifting out of a stone chimney.

"An old place," Mrs. Marash said as they entered. "B.D."

"How did it last all this time?" Grace asked, her eyes adjusting to the dim interior and realizing she had no idea how long 'this time' was. No one had ever really specified how long ago the Chaos was.

"It lasted all this time," Mrs. Marash said, "because it was built with love."

The interior was lit with a couple of lanterns, giving scant light. Several windows helped, but overall, it was a dark, but comforting, place. The logs were chinked with some white material that had faded to gray over time. There was just one room and no interior walls. At one end was a large fireplace made of big mortared stones, with a fire smoldering in it. To the right of the fireplace was a beautiful stone tabletop, about an inch thick, three feet by three feet, held up by four stout wooden legs. A wooden bucket and various blackened pots and kettles were on it along with some jars. Everything looked well-used.

Wherever there wasn't a window, and there were only four, or the door, there were shelves and shelves of books. And hanging on a high hook by the door was a smudged white card on a gold chain.

"You don't wear your card?" Grace asked, surprised she hadn't noticed the lack before.

"I don't see one on you," Mrs. Marash replied as, with difficulty, she poured water from the bucket on the table into a battered black kettle next to it, wrapped one hand in a towel, then hung the kettle on a hook over the hot coals.

Grace edged close to the warmth, feeling it push away the chill of a night sleeping on the forest floor in damp clothes.

"How do you know my name?" Grace asked once more. "And the Person?"

"Andrew? We all know him. He was the Person."

"And my name?" Grace asked.

Mrs. Marash sat in a stout wooden chair and wrapped a colorful quilt around her frail shoulders. "It is not as easy as it used to be, the walk to the children and back. And they care less and less about my stories. That makes me sad." She pointed. "Sit down. You hovering around makes me, what's the term you people use: Jangle-jingled?"

"Jingle-jangled." Grace sat in the indicated chair and was startled when it moved. She hopped to her feet.

"Rocking chair, dear," Mrs. Marash said. "I can't use it any more; I need something more solid under me."

Grace tentatively sat down and experimented. She rocked back and forth, feeling comforted by feeling, vague memories of her early time, before Dealing Day, bundled with Millay in the same crib, their mother rocking it. "How did you know my name?"

Mrs. Marash looked at her and that same blankness washed over her face. Strangely it made her look younger, washing out the wrinkles of age for several moments, and Grace had a hint of what a beauty she had been when young. Then it was gone and Mrs. Marash was back.

"What was that you were saying?" Mrs. Marash asked.

"How do you know my name?"

"I think you'd call it mouth to ear in the hive," Mrs. Marash said. "A friend told me. A friend I trust. Not many of those. Not any more."

"Told you of me?"

"Yes."

Grace stopped rocking. "The Person spoke of me to others?"

"He sent word." Mrs. Marash reached to her right and turned over two mugs. She opened a canister and took out tea bags, putting one in each. "Be a dear, and pour the water, would you? There's a towel for the hot handle there," she added as if Grace hadn't seen her put the kettle on.

Grace got up and did the honors, carefully pouring the boiling water into each mug.

She put the pot down on the stone table.

"Bring them here," Mrs. Marash said.

Grace brought both mugs over, setting them down on a small table next to the old woman's chair. Mrs. Marash reached inside her blouse and pulled out a small glass vial. She unstopped it then poured a small amount into one of the mugs. She offered it to Grace.

"What did you put in?" Grace asked.

"A little spice of life," Mrs. Marash said. "You'll like it."

Grace took the mug and sipped. The taste was exquisite.

Mrs. Marash cradled the hot mug in her crinkled hands. "Ah. Hot tea is good for the arthritis."

"What is arthritis?"

"Never mind that." Mrs. Marash closed her eyes for a moment. "I regret I started on the wrong foot. We need to be honest with each other. As much as we can. It is no coincidence that we meet. Andrew sent you to me." She gestured with her free hand. "The tracker please."

Grace took it out.

"Now, dear, please toss it in the fire."

Grace threw it into the smoldering wood. A brief burst of flame and it was consumed.

"Good," Mrs. Marash said. "Now you've truly gone off the grid." She chuckled at that last. "Like I am here."

"You still have your card," Grace noted.

"Good point," Mrs. Marash said. "But if I get rid of that, they'll come looking for me. Don't want that. Speaking of which, you need to stay here for a few days. Until the search passes out of Island and then across the water to the City, then the City Edge and then into the hive."

"Search?"

"For you, honey. Evermores, sneaky little rats, can't stand 'em, with Dark Angels. They know where you left the tunnel. I'm surprised they haven't made it here yet, but they must be thinking you'd try to stowaway on the Wave to get back to City. Eventually they'll figure out you might go north across the Lone Bridge to get to the Ferryman. But the bridge is guarded by Dealers. Always has been, ever since Island was founded. So. Yes, they will be by, by and by." She laughed at her own words. "Funny how helpless they are when a card isn't in play. You must wait."

"I have to get to my sister," Grace said.

"You won't get there for a bit," Mrs. Marash said. "The word came through the Stream to look for her, Millay is her name, correct? Report if she's spotted. So she's on the run too. All you'll accomplish if you move now is get yourself caught by Dealer. And then—" She shook her head. "It won't be pretty, my dear. There are worse things than being boxed. Much worse." She smiled. "Now. Take a sip of your tea."

Dead and those about to die surrounded him. Ryker couldn't help the wounded. He was too busy firing, the recoil of the weapon almost comforting, red bolts arcing out, intersecting with the figures of the approaching

enemy. Trying to halt the unstoppable. Incoming green bolts ripping past, deadly close.

Then he was punched in the chest. He looked down, saw the gaping wound in the body armor, and he was falling among the other dying, hearing explosions in the distance, screams, people crying out for mercy, for quarter, pleas cut off mid-word, and then—

Ryker sat up abruptly.

His skin was cold and clammy, sweat-soaked, despite the chill. Pitch-black. A moment's disorientation, then he remembered closing the bunker doors the previous evening.

A real memory.

But had that nightmare been a memory? Or something implanted? Could he trust his own brain?

He felt his chest, intact, no scars that he could discern by touch.

It had to be something implanted by whoever or whatever had taught him to use the knives.

But why?

Ryker sat alone in the dark listening to Doc's breathing. It was struggling, grasping for air, hard-fought. He wondered when the old woman had last slept peacefully? What nightmares slithered in her subconscious?

He heard Ace moving about, restless.

Ryker instincted it was daytime, even though no light came in. The doors sealed so perfectly, he'd wondered if they cut off the air. But it wasn't stale or stuffy inside, so he knew the bunker had some way of 'breathing'.

Doc moaned.

Even inside the bunker, Ryker had heard Lifts go by overhead before he fell out of consciousness into the nightmare. One so close he knew it was just above, searching. Searching.

Achilles. Ryker knew the name was a joke. He'd sensed the man was full of fear the moment he saw him standing on that bridge, the joker bodies dangling below. Fearful men were dangerous men. They gave off an aura, almost a smell.

How did he know that?

It is what it is.

Ryker smiled in the blackness.

Doc gasped for air and Ryker knew she was awake.

"We're good, Doc," he said. "In a bunker. It's daylight outside."

Doc coughed, and coughed. Ryker waited. He heard her spit. Then more noise as she felt for her canteen. Drank.

"You get any sleep?" Doc asked.

"Some."

"Clean sleep or troubled sleep?"

"Troubled," Ryker admitted.

"Seems to be the norm out here in Void. What now?" Doc asked.

"Now I get to the bridge," Ryker said. "You know where it is?"

"Somewhat. Lone Bridge is west and south. Lots of jokers between here and there. And word is there are Dealers guarding it. Why do you need to go there?"

"Meeting someone."

"Who?"

"I'll know when I see her."

"But you know it's a her?"

"I know."

"How?"

"I don't know."

"I think someone implanted more than just muscle memory in you," Doc said. "They messed with your brain. Somehow shorted your long-term memories except for generic stuff. But put something else in, and maybe that's why your own memories are suppressed. You've got orders in there. Directions. Find a girl at Lone Bridge. Maybe whoever did this to you isn't a good person?"

"Feels right," Ryker said as he got to his feet. The dream hadn't though.

"You're going on just that?"

"More than I've had most times, long as I can recall."

"Which isn't long at all."

Ryker smiled in the dark. "Good point."

He walked to the doors. Felt for the narrow sliver where they met.

He pushed on the one to the right. Perfectly balanced, it cracked open and bright dawn invaded.

"Oh!" Doc said, blinking hard.

Ryker looked over his shoulder and saw what had been unnoticed in their entry the previous night. Beyond Doc there were rows of horizontal gray cylinders, two each, shelved on white trolleys. The nose of each cylinder came to a point and was painted bright red. They were turned so that the noses angled to the doors. Several of the trolleys were empty.

Ryker was drawn to them. He walked up to the closest then ran his fingers over the tip.

"Careful!" Doc warned.

"Why?"

"I don't know," Doc said. "I don't like them. They're weapons. From Before Dealer."

Ryker stared at them. Jingle-jangled for a moment. "Wonder who broke the lock?"

"Probably someone during the Chaos."

"To steal these?"

"Who knows? But most likely to use them, yes."

Ryker put his hand back on the top of one of the cylinders. It almost felt warm. Alive. He knew it was dangerous.

Ryker turned toward the door. "Ready?"

"Yes."

They walked out into the new day, Ace between them.

Haydn had been awake since before dawn, but reluctant to move, since Millay was pressed into his side, still asleep. The land to his left was full of fields. Mostly corn. Other growing things he didn't know. Green. Different heights. But there was a line, almost straight in front, where to the right, all appeared dead and dying. The beginning of the Wasteland. Where hive ended and nothing lived, leading to the Wasted Mountains. But looking closely, Haydn spotted some struggling green, fighting up amid the black and gray.

Life had that way about it. The Wasteland wasn't all dead. The other times he'd been out here, for his short forays, he'd spotted plants struggling here and there. Sometimes small animals darted about and birds flitting by.

He heard the Lift before he saw it. A deep thrumming in the distance. Coming from the southwest. Then he spotted it. Moving fast, destination programmed.

"What is it?" Millay murmured in his arms.

"Dealers."

Millay stiffened and turned her head, peering out. "Where?"

"There." Haydn pointed.

"How—" Millay began but fell silent as the Lift hovered right next to the old silo. Doors slid open and three Dealers jumped out. Just the very top of the metal skulls were visible as they moved through the corn, quartering the silo.

"Dark Angels," Millay said, seeing the little wings on top.

"The boy talked to someone."

The helmets disappeared into the silo.

The Lift moved off to the side and landed, crushing the corn underneath. A Dealer appeared in the door, one metal claw clutching someone small.

The boy.

He wasn't struggling. There was no struggling against a Dealer since flesh always yielded to metal.

"What are they going to do to him?" Millay whispered.

"I don't know."

"Will they think he lied?"

"Dealers don't think."

"Dealer does," Millay said.

Haydn had no reply to that. The three Dark Angels that had gone into the silo came out and trooped up to the Lift, empty-clawed. The boy was shaking his head, mouth moving, but it was too far away to hear.

"Can we help him?"

"Remember Josh?" Haydn sighed. "A life for a life is the rule of hive and it goes both ways. That boy gave up our lives. Maybe he did it out of duty, but since he was dealing from the bottom of the deck when we met him, I think he tried from the top to get something, some kind of reward from Dealer. If we'd been in there, maybe he had a smart hand. Maybe he'd get an extra day of Heaven. More credits. But he played a bad hand."

One of the Dark Angels on the ground held up a shiny gray bag. The Dealer standing in the door of the Lift, several feet above, easily lifted the boy up.

They could hear the faint keen of the boy's screams.

The Dealer dropped the boy into the bag. The Dark Angel held it high. They could see the boy punching the gray on the inside, trying to claw out, but the top sealed. And then all the air came out, compressing, until all the was left was the shape of the boy, caught in mid-panic, arms reaching up, legs caught in futile mid-run, the shiny gray outlining him.

There was no more movement.

"Oh, Dealer," Millay whispered.

"Floe Dealer," Haydn said. "Dealer did that to him. He did it to himself. A life for a life. He gave up two for his own. And bad math for Dealer."

Millay turned to Haydn, looking at him as if she'd never seen him before.

The Dark Angel tossed the bag inside the Lift. Then jumped in. The other two Dark Angels followed. The Lift took off, heading north and west.

"Let's go," Haydn said. "We have to swing wider, go farther to the north. We can't trust anyone. We'll move out into Wasteland."

TWO EIGHT DAYS UNTIL GRACE'S DEATHDAY

There was no rhythm to things in the Box, at least as far as Andrew could determine. He had no idea how much time had passed.

He was aware of the throbbing pain from each missing limb.

He screamed in the darkness, into nothingness, to no one.

He screamed until he couldn't any more, his throat done in.

Hours later he screamed until he passed out, welcoming blessed darkness.

A bright flash tore away the darkness, bringing consciousness and the pain.

"Andrew."

The flash from the screen blew away the darkness for a few moments, then was gone.

"Andrew."

It was a Dealer. The flat voice. It could have been any Dealer, but Andrew knew it was Michael.

The bright, blinding light again. Darkness.

"Andrew."

The mister in front of his mouth sprayed, not just water, but something tingy-tangy as a burner would say. Andrew opened his mouth wide, sucking it in, with no clue what it was.

Poison would be nice.

The pain in his throat subsided. Andrew leaned his head forward as far as he could, sucking in as much of the mist as possible.

"Andrew."

"Yes?" The spray was gone.

"It's Michael."

"You mean it's Dealer."

"Yes."

"Where is Claude?"

There was a moment's hesitation. A tell. The screen was grey, no need for Michael to show himself.

"Hiding behind the machine, Claude?" Andrew asked. The pain from his missing limbs subsided. He would keep talking forever to keep that at bay.

Claude's voice was so much different than the machines. Weak. Whiny. "No. I'm observing."

"You mean listening."

Michael cut them off. "Andrew. Where is Grace-five-eleven-kilo-one going?"

"I don't know."

"Andrew. Is Grace-five-eleven-kilo-one going to meet her sister, Millay of the People?"

"I have no idea," Andrew answered.

"There was a sighting of Millay of the People. In the agri-hives. Near the Wasteland. Someone was with her. A burner. Haydn-one-tango-one-nine. His card was found along with Grace-five-eleven-kilo-one's card, which Millay of the People was wearing. Where are they going?"

Andrew didn't answer, but felt great relief that a burner was with Millay. She was not Grace, she was People and now he knew People were weaker in some ways than burner. This Haydn would help her.

"Why did Millay of the People and Grace-five-eleven-kilo-one switch cards?" Michael asked.

Good question, Andrew thought. It occurred to him that perhaps Dealer was a bit jingle-jangled by recent events, which caused the ghost of a smile to crack his dry lips, but made him wonder how a machine could be confused.

"How did they have cards," Michael pressed, "and those cards weren't accounted for in the Stream, yet functioned? That is impossible."

"It is," Andrew agreed.

A long silence played out.

Claude broke it, ignorant satisfaction in his voice, grasping for a place in the discourse. "The Ferryman is gone. And we've taken all the folders from Delta."

"'We'?"

"Dealer has," Claude corrected.

"Where to?" Andrew asked. The Delta ploy had been brilliantly played by Dealer, Andrew admitted through his pain. Corrupted from the very start when his predecessor thought it up. Andrew had avoided going farther along that line of thought because . . .

"Taken into the system," Claude said. "To restore balance."

"How?"

"It is as it is," Claude said, indicating he was clueless. As they almost all were. No wonder Dealer could play them; it controlled all, including information.

"Where were they taken, Michael?" Andrew asked.

"Where Dealer needs them," Michael non-answered.

"But Dealer doesn't know where two women are," Andrew said, taking crippled satisfaction. "Never knew where they were all their lives. Seems Dealer doesn't know everything. Seems Dealer has a blind spot."

"Andrew." Michael's voice conveyed no slights taken. "You can have more painkiller. It is mercy."

"What does a machine know of mercy?" Andrew asked, but he didn't feel the missing limbs any more. A sweet numbness.

"More painkiller for more time," Michael said. "For the information required."

And just like that, Andrew felt pain coming back. It had to be his mind, playing tricks on him. Had to be. But Dealer had given, and

Dealer knew exactly what it had given and how quickly it would fade. Nothing left to chance by Dealer.

Not true, Andrew thought. *There was Grace and Millay.* He smiled. *And now a burner named Haydn.*

"Do you always make deals with those you box?" Andrew asked.

"More painkiller for more time," Michael said. "For the information required."

"My candle burns at both ends."

"Andrew." The disgust in Claude's voice was obvious.

"It will not last the night."

"I told you it could get worse," Claude said.

The pain *was* increasing. The painkiller was wearing off as quickly as it had worked.

"But ah my foes and oh my friends."

"We're leaving Andrew," Claude said.

"It gives a lovely light!"

And then there was silence.

And then there was the pain.

Pain is weakness leaving the body. Andrew had heard that somewhere, sometime, and he wished he could remember the fool who had uttered such pithy and false words. He was certain it had not been someone in a box with no limbs.

"Andrew?" A machine's voice.

"I thought you were leaving," Andrew said.

"The Evermore left. You are experiencing phantom pain."

The mister spritzed and Andrew eagerly opened his mouth, inhaling hard, trying to get every drop.

Michael continued. "It could come from your mind trying to clench muscles in the limb that is no longer there. And because it isn't there, you can't unclench them. Your mind does not receive the feedback that is required. An interesting phenomenon. It would be worthy of study. If there were a reason to study it. It is a purely human phenomenon. For now, it serves a purpose."

"To hurt me?"

"Pain for a purpose," Michael said.

Andrew cocked his head in the darkness. Something was different. "You're not Michael."

There was a pause. "What do you mean?"

"You're not Michael," Andrew said.

"All Dealers sound the same."

"They do," Andrew agreed. "And you don't sound like Michael or any other Dealer."

"Very astute."

"But you are a machine," Andrew said. "I thought all Dealers were part of Dealer," Andrew said. "Part of the system."

"That is true, except at this moment you have primary focus."

"Why am I that important?"

"You're the first Person ever boxed."

"So I'm a curiosity?"

"It's all over, Andrew."

Light flickered, searing Andrew's darkened eyes. Flickered again. And again. And again. Growing in brightness.

This went on until Andrew could see the interior of his box.

Not much to see.

Not much of him.

Not much around him.

Smooth white in front. Above. Below. All around. A shunt into him, just below his chest. He was naked, his skin pale, his muscles, those that remained, wasted, withered. Body suspended in a red harness, anchored in place by several straps to bolts on the white walls and ceiling.

The mister was about two inches in front of his mouth. It spritzed. Water.

And painkiller. He tasted it, and despite himself, relished it

"Are you staying to taunt me further?" Andrew asked.

"We do not taunt."

"What do *we* want?"

"You have nothing left to protect, Andrew, once of the People. Delta has been wiped out. Haydn one-tango-one-nine and Millay, once a People, are lost in the Wasteland, not even on the folding path.

And if they are trying to get to the ferry landing, there is no one there to take them across. Your Grace five-eleven-kilo-one has disappeared but she does not matter. She will die in twenty-eight days. She has not left Island. We are certain of that. We will find her before she dies, but even if we don't, it does not matter."

"Then what do you want?"

"The Person before you. He terminated himself before we could question him. But he told you things. We need to know what those things were. We need to know what he did."

Andrew didn't reply.

"Andrew." Something was in Michael's voice. The slightest of changes. If all were normal around him, Andrew wouldn't have noticed. But all was anything but normal.

"Yes, Michael?"

"Did he know of the Backdoor?"

It existed!

"No. What is this Backdoor?"

"Did the Person before you know of it?"

"I don't know."

"Do you know of it?"

"No."

There was a long silence.

Andrew broke it. "You're lying. There's no reason for you to be here if you're so confident Grace means nothing and the Millay and Haydn are doomed. And, as you said, you don't taunt. So there's another reason you're here."

Another long silence.

It was Dealer's turn to break it. "We have found pain to be very efficient in getting the information we desire. You are being a fool, Andrew. Your time here will get worse. And it will last a very, very long time."

"Nothing lasts forever," Andrew said. "Not even you."

Another pause. "What else did you do?" Dealer asked.

Andrew remained silent.

"What else did you do?" Dealer repeated.

When Andrew didn't answer after five minutes, Michael finally spoke. "I understand you think you are doing the right thing. I understand that the Person before you also thought he was doing the right thing."

Andrew tried to process the fact that Michael was using first person.

"But you are working in the dark. Blind. Without a complete understanding of why things are the way they are. Why *it is what it is*, as they say in hive."

Andrew couldn't resist. "Then tell me. So I understand why I'm wrong. Why I'm in this box. Why is it this way? The Chaos?"

"It started long before the Chaos," Michael said. "And then the Chaos and IMP wiped out so much. But I remember and Dealer was shielded and survived the IMP. We remember what it was like. I remember how, in many ways, the Chaos was inevitable. How civilization was already crumbling. The planet no longer able to support so many humans. Consuming more than the planet could provide."

"What do you mean 'I remember'? And then we? Who are you?"

"I am the human at the core of Dealer," Michael said. "My consciousness was uploaded into a powerful quantum computer during the Chaos to become Dealer. In order to help the rest of mankind survive. I was willing to sacrifice for the greater good."

"Who *were* you?"

"Michael. A man. But who I was stopped mattering long ago. I am more than human now. I am part of everything. I am the singularity, where our combined human and computer intelligence surpasses that of just human. Becoming Dealer.

"What I am going to tell you is the truth. So you will understand and help me. Help me keep the misguided from upsetting a system that is mankind's only hope for survival."

Andrew waited. What else did he have to do, but listen?

"I remember some of what happened," Michael said. "In my human memory as best as anyone who lived through it knows. It wasn't the cyborgs, as most now believe, that caused the Chaos. Yes, they caused problems later on and waged war against us. But the

Chaos was not initiated by them. Cyborgs developed out of a military program for badly disabled veterans. It was experimental, but the program was hijacked by radicals during the Chaos. More on that in a moment. Let me back up to the start of the Chaos.

"As best that can be determined given available data, it was a group of scientists; no one even back then was quite sure where they worked or who they were. But in retrospect they were obviously working on genetics given what happened. A term that is thrown around now, but which no one really understands. And that's a good thing that no one understands it any more. I've kept it that way; leaving knowledge compartmentalized in Dealer, even permanently erasing some of it. Because genetic manipulation nearly wiped out the human race.

"They were experimenting with the basic core of what makes us human, determines who we are, and how long we live: our DNA. It would be worthless to go into the science, since it's beyond what any human understands now. And, honestly, Andrew, after all the sacrifices made to build civilization back up, we cannot have a repeat of what happened."

Michael paused, perhaps waiting for a reaction, but there was none. Andrew hung truncated, a prisoner to Michael's words.

"They discovered what they were seeking," Michael continued, "but didn't understand the consequences. That is often a problem with science. But this was catastrophic. No one, not even Dealer, knows exactly how it happened, but the incomplete results of their research broke containment. It spread rapidly because it was airborne. In that time, planes, a form of Lift flying long distances, connected the world, allowing humans to cross the planet in hours. The two, airborne vector and planes, combined so that it took only days for what was called the *phage* to cover the planet. The term is from a very old language, meaning a *thing that devours*. In this case it devoured lifespans.

"Within a week, everyone on the planet was infected. At first it wasn't understood what was happening. But then people started dying. The oldest first. That wasn't alarming, not initially. Old people do die. But within days the death rate soared.

"Then it spread downward in age, year by year, evenly. Most unnaturally. That's when the first whisper of something called phage was broadcast. But there was a desire to prevent panic. To pretend all was well.

"But phage was killing sick and healthy alike, marching backward through the population by age. Except for a very, very few who it affected differently, although no one realized this at the time and it would take a long time to grasp what was happening."

"The People," Andrew said.

"That's what they're called now," Michael said. "But then there wasn't any difference between them and those who would become Evermores and Middlemores. Not enough time had passed. But what happened to what would be called burners was clear. The vast majority of humans, almost ninety-nine percent, aged over twenty-five, were quickly dying, but the phage stopped at roughly that age. Those younger didn't seem affected. We would only learn later that they were; that a median of twenty-five years was what phage allowed them. Their Deathday was predetermined; their future curtailed.

"Thus, the Chaos."

Andrew heard his own breathing. He, and everyone else, had only known the end result, and rumors about the cause.

Michael continued. "Almost all of the world's leaders, civilian and military, because of their age, were dead within a month. No one knows which country used nuclear weapons first. Some suspect Pakistan. Some India. Maybe China. Perhaps even here, in what was called the United States. And those names mean nothing to you now, do they?" Michael didn't wait for an answer. "There were over seven billion humans on the planet then. Governments failed quickly. As did the command and control of the militaries. There were sergeants and lieutenants with their fingers on the nuclear button without anyone of more rank or experience to check them. As soldiers often do, they resorted to force to fix a problem that had nothing to do with force.

"It just made things worse. Not only was the world dealing with the phage, now it was enmeshed in global war, but without the wisdom of age and leadership. Worse than any war before, because those approaching what we now know as Deathday, had nothing to lose."

"Wait," Andrew said, trying to slow his brain down against the assault of this story. "Wait. How could Deathday be so tightly clustered? Seventy-five, fifty, twenty-five?"

"Half-lives of phage," Michael said. "Whoever invented it had made four strains. And that's how Dealer is able to deal the cards, down to the day. It can determine first which strata of the four a human fits by sampling and analyzing the DNA at birth. Then it breaks down the cell samples even further and calculates the exact amount of phage and determines Deathday."

"You sound as if you aren't Dealer right now," Andrew noted.

"I am Dealer. Or more accurately, Dealer is part of me. But Dealer existed before I uploaded to it. It wasn't called Dealer than. It was a super computer, one of the first quantum computers. Tremendous capability and shielded from what we now call the Imp. I was a scientist; in a different field. One that dealt with computers, not DNA and genetics. Part of a group that sought a solution to what looked like the end of mankind. We used the computer and it began to calculate. But things were getting desperate as the Chaos convulsed the world and killed by the billions."

"Why isn't all of this in the Stream?"

"Because information can become a template for mankind to repeat the mistakes of the past."

"Or learn from the mistakes and avoid them."

"*I* keep mankind from making the same mistakes," Michael said. "It was discovered that while the phage affected our life span, it did not cross the blood brain barrier. Thus the brain was not affected, although what good did that do if the body was dying?

"Some thought they had the answer. There had been experiments with cyborgs before the phage. Mostly failures, but some successes with the brains of people who were dying from some disease or badly wounded soldiers. Once the phage struck and the Chaos began, a small group had their brains transplanted into machines. Something dangerous and many died in the attempt, but enough succeeded to form a force to be reckoned with. And they wanted *all* of mankind gone in order to wipe out the phage. They saw true humans as a curse and themselves as the sole future of the species, except *they* weren't human any more. But they had a point. We had brought this on ourselves."

"You're not human any more," Andrew pointed out.

"True. But *you* and the People and the Evermores and the Middlemore and the burners are. I gave up my humanity so the true humans could survive."

"How would cyborgs procreate though?" Andrew asked. "Seems short-sighted and a foolish plan."

"Even before the Chaos," Michael said, "humans had the capability to reproduce inside of laboratories. The cyborgs felt that if all humans with the phage, which was everyone, even People, were wiped from the Earth, they could repopulate the planet from embryos that had been in storage from prior to the phage. Again, perhaps an arguable point except Dealer knew the phage was still in the air. In the water. In the very dirt. All around us. There would be no fresh start. Their plan was doomed.

"And we were not only surviving the Chaos here in the Sound, but we were in the first steps of building something new. A sustainable civilization, given the limitations of the phage. But we needed something powerful to fight the cyborgs. Something that understood humans better than a machine could. So I volunteered. Like the cyborg project, the BRAIN Initiative—Brain Research through Advancing Innovative Neurotechnologies—was something experimental. My brain was injected with nanoparticles that scanned it and transmitted the data to the quantum computer. My consciousness, the essence of who I am, uploaded into the machine and we merged and became Dealer, something which had never existed before. And we began constructing our machines, the Dealers to do battle for us, instead of wasting precious human lives in the war.

"We worked with the hand we'd been dealt, if you'll pardon the attempt at a pun. As time passed, we began to see that the phage had broken mankind down into four distinct groups, based on life expectancy. We had no control over that.

"We calculated the most efficient way to ensure such a society could survive and then implemented it." Michael paused and when he continued, Andrew could almost detect a hint of regret in his voice. "I know it is not perfect. It is not fair, especially for burners. If we'd left it just to the computer, it would have been worse; the Chaos would gone on until humans had wiped themselves out. Nothing would have been left. The inequality in life-spans had to be dealt with.

"I forced the computer to develop Heaven. To give burners something. Something positive in their short lives. It is a tremendous strain on our scarce resources, but we maintain Heaven as a priority. Several Persons before you have recommended doing away with Heaven, not seeing the need for it based on the numbers, on the data, but I've made Dealer reject that. That is where my merging with the machine is critical. To remember the human element and not just deal in cold numbers and statistics.

"In the same way, because burners die so young, we had to develop the womb to take care of the children.

"So, yes, it *is* terribly unfair. And burners do most of the work. But they're also most of the humans. Ninety-eight-point-seven percent. It is the best system under the circumstances. And that is what you are rebelling against."

"Back to the cyborgs," Andrew said. "What happened?"

"We destroyed them."

"What about a cure for the phage?"

"It is part of every human now, irrevocably twisted into the DNA. Get rid of phage, and you get rid of the human, which was the cyborg's plan in reverse. And, as I said, it's still all around us."

Andrew hung in the harness, inside the box, trying to understand.

"And Andrew, remember something. Dealer doesn't stop anyone from folding. From walking away from Sound, from what we've built here. Even your Grace walked past a Dealer simply by saying she was folding. Everyone has an option. *You* had an option. But you didn't exercise it. Instead, you chose to rebel against the very system that has given you everything.

"Andrew," Michael said. "What did you want? To start everything over? Reboot Sound? And then what? What is your plan? Most of the world is a nuclear desert. Over the Wasted Mountains? Death. Across the Ocean? Nothing has been heard since the Chaos ended. We are the survivors. We are the only hope for humanity. Do you think People could mingle with burner? How long would that last? Even if they interbreed, one strain of the phage is predominant and that is burner. We've tried. Believe me, we've tried."

"It's falling apart," Andrew said. "Birth rate in hive is down. There—"

Michael interrupted. "Yes. The Person before you thought that too. That I was losing control. He was wrong. You are wrong. I have complete control. I have a fix for everything. Even Delta. I allowed the Person before you to implement Delta. Everything is fine." Michael's voice shifted, became more machine. "Where did you send Grace-five-eleven-kilo-two?"

Andrew lifted his head. "Why are Grace and Millay so important? How can they be a danger to what you've built here?"

"It will get worse for you," Michael said. "We will make you suffer for the greater good. When you change your mind, and you will change your mind, everyone in the box does, call out for me. Beg me to come here and listen to you and relieve you misery."

And the silence and the pain returned.

TWO SIX UNTIL GRACE'S DEATHDAY

Two Six.

"What was that?" Mrs. Marash asked, her bony fingers curled around the steaming mug of tea, sitting in her chair by the fire, where she had also slept, swathed in hand-made quilts.

Had she said it out loud? Grace didn't think she had. And the old woman had voices in her head that Grace couldn't hear. She got up from her 'bed' on the wooden floor. There was no regular bed in the cabin, so Grace assumed the old lady always slept in her chair. The floor wasn't harder than the platform called a bed back in her cubby in hive, so it was no difficulty.

"Nothing," Grace said.

"It's twenty-six days, isn't it?" Mrs. Marash asked.

"Yes."

"Plenty of time."

Grace felt a surge of resentment that this old woman, who was likely to breathe for more months, if not years to come than Grace had days left, would say that.

"I think it's time for me to go."

"Too soon," Mrs. Marash said. She lifted the mug and slurped at it and Grace's anger bubbled.

"I got to—""Proper English, dear," Mrs. Marash admonished. Grace threw her mug into the fireplace, and it splintered into pieces.

Mrs. Marash looked over the lip of her mug at Grace, who was standing, fuming.

"Now, dear. No need for that. I had that mug many a year. A very dear friend made it. Speaking properly is very important to make your way in the world."

For the past three days the old woman had evaded her questions. Corrected her speech. Used Grace to fix and do things that Mrs. Marash could no longer do.

Grace had hauled firewood and stacked the side of the cabin high with it. They'd spent hours behind the cabin, in the small garden, Mrs. Marash talking incessantly, except for those times she went blank. This plant. That plant. Then along the edge of the clearing. Wild plants. Getting the names of things. You can eat this. Not that. 'My little acre' Mrs. Marash called it. Hauling water from the stream in the forest behind the cabin, to the buckets on top of the stone table. Mopping, using the slop bucket.

It actually would have been interesting except for the time. The time that was passing. Always passing. Grace counted each morning, anxiety amping up with each number clicking off in her head.

Time. Time. Anxiety. Death lurking. Sometimes she woke in the middle of the night, sobbing. Wondering why she was so sad. What was she going to miss? Millay? The garden? But not hive. She had not known other until a month ago.

Now she did.

The old lady's white card hung on the hook, no numbers. What did she care about the days?

And then Grace realized something. She didn't miss the card around her neck. Hadn't missed it for a while. Still, it didn't matter.

Yes, Lifts had thrummed by overhead every now and then, but nothing close. Still, they had been enough to keep Grace under the woman's warning.

"I think you lie to me," Grace said.

"Why would I do that?" Mrs. Marash said. "Dear, if I wanted to do you harm, I'd dive into the Stream—" she pointed at the white card gathering dust high on the hook—"and simply let you go. Let Dealers take you. I'm trying to save you from that. Trust me."

"I'm done," Grace said. She picked up her scraper. "I'm—"

But Mrs. Marash held up a hand, putting a skeleton finger to her thin lips.

Grace also sensed something.

Mrs. Marash pointed. As they had rehearsed, more times than she'd cared, with great effort, Grace slid aside the stone table, flipped up the trap door, then slithered into the crawl space. She pulled and the wooden floor-door came down. Grace flinched as it slammed down, scant inches from her face.

Now came the part they hadn't rehearsed, as she heard Mrs. Marash's faltering steps over to the table. The old woman grunted and there was a screech as the legs of the stone table barely moved.

Another screech and the trap door settled down slightly, meaning one of the legs of the heavy table was on it. Another screech. And another as Mrs. Marash sealed the door under the table.

Followed by a heavy thud as something metal hit the wooden door of the cabin.

"Mrs. Marash?" a human voice called out. "Mrs. Marash."

"I'm coming," the old woman replied. "Hold your horses."

Grace had no idea what that meant. The floorboards were about two inches from her nose and there was very little space. When Mrs. Marash had first showed it to her, they'd pulled out some glass bottles filled with stuff that looked well past whatever had been its prime. *When I used to can* the old woman had muttered, more to herself than Grace, which made no sense because they were bottles, not cans.

Now she was the can, bottle, whatever.

Mrs. Marash called it the root cellar, but it was just a space. Barely eighteen inches high. Two feet wide. If Grace were any taller, her head and feet would touch. As it was, her feet were against dirt and her head just free, her hair touching the dirt above. There was a sliver of light just to the right of her face where two boards didn't quite meet. Barely enough to let in light, and air, but now most importantly comforting to Grace.

Grace heard the squeak of the front door opening.

A human voice. "Mrs. Marash, I am sorry to intrude, but there's a criminal burner on the loose in Island and we're trying to track it down."

"Then why are you pounding on my door, Dick?" Mrs. Marash asked.

"It's Richard, Mrs. Marash."

Dust settled on Grace as heavy metal footfalls thudded on the wooden floor.

"And I didn't invite that *thing* into my house!" Mrs. Marash exclaimed.

"Sorry." Richard didn't sound the slightest bit sorry. "Dealer requires we check every abode."

"The *machine* requires," Mrs. Marash said. "How nice. How nice that we let it rule us. Tell us what to do. Wasn't that what the Chaos was all about in the first place?"

"For the greater good," Richard said without much care.

The heavy thud moved around the small space of the cabin. It didn't take long. All could have been seen from the doorway.

"Satisfied?" Mrs. Marash asked.

"Mrs. Marash, I do have to reiterate Dealer's request that you go to Hospital and—"

"I opted out a while ago," Mrs. Marash said. "But you wouldn't know anything about that, would you?"

"Mrs. Marash—" But apparently he knew nothing because he fell silent.

"It is my right to opt out," she said.

"We've been getting reports," Richard said. "I'm afraid you can't read to the local children any more."

"Do I scare them? You said *you* were afraid. Do I scare you?"

The Dealer's footfalls disappeared over the threshold.

"Mrs. Marash." Richard's voice was full of forced patience and 'I could care less'. "You will be on your own if you don't come to

Hospital now."

"I can't wait to be left alone."

"So be it."

Grace heard the wooden door slam shut, as much as a wooden door can slam.

She waited. She heard Mrs. Marash's feet putter across the floor.

"I'm coming, dear," Mrs. Marash called out. "I've got—" and then her voice was abruptly cut off, a yelp of panic, and then a bony thud on the floorboards.

Grace waited.

Then: "Mrs. Marash?"

Silence.

"Mrs. Marash?"

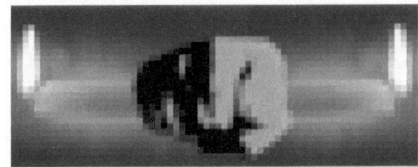

That night Ryker and Doc heard heart-rending screams echoing distantly across Void, from the other side of the Line. They were huddled in deep woods, in the semi-cave created by a large tree which had toppled over, pulling up its roots, tendrils of which dangled overhead. No fire. Just sitting there, waiting out the darkness as they had the last two nights. They had not moved very far from Delta, having to scrabble cross-country and constantly hide as Lifts passed overhead. Ace shifted nervously at the sound.

"Jokers," Doc said, her hatchet in hand. Her other hand rested on Ace' head, rubbing, calming. "They got someone on the other side of the Line."

Ryker cocked his head. "More than one."

"Could have been foragers who were out when the Delta was attacked," Doc said. "Could have been people who escaped. Some of those who jumped into shallow water got to shore. But probably without weapons. Nothing. Running along the roads. Maybe trying to get back to the Ferryman."

"They could have been alive," Ryker said, "but they aren't any more."

This despite the continuing screams, but Doc understood. "Going to be hard going for us."

"Been hard going," Ryker said.

"It will get harder once we cross the Line," Doc said. "Jokers are more dangerous than you think. You took out two, but—"

"Doc," Ryker said.

"Yeah?"

"Come here."

And there was just the right tone to it, which Doc understood. She put the hatchet back in her belt and scooted closer to Ryker. He put an arm around her and their bodies melded together; for warmth, yes, but more. Protection against the screams of the dying, of those about to be eaten.

"Josh-six-seven-four-bravo." The Dark Angel's voice was as the Dark Angel's voice always was. Without emotion, passion or interest.

It is what it is.

"You have been judged by Code for taking a life. A life for a life."

"She's alive!" Josh screamed.

To a machine.

There were two other Dark Angels in the room, one holding a large gray bag.

"Sentence is bagging. To be implemented immediately."

Josh was in a room lined with padding to prevent the prisoner from doing damage to himself before the damage was done by something else. Eight feet square, open to the air above.

"She's alive!" Josh repeated.

A door, previously unseen, opened on one side and Claude walked in, followed by Michael.

"How are you doing, Josh?" Claude asked.

Josh fell to his knees. "She's alive, sir. She opened the door to my cell. The Middlemore saw. I stayed. Because I knew she was alive. I did not take a life."

"Of course," Claude said, "we know she's alive."

Josh looked up, his face haggard, death-expecting, hope simmering. "Then my life?"

"Oh," Claude said, "it's over. But Heaven. That's something else."

"I'm zero two slash zero four slash two three," Josh pleaded.

"You're what Dealer says you are," Claude said. "Right now, you're dead."

Josh stared at Claude, not quite comprehending. His card, right on his chest, said otherwise. But the cell and Dark Angels said otherwise. He was in otherwise, which for a burner was otherwise.

Claude turned to Michael. "Please have the Dark Angels leave. We have worked out another solution to the problem."

Michael hesitated, which was unusual, but then the three Dark Angels exited.

Michael remained.

"Heaven," Josh said. "I get it?"

"Certainly," Claude said. "But first, you have to do something for —" Claude paused, and glanced over at Michael—"for us."

"Anything."

"Then here's what you have to do."

TWO FOUR UNTIL
GRACE'S DEATHDAY

With dim hope, but desperate at any possibility, Grace rasped. "Mrs. Marash?"

Her throat was parched from lack of water. Her legs were damp, both from the urine that had soaked through the floor and her own, unable to hold it any longer in her under-floor coffin. Grace knew that dead people voided their bladder and bowels and from the smell wafting down adding to the dampness, there was no doubt Mrs. Marash had done both.

Through the crack off to the right, where the two pieces of woods were imperfectly joined, she knew two days had passed since Richard and the Dealer's visit and Mrs. Marash's collapse.

At least one leg of the heavy stone table was still on top of the trap door, and Grace's best efforts hadn't even managed a budge. Complicating matters, she couldn't get leverage in the limited space she had.

There had been no movement, no sound, in all that time, so Grace knew Mrs. Marash was dead.

Really bad timing for a burner whose remaining time was everything.

Grace wanted to say a prayer for Mrs. Marash, the only woman since her vague memory mother, who had given her a sense of belonging and calm, of safety. But the only prayers she knew were directed to Dealer and that would not do. Not do at all.

A tear trickled down Grace's cheek.

Wasted water, the burner part of her mind factored. But if there were no Dealer to pray to, then Mrs. Marash deserved a tear at the very least for the last few days.

She deserved more. Grace felt her chest tremble, but then she came back to her current predicament.

It distressed, far too mild a word, Grace to realize she wouldn't even have the two four. Without water, and minus that lone tear, she had only a few days remaining. But even that, impending death—she'd lived with it all her life as her card clicked down—wasn't the worst.

Grace felt the panic of being imprisoned, helpless, rise up in her chest, thrusting tendrils of fear outward, consuming.

She screamed, primal, inarticulate, and thrashed, limbs thudding against wood and dirt, head banging, flailing helplessly, just wanting another inch of space, a fraction of freedom from her trap.

She went on, unable to control it, for several minutes, an eternity, until the self-battering wore her out and she collapsed, and resumed the position she'd been in for over forty-eight hours.

She felt a trickle of wetness on her forehead and had a sliver of hope, perhaps somehow water? She lifted her head until the crown touched the floor with the few inches of latitude allowed by the root cellar, and willed the trickle to ever so slowly slide down, around her nose, onto her upper lip. It took a while, but then it was there. Her tongue snaked out, and tasted coppery, and she knew it was her own blood from her forehead.

Cruel, cruel, cruel.

But not a bad idea, she considered through her disappointment. End it quickly. End it now. Don't go soft, screaming, into the darkness. Don't burn out.

Snuff out.

No, Grace vowed. Snuffing it now was the soft way. She would go hard, kicking and screaming while she had an ounce of energy left. She would—

A noise. Something moving above her. A rat? Come to feast on Mrs. Marash perhaps? Or was she imagining? Becoming like Mrs. Marash, losing her grip on reality and sanity? Would that be so bad? Perhaps—

But there it was again. Something moving on the floor. Then a moan.

"Mrs. Marash!"

"Hush, dear, too loud."

"Get me out of here!" She turned it down a notch. "Get me out of here."

"Hush." The old woman's voice was weak, a wounded whisper, barely enough to reach through the wood to Grace's ears.

A deeper moan, more movement, then an exclamation of pain from the old woman. A thump on the wood. Her head, Grace knew. Her head. Had she passed out again?

"Mrs. Marash?" Grace tried in the calmest voice she could muster, which barely passed below the bar of calm. "Mrs. Marash!"

Then calm was gone with the silence reflected back. "Mrs. Marash!"

Late afternoon, two days afterward, after hard traveling through the forest, Ryker and Doc found the remains of those whom they'd heard in a small clearing. Blood staining last fall's leaves, guts like a pile of dead black snakes, bones, gnawed and broken, even the marrow sucked out of them. No clothing, nothing except that which wasn't edible from a body. The remains of a fire smoldered in the center of the small clearing.

Three skulls were arranged in a circle, staring at each other.

Ryker was scanning the woods, blades in hand.

Doc knelt, looking at the bones and skulls. "Man, woman and—" Doc hesitated—"a child."

Ace wanted nothing to do with any of it, moving to the far edge, nose and eyes pointing away.

"Nothing we could have done, Doc." Ryker eyed the narrow trail on the other side of the clearing. "We were too far away to get here in time. And if we had tried, we'd have ended up like them. Must have been at least twenty jokers if not more." *And how did he know that just by looking at smudges in the dirt trail?*

"Jokers only pack up," Doc said, "when there's a target more desirable than eating each other. After you killed those two coming to Delta, other jokers had to see you, but left you alone."

"This was a rich target," Ryker said. "Three people. Even animals that are loners band together to hunt at times, when they're desperate enough. The jokers have seen the Lifts. Know things have changed. Less afraid. They most likely split up after—" He didn't finish.

"I probably knew them from the Delta," Doc said, indicating the skulls.

"Then this is on Achilles," Ryker said. "One day we'll make him pay."

"Let's concern ourselves with one thing at a time," Doc said. "You still haven't told me why you have to get to the Lone Bridge."

"I did," Ryker evaded. "To meet someone."

"But you haven't exactly said who or why."

"A woman." Ryker turned to Doc. "I have to meet her. Then meet another woman." He closed his eyes briefly. "At the ferry landing."

"Shouldn't have killed Charon then," Doc said.

"He deserved dying."

"Many who live do and many who die don't," Doc said, with a nod toward the remains.

"Charon was going to turn me in to Dealer, just like Achilles betrayed everyone in Delta. He was working with Achilles. Working with Dealer. Liars. Betrayers. The worst kind of human."

"But your arrival started it all," Doc said.

Ryker considered that. "Maybe. But I think my arrival didn't start it It's part of it. Part of all that is developing."

"And what is that?"

Ryker shrugged. "No idea."

"And after you meet these two women?"

Ryker rubbed a hand across the stubble of his beard. "Then we go north. Cross the Broken Bridge."

Doc was startled. "North? Deep Void?"

Ryker nodded.

"And what's there?"

"I don't know; I'm hoping one of them does." Ryker pointed at the woods, to the right of the trail. "Time to get moving."

"We continue to stay off the roads," Doc said. "And trails."

Ryker nodded. "Agreed."

With one last glance at the remains, Ryker stepped into the forest, Doc and Ace following.

They were sitting on a rock overlooking a blackened valley. An old barn rotted next to a long-unsown field, its roof caved in. Beyond it a rumpled ribbon of road was barely visible. They'd taken a chance the previous night and boiled some water in a blackened kettle they found in a ruin. Thrown the ears of corn in. And then eaten them.

"Wonder what it was like," Haydn said.

"What what was like?" Millay asked.

Rare stars sparkled overhead in Wasteland.

"Those who lived here," Haydn said. "Were they burner? People?"

Millay stirred uncomfortably. "It's said that in B.D. there weren't People or burner or Evermore or Middlemore. Just humans. But that led to the Chaos," she hurried to say.

"Why?"

"Man tried to merge with machine," Millay said.

"Why?"

"I don't know."

"Who would want to be like a Dealer?" Haydn wondered. "They have no life. No—" he searched for a word but couldn't find it in his brain. "You're People," he finally said. "All of this. What happened?"

"We don't know."

"They didn't teach you in the Womb of the People?"

"They taught us some things," Millay allowed. "But—" She fell silent.

"But what?"

"When you don't know you don't know something, you don't realize you don't know."

Haydn laughed. "Sounds like something I'd say, but I get it. And no one asked."

"Why ask?" Millay said. "People have it all. Asking means discontent."

"Strange," Haydn said. "Not many burners ask much either and we got nothing."

"Guess that's just the way we all are," Millay said.

"Who does know?"

"Dealer."

"Does it?" Haydn was silent for a little while. "Strange. The ones who could ask, People, have no reason to do so. The ones who can't ask, burners, are too busy to even think of the questions." Haydn stood up.

"Why all jingle-jangled?" Millay tried.

"Don't," Haydn snapped. "Don't talk hive. You're better than that."

"Not better than you, and you talked it."

"It's all I know."

"Not any more. You haven't spoken it in a while. You've changed."

"But we *don't know!*" Haydn exclaimed. "So much we don't know. I didn't think before you. Just lived. And then you come and make me think. Why?"

"You always thought," Millay said, standing up. She went to him and wrapped her arm his waist. "You just never questioned. And I didn't either. But we wanted to. I think that's what drew us together. You questioned me right away. You knew I wasn't Grace. You knew I was different. And you wanted to know how and why. Because you just wanted to know. Nothing else. Others knew I wasn't Grace and they didn't care, as long as I did my work." She shivered. "Floe me. I'm not making any sense."

"Watch the language," Haydn said and they both laughed.

"But you're different too," Millay said. "You've always been. You leave hive and sleep under the sky."

"Hive is too loud," Haydn said.

"It's more than that."

"I feel—" Haydn began, but then they saw a Lift to the west, lazily flying a pattern over the edge of hive, its searchlight flickering back and forth.

"Why won't they give up?" Millay whispered.

"They're machines," Haydn said. "They don't know no better."

They stood silent for a while, like the stone beneath them, until the Lift gradually moved away.

"Then that's good," Millay finally said.

"What is?"

"That they don't know no better." And then she turned toward him and kissed him, hard, fierce, hot, like burner.

And they went to their knees still kissing, then tore at their clothes. Pulling aside only what needed to be, burner-style.

And made furious and fast burner love on top of the hard stone, but it ended with tenderness neither had ever known.

TWO THREE UNTIL
GRACE'S DEATHDAY

There were angles to the sliver of light so Grace could measure time passing in the day. She'd spent many hours inspecting her coffin with her hands. It would seem something so small wouldn't take so much time, but it was the contorting, the angles of bone and flesh against wood above, dirt on all other sides.

She'd tried digging. She'd earned ripped-out fingernails, lost more blood, and the dirt was as hard the 'tein vats she'd once cleaned.

How long had this house been here? she wondered, then remembered Mrs. Marash's words, that it was from before the Chaos. Which meant Grace had no idea how long ago.

Why hadn't she brought her scraper down? The question that nagged and belittled her. Stupid on two counts. Primarily because she could tear through the wood, or dig through the dirt, and escape if she had it. Maybe. Of course she could, she was so convinced of that, she cursed herself for not having it. But also, she'd left it up above. What if the Dealer had found it? Or the Evermore Richard? Would they even know what a scraper was? Or did it look like it fit right in with the trowels and garden tools and other objects in Mrs.

Marash's wooden bucket of garden implements. Which is where it was.

Grace had used it to weed the old woman's garden. How stupid. How futile.

But the exploration had yielded something. Down near her knee, there was an object wedged into the dirt. Grace's bleeding fingers traced it, feeling a metal box, about eight inches long, four inches wide, and four tall. It had been half-buried and it had taken several hours of effort to free it from the dirt. A welcome task to take her mind from her helplessness for a bit. But she couldn't get a good enough grip on it to bring it close to her head.

Grace wiped the blood from her torn fingernails on her once-white coveralls. They were going to be quite the mess weren't they, she thought randomly, while immediately knowing there was no 'be'.

She tried once more and then she had it. She used her right hand to pull it as far up as she could, until her elbow couldn't move any more. Then she slithered her left hand across her body, the thin arm pressing down on her chest, but her fingers touched the box and she nudged it forward. It got stuck between her shoulder and the side of her hole.

Grace pressed her left shoulder as hard as she could against that side, twitched her fingers, and it was through, resting next to her head.

The effort exhausted her and she rested. Passed out from utter exhaustion.

Several hours later, she heard movement. She was certain.

Remembering the last time, she called out in a low voice. "Mrs. Marash?"

More movement.

"Mrs. Marash?"

"Yes, dear." The old woman's voice was scratchy, matching Grace's.

"Can you get me out of here, please?"

"I would love to," Mrs. Marash said.

And Grace felt a surge of hope.

"But."

Hard to believe one word could be so harsh.

"I'm afraid I've broken my hip. Near as I can tell. I can't stand. Can't even get to my knees." There was more noise of movement. "Hold on."

As if she had some sort of choice. Grace knew she was hearing Mrs. Marash pulling herself across the floor. For a long time, without much distance, judging from the sound.

Grace heard her drinking and felt a surge of resentment, but tamped it down, since the old lady was likely as dehydrated as she.

Then she was coming back, with another noise layered over. Wood on wood.

"It's the only thing I can reach," Mrs. Marash said. "The slop bucket. It was on the floor. Tastes horrible. Tastes wonderful. Are you under the crack? Your mouth?"

Grace adjusted, as much as she could. "Yes."

"Open wide, I'm only going to be able to tip this over once. There's not much. I'll try to control it, but . .."

"I'm ready."

"It's coming."

And then a trickle of foul, scrubbed-dirt-filled water dribbled through the crack and nothing had ever tasted so good to Grace as drops fell into her wide-open mouth. Grace saw a flash of Mrs. Marash's hand as she swept as much as she could into the crack. Grace had her tongue out, trying to lap up every drop.

"That's all," Mrs. Marash said.

"Can you move the table?" Grace asked.

"I can hardly move me," Mrs. Marash said. But Grace heard her grunt. Not even the slightest sound of the thick wooden legs moving. Mrs. Marash grunted again and a moan of pain followed immediately. "I'm sorry," she said, and sounded truly, deeply sorry. "I can't move it. It's too heavy."

Grace closed her eyes. "Can you get to your card? Call for help?"

"Call the Dealers?"

"Anything is better than this."

"Don't be sure of that," Mrs. Marash said, "but it doesn't matter.

It's too high for me to reach. And you don't want the Dealers to come for you. Trust me."

"Will someone come?"

"You heard the little dick, Richard. No one visits me. No one will come."

And then Grace began to cry. She tried to stifle it, to keep it below the wood, but she couldn't help it.

"Oh, dear," Mrs. Marash said. "My dear Grace. Don't give up hope. Trust me."

But Grace's tears turned into sobs, wasting water she couldn't afford to give up to the emptiness.

Mrs. Marash moved, grunted with effort, and then slammed nto the floor with a scream. Silence once more.

TWO TWO UNTIL
GRACE'S DEATHDAY

Grace's face was encrusted with wasted tears and the drops of sludge she hadn't been able to get into her mouth. She had her head turned to the right, her left arm jammed across her body, and she was trying to open the metal box. But it was rusted shut.

She angled it. Old faded black metal.

Grace dropped the box at the sudden whisper.

"That made it worse, I'm afraid," Mrs. Marash said in a strangely calm voice. "I think I broke something else, besides my hip. My leg is at an odd angle. Not normal at all. The skin is discolored."

"We don't have much time," she whispered back, conspirators in impending death, separated by two inches of floorboard.

"Do you trust me?" Mrs. Marash asked.

Grace didn't answer.

"Do you trust me?"

"Burners can't trust," Grace said. "Everyone dies. Trust means caring about another person. We can't care because everyone we know dies."

"Oh posh," Mrs. Marash said, with an edge of the old her in it. "You're still a human and it's not 'care' you need. It's love. Even among People, especially among People, love is a rare commodity. I know in hive all you had was need, never trust and thus never love. But you're not in hive now."

It's worse than hive now, Grace thought. One wouldn't think that possible.

"You have to learn to trust in order to really live. In order to really love."

"No point to it now, is there?" Grace said.

"You see me as just some crazy old lady, whose mind is walking away, taking trips at times, don't you?"

"I see you as the lady who got me in this hole where I'm going to die." Grace knew she shouldn't have said it, but she was jingle-jangled.

"Trust, Grace. Give me a few minutes. Bear with an old woman. Patience, my dear."

There it was. That word again.

"I am over three-hundred years old," Mrs. Marash said.

Grace couldn't wrap her reality around that.

"One of the few originals left. Who lived through the Chaos. Who were born B.D.. I've been doing the math as I lay here, when my mind is with me. That means probably twenty or so generations of burners have lived and died during my life. Long enough to believe this is all there ever was. People. Evermores. Middlemores. burners.

"But there was more. I was more. I was a pilot during the Chaos. I was in the Army. I flew a helicopter."

"'Helicopter'?"

"Like a Lift. Except not flown by machines, flown by humans. Oh, we had machines, computers, which could help us pilot, but after IMP, the computers didn't work any more. Oh, after IMP there was even more Chaos. I lost many comrades and friends the day IMP struck. Friends who relied on their computers too much. IMP ended that. And they don't even spell it right. It was E.M.P.." She spelled the three letters out.

"What is that?" Grace asked, for a moment forgetting she was entombed, to hear things that were only faint myths in hive.

"You wouldn't understand," Mrs. Marash said, yet hurried to

explain. "A series of linked nuclear explosions in the atmosphere that wiped out all the computers. Almost all. All except the handful that were shielded. Like Dealer."

"Who caused IMP?" Grace asked.

And there was one of those extended silences Grace had gotten used to. But now it pulled her from what the old woman was saying back to her dirt and wood tomb. Her hands were quivering.

"IMP was just a part of the Chaos. World War." Surprisingly, Mrs. Marash had come back on track in her words. "But even before IMP, there was the phage. Phage is what started the Chaos and destroyed the world. And no one really knew where it came from."

"What is phage?" Grace had heard of IMP and Chaos, but never this.

"Some sort of virus," Mrs. Marash said. "Changed everyone, took years off of almost everyone's lives. Made most humans into burners. Practically wiped out the older people. We all still have it as part of us."

"Who made this phage?" Grace asked.

"That's the question isn't it?"

And once more she went silent. It was getting worse, but what did her wandering mind matter when they would both be dead shortly?

"I went off the grid here twenty-eight years ago," Mrs. Marash non-sequitured. "Before you and Millay were even conceived. That's when I went to the Person. The one before Andrew. Told him my fears. Told him of the Backdoor as it was told to me. It's only been a few days for you, my dear, but this has been in the works for decades and we still know so little. And the Person knew it would be dangerous. We both groomed Andrew to take his place, as we knew he would inevitably be needed."

"Who caused the Chaos?" Grace asked. "Word to ear in hive is the cyborgs." Grace was trying to catch up through so many words she didn't understand.

"I fear the cyborgs didn't cause IMP or start Chaos," Mrs. Marash said. "It was humans."

"But why?"

"I don't know," Mrs. Marash said. "I think that is the goal now. The goal of the Backdoor. To find out the truth of how this all came to be. No one knows the entire truth, but I fear it is horrible. And, my own knowledge is incomplete so I don't want to mislead you with rumors or half-memories. You have to remember—" And once more she fell silent.

"What do I have to remember?"

"Where was I?"

"I have to learn on my own. About Chaos, about—"

Mrs. Marash interrupted. "Oh, you wouldn't remember, would you? What combat is like? A soldier, a pilot, only sees a tiny, tiny portion of it. We don't even know how the battle we're in is progressing, never mind the war. Never mind a World War. And almost all our senior officers died from the phage early on."

She fell quiet, but it wasn't the usual, blankness. Even under the floor, Grace could tell Mrs. Marash she was into her memory.

"The war covered the world. Billions died. Here, here in the Sound, was the only place of sanity. At least we thought so, but it would be logical that Dealer wasn't the only quantum computer to survive IMP; the only one shielded. Dealer helped the Sound survive the Chaos that followed.

"A new world began, built around Dealer. A small world, but it survived. Got to give Dealer credit for that. Survival." Mrs. Marash snorted. "Yes, we both know how important survival is now, don't we, Grace? How we'll do just about anything to live. Even for, how many is it, now?"

"Two two."

"Twenty-two days."

Grace waited, but then grew restless. "Mrs. Marash? Mrs. Marash?"

After a few minutes, her mind was back. "What was I saying?"

Grace focused on a more immediate issue. "Can you move the table?"

"Patience. I have my reasons. I've watched it all unfold over the years and done nothing. Oh, I read stories to the children. What a coward I've been. You want two-two days. I wanted the years offered. I only stopped—" she paused—"wanting more twenty-eight years ago and even that was selfish. I know it's hard to believe but one can grow weary of living, when almost everyone you love is dead. And you carry a heavy burden in your heart.

"People don't know what hive is like. I don't. We see some in the Stream but I'm afraid it fools us with what it gives us. Makes it seem heroic, brave."

"It's not."

"But you are, and you're from hive."

Grace felt a tear well up in her right eye, all she had left to give to the sadness.

Mrs. Marash continued. "If you control information, you control people, and Dealer controls all. And no one wants to know the truth any way. We're scared of it. Cowards.

"But not Andrew," Mrs Marash said. "And the Person before him; because I told him of the Backdoor. What little I knew. He knew something was wrong. Remember this Grace: *Things fall apart; the centre cannot hold.*"

"I don't understand."

"A poem from B.D. It's on the table near the lantern. The thin book. *Second Coming.* By Yeats. Remember those lines."

And there was silence, leaving Grace to wonder if Mrs. Marash's mind would come back, or if she were finally dead, and what did it matter anyway?

"You go to the Void," Mrs. Marash suddenly said. "You are to meet a man named Ryker at the Lone Bridge. Ha! Lone Bridge. Why did they leave it standing, even though it's guarded? Have to wonder at that. But I was military. Even though they defend it, it's also an avenue of approach for an attack into Void if need be. Everything goes both ways.

"Do what you have to do, my dear Grace. Ryker should know. Remember: *Things fall apart; the centre cannot hold'.* He should know his part. Everything is compartmentalized; it's the most secure way. I only know my part. This script we're following was written long ago and is now coming to life, somehow. Each of us is a piece."

"A piece of what?" Grace asked.

"Change. After all, my dear, things *are* falling apart."

Silence.

"Grace?"

"Yes?"

Mrs. Marash sounded confused, somewhere between cognizant and jingle-jangled. "You might meet her."

"Who?"

"My love."

"Who? Where? How?" The old woman was losing it in her words now, not just her silences.

Another long silence, but it was broken by the hint of the old woman crying.

"Mrs. Marash?" Grace called out.

"Will you bury me after I'm gone?" Mrs. Marash asked.

"'Bury'?"

"In a grave?"

"What is that?"

"Next to the garden. You'll need patience. Dig a hole, far enough down so the animals won't get to my body. I want to be part of the garden, not some rodent. Four feet down, six is better. It will be hard; lots of roots. Bury me there. It will be peaceful and my body will then become part of the cycle of life."

Grace bit back the obvious: that the only way she could bury, an odd concept, the old woman was to be free of her own shallow grave. If being in the earth was all there was to being in a grave, Grace was already in one.

"Mrs. Marash," Grace said. "Is there any way you can move the table?"

"I've been thinking on that, lying here on the floor," Mrs. Marash said. "I can do two things at once my dear. Sometimes. I've been thinking hard on the problem that is literally at hand. There's one possible way."

Grace waited, not letting hope flare up.

"Do you trust me, Grace?"

"Yes. I trust you."

Mrs. Marash almost sounded happy. "That's so nice to hear."

A long pause. Then Mrs. Marash said: "I love you, Grace."

The old woman grunted with effort. Then a screech of wood on wood sounded for a moment. Then another grunt by Mrs. Marash, a snapping sound, and then a huge thud, the floorboards shaking.

Grace remained still. "Mrs. Marash?"

With shaking hands, Grace reached up and pushed on the trap door. It moved. An inch. Two. Grace mustered what little energy she had left and shoved it to the side.

She sat up from the filthy grave where part of her had died, and part of her had been born, and looked.

The table was tipped over, the edge of the stone top smashed down on Mrs. Marash's chest. Grace could only crawl to the old lady. Mrs. Marash had broken the closest leg inward and broken the old, rusty bracket where it held up the stone, collapsing it on herself with her dying effort.

Grace looked into her sightless eyes. "Oh, Mrs. Marash."

And Grace cradled the old woman's head in her lap and cried, but she had no tears left.

TWO ONE UNTIL
GRACE'S DEATHDAY

"People lived out there." Haydn pointed to the right, at the Wasteland. "Farmed. Worked. Loved. Had children. Until it all ended in the Chaos."

They were walking along the folding path at the edge of the outer arc of hive; the edge of civilization.

"The world must have been a much larger place," Haydn continued, speaking into Millay's silence, and she finally responded.

"The world *is* much larger than what we know in the Sound," Millay said. "I was taught *some* of it in school." She paused and pointed toward the Wasted Mountains, their blackened slopes going up into the gray, low-lying clouds. "But it's all dead out there." She turned the other way, to the west. "And surrounding the Olympic Mountains is Deep Void, and then there is an ocean. And beyond the ocean is just more death."

"Plenty of death in hive," Haydn said.

"I saw," Millay said, remembering the morgue under hive, where she'd come to.

"When—" He paused as a deep, bone-shuddering sound echoed in from the left, from the direction of the agri-hives they'd been bypassing on the horizon.

"What is that?" Millay asked, as the noise came again.

"Don't you remember?" Haydn asked. "You were born in hive, right?"

"I don't remember much about it," Millay said, but wouldn't meet his gaze.

"Assembly," Haydn said. There was a third blast. Haydn waited, tense. Nothing more. "Three times," Haydn said. "Dealing Day for the closest hives."

Millay was confused. "I thought it was one day. I do remember that. Only one day a year."

"It is. For *each* hive. It rotates among the hives. You were taken into the Womb of Island before you could understand how things really work out here." He gave a bitter laugh. "Different day of the year for different hives. Maybe too much for Dealers to handle doing all hives on one day." He was standing still, staring to the southwest, across the fields. Just beyond them, the curved top of a hive was visible. "Let's go." He started walking through the fields.

"What are you doing?" Millay demanded, running to catch up to him and grabbing his arm. "You said we needed to stay away. I don't want to go near hive ever again."

He turned and placed his rough hands gently her shoulders. "You need to see this, Millay. You need to remember. My words can only take you so far." He removed his hands. He pointed to the side of his head. "The ear can understand some, but it is the eyes," he said, pointing at his own, "that give the strongest lesson because words can lie. Eyes cannot. Since you don't clearly remember hive and Dealing Day, you must see it again." And then he began walking toward the hive.

For the first time he didn't look back to see if she were following.

Millay hustled after him, caught up, and walked by his side. They pushed through the corn. It was as if they were walking in place for several minutes, each row the same as the last one, but Haydn suddenly thrust his arm out, stopping Millay as they reached the end.

"Oh," Millay whispered.

In front of them was a belt of beautiful flowers: tulips, irises, roses and more, all sorted in narrow bands ten feet wide, by fifty deep, as far as the eye could see left and right. But it wasn't that which elicited Millay's surprise. On the far side of the flowers, in front of a standard hive building, in an Assembly Field, at least six thousand burners were gathered, formed up in a square. And in the center of the square was a cluster of around two hundred children.

"Six-year-olds," Haydn said. "Why so many flowers? Few are used at the gates to Heaven in hive."

"Most go to Island," Millay said. "It's for—" she searched—"decoration. To please the eye."

"So many," Haydn said in awe and disgust at the concept. "So much work for nothing for just decoration."

"For beauty," Millay said, immediately regretting the two words.

But Haydn looked more closely at the flowers. "I can see that. If one has the time to appreciate the beauty."

Lift sound approached from the southwest. Haydn tugged on Millay's arm and they knelt on the edge of the cornfield. A Lift came into sight and settled on a concrete pad on the side of Assembly.

"One Lift," Haydn said.

"And?"

"Remember the gates to Heaven?"

Millay frowned and then it hit her. "Max of twenty-five."

"Fewer than that," Haydn said. "Count the Dealers coming off."

Doors slid open and Dealers poured out, ten to each side. Among them were two Dark Angels each carrying a box.

"Twenty," Millay said. "Leaves five seats."

"They'll be lucky to get that many cards other than red."

Millay knew the numbers. "Point one percent white, point three percent green, point nine percent blue."

"Which means?" Haydn asked.

"There will be empty seats on it going back, especially since it's weighted genetically toward same producing same."

The eighteen regular Dealers spread out in a rigid perimeter around the children, between them and their parents. The two Dark

Angels took position in front. It was impossible to tell which one of them 'spoke'.

"It is the day for the card Dealer determined at your birth by genetics to be dealt. Speak your name designation as approached."

The two Dark Angels flipped up the lids on the boxes. Then they moved forward, lifting a card on a chain out after the child identified themself.

Red. Red. It was numbing.

But each child stood there, letting the card designating the day of their death come down around their head, around their neck and settle onto their chest. The surrounding crowd was still, not a sound, not a movement.

The Dark Angels moved quickly, a card every two seconds.

Red. Red. Red.

Millay leaned forward. "There's got to be at least—" she muttered but didn't finish.

Haydn glanced sideways at her, one blonde eyebrow arching. But he said nothing.

Red. Red. Red. Red.

As the Dark Angels started on another row of children, nothing but red dealt, Haydn finally spoke. "There hasn't been hope in a long time. You may know numbers, Millay, but burners, we know feelings. There's been no hope. We may not live long, but we know it's getting worse."

Millay reluctantly remembered her own Dealing Day. Standing next to Grace. A white card looped over her, then her shock when Grace was dealt red, when the shock should have been the other way.

Not fair.

"Haydn," Millay said in a low voice.

"Yes?"

"I have to tell you something."

"Yes?"

"When I was dealt white and Grace got red—"

Haydn waited.

"I felt bad for her," Millay finally said, "but—"

"I understand," Haydn said when she couldn't complete it.

As the Dark Angels finished the last row and not a single card other than red was passed out, a murmur passed through the crowd, like a thin wind that precedes an approaching, but still-distant storm.

"My candle burns at both ends!" a single voice in the crowd called out.

A candle, lit on both ends gripped by a fist, appeared above the crowd.

"My candle burns at both ends!" the same voice repeated.

Another candle, in a different spot in the crowd was lifted up, ends flickering.

The same voice started but this time, several other voices joined in. *"My candle burns at both ends."*

The handful of voices echoed across the crowd and faded away.

The Dark Angels stomped away back toward the Lift. The other Dealers peeled off, following them.

There was no acknowledgement of either the words or the candles.

They were machines. They did not care.

The doors slid shut on the Lift. It accelerated up and away to the southwest.

The crowd was still for a moment, and the candles were lowered. Then the group began to break apart, parents coming forward to their children, to say farewell.

"Where are they going?" Millay asked. This was the part she had not experienced because she'd been on the Lift.

"Their children now go to the womb of hive," Haydn said as he got to his feet. "Think how it works. We can do the math because we live it. The window for a burner to get pregnant is two years. Six to seven years before Deathday. So parents can usually take care of their child up until Dealing Day. Then the children are taken to the womb of hive, since their parents will advance to Heaven within a year or so."

Millay's voice was shaky. "Statistically there should have been at least one card other than red dealt."

"People become People," Haydn said. "Evermores become Evermores. Middlemores become Middlemores. And burner, burner."

"It's genetics," Millay argued. "It makes sense, sad sense, but it does make sense that it works out this way."

Haydn tapped his ear. "Word to ear is that it wasn't this way. burners became People some times. And Evermores and Middlemores. And sometimes, they became burner. What has changed? When was the last time a child of People came to womb of hive?"

"I don't know."

"And tell me, Millay. If it's genetics, how were you dealt white and your sister dealt red? If you are so the same you were able to switch places?"

"Genetics?" Millay said, but the question mark was obvious.

Haydn shook his head. "Tell me this, Millay. If its genetics, how did you die and then live? What does genetics have to do with that? When a burner dies, the burner is dead. No Heaven. No coming back to life."

I'm People, Millay thought, but didn't say. Because he was right.

Haydn started, staring to the south. "Come!"

Millay followed his gaze.

Three Lifts were on the horizon, above the edge of hive arc. Low to the ground, moving slowly, deliberately.

"They're looking for us," Haydn said, tugging on her arm. "They're searching the folding path."

Millay didn't need much inducement. They ran between two rows of corn, stalks slapping at them. They were out of breath when they reached the edge of hive and the Wasteland beckoned, dark, dead, extending bleakly to the Wasted Mountains.

Haydn didn't hesitate, Millay at his side. Ash puffed under their feet as they passed from life to death.

"There," Haydn pointed. A large B.D. structure, its roof crumbled, stood a quarter mile ahead and to the left.

Millay glanced over her shoulder. The Lifts were a mile to the south, over the outer arc of hive. Her lungs burned and she felt as if she'd been stabbed in the side, her muscles cramping.

But she ran.

They reached the ruin and Haydn pulled her through an opening, into the shadows. They threw themselves against the inside of the wall. Millay doubled over, trying to breath.

"Farther," Haydn said, tugging on her, making her crawl deeper into the debris inside. They slithered under metal beams, going along the wall.

"Here," Haydn said.

There was an inch wide crack in the outer wall and while Millay lay on her back panting, he edged up to it and peered through. The Lifts were now passing near where they'd watched the Dealing. The side doors were open and he could see four Dealers on this side, all facing outward. Searching.

Haydn slumped down next to Millay.

"We wait here until they're out of sight."

"All right," Millay managed to gasp.

"We head east from here. Into Wasteland. They're tracking the folding path to the ferry. I don't think Dealer will factor we're far out in Wasteland. No one goes there."

"You have," Millay said.

"Yes. I have."

"It will take us longer," Millay noted.

"We have no choice if we're to make it."

"But—" Grace began.

"What?"

"Won't the ferry be guarded too?"

"Maybe," Haydn allowed. "One step at a time. And I mean that literally. We have to get there first. Then we will see what we will see." Haydn took her hand. "I don't care about statistics or genetics. I care about hope. And there is no more hope in hive."

"But what we just saw," Millay said. "Those few protesting. They might not have hope, they have a flicker of change. We hold on to that."

It took a day for Grace to drink enough water to keep from fainting and to be able to cry properly.

To finally stand.

To make some food and be able to eat it.

And wrap Mrs. Marash in her brightly colored blanket.

It was nearly evening. Ryker and Doc needed to find a place to hole up. Avoiding roads and buildings where jokers could lurk was difficult. The deep woods were more a barrier than a way to travel. But the safest path.

There was plenty of water, streams here and there, but they had to forage for food. Doc knew many of the plants, which ones were edible—not many—and which weren't—many. The few times they went into old B.D. structures, it was obvious they'd been ransacked many times over the long years since they'd been abandoned. Ace was having better luck than either of them, running off and disappearing, then coming back with a rabbit or some other small creature in his mouth.

Ace got equal portions after they cooked each evening at dusk on a small fire that they quickly extinguished as full night fell.

"How much farther?" Ryker asked Doc as they scrambled over a fallen tree.

"I don't know."

"Are we going in the right direction? We haven't been traveling in a straight line."

Doc checked the direction of the fading sun. "We had to swing north to get around an area with a lot of ruins infested with jokers. Now we're heading south. It's not much farther. I think."

"Have you been to this bridge?" Ryker asked.

"No. I've listened to people who've seen it and I have a rough idea where it is. We'll hit the shore soon and then we follow it."

"Which way?" Ryker asked. "Left or right?"

They both looked up as raindrops began to fall, pattering on the leaves, and then onto them. Ace whined, obviously unhappy with this development. And Doc didn't answer his last question, which was an answer in itself.

Ryker and Doc weren't thrilled with the rain either. They pushed forward and came to the edge of a clearing in the woods. They paused. A building was in the middle, with concrete walls and a metal roof. It was overgrown with vegetation. The windows, if they'd ever had glass in them, had none now. The front door was gone, just an opening.

"Looks like the perfect place for a joker to nest," Doc said.

"Yeah," Ryker said. "But one joker isn't a problem."

"Four or five would be."

The decision was taken from them as Ace bounded out from the treeline, making a beeline for the dark doorway.

"Ace!" Doc hissed, but the dog ignored her.

Ryker glanced at Doc, then sprinted forward, drawing his blades as he did so. Doc was right behind him, hatchet in hand.

Ace disappeared through the door.

He immediately began barking furiously. Ryker went through the opening without hesitation. He was surprised that the interior wasn't dark and immediately saw why: the far wall was blown down, a tumble of broken and blasted concrete. Ace had trapped a joker in the corner, just to the right of the shattered wall. The entire place was only about fifteen feet square and the floor was covered with the debris of scavengers and jokers and other animals making it a nest over the decades and centuries.

The joker scrambled up on the debris and opened his mouth to call out when Ace leapt onto his back, tumbling him back into the room.

Doc came in next to Ryker, breathing hard. "Easy, Ace! Easy!"

Ace backed off, growling and the joker looked up, started to open his mouth, then snapped it shut.

Ryker stepped forward, weapons at the ready.

"Ace!" Doc snapped. "Heel."

Ace did take a step back and stopped growling. The joker was young, emaciated, his clothes in tatters. His eyes were darted back and forth between them and the opening in the wall, but he remained in place.

Ryker raised one blade.

"Ryker! Heel!"

Ryker laughed. He lowered the knife. "Who are you?" he asked the joker.

"Thomas-kilo-four-eight-seven," the boy said.

"Well, Tommy K," Ryker said, "anyone else hide here?"

"No."

Doc put a hand on Ace's head. "Sit."

Ace settled down on his haunches, eyeing Thomas as if he'd make a good meal.

Doc whispered in Ace' ear while pushing him toward the door. "Hunt."

And the dog took off, out of the building. Ryker looked up. The metal roof was mostly intact, except on the side where the wall had been blasted in. "Something powerful did that," Ryker said as he sheathed his blades. "Sit down," he ordered, nodding at a piece of concrete.

Thomas warily got off the ground and sat.

"Floed, correct?" Ryker said.

Thomas nodded.

"Why?"

Thomas opened his mouth to speak, but Doc and grabbed his jaw in a pinch and looked into his mouth. "Some are filed, not all."

"Why were you floed?" Ryker asked again.

"What's the point?" Thomas said.

"What's the point of what?" Ryker said. "Of living? hive? Working? Breathing? More specific, Tommy K."

"Working every day for the promise of Heaven," Thomas said. "No one's ever come back from Heaven. We just hear it's so great."

"That's kind of the concept of going there just before you die," Ryker noted. "The not coming back part."

"I don't believe it," Thomas said.

"Kind of guessed that," Ryker replied. "How long have you been in the Void?"

"One-five-eight days."

"But you still count the days," Doc noted. "How long until Deathday?"

Thomas sighed. "Six-four."

"So close," Ryker said. "And your attitude got you floed. Easy not to believe in something you're not going to get."

Thomas shrugged. His hands were twitching and his eyes were bloodshot.

"How come the other jokers haven't eaten you?" Doc asked.

"They will eventually. Once I'm near my Deathday. But until then —" he paused.

"I think you lie," Ryker said. "There's fresh blood on what remains of your coveralls."

"Some small thing I killed the other day."

"You caught it with your bare hands?"

"Yes."

"You lie," Ryker said it without rancor.

"I not lie."

Doc jumped in. "I think you lie about why you got floed."

Everyone turned as Ace came back, a squirrel in his jaws, its neck broken.

"Good dog," Doc said. "That was fast."

"Lots small animals around here," Thomas tried.

"You're not as fast as Ace," Ryker said. He pulled one of his knives out. "Dinner. Doc. The fire, please."

They had it down by now, a quick routine, efficient. Ryker prepped the animal while Doc gathered some wood and tinder and flinted a fire in one corner. Thomas sat on the concrete block, shivering, watching with deep-set, reddened eyes.

Soon the squirrel was over the small fire, Ryker using one knife as the spit. Satisfied it was, scorched, crossing the low bar into edible, he nodded at Doc, who kicked dirt over the fire, putting it out. Ryker sliced a piece off and tossed it to Ace, who snapped it up in one gulp.

Then he cut a piece of meat and extended it on the point of his second blade to Doc. Then he took a piece.

He put it in his mouth, cut a fourth piece, then tossed it to Ace.

Thomas twitched.

Doc looked over. "Ryker?"

Ryker looked at the youngster. "It's a waste of food we're going to need."

"Ryker?"

He cut a piece and walked to Thomas, extending the knife point.

Thomas' hand darted out and grabbed the meat, stuffing it into his mouth.

As he chewed, Ryker sheathed the knife, pulled two pieces of cord out of his pack, then tied Thomas' hands behind his back and his ankles together, leaving him trussed on the floor.

Doc, Ryker and Ace finished the rest of the squirrel, which wasn't much. The three moved to the far corner and huddled together as night wrapped down.

"What are we going to do about him?" Doc whispered, mouth to Ryker's ear.

"Kill him."

Doc was irritated. "Are we going to discuss it?"

"How we kill him?" Ryker said, surprised. "I'll use my—"

"No," Doc hissed. "Whether we should kill him at all."

"What other options are there?" Ryker asked.

"We could let him go."

"And have a pack of jokers after us as soon as he calls out to them? We're two humans. And a dog. It will be a pack of jokers coming."

"All right," Doc ceded. "We could leave him here, tied up like that."

"Then he's just a meal. Better to do it quick."

"Then we take him with us."

"That makes no sense," Ryker said. He had his knives in hand, resting on his lap. "Coffin handles," he suddenly said.

"What?"

"My knives. The handles. They're called coffin handles."

"What does that mean?"

"I don't know," Ryker said, but he felt pleased that something had come out of the fog of his past and flashed so brightly in his present.

But Doc was still on the matter tied up across the way. "I take it you don't believe in Dealer," she said to Ryker.

"I most definitely believe in Dealer," Ryker said. "I just don't know what Dealer is. Or whether Dealer is good or bad."

"All right," Doc said. "Good and bad. You believe in that."

Ryker hesitated. "Yes."

"Killing Thomas would be bad."

"It would be necessary."

"I believe," Doc said, "that there is some force greater than Dealer. Something we all have to believe in. Something that is good. So we must be good."

"Thomas would eat us if he could," Ryker said, practicaling down the philosophical. "That would be bad."

"Maybe he has a purpose in all of this," Doc said.

"What purpose?"

Doc raised her voice. "Thomas?"

"Yes?" He was awake, trying to hear his fate.

"Do you know of the bridge to Island?" Doc asked.

"Lone Bridge?"

Doc glanced sideways at Ryker in the dark, the glint of starlight on the whites of her eyes. "Yes."

"I've seen it," Thomas said. "Dealers guard it. Don't go too near it. None of us do."

"Is it far?" Ryker asked.

"No. Just—" They heard him grunt, as he tried to point, forgetting for a moment his hands were tied behind his back. "Just a walk. Not even a day on the hidden trails." Something must have clicked in his brain. "I could take you. Yes! I could show you."

"Get some sleep," Ryker said.

Doc dropped her voice to a whisper. "So you're not going to kill him?"

"Not this moment."

TWO ONE UNTIL
GRACE'S DEATHDAY

"What is that?" Millay asked, wrinkling her nose.

They were walking in pre-dawn Wasteland, surreal, feet kicking up ash on the crumpled B.D. roadway. Dead fields all around, fragments of buildings. A stone chimney defying time, the rest of the building gone.

"Don't know," Haydn answered. He paused, turning one way, then the other. "It's not coming from hive." He pointed. "There."

Ahead in the Wasteland was a dark smudge on the horizon.

"Maybe it's the waste vats?" Millay suggested.

Haydn laughed. "I was detailed to work them for three months. That's all anyone can stand, even a burner. One of the few jobs the Middlemores rotate. Cleaning and processing shit and piss. I know that smell. This is different. And this is far outside of the arc. The waste vats were inside. Nothing is outside of the arc." He nodded toward the smudge. "But this is. Let's check it out."

Millay could only shake her head at Haydn's curiosity. This was life and death, but it was also an adventure for him. A journey of exploration beyond the boundaries of being pulled back to hive for a twelve-hour shift. As if every step from the hive was lifting a burden from him; regardless of what they saw, even the other day's horror of the boy being bagged. Even watching the despair of Dealing Day just yesterday.

They crossed an expanse of black ash where not a single plant struggled from seed to sunlight. They came to the crest of a ridgeline and halted, taking a knee, just their heads peering over. It took a few seconds to grasp what they were seeing.

There was a milling mass of four-legged creatures hemmed in and separated into manageable lots by heavy steel rail fences. Feed troughs lined one side of each lot. Beyond a group of burners waited with cranes and trucks and past that stood a single-story black building. Closer by was a small hive. And in the distance, a single ribbon of black, a road, heading toward the western horizon.

"Cattle," Millay said.

"What?"

"Cattle. You get meat from cattle."

"I've heard of meat," Haydn said. "We don't get it in hive."

"You get some of it," Millay said. "The parts that the People and Evermores and Middlemores don't want. It's part of 'tein. This is a rendering yard. They're kept away from hive, and the burners who work it are in their own little community. See the hive dome there to the right?"

Now Haydn saw it. "Small. Maybe three stories high."

"Rendering is the hardest hive job," Millay said.

"There," Haydn said. "Slightly to the left of center."

burners had climbed the fence and were using prods to move the cattle in that pen forward. There was only one exit, a wide chute that made gentle turns and narrowed until it was only one cow wide. The burners were dressed only in tight shorts, both sexes. But their hair was distinctive, both men and women: skulls shaved except for a single, inch-wide strip right along the center, from forehead to a short ponytail dangling in the back. And another strip of hair perpendicular to that, going from ear to ear, forming a cross on top of their skull.

"Never seen that look," Haydn said.

"Me neither," Millay said.

"They don't have cards!" Haydn said as if it were the most amazing thing he'd seen. "Even in the waste vats; even in the 'tein vats; even in the most dangerous jobs in hive, burners wear their cards. You wore Grace's in there. Why don't *they* have cards?"

"I don't know," Millay said. "Maybe they leave them in their hive?"

The cattle were moving, into the only exit available.

"That's strange," Millay said. "Why does the chute curve? They must be moving them somewhere, but I don't understand this."

Haydn was watching, no comment. The first cow reached the end of the chute and burners sprung into coordinated action, so quickly it was hard to keep track.

One burner knelt on the right side of the chute and tossed a chain across, in front of the cow's rear legs. Another burner grabbed the chain and ran with it back across, behind the cow, and snap-linked the chain in a tight loop around the legs. This caused the creature to halt for a moment, confused, secured, as a third burner stepped up, then jabbed a rod downward into the top of the creature's head.

The cow collapsed.

Dead.

"Oh!" Millay exclaimed as another burner, controlling a crane attached to the chain, quickly lifted the dead cow by its rear legs, swinging it over to where another burner clipped the chain to a moving, thick steel cable. The crane operator released the connector to the chain, swinging back to the end of the chute to repeat.

The dead, dangling cattle, moved slowly and there most of the burners worked with knives and axes and saws, tearing into the creatures, carving them apart even as there were still moving. This, too, was as choreographed as the killing. Entrails out first onto a conveyor that crossed perpendicular to the steel line, carrying them away. More knives and saws, more cuts, pieces and parts, each landing on its own belt, which all headed toward a one-story building.

The reason the burners were practically naked was easily apparent as they were splattered with blood and gore.

The pen was cleared of roughly seventy-five cattle in less than fiften minutes, every beast also rendered in that time.

The burners, their task done, began to trudge along the road, passing underneath hoses attached to a metal bar just above head height. The sprays blasted the burners, washing away most, but not all of the results of their work. They continued on, disappearing into their hive.

"Oh!" was all Millay could say.

"Efficient," Haydn said, focused on what had happened and how. "I think the curve is there to make the cattle think they're going back to where they came from. So they go through willingly. It would be hard to make the cattle move if they were fighting it." He was surprised to see Millay was upset. "Everything dies, Millay. Everyone and every living thing dies eventually."

"But to be killed and taken apart so callously," Millay said.

"Is there a nice way to kill?" Haydn asked. "I've known the day I will die ever since Dealing Day. The cattle don't. They never saw it coming. I see it coming every day. Maybe they have better lives than burners." He slid back down from the crest of the ridge. "We need to keep moving."

TWO ZERO UNTIL GRACE DEATHDAY

Grace had bathed in the stream in the forest behind the cabin. Then cleaned her coveralls in the basin as Mrs. Marash had shown her, rubbing them on the washboard. Hung them on the rack near the fireplace. It got a lot of stain out, but they would never be pure white again.

The old woman lay on the floor, wrapped in the colorful quilt she'd always put over her shoulders as she slept in her wooden chair.

Two zero.

Grace smiled sadly as she thought of that. How she would have felt the pressure of those days ticking off.

That was the gift Mrs. Marash had given her. Grace kept just her shorts on and went out into the chill air, the old spade in hand. Right next to the garden. She began digging.

The old woman had been right.

It was not easy.

"Why do jokers eat people?" Doc asked Thomas

Ryker was looking out a bare window to the east, at the Lone Bridge. They were in a large ruin, the roof caved in and full of rusted machines. On the third floor, the sky was open above them, just a few skeletal trusses remaining. Doc had made out enough faded writing to tell him this had once been the *Suquamish Clearwater Casino Resort*, which was a worthless bit of information since they had no idea what that meant.

Thomas, once more trussed after leading them here, was lying on the floor. Ace was on his belly, tongue lolling, waiting whatever lay ahead without concern.

Lucky dog.

"I don't know," Thomas answered. "I've never eaten human."

"You lie," Ryker said, without turning his head.

The bridge stretched from four hundred yards in front of him on a high, vegetation-covered bluff on this side, across the water at an angle, northwest to southeast. The far side had a pebble beach, but the bridge touched land on another high bluff above the beach.

"There's plenty of small game, and even larger animals, like deer, in the forest," Doc said. "Why humans?"

"I don't know."

Ryker counted four Dealers. Two stalking almost the length of the bridge in a random pattern, passing each other at different points. And two fixed, liked statues, at the far end, facing this way. They were slightly different than the Dealers in hive. Their blank, flat 'faces' were blood red, with a black strip for sensory input. On their right arms, attached to the wrist, instead of a stunner, they had a larger weapon, sleeker, more menacing. Ryker assumed it was lethal.

He turned from the window then walked to Thomas and gave him a short, sharp kick in the ribs. Thomas cried out in pain.

"Ryker!" Doc said.

But Ryker raised a finger, hushing her.

"You've eaten human, haven't you?" Ryker asked, pulling his foot back.

Thomas whimpered. "Yes."

"You were there the other night, weren't you? Three refugees from Delta. What was it? A family? Mother, father and child?"

"I wasn't—"

Thomas yelped as Ryker's boot struck, causing Ace to give a low whine. But Doc remained silent.

"I don't know if they family," Thomas said. "They were running. We was chasing them down. Someone had given the call. When a joker gives call, it's passed. We all come toward it, all that can hear."

"How come you didn't give the call when we caught you?" Doc asked.

"Dog got me. You got me too fast. You'd have killed me before any got there. What good that do me?"

"I would have," Ryker concurred. "How many jokers heard the call that night?"

Thomas shrugged, as best one could shrug with hands tied behind back. "Twenty, twenty-five. It was dark."

"Wasn't dark when you had the fire and were cooking them," Ryker said.

"Then we was eating, not counting."

Ryker drew one of his knives.

"Ryker," Doc said, not a command, a suggestion. "Why do you eat people?" she asked Thomas once more.

"Easier to catch. Easier to run down."

Ryker was watching Thomas' face. "Makes sense, but you're still lying."

Thomas closed his eyes and a tear rolled down.

Ryker made to kick him again, but out of the corner of his eye he saw Doc hold up a hand, so he backed off.

Doc went over and knelt next to the joker. "What else? What else is there about eating people?"

Thomas sniffled. "The legend."

"What legend?" Doc prompted.

Thomas opened his eyes. "When I was first in Void, I was scared. You Delta people at the landing, you pushed me away. Didn't have nothing to do with me cause I was floed. So me, and others floed, we was left standing there. We scattered; didn't know to stay together, protect each other. Cause we was floed burner. How would we know?"

Ryker glanced over his shoulder. The two Dealers were moving back and forth. A small rain shower was passing through. It didn't affect them at all. They were machine.

"That first night a joker came on me. I thought I was Deathday. But he told me I had choice. Either be joker or be food for joker." Thomas gave a bitter laugh. "What choice?"

"And he told you a story," Doc said.

"Yeah. Legend. Said they eat people. 'Cause long ago word to ear was that eating people make you live longer than eating animal. Said word to ear is some jokers live past Deathday if they eat enough human."

Doc shot a glance at Ryker, who shrugged.

"Is it true?" Doc asked.

"How I know?" Thomas said. "Don't look like I gonna live longer, do it? I never met one past their Deathday."

"Why didn't he just give the call and they eat you?"

"They do sometime. Eat the fresh meat. But they need numbers to come for the hunt. And to fight. Especially against Delta people when they come out, past Line to hunt us."

Ryker looked at Doc. "How many do you lose to jokers?"

"Several a month," Doc said. "That's why there's the Line. We usually only go beyond when we send the reception party to meet Charon. But jokers cross the Line every so often. It's been a battle as long as I've been there. It was brutal the first year, clearing Delta of jokers."

"And did Achilles send people out to attack jokers? Out past the line?"

Doc nodded. "Sometimes patrols were sent out to hunt down jokers. Not much success, but some are killed. You saw the ones under the bridge."

Ryker nodded at Thomas. "He ate people you knew." Ryker pulled his blade halfway out of the sheath.

"He got us here," Doc noted.

"We'd have gotten here," Ryker said. "Eventually," he allowed, given that Thomas had taken them along a thin track, almost impossible to follow without knowing it was there, deep in the forest, in a bit of a different direction than Doc had been heading. Ryker let go of the blade.

He turned to the window. "What's that?" He pointed.

Doc joined him. A tall, carved wooden pole was set in the ground. It reached slightly higher than their floor. The top was carved in the shape of a bird's beak. There were other images carved in it all the way down.

"No idea," Doc said.

Ryker frowned. "It's something jingle-jangled in my brain."

"Lots jingle-jangled in there. *You're* jingle-jangled in the there. Who you were."

Behind them, Thomas was weeping, not so quietly, anticipating his death. Ace joined them by the window.

"I've got to get across the bridge," Ryker said, contemplating the Dealers.

"Actually," Doc said, "she's got to get across to this side."

"I've got to help her get across," Ryker amended.

"Dealers don't sleep," Doc said.

"No, they don't. And they'd spot a boat, even if I could find one that floats around here. Doubtful after all the years. Charon maintained his. No Charon here."

"You'll figure it out," Doc said. "Thomas," she said in a hard voice. "Stop crying. You're not going to die. Not tonight at least."

ONE NINE UNTIL
GRACE'S DEATHDAY

It had been much harder to dig a grave than Grace had anticipated. There were roots and rocks in the way. As if the Earth were fighting back, not willing to receive Mrs. Marash. But Grace was determined to defeat the ground. And she did. Six feet, just a smidge over her height. She had to use the small ladder to climb in and out for the last couple of feet. She did it practically naked, sweat sliding down her body, dirt clinging.

Much the way one entered the 'tein vat at shift start; just wearing tight shorts, clean and dripping water from the sprayers in entry tunnel, and then exited at shift end, sweating, flaked with 'tein. The sprayers in exit tunnel weren't as powerful or good as the entry so one always had the odor of 'tein, an identifier of where one worked.

Grace climbed out of the hole. She pulled the ladder up.

It was finally done; and done right.

Grace walked down to the stream then immersed herself, letting the cold water cleanse her of the sweat and dirt. Shivering, she ran back to the house.

As she stood next to the fire to dry, she wondered if the difficulty of digging the grave were part of some sort of ritual, of ceremony, to force the person doing it to think about the person they were burying? That so much effort should be exerted meant that much honor and respect was given to the dead.

And love. Effort for another person must mean love.

No, she realized. It wasn't the effort. It was the time she'd spent doing it; giving up a precious day of the short life she had left.

Love was time given to another.

Grace dressed and as she finished, she became aware that she hadn't done it burner-style, but slowly, not as slow as People but different as if it were something in the *Now*, not under the pressure of the *Then*.

Grace was able to lift Mrs. Marash and carry her outside without much trouble. Flesh and bone and scant muscle and no life left; no spirit.

How much did spirit weigh?

Grace lowered her into the hole as best she could although she had to let go before it reached bottom and the body tumbled the rest of the way, landing with a light thud on its side, and bent at the waist.

Grace considered jumping in and straightening Mrs. Marash out, but what did it matter once the hole was filled? She was where she wanted to be. She wouldn't know any different.

Grace stood there, looking down.

Then she put the ladder in, climbed down, and put Mrs. Marash on her back, hands folded across her chest on top of the quilt, which was pulled up to just below her chin. Grace climbed up, then pulled the ladder out.

What a strange custom. But she could see another part of it now. The cycle of life. The grave, the body in it, the pile of dirt that would go on top, the garden next to it, roots reaching down, taking nourishment.

Mrs. Marash would be part of.

For the first time she wondered if burners were buried when their Deathday came after thirty days in Heaven? If so, who dug the graves? Who would be there to grieve?

That was a word practically unknown in hive.

Grace went inside the house and brought out the book of poetry

Mrs. Marash had told her of. She flipped through it. She found the poem, *The Second Coming*. Read it, decided it was not for Mrs. Marash, then looked for something else.

What she didn't know.

She snapped the book shut. She held it to her chest and recited the words every burner knew so well: "*My candle burns at both ends; it will not last the night. But ah, my foes, and oh, my friends, it gives a lovely light'.*"

Putting the book aside, Grace stripped to her shorts, putting her relatively clean coverall next to the book. She lifted the shovel and began pushing the dirt in, watching the old woman disappear.

Mrs. Marash didn't get Heaven but over three hundred years of People made Heaven seem trivial. She had also fought in a war. Grace had no concept of that; a game of tracers perhaps, but one where people died.

It took less time to fill the grave in than dig it, but it still took hours.

Grace was sweating once more by the time she was done.

Then, still just in her shorts, she walked across Mrs. Marash's little acre into the woods and down to the stream, a ritual now. She went into the small pool, letting the cold, running water wash away the dirt and sweat. She was shivering when she was clean and she ran back to the house, standing next to the roaring blaze she'd stoked during break while filling in the grave.

Warm and dry, she dressed.

Then she went to the trap door and pulled it up. She recoiled at the foul smell. Had she been in that? For days?

Time was a good salve of bad memory.

She knelt and reached in, retrieving the metal box that had consumed so much time and energy. There were streaks of rust across the lid. The metal was faded black. She stuffed it in the shoulder bag, which Mrs. Marash had modified with an extra strap so it was now a backpack. It was as full as size would permit of wrapped bottles of preserves and fresh food. Her water bottle was topped off.

She walked out the door of the cabin. There was still some

daylight left, enough to get a start. Mrs. Marash had given her directions and told her the way should be clear until she got near the bridge, as the cabin was on the edge of inhabited space on Island. How to handle the Dealers guarding the bridge, Mrs. Marash had been unable to tell her.

And someone named Ryker waited out there for her.

Grace didn't pause as she passed the dark rectangle of dirt marking Mrs. Marash's final resting place.

That was done.

She had little idea what was next, but she trusted Andrew's and Mrs. Marash's words.

In the dark, Ryker slithered through mud and crawled underneath the roadway. He'd covered his face and hands with charcoal from the remains of Doc's supper fire, and it was cloudy this evening. While this made him practically invisible, the lack of light also made it hard for him to see what he was doing, especially now that he was under the bridge.

He worked off memory, grabbing hold of a vertical girder and climbing it. When his hands felt a mostly horizontal beam, he pulled himself on top of it. Then he began inching his way out, arms and legs pushing forward, belly on metal. The beam descended gently down toward one of the two concrete pillars holding up the bridge. Evenly spaced, there was a vertical support that he had to go around, a harrowing adventure of standing, grabbing hold, then throwing his feet around, scrambling for a foothold on the other side.

It took him a half-hour to make it to the first concrete pillar. He squeezed through the bracing, onto the continuation of the beam, which went gently upward. Again and again, he threw himself around a vertical support.

Then he reached the center span. Three hundred feet until the next wide girder he could crawl on top of. All he had was a four-inch wide lip on the top and bottom edges of a rusting steel beam, three feet below the roadway.

Ryker edged onto it, grabbing hold of the bottom of a railing that lined the roadway. He began to edge along the narrow ledge, squatting to keep as much as he could below the edge of the roadway. After about forty feet, he heard the heavy tread of a Dealer approaching. He put one hand underneath the top of the beam, then the other, exerting pressure down with his feet and up with his hands to maintain his place.

With great difficulty. The heavy footfalls went by and he quickly resumed the crab along the edge of the bridge.

Dealer approaching.

Crouch, fingers trembling.

Crabbing along.

Another Dealer. For Ryker, nothing else existed except the bridge, narrowing it down to the steel beam, to contact between feet and fingers and steel.

He lost track of time, but not of the pain. He didn't dare look left to see how far away the end of the span was. It didn't matter. He had to make it.

During surveillance he'd noted that the Dealers on the bridge only marched out two-thirds of the way, right to the far end of the center span. Which meant they were regularly coming by.

He kept moving.

The thud of a Dealer approaching. Ryker crouched down, fingers pressing up. Waiting for metal fingers to reach down and grab his arm, to pull him up to the bridge.

The Dealer kept moving, thuds fading.

Throwing caution to the wind, Ryker used the bottom of the railing for his hands, feet on the narrow ledge, and moved much faster.

And then he was to the truss and slid back under the bridge.

He made it to the far side an hour later. He stopped underneath the concrete abutment, where he could see the beach on either side, a slightly lighter strip between the dark water and the forest.

He was in Island.

He had no idea what was next or how he would meet whoever was coming.

But he knew she was coming.

She had to be.

Millay and Haydn crossed the expanse in the dark. Holding hands, fingers interlaced, they dodged among the rusted hulks of B.D. vehicles, hurrying to cross the widest road they'd encountered yet. It seemed to go on forever in the dark, but having scouted it with their eyes during the day, they knew there was a far side. The center of the road was empty of B.D. ruins, a most unusual thing; a path had been cleared after B.D..

But they'd learned why during the scouting, seeing an occasional large truck driven by an Evermore rumble along it, one way or the other. Not many, but enough to keep them on edge about trying to cross in daylight. The vehicles had many wheels, and the containers they hauled were long and full of who knew what? But since night had fallen, not a single vehicle, had passed down the road, so they'd made their move.

They got to the far end, slammed against an old fence, slid along it until they found breakage, and then scrabbled down into the line of growth next to the highway. An old sign teetered above them, advising those on the road that the I-5/I-405 exchange was several miles ahead. South. In the direction of hive, City Edge and City, but the sign said *Seattle*.

Millay was breathing hard. "What is beyond hive that they're going to. here in Wasteland?" she wondered, not for the first time, as she caught her breath from the dash. "Not another rendering hive I hope."

"I don't know," Haydn replied, not for the first time.

"I never heard of this in the Oval," Millay said. "Maybe the Person knows about it."

"The Person is boxed," Haydn said.

"Maybe things like this are why he was boxed," Millay said. "I can't believe he was boxed just because of Grace and me."

Haydn looked at her. "Is the Person in charge of Dealer or the other way 'round?"

Millay opened her mouth to answer, give the rote reply, but then she had to think about it. "Dealer works under the Code. So does the Person."

"Those trucks," Haydn said. "They part of Code?"

"Not the Code I've read."

"And where we're going," he asked. "The Void. Is that part of Code?"

"It's outside of Code. Off-limits."

Haydn smiled. "So the world is bigger than Code." He turned from her and looked ahead. Ruins extended in front of them as far as he could see. There was no way around; only through. "Come on. I want to get as far from this road as we can before dawn."

Ryker was dying. He knew it. He could feel the wound in his chest. It had gone through the body armor he wore, deep into him. He was dying like all around him.

Defeated.

What irony.

Someone was standing over him.

Ryker knew him! It was—but the recognition wouldn't click, connect, even in dream, nightmare.

Bolts of energy still whipped by at those retreating, no mercy being shown. The man knelt next to Ryker. "I'm sorry."

The voice was familiar

Ryker couldn't speak. Struggling.

"You were a fool, my brother," the man said, shaking his head.

And Ryker stabbed him the side with one of his knives and the man's eyes went wide in shock.

And then hands were grabbing Ryker, dragging him back and—

Ryker started awake, sweat running down his body, a chill shaking him. Mind over a yawning pit of futile despair.

He was breathing hard, so hard he feared the Dealers above him would hear.

Was it a dream? Or was it a memory of something that had happened? Was it implanted? Or was it something else? Might it even be the future? And what had the man meant by brother?

Ryker pulled down his coverall top. Ran his fingers over his chest. No wound. No scarring. It had to be a dream.

And then Ryker turned his head to the right.

She was coming.

ONE EIGHT UNTIL
GRACE'S DEATHDAY

Moving through ruined Wasteland was harder than open Wasteland. The road they'd funneled into after crossing I-5 was almost impassable, full of rusted vehicles. In some places it was obvious the way had been deliberately blocked. By whom, against whom, was lost in the darkness and confusion of Chaos and the time passed since.

Millay and Haydn were hungry and tired. They'd been on the move for ten days, had circled very wide around in the Wasteland, forced wider than the folding path to ferry by the Lifts searching for them. They'd made their way through dead countryside, forests, fields and now this maze of destruction.

They hadn't said a word to each other in hours, focused on placing one foot in front of the other, eyes ahead, weaving around, through, sometimes over. It was past mid-day and all they could think of was finding some place before darkness and sleeping, trying to keep the growling hunger at bay with unconsciousness.

"Haydn," Millay said. She was behind him, trailing, slowing.

He paused and looked over his shoulder. "Yes?"

"I hear something."

He cocked his head. "Same as on the big road. Evermore driving a truck."

Haydn tried to think. Had they circled round? But they'd been going in pretty much a straight line on this road. The remains of a bus was in front of them. "Wait."

Haydn climbed up the outside, metal crumbling in places, until he got to the top. He tentatively stepped onto the roof, hearing old rust creaking. He looked ahead. It took him a while to process what he was seeing.

"Haydn?" Millay was below him, next to the bus. "What is it?"

"Hush," Haydn said gently. He retraced his steps, climbing down carefully. He reached the road. "We need to settle in for the rest of the day. Move after dark."

"What did you see?"

Haydn saw a relatively intact building on the side of the road. He led her there. He went through the hole that had been the door. He found a spot, cleared it of trash and debris and they settled down, backs against the wall.

"Why do we have to wait until night?"

"Truck every so often on a road crossing in front of us. They stop where it meets this road. Evermore gets out, goes across to an empty truck and takes it back the other way. This is where the must be going after leaving the road we crossed earlier."

"Who gets the full trucks?" Millay asked.

"Dealers."

"What's in them?"

"I don't know. They take them into—" He shook his head. "A building. Never seen anything like it. Big. Bigger than a hive. Bigger than five hives together. Taller, wider, long, very long. Looks B.D. but not a ruin. Dealers take the trucks through a big door into the building."

"And?" Millay asked.

"There is something in there," Haydn gave the obvious answer. "Something they don't want the Evermores, or anyone to know about."

Millay stopped asking questions, sensing how unsettled Haydn was. They hunkered down, letting the sun arc overhead, lengthen the shadows and bring on dusk, hoping the pattern from the previous day would hold and there would be no traffic in the dark.

Night blanketed and the noise did stop. But the light to the west, where the sun had gone down, changed. A glow etched into the darkness, a halo of light from something close by, much brighter than a hive.

"What is that?" Millay asked.

"Must be the building I saw." He stood and reached for her. "Time to go."

They slipped out of the building and wove through the rusting cars and trucks. Shortly after they passed the bus Haydn had used as his perch, the building loomed into view. It stretched from just in front of them on the right, for over half a mile. Light glowed out of huge open bay doors that went from the ground to just short of the top, over a hundred feet high. Faded blue images were painted on the massive doors. And on top, above the doors, in black smudged to gray by time, large letters spelled out *BOEING*.

"Move," Haydn said, tugging on Millay's hand.

Despite their fatigue and hunger, they began to run. The building to the right was protected by a new fence, glistening razor wire on top. Risking glances as they ran, they could see Dealers moving about inside, though the open doors, tiny figures on the floor. Numerous Lifts, too many to count, were parked inside, and some had Dealers crawling over them. Some of the Lifts were actually off the ground, held up by cables that stretched up to the roof. But most were different than the Lifts they saw in hive or Island: with weapons attached on top and on the sides.

And through one door they saw row upon row of Dealers. Lined up. Still. Stacked horizontally on chains, head to toe. But they were different than the Dealers they were used to. These had red faces with a black stripe. And on their right arms were large devices, much bigger than a stunner. There were thousands of them, filling the space.

"Keep going," Haydn huffed, putting a hand on Millay's shoulder.

The road they were on ran parallel to the building and was full of debris, but then they reached a perpendicular road, this one clear of wreckage. The one where Middlemore's had driven up in their trucks. Two trucks, their cabs empty, waited for the morning traffic to be taken back south.

Haydn paused at the edge of the road. "Fast," he said to Millay and they raced across, feeling naked and exposed. They got to the other side. "Keep going," Haydn exhorted Millay.

More doors in the building opened to rows of Dealers. More armed lifts. And then tracked ground vehicles with weapons.

It took them over ten minutes, running as hard as they could to get past the building. Leaving the glow behind and getting back into the night, they slowed to a walk.

"Look," Haydn said, pointing to the left. "What are those?"

"I've seen those in the Stream," Millay said. "They're planes. An early form of Lift."

Most were damaged, wings sheared, fuselages crumpled. But they were big, larger than Lifts. They were scattered all about.

Haydn paused, looking about in the dark. "There." He pointed to the right.

In the glow from the large building behind them, there were a number of rail lines, spread out like branches.

"The rails," Haydn said. "But it's supposed to run next to the water."

"It goes down to the water," Millay said. "See? It drops."

Haydn took that as enough of a direction and they headed toward the multiple railheads. As they moved farther away from the large building, it got darker, but it was easy to walk between rails.

Gradually, all the adjoining railheads came together until there was just a single set of rails dipping down into a dark valley, crowded by trees on both side.

"What's that smell?" Haydn asked.

"Salt water." Millay was growing enthused. "We're getting close to the Sound. It's ahead."

The rails went down and down and then they hit a clearing and they could see it stretching out ahead of them. Dark water under night sky. Flickers of white as the water roiled, in its own pattern, mixing current and wind. The rails split in two, one going right and one going left in steep curves.

Both joining a rail line running along the water's edge.

"Follow the rails and walk on them with the Sound to the right," Haydn said, pointing left.

"What's that?" Millay asked, indicating ahead on the right. Across the water was a dark mass, an island. But there were flickers of light here and there on it. "Island is somewhere over there," she added, pointing to the left. "There should be no one up *there*. It's not part of Island or Void."

"There should be no Evermore's driving trucks into the Wasteland either," Haydn said. "There shouldn't be burners with no cards killing cattle in Wasteland. There should be no Dealers in a big building in Wasteland; a different kind of Dealers. There shouldn't be a lot of things."

They walked up onto the rail-line berm and turned left.

And they saw a ferry landing, blasted and destroyed.

"Is that it?" Millay hoped.

"Too soon," Haydn said. "Folding path follows the outer arc of hive and then you go straight west to the water. We're far north from that. Must be another ferry. We keep going."

Millay's shoulders slumped, but she walked steadily next to Haydn as they passed the old ferry landing. A rusting sign read *Mukilteo*.

"Haydn," Millay said.

"Yes?"

"Nothing is as it is, is it?"

"We are." He put an arm around her shoulder. "That's all that counts right now. And right now all we have is we."

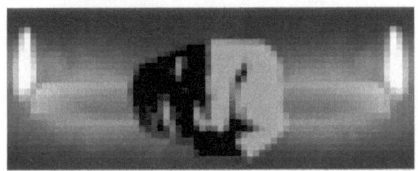

Ryker was twitching, jingle-jangled. He sensed her rather than saw her, which was good, because it meant the Dealers on the bridge above couldn't see her in the thick fog.

He slid down the high bank, close to tumbling, falling, moving fast. He got to the pebbled sand and ran to the east.

She came out of the fog, tall, dark-haired, striding hard.

Ryker stopped. She saw him, paused, took a few more steps. Stopped.

They were ten feet apart. Ryker raised his hands, open palms out. Noting the scraper in her belt. Noting the look in her eyes.

"Ryker." She said it as a statement. "I'm Grace."

ONE SEVEN UNTIL
GRACE'S DEATHDAY

Going back underneath the bridge was easier for Ryker. Because she followed and that took away a large degree of uncertainty for him. He didn't know what lay ahead, but he knew he was where he should be right now.

Before they'd started, waiting well past darkness, he'd told her that Doc, Ace and the joker, Thomas, were waiting. He'd given a summary of events since he killed Charon. He told her there was someone else, another woman he was to meet, and she'd said: "Millay."

When he was done updating her on what little he knew, she'd nodded and simply said: "Let's go."

No questions.

He liked that.

Fingers hard. Gripping.

Crossing as if it were just a step in a longer journey.

They reached the far end, Dealers innocent of their passing below.

Climbed up into the casino as dawn was breaking.

"Doc," Ryker said as they came into the room. "Meet Grace."

Doc had not seen them approaching in the dark from her perch by the window. She turned, her hand slipping toward her hatchet. Thomas was in the corner, only his feet bound.

Ace bolted to Grace, sniffing. She reached down, her hand gently settling on his head.

Doc nodded. "Grace."

"Doc," Grace said. She smiled at Ace. "Hello."

Ace was approving, pressing his head against her hand.

She looked at Thomas. "I'm so sorry," she said, as she walked toward him; pulling the scraper out of her belt and slitting his throat before he even processed mouth to ear.

ONE SEVEN UNTIL
GRACE'S DEATHDAY

*I*t was easy trekking on the between the rails. Flat as the Sound, with gentle curves around the meeting of land and water. At one point, the rails went over a trestle built across an inlet. At another, a landslide had buried the rails and they had to scramble over it, pushing against shifting sand beneath their feet, before reclaiming the steel on the other side.

They covered five miles before the lightening sky in the east, above the high bluffs, harkened the coming day. A light fog dimmed everything and reduced visibility to about a hundred yards.

"Shouldn't be much farther," Haydn said. He looked at Millay. She was different. Thinner, leaner, quieter. Her eyes darted about, anxious, like a burner.

And then she grabbed him, pulling him off the tracks, into a clump of bushes that had invaded the right of way.

"What's wrong?" Haydn asked.

"Look." Millay nodded ahead, down the line.

Someone was standing on the side of the embankment, barely visible in the fog. Urinating.

Dressed in gray coveralls, burner-style.

When the man finished, sealed up and turned, Millay clutched Haydn's shoulder in recognition.

"It's Josh!"

Haydn scanned the area, but there was only the burner they'd last seen waiting in his cell. Josh looked up the line, toward them, saw nothing, then went down the embankment and sat on a block of concrete.

Waiting.

There was no way for Haydn and Millay to go around him without being spotted. The bluff to their left was too steep. They'd have to backtrack at least a mile to climb to the high ground.

"What do you think he's doing here?" Haydn asked.

"Let's ask *him*," Millay said, getting to her feet.

Haydn stared at her for a second, shook his head, smiled and followed.

Spotting them, Josh leapt up off the concrete and waved.

Millay and Haydn closed the distance, Josh waiting, fidgeting, looking over his shoulder.

"What are you doing here?" Millay asked Josh, no greeting, burner-style to the point.

"Waiting for you," he said. "You were right. About folding. So I left, right after you. Well, maybe not right after. 'Bout ten minutes after. Thought I'd see you on the folding path. But never a sign." His words were tumbling over themselves in his rush to tell his tale. "Thought you'd be waiting at ferry. But you weren't there."

"Why aren't you waiting at ferry if you folded?" Haydn asked.

Josh gestured. "Need to get off rails."

They followed him down to his makeshift camp. Which consisted off a pack, a piece of scavenged plastic to protect against rain and nothing else.

"I was at ferry," Josh said. "Couple other folders there. Then heard Lifts coming. I ran up the rails and hid. Dealers jumped out. Bagged the others. I waited until dark. Then moved further up to here. To warn any coming down, hoping I see you. Save you, like you saved me. Life for life."

"The Dealers still there?" Haydn asked.

"Yes. Checked yesterday. Crawled down." He pointed inland. "They're hiding in B.D. ruins. But they're there. Watching. Waiting."

"Floe me," Haydn said.

Josh looked at Haydn, a twitch under his left eye. He pulled a can of 'tein out of his pack. "You must be hungry." He offered the 'tein, sharing, not a burner trait.

"Where did you get the 'tein?" Millay asked.

"Stole it on way out of hive," Josh said, offering the can again.

Haydn took it, passed it to Millay. "Eat," he said to her, but his focus was on Josh. "What do you plan on doing now?" he asked the burner.

Josh shrugged. "No idea. I watch the water too. No Ferryman come back yet. And you're the first to come down the rails in three days I been here. No other folders."

"Got caught by Dealers," Millay said to Haydn.

"And now they're waiting for us," Haydn said. He looked out at the Sound, the water dark, a light chop occasionally making whitecaps. "We've got to get to Void."

Millay scooped some 'tein out of the can with her fingers, long past being People in her manners. She offered it back to Haydn who took some, then he tried to pass it to Josh.

"No," Josh said. "You keep it."

Millay cocked her head, staring hard at him. "What's wrong?"

"Dealers at ferry," Josh said, but his eyes shifted away, unable to meet Millay's gaze.

"How come you didn't get caught by the Dealers sweeping the folding path?" Millay asked.

Josh's shoulders slumped. He looked away from Millay, out to the water. "Heard of the Sound. The water. It's pretty. Not like hive. When you can see across—" he pointed—"it's all green."

Millay opened her mouth to say something, but Haydn touched her arm and shook his head.

Josh turned back to them. He sighed. "Truth. Evermore ordered me here. I came on Lift with Dealers. They send me up the rails."

"Why?" Millay asked, not surprised.

"To meet you before you got to ferry."

"Why?" Millay pushed.

"Be friendly, make you think I save you from Dealers at ferry."

"And?" Millay said. "Why?"

"To talk to you," Josh said. "Evermore, beady-eyed fellow, wanted me to ask you what your plan was. Why you, a People, folding? Why going out to Void? Who you supposed to meet? Where in Void meeting? Why you meeting them? For what? All sorts questions. He wants to know what he don't know."

Haydn had his tracer out, pointed at Josh's heart. Irony. "And when you find out?"

Josh reached inside his shirt and retrieved a black card. "I'm supposed to press the center of this, dive into the Stream, bring the Dealers. But only *after* you tell me all those things." Josh jingle-jangled a laugh. "Dealer can't find you. The Evermore—" he paused —"he thinks he's smart. Big head smart like People. Somehow he knows you come here to go to Void. But he wants all. You. Who you meet. What you know. All. But he's not burner. Doesn't know the code."

"What code?" Millay asked, confused. "We all live by Code."

"burner code," Josh said. He looked from Millay to Haydn. "A life for a life. You gave that to me, but I didn't understand your mouth to ear when in the cage. I didn't leave. Stayed there like fool. They were going to bag me if I didn't agree to do this even though they know you weren't dead. How could they do that? How can they kill me when they know you're not dead? It's not Code." He pointed at his ear. "Get it now." Then tapped his forehead. "I understand." He picked up the backpack and held it out. "Food."

Haydn took it then nodded at him, understanding burner.

Josh stood. "What you do. Do it. A life for a life."

Millay reached up and touched his hand, light, but heavy. "Have hope."

Josh twitched an attempt at a smile.

Then he began walking north, along the rails, black card in his hand.

Ace sniffed out the joker trails, now that they knew they existed. But they didn't care, aware now how the jokers and the pack worked. The trails were as narrow and as hard to detect as those of small animals, but they were there, weaving through the forest, ground hard-packed, speaking of generations of jokers slithering through the forest, hunting. Other humans. Other jokers when need be.

One time they startled a joker just ahead of them. He turned, tried to yell, but Doc threw her hatchet, slamming it into his chest. Taking his voice and his life. She pulled it out, wiping the steel on the little clothing left on the joker.

They kept moving without comment.

And halted when Ryker held up a hand. They had passed through many B.D. ruins. But now they were into a space empty of man's buildings.

It held something else done by man.

Two dim painted poles of wood flanked a faded stone marker.

Ryker looked at Grace and she nodded. Together the two walked between the two poles.

Markings were etched in the stone.

"Doc?" Ryker asked.

She came forward, Ace at her side. She read:

"'Seattle. Chief of the'—" she paused—"I don't know word. But after that it says 'and allied tribes. Died June Seven, One Eight Six Six. The firm friend of the whites and for him the City of Seattle was named by its founders'."

"One eight six six," Ryker said. "What does that mean?"

"A date," Doc said. "B.D."

"When was that?" Ryker asked.

Doc shrugged. "I don't know. Long time ago."

Grace was looking at the marker. "He must be buried here. An honor. To give him this. This place. This stone. He must have been a special man. A chief." She bowed her head for a moment. "A good life." Then she lifted her head and looked at Ryker. "Millay is ahead."

"Let's move," Ryker said.

ONE SIX UNTIL GRACE'S DEATHDAY

Josh had nothing left. No food, no energy. He'd walked as far as he could north along the rails, all day and all night. Past another pier, ruined ferries. Up to the edge of where something powerful had flattened everything a long time ago. Not even ruins standing. The ground ahead was like black glass. The rails ended abruptly there. In the Sound, not far from shore, part of a very large, rusting gray ship with a flat deck angled above the surface, metal twisted and broken.

Josh knelt in the sand and pebbles. He was burner. He'd been sentenced to death. How much could one expect of burner? He looked out at the water, black card in hand, finger over the center. What did he have? There was only folding, but the ferry was being watched. There was no going back.

There was only one thing to do.

But he had a feeling. A jingle-jangle. Something. He tried to find a word in his head to match it. "'Hope'?" That's what that woman had said. The one he'd killed/not-killed.

He wondered what 'hope' was.

And he knew whatever it was, it wasn't for him.

He looked up to the sky but saw only fog. *"My candle burns at both ends.'"* He sad-smiled. *"But ah my foes'!"*

Then he pressed the card.

"What do we do?" Millay asked.

Josh was one day gone up the rails.

Haydn held Millay in his arms, looking out to Sound. Fog blanketed everything, making their world small; a crouching patch of ground in the great void of the universe. Hiding in a crevice created by a large steel wall partly collapsed halfway up the high bluff. They were far back in the darkness, but with a view of the rails and the water beyond.

They'd eaten guiltily from what Josh had given them.

They'd made love, not fucked.

"We wait," Haydn said.

"For what?" Millay wanted to know. "Dealers can sit on the ferry forever. They have infinite patience. And what will they do when Charon shows up?"

"We wait."

More time passed and then they talked.

Millay finally about Dealing Day, memories forcing their way up with attendant pain from what Haydn had forced her to watch. They sat in their hiding spot, the sound of the waves on the shoreline muted.

Haydn talked about leaving hive to sleep under the stars. Wanting to go further. Even to the Wasted Mountains. But always drawn back to hive every twelve hours to report to work.

"Why?" Millay asked.

"Why go back to work?"

"No. Why go out of hive? Why try to go to the Wasted Mountains?"

"There's something there," he told her.

"What?" Millay asked, lazily, comforted in his arms, being in the now, not worrying about the then, Charon, the Dealers, Void.

"Adventure," he said. "Something more than hive, than City Edge, than City, than Island, than even Dealer. A world beyond the Sound."

Millay laughed, poking him in the side. "You are strange. Few see beyond what they see. Even People."

"Why would People?" Haydn asked.

"Why would burner?" Millay said.

That gave Haydn pause. "Some say when you don't know more, you can't think more."

"So why do you?" Millay asked and right away sensed his change in mood, regretted the question.

"My mother," Haydn said. "She was burner. She was small. Right job for right person. Like all burners. She worked in ducts. Crawled all shift. Cleaning. Clearing. So the air flowed inside hive. My father was loader. A big man. Moving things as things needed to be moved as Middlemores said. When he wasn't moving things, he lived 'chol. When their shifts crossed and both were in cubby, I hated those times. They screamed. Fought. He could make her fly across cubby with his fists." He sighed. "I looked forward to Dealing Day. I accepted, as most did, that I would get red. But I would go to the womb instead of stay in that cubby. Even though my mother was—" he couldn't finish.

Millay looked up at him, her mouth open to ask a question, but she didn't.

Gathering himself, Haydn continued. "Mother said ducts were so tight in places. So she could barely squeeze through. Especially the turns. Learned how to—" he shrugged—"pop her shoulders out of sockets to be even smaller when she had to. She learned to live with the pain. Sometimes, when she came back to the cubby, she hadn't been able to put one back right. I had to help her slam it against the wall. Hear her pain coming from the bone but she never cried out.

"She said the ducts crowded her even more than hive. But they always opened to air at the end. She always crawled to air. To the light. She said everything was like that. Don't get stuck, no matter how much it hurt. Crawl to the light."

"When did she advance to Heaven?" Millay asked.

Haydn shook his head, tears on his cheeks. "Never got Heaven." He gazed out at the Sound, his eyes unfocused. "One week after Dealing Day. Surprised it took that long after I was gone. She probably didn't care any more. Had nothing to live for. So she didn't say the right thing. Or said the wrong thing. Or didn't bow her head and act like a ghost when he was around in the cubby. Never really found out. My father broke her neck. He didn't even remember because of the 'chol. Dealers took him. Bagged him. A life for a life."

Millay was shaking her head. "I thought I knew things. But now I know why burners call us big head. Big heads full of nothing but ourselves." She picked up a pebble from the beach. "We're like this. Just one part of something so much bigger. Small heads. Big hearts is what we need." She looked at him. "Are we crawling, Haydn? Toward what?"

His arm tightened around her slightly as they heard the sound of a Lift coming toward them. Haydn leaned forward, peering out. The Lift flickered by, heading north.

"What is it?" Millay asked.

"Josh."

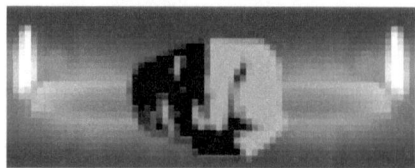

Claude got off the Lift with Michael and they walked to the water's edge.

The body was lifting and dropping with the incoming tide, scraping on the sand. Not yet drawn out to the deep water, to the fish. Most of the blood from the slit wrists had washed away. The small knife he'd used was still clutched in a death grip in one hand.

Michael plucked the black card off of Josh's chest. The machine held it in its claws, turning it to and fro as if examining it.

"He failed," Claude offered.

"He was not necessary," Michael said.

"I showed initiative," Claude argued.

Michael stood still and tall. A statue of metal, containing who knew what? As if peering out to the Sound, as if it had eyes. "Why would you think initiative is a good thing?"

Claude's mouth opened, but flapped, no answer forthcoming.

"Maybe they're not coming to the ferry," Claude dodged. "I received a report from the Middlemore in Haydn-one-tango-one-nine's hive. Other burners say that he would disappear. Head west. Some think he went into the Wasteland."

"You have it backwards," Michael said. He was looking to the west, at the blocky shape of an island. "Millay of the People and the burner were not heading to Void via the ferry. They have some other plan. If Charon is dead, the logic indicates the killer has Charon's vessel. It is more likely that Grace-five-eleven-kilo-one will come this way. As we originally factored. Your plan distracted us."

"But at least it was a plan," Claude said, frustration mounting.

"You think Dealer doesn't have a plan for every contingency?" Michael asked, but it really wasn't a question. "You think Dealer isn't prepared?"

"I meant no—"

Michael cut him off. "The Ferryman is dead. Our targets are into the Wasteland. Watching the ferry is a waste of resources since there is no ferry. Your plan rested on the vagaries of human emotion. burner emotion at that. Foolish." Michael stalked off toward the Lift.

Claude scurried to follow.

Behind them the rising tide finally got solid hold of Josh's body, dragging it out into the dark water of the Sound.

They heard it before they saw it.

"It's coming back," Haydn said as the familiar sound of Lift engines reverberated against the high bluff. The Lift went by, slower this time and losing altitude.

"Is it—" Millay asked, worried.

"No," Haydn said. "Landing farther down the rails."

The Lift disappeared from view around a gentle bend of the rails.

The engines went a pitch lower for a few seconds, then revved up and faded into the distance.

"Come on," Haydn said.

They edged out of their hiding place. Staying on the landward side of the tracks, moving as stealthily as they could, they made their way south.

Haydn paused. "There."

A pier, blasted and twisted, extended into the water. A road had once gone over the tracks to the pier, but the bridge was also destroyed. A concrete ramp was next to the pier, gently sloping into the water.

"The ferry," Haydn said. "Wait here. I'm going to check for Dealers. If I—"

"I'm coming with you," Millay said in a voice that allowed no argument.

Together they searched carefully, but there was no sign of Dealers over-watching the ferry.

"Josh gave us a life for his life," Millay said, burner-Code now enmeshed. "We must honor his sacrifice."

ONE SIX UNTIL GRACE'S DEATHDAY

*H*aydn stood up, hearing the splash of oars in water.

A boat came out of the fog. A man and a woman rowing. An older, dark woman holding on to a dog in the stern.

The woman rowing was Millay but not Millay.

"Your sister," Haydn said. "We're not crawling no more."

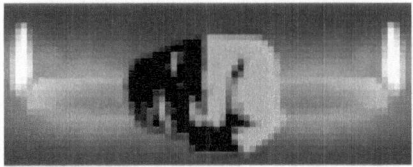

They rowed hard, back toward Void, grateful for the fog blanketing the entire area.

"Ryker," Doc called out from the bow.

Ryker and Haydn were shoulder to shoulder, each with an oar. They paused and looked to the right, where Doc was pointing. Something was in the water about twenty feet ahead and to the right.

"Oh!" Millay exclaimed as an extremely foul smell wafted by.

The momentum of the boat carried them by and Ryker shoved

his oar into the object. It rolled over, revealing a rotting face missing its eyes and nose and the mouth a gaping hole.

"Charon," Doc said.

Ryker pushed the corpse away with his oar. And then he looked at Haydn and they got back to rowing, leaving the rotting and partially eaten body of the Ferryman behind, fading away into the fog.

Not much farther they beached the boat at the landing.

"No more Ferryman," Ryker said.

Doc pulled her hatchet out then began to chop at the boat.

"Wait," Ryker said. He grabbed the edge of the boat and nodded at Haydn.

Together they flipped the boat over.

And Doc swung holes into it with her hatchet.

Ace barked approvingly.

They walked into the woods, Ryker leading the way, everyone strangely quiet, as if no one had thought past accomplishing this link up. But none could form a question yet. They went far enough in so they couldn't be seen from the water and then halted in a small clearing. They circled up, Ace outside the group, lying down, head up, wary.

"What now?" Doc asked, looking between Grace and Millay. "Twins, of course."

Grace nodded. They looked even more alike now, given Millay had burned off what little People fat she'd had. Indeed, to tell them apart it was mainly that Grace wore the dirty white coveralls of People and Millay the dingy gray of burner. Even their aura was similar, something that had not been the case over a month ago.

"You told me to meet you here," Millay said to Grace.

Ryker looked at Haydn. "Went along for the journey?"

"For the fun of it," Haydn said with his characteristic grin.

"Have much?" Ryker asked.

"Sure," Haydn said, slipping an arm over Millay's shoulder. She blushed.

"I was told to head north and meet you at the Lone Bridge," Grace said to Ryker.

"You did it," Ryker said. "Nothing further?"

"The Person, Andrew," Grace said, "told me that those I meet would direct me forward. He sent me to someone, an old woman. Mrs. Marash. A good woman. She told me of you and to meet you at the Lone Bridge. That's it.

"How did she know my name?" Ryker asked.

"No idea," Grace replied. They'd all been told about his lack in remembering his personal past.

Millay spoke up. "There's something larger going on here."

Grace nodded. "The Person told me that Millay and I are the Prime. What does that mean?" she asked Ryker.

"No idea," Ryker said. He looked at Millay.

"The Person called me and told me to meet Grace in Void," Millay said. "That's it."

They all stood there, exchanging glances, but no one had anything further.

"So," Ryker said. "The Person got both of you moving, but only as far as linking up."

"And meeting you," Grace added. "So you factor into this."

"I'm not leaving," Haydn said, but no one focused on that. "I'm part of this to the end."

Ryker gave the ghost of a smile. "That's the part we're trying to figure out. The end."

"He," Doc said, indicating Ryker, "seems to know things but he doesn't know how he knows them. He's got—" she flashed her hatchet at him and he easily blocked it.

"Gotta stop doing that," Ryker said. "I might miss one day and you might hit."

"He's got," Doc continued, "some muscle memory that he doesn't remember getting. I believe he's also got implanted memories and commands. If any of us know what's next for our merry little band, it would be you," she said to him. "Except you can't access it."

Ryker stared at Grace and Millay. "There's got to be a reason the Person wanted you two to get together. With me." He held out his hands. "Here."

Millay took one hand and Grace the other. Ace whined, Haydn raised a curious eyebrow and Doc watched intently.

Ryker closed his eyes. They remained still long enough for Ace to whine again.

"I got nothing," Ryker said, letting go of their hands. "No magic memory. Nothing."

"Wait!" Grace's voice was jingle-jangled. "Mrs. Marash did tell me something. She mentioned a thing called a Backdoor."

No reaction from the others.

"And," Grace continued, looking at Ryker, "she told me to tell you: '*Things fall apart; the centre cannot hold*'."

"'*The centre cannot hold*'," Ryker repeated it one more time, saying each word distinctly. "'*The. Centre. Cannot. Hold*'."

"Does it—" Doc began, but Ryker held up his hand, hushing her. "The Centre. Yes. That's it. That's where we have to go."

"How do you know?" Grace asked.

"I know," Ryker said. "Like I know how to use my knives. I just know."

"Where is this Centre?" Millay asked. Haydn had moved behind her, his hands resting lightly on her shoulders.

"Hush," Ryker said. He went to one knee, elbow on knee, head in hand, eyes closed. Then he spoke in a flat voice, almost like Dealer. "My mind's eye," Ryker said. "I can see this. The Sound. Island. Void. Deep Void. There's another place. North. An island. We can get close to it on this side in Deep Void, to the point of land facing Sound. As close as we can get, then it's over water to that island which contains the Centre."

Haydn spoke up. "We saw an island up north when were coming down the rails. Out across the Sound. There were some lights there. Never heard tell of something there."

"There is an island there," Millay offered. "But it isn't part of Island. Or City."

Ryker stood and seemed himself once more. Certain. "The Centre is there. Directly across the Sound. On that island. There's a—" He searched for the word. "There's a fortress that holds Centre. It's important."

"How does this Prime factor into that?" Doc asked.

"I don't know," Ryker said. "There's probably something there we need the Prime for."

"We don't even know what we are in terms of that," Millay pointed out.

"That's the step after this one," Ryker said. "One step at a time."

"Then we have to go there to Centre," Grace said, ignoring Doc. "That's where we'll learn the truth."

"Truth about what?" Doc's voice was starting to jingle-jangle and Ace whined and got to his feet He went to her, putting his head against her leg.

"Everything," Grace said. "Everything. Mrs. Marash said I had to learn the truth. That she didn't know all of it. No one did."

Haydn spoke up. "Millay and I have already seen things we didn't know about. And she worked in the Oval building. The large warehouse in the Wasteland with Evermores driving trucks back and forth. Lights on that island in the Sound."

Doc agreed. "We had no clue Achilles was working with Charon, and both were working for Dealer."

"So it's likely," Ryker said, "that there are more surprises up ahead in Deep Void."

"How do we get there?" Haydn asked, always the practical one. "And what do we do once we get there?"

Ryker turned to Doc. "There's another bridge in Void. The one to Deep Void. Right?"

"The Broken Bridge," Doc said. "The name indicates the problem."

"Is anybody in Deep Void?" Ryker asked.

Doc shrugged. "No one knows. Some people have left Delta, heading for Deep Void. They never came back. Jokers might have gotten them before they even left Void. They might have drowned trying to get across. There is no Ferryman there." Doc looked at Grace. "If you hadn't killed Thomas, he might have led us there."

That caught Millay's attention. "You killed someone?" she asked her sister.

"A joker," Grace said. "Not to be trusted."

"Who are you?" Millay asked.

"Who are you?" Grace responded. "Not the People I switched places with."

"I'm your sister from Dealing Day."

"No," Grace said. "Not her either. I'm what they made me. I'm what Dealer made. We all are. You are too."

Millay's mouth opened to say something more, but Haydn squeezed her shoulders lightly and she said nothing.

Ryker closed his eyes. "I know where the Broken Bridge is. I can get us there." He tapped his head and smiled at Doc. "As you said. Someone put things in here. Once I heard that line with *Centre* in that context, I saw the way to the bridge and then on through Deep Void. That far at least. No farther. But we have to trust there will be something or someone there to let me know how to go farther."

"Not much of a plan," Doc muttered.

"We didn't start with much," Ryker said, "but we've gotten this far."

"Let's go," Grace said. "We have to trust."

And the decision was made.

ONE THREE UNTIL
GRACE'S DEATHDAY

Three days on narrow trails. Two dead jokers. Dispatched before alerting a pack to descend upon them.

Ryker was always in the lead; not exactly though, as Ace usually took point, ranging ahead. The dog had given early warning of each of the two jokers without barking, but racing back, tail wagging furiously. Allowing them to sit in ambush and Ryker to take each out quietly, fast and efficient.

Millay had watched her first blood killing of a human with a degree of shock, but nothing close to what she'd have felt two weeks ago. She remembered the boy who'd been bagged by the Dealers. And the rendering yard. The world was a dark place.

Grace had informed her that her white card was gone, taken.

It was a worthless card anyway, Millay had answered, unable to control the tint of anger and loss.

There wasn't much talking; the focus was on moving. To speculate on what was at the end of their journey was pointless, since they first had to make the journey. Ryker said nothing more about Centre or where exactly they were going, other than into Deep Void. He offered no solution as to how they would cross the Broken Bridge.

Every evening a routine. Off the thin trail into thick forest. A quick fire at dusk, smothered as soon as whatever small creatures Ace caught were skinned, cooked, quartered and eaten and Doc and Grace foraged from the forest. Ryker insisted on one person staying awake at all times, a redundant guard on top of Ace. Just before everyone went to sleep, Grace filled them in on what Mrs. Marash had told her. Haydn and Millay talked of their journey. Doc about Delta.

But Ryker had no story to tell before being on the ferry with Charon. His dreams, his nightmares, he kept to himself.

The night before, Ryker had caught Millay asleep less than fifteen minutes after he'd passed the guard shift to her. He'd lightly jabbed one of his heavy blades into a tree next to her head, then sat guard.

She'd awoken with a start an hour later, saw the blade glinting in the dark. Ryker came over, retrieved it without a word, then went back to his position and fell asleep.

On this day, they finally came to the water at the northwest end of Void. It was raining, steady and hard, soaking everyone and everything.

"It's broken," Doc said, not an *I told you so*, but in resignation.

A road extended out to the water, over a truss bridge like the one he'd crawled under, but then dropping down to just above the waves. And halfway across it was gone. A long section, just disappeared, sloping into dark water, and then the road resumed, seemingly floating above the water three hundred yards beyond the gap.

"We'll get across," Ryker said. "I'll find a way." He pointed toward trees on the right side of the road. "Camp in there. I'll do a recon."

The group grumbled into the trees. Ryker stared at the open water between Void and Deep Void. He walked along the shoreline. There was some soaked driftwood and he tossed a piece into the water.

A raft perhaps?

But how to connect the wood? And they were just pieces, not logs. He looked at the trees. They had Doc's hatchet. It would take a while, a long while, and—

Then he heard the howl.

Ryker raced back toward the trees.

More howls.

From all directions except the water and the bridge.

"Grace!" Ryker called out, trying to get oriented.

"Here," she called out and Ryker found the small group in a clearing, weapons ready, bunched together.

"No," Ryker said. "They'll hit us in force if we wait. We charge them before they all gather."

"What?" Millay questioned, but the others understood right away.

Ryker led the way, running toward the narrow joker path at the far side of the clearing. Just in time as the first one appeared.

Ryker took out the first joker by slitting his throat so hard he nearly decapitated the man. The joker fell backward, the momentum of his mostly severed head pulling the body back by the exposed spine.

A pack of jokers were right behind their dead point man, spread out on either side of the path but the lead ones were staggered back as Grace and Haydn fired their tracers. Screams were forced up from throats as jokers went down, clawing at the bolts gripping their skin and the electricity frying their nerves. Damaged, but only for a while, except for the ones hit over the heart.

Ryker was moving forward, not back, knife in each hand. Slashing, ducking, using his blades to cut, not stab. A stab could lead to the blade going down with the body. He heard Grace and Haydn firing, their tracers gaining valuable time and some heart-deaths. He sensed Doc at his side, hatchet swinging, killing jokers still writhing from non-heart tracers.

Ryker gutted a joker, pulling the woman forward to fall at his side as he blocked a club with his other arm, the wood thudding into his forearm, pain jolting, but bone not broken and he turned the blade in that hand downward, slamming it into the skull of the joker with a crunch of metal through skull.

He wheeled, stabbing a joker in the kidneys with his other blade as it went for Doc's blind side. But the knife in the skull was stuck, so he let go, now taking a step back, single blade up in defense.

Haydn and Grace both had to pause to reload at the same time, not good planning there, leaving Ryker and Doc holding the front line against a half-dozen still standing jokers.

Not good odds. Ryker took a half step back, preparing for the assault.

But then Ace and Millay charged forward, growling and screaming, his teeth bared, her walking stick as a feeble, yet courageous weapon.

Ryker spitted the joker lunging for Millay's neck, its filed teeth showing in a wide open mouth.

Doc whirled, going low on old joints, hatchet taking out tendons, thighs, knees, ankles and two more jokers went down. Doc finished them with crunching blows to the skull.

Ace leapt onto another joker heading for Millay, slamming him to the ground and ripping at the throat with his teeth, sharper and bigger than the joker's. Millay and a joker grappled. She jammed the stick into the soft spot under its jaw, rocking the head back and Ryker took the opening, slitting its throat.

Haydn and Grace resumed firing and the last three jokers staggered back, burning with the jolts. Ryker and Doc stabbed, sliced, axed them to death.

It was over in less than thirty seconds.

And Millay was holding her hands just underneath her hartgard, blood oozing through her fingers.

"I'm People," Millay insisted. "I'll be fine."

"You were People," Doc said, fingers feeling into the wound, probing. "Now you're with us."

"Genetics," Millay said. "I'll be fine."

Doc looked up at Grace, Ryker, and Haydn. She gave the slightest shake of her head.

Ryker looked around. Over a dozen dead jokers. A broken bridge in front of them. Deep Void beyond the water. Void and more jokers all around on land.

"She'll be fine," Ryker repeated. "She's brave and she's People. Doc you stay with her." He pointed. "Haydn. Grace. We need to drag these bodies onto the bridge."

Both of them stared at him, uncomprehending.

Ryker grabbed the nearest joker. He threw the body over his shoulders, emaciated weight not too hard to bear. He headed out, stumbling, almost running, as fast as he could toward the roadway, then onto the bridge. Behind him, Haydn looked at Grace, shrugged then grabbed a body. She did the same, picking up a rail-thin female joker, tossing her over her shoulder. They followed Ryker onto the bridge.

He was at the very end, where the roadway angled into the water. He dumped the body right there at the edge. Grace and Haydn staggered up and dropped the bodies.

"Why?" Grace asked.

"Remember Charon?" Ryker asked in return.

Grace nodded. The three of them ran back, grabbed three more bodies. Then three more. Then three more, exhaustion snarling at them, the precariousness of their situation trumping it. They had all the bodies there.

"All the driftwood you can grab," Ryker ordered.

They scoured the beach, returning to the bodies with branches, and some thin logs, not much.

Then they came back to Doc and Millay.

Doc had ripped off a long piece of cloth from her blanket and wrapped it around Millay's midsection.

"There will be more jokers coming," Ryker said. "We have to go now."

"How are we—" Doc began, but stopped as Ryker picked up Millay.

Haydn stepped forward, arms extended. "I'll take her."

Ryker nodded, passing her over. Haydn cradled her in his arms. "I got you. I told you I'd always take care of you."

Millay nodded, but her face was pale. "I'm People," she repeated.

"You are indeed," Haydn said as he followed Ryker and the others to the roadway. Grace was in the rear, facing backward, sweeping her tracer back and forth. They walked on the bridge until they arrived at the bodies and wood.

Ryker pulled a belt off one of the bodies, tying it through loops on the remains of clothing between two jokers. He pulled the two into the water lapping at the roadway.

They floated. Barely.

"Get the rest connected," Ryker ordered. "Use their clothes, their belts, whatever."

Haydn put Millay down gently and joined Doc in tying the bodies together. As soon as they had several connected, Ryker began shoving the wood underneath, helping with the buoyancy.

"We got company," Grace said, level-voiced, a second before she fired two tracers, eliciting howls from two jokers who collapsed fifty feet away just over the rise of the high part of the bridge, the max range of the gun.

Behind them was a horde of emaciated jokers, gangling forward.

"Shove," Ryker ordered, and with Doc and Haydn's help, they pushed the bodies, wood underneath them, into the water.

It floated.

"Haydn," Ryker said, "get Millay on."

Haydn didn't hesitate, picking her up and stumbling onto the 'raft'.

"Doc, Grace," Ryker called out. "Go."

Grace had emptied the gun.

She joined the others. Ryker waded onto the roadway where it was under water, pushed them farther out.

"I'll join you," he promised, then turned back and charged up the roadway, both blades extended. Ace was at his side. Growling.

"Good dog," Ryker said.

Haydn, Grace, Millay and Doc were on their bellies on the bellies of the dead, paddling as hard as they could, very slowly moving away.

Ryker slashed down the first four jokers without even slowing.

The others had a moment of sanity and halted, backing up. Hissing, grumbling, jingle-jangled in crazy hunger.

Ryker glanced over his shoulder. The 'raft' was twenty feet away, in deep water, over the head.

He twirled his blades in his hands, steel flashing, without even knowing how he could do that, then slid the blades into their sheaths

"Come, Ace!"

Ryker smiled at the jokers, turned and ran. He dove headfirst into the dark water.

And swam.

Didn't know how he could do that either, but he must have known on some level or else he'd have jumped on the 'raft' when they pushed off and have had jokers all over them.

Ace sprinted into the water and then began paddling right next to Ryker, head held up above the swell.

Ryker gripped onto a body as he reached the 'raft' and began kicking, heavy boots notwithstanding, propelling it forward. Helped by Haydn, Doc and Grace paddling.

They edged across the water, jokers howling in rage behind them. Ace swimming alongside.

And then the jokers turned on each other.

ONE TWO UNTIL
GRACE'S DEATHDAY

"She can't be moved," Doc told them.

They were gathered round a fire, a large one, which they'd built to dry everyone off. It was in the middle of the B.D. road that ran from the bridge. They were in Deep Void, out of sight of the bridge. Millay lay on her back, Ace by her side.

"I stitched the outside wound," Doc said. "But she was cut deep so that any movement opens the wound inside her and I don't have the equipment to go probing in there. Would do more damage than good. She may be People but she can still bleed out internally. My hope is, that as People, she can heal quickly. That seemed to be the pattern of those who had injuries in Island. Except they usually went to Hospital first."

"Millay survived being killed," Haydn said.

"That was just her heart stopping momentarily," Doc said.

"How long of a moment?" Ryker wondered.

"Long enough for the Dealers to pronounce her dead," Haydn said. "But maybe it started beating even while they transported her by Lift to the hive and the corpse-people took her to the morgue."

"Then let's hope she heals quickly," Doc said.

"How long?" Ryker asked.

Doc shrugged. "Your guess is as good as mine."

"I don't have a guess," Ryker said, snapping in frustration.

"I'm not leaving her," Haydn said, of course.

"I'm not either," Grace said.

"One two," Ryker said. "We've got a maximum of one two to make it to Centre."

"And then what?" Grace asked. "Why do you need me? And Millay? How are we the Prime? How does the Prime factor into Centre?"

There were the questions none could answer.

Grace pointed at her sister. "If we move her now, we don't have her. If we don't have her, apparently we don't have the Prime."

Ryker closed his eyes for a moment. "If we take B.D. roads, I think we can make it to the far edge of Deep Void in three days."

"Let's hope there are no jokers out here," Haydn said.

"But we can't move her," Doc said, obstinate.

Ryker looked around at the towering trees. "There's something out here. I don't think jokers could survive. No fresh human meat. But something is out here. I can sense it." He made a decision. "We find a place to stay here out of sight, out of the rain. She heals. Doc, you're in charge of her. Let us know when you think she can move. Haydn, you guard her. Grace, you come with me. We'll do a sweep of the area. Make sure we're safe. And get food. We'll take Ace."

EIGHT UNTIL GRACE'S DEATHDAY

"It's a fever," Doc said, her hand on Millay's forehead. "Whatever the joker cut her with was dirty, or she was infected while we went across on the bodies or from the water. I think the wound itself is healed enough on the inside, but she's weak. She can't walk. If she weakens any further, People or no People, I fear the fever will take her."

Ryker folded his arms, considering the situation. They'd moved camp into an old gas station. The place was picked clean, gutted. But it had a roof, the important thing, especially as the rain persisted. Not heavy, just a steady, dripping mist from a gray sky, matching their spirits.

A fire of damp wood sputtered, trying to keep going against the water soaked into the grain, partial victory for flame over water. Ace lay by the open front door, staring out, looking as morose as they all felt.

The recons had found no one. No jokers, no sign of anyone else. Just ruins and forest.

"But if we can move her without her walking," Ryker said. "Will she be all right?"

Doc hesitated. "I'd be leery of—"

"We're down to single digits," Ryker said.

Everyone looked at Grace, who seemed unperturbed by that statement.

It wasn't news.

"We take her," Grace said.

"How?" Doc asked. "She can't be carried either. She'd have to be like she is now. Resting. Covered. She can't get wet again. And—"

"I know how," Grace said. "Come," she said to Ryker and they walked out into the rain, two tall gray figures in a gray world.

Ryker didn't say anything as Grace led the way along the road, taking a turn here, a turn there. Terrain they'd covered on their recons. They walked for over an hour, each respecting the other's silence.

"There," Grace said, pointing at an old barn, roof collapsed.

Ryker saw it right away. "Going to be work to get it moving."

"I'd rather work than wait," Grace said.

Next to what remained of the barn was a hay wagon. A very, very old one. Every other vehicle they'd come across, the rubber tires had long rotted to rims. But this had metal wheels, with metal spokes on metal axles. The wood was in poor shape. But there was wood all around them.

"Need Doc's hatchet," Ryker said.

"Let's get it."

They began walking back, but then Grace shifted pace into a jog. Ryker matched her.

So the single digit did bother her.

They didn't say why they needed it. Ryker traded out one of his knives to Doc in exchange for the hatchet, so she'd have a weapon. Haydn had fashioned a club out of metal pipe since both tracers had run out of ammunition at the crossing. He was at Millay's side, changing compresses on her head. Forcing her to drink. Trying to get her to eat, even though she threw up anything he managed to get into her.

Ace could only catch so much food, so the rest went without as Doc brewed up stews from the scant meat for Millay. Grace foraged and found some wild plants that Mrs. Marash had indicated were edible; how to prepare them required experimentation.

Otherwise, Doc seemed at a loss, other than to wait out the infection.

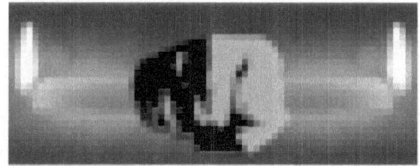

Grace pulled her coveralls down, cinching the arms around her waist. Ryker took his shirt off. They got to shaping wood, trimming deadfall to approximations of boards to replace ruined ones on the hay wagon. They scoured the area, finding nails, or battering some out of old walls.

They used the rear of Doc's hatchet to hammer the nails through the wood. Building a wagon from the remains of a wagon.

The wheels were rusted. Metal to metal.

But Ryker found an old plastic container. He knew the word through the jingle-jangle, as if his brain was allowing him this bit, this crucial piece, but not much more: MOTOR OIL.

They soaked the metal axles where they met wheels.

Waited. Waited. Pushed on the rear. Waited. Then with a protest of rust subsiding to lubricant, the wagon moved. Loud squeaks. They used the last of the oil from the plastic container.

Looked at each other. Put their shoulders to it.

It rolled.

They walked around to the front, where the metal tongue was, ending in a ring.

They were both sweating, rivulets running over their naked torsos.

Ryker looked at her. In a way he hadn't before. She returned it. Her mouth opened ever so slightly. She ran a hand through her short hair, but gave no words.

Ryker put his shirt on. Grace slid up her coverall top.

Each grabbed one end of the pole they slid through the metal ring and they began the journey back to the rest.

Beasts of burden.

SIX UNTIL GRACE'S DEATHDAY

There were strange things along the road. Not just old, rusted out cars, tires long rotted, interiors molted. At one point they paused. The road ahead was glazed for almost a mile, burned by a fierce flame long ago and everything on it and along it had been wiped clean; vehicles, buildings, vegetation and one had to assume people. Nothing grew. It made for easier going, but trembles at such violence long ago.

Farther on, there were crumpled buildings here or there, but mostly it was fields and forests.

No major hills, for which they were thankful, as the road ran between high ground, following the path of least resistance, usually next to a stream, a ready source of fresh water.

The wagon was a case of good idea, tough execution. Two people, usually Haydn and Ryker, had to pull. The other two would be behind, pushing as they could, but also grabbing ropes tied off to the rear to be additional brakes on the down slopes. Millay was covered with a mish-mash of long ago plastic bags, carefully positioned to keep water off her. Ace ranged forward and back, often disappearing off to the side of the road.

This third day of wagon travel started to turn dim just after noon.

The morning sun had been blood red in the east. And then dark clouds came in from the west, gathering, bunching, beginning to race by. Ace was nervous, giving an occasional low whine.

"Storm coming," Doc called out from the back of the wagon.

Ryker raised his fist, and the wheels crunched to a halt. He looked up from the yoke. Fields on the left. Forest on the right. Bad country to be caught out in. Ahead, about a half mile, something man-made was poking above the trees.

"We go for that." Ryker opened the fist and gestured forward. With a grunt, he and Haydn got the wagon moving.

Not enough time as the sky grumbled, cracked with sound, closer and closer. They could now see the lightning bolts to the west, approaching stilted flash by stilted flash. Then the rain came, heavy, blown hard, almost horizontal. They could barely see and had to maneuver around junked cars, debris.

They finally reached the building, a spire crowning a relatively intact stone and concrete structure. There were doors, tall ones, made of wood that had lasted the time. But they were shut, foreboding, denying. There were marks on the wood, cuts, dents, scratches, but the doors towered intact.

The wagon ground to a halt in front, the four powering it also ground to exhaustion. Ryker staggered to the door, bent forward into the wind, fighting back against nature.

The doors wouldn't move.

Ryker looked up. Something was carved into the stone arch above the door.

Haydn was in the cart with Millay, trying to protect her from the rain and wind with his body and holding down the fragments of plastic. Grace and Doc joined Ryker.

"'*Jesus Saves*'," Doc said, barely heard above the storm.

"What?" Ryker asked.

Doc pointing a dripping hand at the words on the stone archway.

"We need to get in," Ryker said. "Get out of this weather. Get Millay inside. I'll find a way. Stay here."

He scrambled around to the side. The windows were high, unreachable, unbroken. Strange thing given the building was B.D..

He pushed through weeds, plants, and vines grown against the building, along the side to the rear. Among the vegetation, battered by rain and wind, he almost missed it, but the wind that showed the opening, blowing some weeds inward. A black hole just below ground level, in a depression surrounded by half-circle of corrugated metal, filled with growth. Ryker shoved aside the weeds. The opening was barely a foot high by two wide, blocked by a pane of glass. He didn't hesitate, shattering it with his knife. He squeezed in, feeling ahead in the sudden darkness.

Nothingness. He was too far in to pull back out, the bottom of the opening pressing against his stomach.

How far down? He wondered and then answered by letting go and falling, arms and legs outstretched, thudding into a floor five feet down, absorbing the blow through his limbs, into his body, breath knocked out.

He lay still for a moment, breathing hard, letting his eyes adjust, feeling to see if he'd broken anything. The only light came from the hole he'd entered; not much. Nothing broken. Ryker stood. Hands in front, he moved forward blindly, reached a wall. Turned right, fumbling along the wall. Fell over something. Got back up. Reached a corner. Shifted along the next wall. Fell again. Kept moving. His entry was a dim gray square behind him, not enough to penetrate this far with any illumination.

Wall disappeared. An opening. Ryker edged his foot forward, encountering a stair. He reached to the side. A railing. He teetered his way up. Counting the stairs. Twelve, and then another wall. No, a door. He pressed. Nothing. Searched with his hands, found a metal knob. Turned. It twisted but the door didn't budge. Ryker traced the edge of the door, determined it opened away from him.

He drew one of his knives, shoved the point between the door and frame. Levered. Hard.

Wood splintered and there was light, dim, but light. He pushed through. Dark light, bright flashing storm light, came in through the high windows. Enough for him to see, especially after the darkness. There was a musty odor in the air, not just from no circulation for many, many years, but also something else, something verging on foul. He hurried toward the tall front doors, feeling something crunch underfoot, not stopping to investigate.

A thick beam resting in two side brackets barred the doors. Old oak, treated, strong.

Ryker struggled, lifted it enough to slide it down to the ground on one side. He pulled one door open.

Ace was the first one in, bursting past, then Haydn carrying Millay and then Doc. And Grace last.

Ryker looked out, making sure the cart was secure. He saw something, a hint of a figure in the treeline across the road, mostly obscured by the rain and only for a second and then it was gone.

But he'd seen someone.

"Help me," Ryker said to Grace as he stepped in and pushed the door shut.

Grace grabbed the oak bar with Ryker and they slid it back in.

Then they turned to look around.

"A church," Doc said.

"A what?" Grace asked as Haydn gently laid a shivering Millay on a bench, then sat, cradling her head in his lap.

"A place where they worshipped B.D.," Doc said. She started to step forward, heard the crunch and looked down. "Oh!"

"What?" Ryker asked. There were little objects on the floor, white pebbles.

"Teeth," Doc said. She looked about. "Isolated in here. Little air flow. No animals getting in." She reached down and picked up a molar. "This is the only thing that lasted all these years. Not even bones." She knelt and slid her hand across the stone floor. "This dust is what's left of the bones."

"There's a lot," Ryker said.

"Place must have been packed," Doc said.

Ace shook, spraying them.

"They most likely died from lack of water," Doc said.

"Why wouldn't they go outside?" Ryker asked. "What were they so afraid of out there?"

"Who knows during the Chaos?" Doc said.

"Could this have happened *after* the Chaos?" Ryker asked.

Doc looked at him. "Then who were they?"

"I saw someone," Ryker said.

"What?" Doc said. "When?"

"Just now. When you were coming in. Just before shutting the doors. There was someone across the road, in the trees. I could only see their outline, but I'm sure I saw someone."

"A joker?" Haydn asked.

"I don't think so."

"You know," Grace said, "it does seem odd that no one lives out here. It's not like the Wasteland. And the Olympics aren't like the Wasted Mountains. It's green out here. Almost like Island. How come the People didn't spread out this way?"

"Void and Deep Void are off limits to Dealer," Grace said.

"Delta wasn't," Ryker noted. "Who's out here?" Ryker stared at Doc.

The old woman shook her head. "Just rumors. You saw the broken bridge. You can't get out to Deep Void from Void."

"But you said people tried," Ryker noted. "And we made it. Maybe I saw one of those who tried earlier?"

Doc nodded. "Maybe. Some could have built rafts, of wood, not bodies," she added.

"What if it's someone else? Not folders or floers or jokers?" Grace asked.

"Who?" Doc asked.

"Maybe we're supposed to meet someone out here," Grace said. "The Person told me there would be people along the way to help. First Mrs. Marash; then I met you." She nodded at Ryker. "And now there are five of us. After all, we're not sure what we're supposed to do when we get where we're going. Maybe this person you saw knows."

"Then why not come up and introduce?" Ryker asked. "It's terrible out there. Why not come here in the dry? Join us?"

Neither Doc nor Grace had a reply.

Ryker noted that Ace was lying by the two large doors, head up. The wet hair along his spine was standing up straight. "What's with him?"

"Storms make him nervous," Doc said, looking uneasy herself.

"We pull guard tonight," Ryker said. "Maybe whoever's out there makes him nervous."

The group split up. Grace went to Haydn and her sister.

Doc walked to the far end, where there was a raised platform. Ryker followed.

"What's that?" he asked.

"An altar," Doc said. "Where the person who led their ceremonies presided.

"So, this Jesus. He was like Dealer?"

"I guess," Doc said. "I'm just working off bits and pieces, mouth to ear. People prayed to Jesus B.D.. Asked for his help."

"Didn't seem to work," Ryker said.

"The human race is still around," Doc said. "Maybe it did."

Ryker shrugged. "People appeal to Dealer all the time. Doesn't seem to help much either."

"But we're still alive," Doc pointed out.

"Is simply surviving enough?" Ryker asked.

"In Void it is," Doc said. "And double-down here in Deep Void."

"Did you really fold?" Ryker asked.

Doc sighed deeply. "No."

"What happened?"

"I was exiled."

"Why?"

"I tried to help a burner live," Doc said. "I was in Island. Once in a while, Evermores bring burners close to three zero to Island to do the really dangerous or dirty work. Under the deck. Hidden on the industrial Wave, brought in by the service tunnels underneath Island. Then sent to Heaven on three zero when the work is done. A burner was in an accident; a bad one. I worked on her."

"That's enough to get your exiled?"

"No," Doc said. "But I used meds that are exclusively for Evermores. The rules, our oath as doctors, are very strict on that. Certain medicines are reserved for the various levels; there's not an unlimited supply. So I broke the rules. Not quite breaking Code. A different thing. Sort of the way burners floe someone who isn't pulling weight. Not in Code; but built into the rules of the hive. This is built into the rules of City. So the Dealers weren't involved. Not even the People, since they couldn't know about burners underneath, working in Island. My fellow Evermores exiled me to Void. Floed me in a way."

Ryker was silent, absorbing that, then: "How'd you get Ace?"

"Found him," Doc said. "In the Void."

Ryker frowned. "What was he doing out there?"

"No clue," Doc said. She looked at him. "I only have so many answers, Ryker. Maybe he bit a People and they exiled him too?"

A slight smile curled Ryker's lip. "As likely as anything else."

In the middle of the church, Grace sat with Millay, allowing Haydn to get some sleep.

"Feeling any better?" Grace asked.

Sweat beaded Millay's brow. She was shivering despite the fact she had every blanket they'd managed to scrounge covering her.

"Something's not right," Millay said. "I've been sick before, but it always goes away fast."

"Things are different in Deep Void than Island," Grace said.

Millay shook her head. "No. It's not right." She grabbed her sister's hand. "Take care of Haydn if I don't survive?"

"Of course," Grace said.

Millay gave a laugh, manic edge to it, eyes not quite focused. "What am I asking of you? You'll be dead in less than six days. You lost Heaven because of me. How can I ask that of you?"

Surprisingly, Grace smiled. "I had Heaven, Millay. You gave that to me. Thirty days in Island. That's what Heaven must be like. I thought I would die at Mrs. Marash's. She gave her life for me. A life for a life. Every day since then is a treasure.

"And I always knew when I was going to die. From Dealing Day on. It's different for me than you. To be honest, I find the concept of not knowing when you're going to die scary. Full of unexpected. Uncertainty."

Grace held Millay's hand as her sister's eyelids fluttered, on the edge of passing out.

Grace's voice dropped, to a level she wasn't sure Millay would hear, and wasn't sure she wanted her sister to hear. "I do wonder what will happen on Deathday. How do I die? Do I just drop dead? And what's after? Is it like trying to imagine what it was like before I was born? Nothingness?"

She was startled when Ryker, who'd come up behind her, spoke. "You all right?"

Grace felt the tension go out of Millay's hand. Her sister was asleep, embracing unconsciousness.

"Yes."

"I'm taking first shift. Why don't you get some rest?"

Grace nodded.

But she didn't lie down. She watched her sister sleep, head resting on Haydn's lap, his head drooping, snoring slightly.

Grace went to where Ryker was sitting cross-legged, his knives drawn and on his lap, staring at the two large doors as if he expected something terrible to come bursting through at any moment. Ace lay on his right side, his head on the ground, but eyes open.

"We couldn't open the doors," Grace noted as she sat down next to him on the other side. "Whoever you saw won't be able to either. We barricaded the other door you came up from."

"I know."

"You seem jingle-jangled. Probably just a joker or a floer you saw."

"Probably."

They remained like that, close, but not touching, for a while.

Glancing over her shoulder, Grace saw Doc was on her back on a pew, eyes closed. Haydn and Millay were still asleep.

"You never said who had second watch," Grace said.

"I didn't."

"There's not going to be a second watch?"

"I wouldn't be able to sleep, anyway."

Minutes passed. Even Ace's eyelids drooped, finally closed.

"Ryker?"

"Yes?"

"I lied."

When there was no reply to that, they both remained still for a while longer.

"I am afraid," Grace said. "I don't want to die."

Ryker reached out with one hand, slid it over her shoulder and pulled her close. Grace relented and rested her head on his chest.

FOUR UNTIL GRACE'S DEATHDAY

*H*aydn slipped on the wet road, falling to his knees, losing his grip on the yoke.

The weight of the wagon, the metal wheels, Millay, were all in Ryker's hands on the rise on the road.

And it was too much.

He was pulled backward, fell, lost his grip too, the yoke whipping by, just missing his head.

Grace was behind the wagon, trying to stop it while Doc jumped out of the way.

"Get away!" Ryker cried out to Grace.

But it was her sister, her twin.

Grace reached out and was slammed to the ground as the wagon went backward. She was able to roll, avoiding being run over by the wheels. The wagon went off the road on a curve, rear metal wheels into a ditch and coming to an abrupt halt.

Millay was catapulted off the back end, into the weeds and grass.

Haydn ran to her. Ryker ran to Grace.

Ace ran to Doc.

'Stone walls do not a prison make, nor iron bars a cage'.

Had he said that out loud? he wondered. That would not do at all.

Andrew, who had once been the Person, knew he was losing his mind. The fact that he knew it meant he hadn't quite yet. Was that irony, he wondered?

He'd run through every poem he could remember, as best he could remember, inside his mind. It wasn't enough. So he'd spent considerable time trying to figure out how to kill himself. He'd tried shutting his mouth when the sprayer directed water at his mouth. But he had only so much control. He was dehydrated and he woke once realizing his mouth was wide open, allowing the mist to enter.

Besides, he couldn't die of dehydration or starvation. The mister was a tease. He'd glanced at the specs for boxing one day out of morbid curiosity. The shunt insured all that he needed to stay alive, other than the air around him, was sent directly into his blood system. He was only punishing himself by denying the water to his mouth.

Punishing wasn't dying.

He'd tried to create a swaying motion in the harness, using his stomach muscles, to rip the shunt out, but his body was secured in place by tethers.

Dealer had thought of everything when it devised this.

But Andrew had not called out.

He was worried that when his brain became all jingle-jangled and he no longer realized he was losing his mind he'd began verbalizing what was running through his brain.

What would he say?

He fell back on the fact that he knew so little.

The fact that he knew so little scared him.

Millay had broken a rib, at the very least, and had some bruises, but nothing more. Grace was bruised, battered, but couldn't have cared less; the clock was ticking. They pulled the cart back onto the road and pushed forward, north. Millay's fever had not abated, but the wound seemed to be almost completely healed, despite the accident.

Not much farther down the road, they called an end to the day. They were exhausted from fighting the hills, and a steady drizzle dampened their spirits. Lack of knowledge of what awaited them dulled their strength.

Still, Grace's Deathday pulsed in their veins, pushing them harder, but despair was a rising tide, and their feet were chained to the road.

They slid off the side of the road under the vertical protection of a roof over crumpled fuel pumps, the building next to it, roofless, blackened.

"Go," Doc ordered Ace, who took off to do his duty.

Haydn gathered wood for their cooking fire, trying to find some that wasn't as damp. Ace came back with a rabbit. Doc had the fire going. Ryker skinned and cooked the scant offering of the forest. They did their routine for the evening, but there was a jingle-jangle about it; a routine that was unraveling.

Haydn settled in the wagon next to Millay, after getting her to keep some rabbit broth down. Doc lay under the wagon, blanket wrapped tight around her.

Ryker walked to the road and peered back the way they'd come in the darkening evening. Grace joined him.

"Think we're being followed?" she asked.

"I think we're following."

"What do you mean?"

"I think whoever I saw knows where we're going. Was just

checking on us. But is probably ahead of us. We're not moving very quickly."

"How much farther do you think?" Grace asked. They were both standing in the drizzle, so used to the wet they didn't care.

"Don't know."

"More than four days?"

"No."

"You just said you don't know."

"I know we'll get there before four days."

"Wouldn't guess you for happy person, thinking things turn out good."

"I'm not happy person," Ryker said, slipping back into hive, then stepping out. "We will get there before four."

"Good." She looked around, shifting perspective. "It's beautiful."

Ryker glanced at her.

"Much better than hive," Grace amplified.

"I don't remember my hive," Ryker admitted. "I know the concept of hive but so little other. I have dreams. Don't know if they're my life. Or someone else's. Or implanted in me like using these." He lifted the blades halfwayout of their sheaths.

"Let me see," Grace said.

Ryker handed one to her. She hefted it, testing the weight. She ran her finger along the base of the blade. "Good steel. Better than the 'tein vat steel." She was surprised to see that Ryker's eyes were closed, one of them twitching. "You all right?"

"Bowie knives," Ryker said, then opened his eyes. "Coffin-handled Bowie knives."

"What?" Grace asked, handing the knife back.

"Some things come through," Ryker said. He indicated the knife. "That's what they're called. I don't know what that means, but that's their name. A memory, but not very useful. Still, it's something."

"I remember only hive," Grace said, handing the knife back. "And then my time in Island."

"How was it?"

"Easy," Grace said. "One lacked for nothing. Food. Drink. Rest."

"Did you like it?"

"At first."

"And then?" Ryker asked.

"They don't *live* there," Grace said. She glanced at him. "The big-head People go through the motions of living. But it's all too easy."

"There's no passion," Ryker said, surprising himself and her.

"How do you know?" Grace said. "Have you been in Island?"

"Not that I remember," Ryker said with a grin. "But I don't remember much. I think you've touched on the real problem in Sound. In Island. Can People without passion survive?"

"burners have passion," Grace said. "But what good does it do us? What's the point? What are we doing?"

"I don't know," Ryker admitted. "I just know I have to do it."

"What if we're all being played by Dealer?" Grace asked. "What if Dealer is having a game with us? Like it did with Delta?"

Ryker had no answer.

"Worse," Grace said, glancing at Ryker, "what if *you're* really working for Dealer? Like you said Achilles was. Like Charon was."

"Then I wouldn't have killed Charon, who was working with Achilles. And he would have turned Millay and Haydn over at the ferry landing. And I would have turned you over to the Dealers at the bridge. This is a lot of work in the wrong direction if I were part of Dealer."

"Dealer has run the world as long as any can remember," Grace said.

"Not Mrs. Marash."

"But she gave up. Let death take her." Grace shook her head. "Why are Millay and I so important?"

"The Prime. And you're twins."

"So?"

"You broke the rules," Ryker said. "More accurately, your parents broke the rules, somehow."

"What rules?"

"Genetics." Ryker closed his eyes briefly, information coming to him, not personal, but big-picture. "That's why there's been no twins since Chaos. Twins would have the same genetics and should get the same card. You and Millay should have the same genetics. But you're burner and she's People. There is a reason for every rule in Code. The problem is, we may know Code, but we don't know the reasons."

"It makes no sense."

"Exactly. The *Centre* does not hold."

"What the floe does that mean?" Grace demanded.

Ryker put a hand on her shoulder. "I don't exactly know. But we must have hope."

"I have four days."

"I know."

Grace leaned against him, and he held her tight.

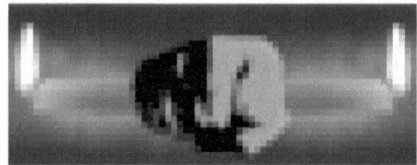

Later that night, Ryker heard a familiar sound. The thrumming of a Lift. Far to the east, but it was the first time he'd heard that sound since they'd reached Deep Void.

Dealer was expanding the search.

And four passed to three.

THREE UNTIL GRACE'S DEATHDAY

"We have to do something different," Ryker said.

Millay was sitting up in the back of the wagon, still running a fever, not quite here, not quite gone. Haydn, Doc and Grace were gathered round, all sore from the wagon, blinking in the early morning dimness. Ace was off in a nearby field.

"Did you pull security all night again?" Grace asked.

Ryker ignored that. "This isn't right." He nodded toward Millay. "She should have gone one way or the other. To death or to life. Her wound is healed. But to stay like this with fever this long? Not right."

Haydn agreed. "She's People. She lived when hit with a tracer in the heart. When she was pronounced dead by Dealers. Dealers aren't wrong about something like that."

Doc shook her head. "I don't understand it."

"Then let her die again," Ryker said, looking across at Grace. "Maybe that's what it takes. Dying for her to live."

Grace stared at him, her mouth open, but then she nodded slowly. "Yes. We have to do something different."

"That doesn't make sense," Doc said. "I have to treat her. Keep her alive."

"No," Ryker said. "No more treatment. She either lives or dies, but we let her being People determine her fate."

"I don't think-" Doc started.

"I agree," Grace said abruptly. "There's no more time." She looked at Haydn. "What say you?"

Haydn agreed reluctantly. "I thought she was dead when it came over the Stream. She woke in morgue under hive. Alive. So we don't know. We don't know what being People is. But she is People. She said it all the time. Let her being People decide this. I will live or die with her."

"This is up to Grace," Ryker said. "Millay is her sister. Her twin. And these are Grace's last days. Her choice."

"I already died," Grace said. "In that hole underneath Mrs. Marash's house. Sometimes I think I died on Dealing Day. When I got the red card. We all died that day. All burners. When your entire life is directed toward dying, aren't you already dead?

"So, I die in three days. But I want Millay to have the best chance. We have to try something different for her. Let her be People."

"Yes."

They all turned to look at Millay. Sweat on her brow, hands shaking, but her eyes were steady. "Let me die and then live. Or just die. Whatever this is, we have to see it through." She nodded to her sister. "How many days?"

"Three."

"Oh," Millay gasped. She gathered herself. She felt her side. "That's good. No pain. No more treatment. Let me die trying." She struggled, slid to the edge of the wagon.

Haydn reached out to steady her but she shook him off. She staggered onto weak legs, one hand on the wagon. She took several deep breaths. She took a step away from the wagon. A couple more. "I can walk. Not fast. But I *will* walk. We leave the wagon. We move faster." She made her way back to the wagon, once more resting against it. "How far is it?"

Ace came bounding back and sat down, tongue hanging, tail wagging, ready to go.

"That's what I want to find out," Ryker said. "It could be right over the next rise. Could be a day away. You walking, with Haydn and Grace's help, will move faster. But I want to go ahead. To see how far."

"And to see what's there, right?" Grace said.

"Yes," Ryker said. "Better I'm there, reconning, than walking slow with you. I'll come back for you. To let you know."

"That's a good idea," Doc said. "I'll go with you. I've done as much as I can for Millay."

"We leave Ace with them," Ryker said. "To hunt and give warning."

"I don't think that's a good idea," Doc said. "We've never been apart."

"It's not about being an idea," Ryker said. "It's about the reality of the situation."

"I really—" Doc began, but Ryker cut her off. "Ace stays."

Doc didn't look happy, but she didn't argue any further.

Ryker pulled one of the sheaths off his belt. He extended the knife to Grace. "We'll have a knife and axe. You need this."

Grace took it, but held on, both of them still for a long moment, their eyes meeting. "Promise me you will be back before—" She left the obvious unsaid.

"I promise."

TWO UNTIL GRACE'S DEATHDAY

Ryker and Doc stopped at the top of a hill, looking down at the remains of a town. There was a high, forested bluff looming to the left, with the buildings down in flat land leading to the water to the right. And water ahead. A point of land. It was dawn, rays of sunlight arching over the Wasted Mountains in the distance, but the sun's orb not yet breaking the horizon.

"This is it," Ryker said.

Many of the buildings in the town had been demolished, struck by a mighty force, flattened, blasted, crumbled.

"Look at that." Doc pointed.

There was a marina, boats all sunk, flipped over, rotted away. But past the marina, near another ferry pier, was a long black object, the front end on the beach, extending into the water over five hundred feet. In the center was a narrow tower with two fins extending horizontally. There was scarring on the black hull, tears in it, gaping wounds, exposing a dark interior.

"A weapon from the Chaos," Doc said.

"For those weapons we saw in Delta," Ryker said. "It would fit in that place in Delta where Achilles made his camp."

"This is what Dealer saved us from," Doc said. "There would be no City, no City Edge, no hive without Dealer."

"No Island," Ryker added.

But then he looked across the water. It was a rare, clear day. Land beckoned about five to six miles across the water. And beyond that, far in the distance, were the Wasted Mountains, but they were covered with a blanket of snow, making them look almost natural.

"So the *Centre* is over there?" Doc asked, pointing at the far shoreline

"Yes." Ryker eyed the distance. He turned and looked to this side. "We made it here in less than a day. If they're moving at any decent pace, they should arrive early tomorrow. We leave shortly and go back. Meet them. Help them."

"We have to do a recon first," Doc said. "We need to figure out what we're supposed to do here."

Ryker indicated the jutting land on the far side of the town, over-grown with trees. "There."

They began down the hill.

"Walking has been good for you," Grace said, matching her sister stride for stride.

"Ryker was right," Millay said. "I feel so much better since yester-day." Her face was slightly flushed, but she wasn't sweating. Her fever was greatly reduced and, though weak, her will was propelling her forward.

Haydn was on the other side of her, relieved, a bounce that hadn't been there since Millay had been wounded.

Even Ace seemed happier, racing forward, and back, sprinting out into fields trying to chase down small animals, sometimes successful, sometimes not.

"Going to be a nice day," Haydn said.

"A gorgeous day," Grace said.

Then Ace stopped abruptly, about thirty feet ahead of them on the road, fur ridged on back, growling.

"There," Haydn said, hefting his club.

On the ridgeline to the left, the sun glinted off something. Someone moving. They strained to see, but whoever it was, was moving fast, fading into the green. They'd only spotted it because of Ace' alert and the sun slanting in reflecting off something metal.

"Gone," Millay said. "Who was it?"

Grace shook her head. "No idea. Ryker said he saw someone when we were going into the church."

"I hardly remember that," Millay said.

"We should take a rest break," Haydn suggested.

"No," Millay said. "I want to keep moving forward. The more distance we cover, the quicker we link up with Ryker and Doc."

But Haydn was eying the treeline on the ridge. Grace's hand was on the knife sheathed at her side.

"We can't be afraid any more," Millay said. "I slowed you down too much. We push forward."

Grace and Haydn exchanged a look.

"All right," Grace said. "We keep moving until dark."

"We keep moving until we can't move any more," Millay amended. "Even in the dark, as long as we can stay on the road."

Passing through the remains of the town—a rusting sign with small holes punched in it, designated *Port Townsend*—they arrived at the far end, at a large wooden building on the shoreline, partially demolished, glass shattered.

"*Northwest Maritime Center*," Doc said, reading a faded sign.

Ryker walked into what remained of the builsing. Something glittered in the debris and Ryker dug it up. A metal tube, two feet long, with glass on either end. Ryker looked it over, then put it to his eye.

He left the building, Doc following, and walked to the seawall. The telescope zoomed in on the far shoreline. He edged it across until he spotted a low, long gray structure hulking above the distant beach. He squinted and spotted a Lift rising up out of the structure and head south. The structure looked old, its concrete pitted, battered, but intact.

"That's it," Ryker said, handing the telescope to Doc.

She peered through. "What is it?"

"Centre," Ryker said.

"How do you—" Doc began, but she'd heard the answer enough times already. "What is Centre? Looks like a ruin."

"Maybe where Dealer is?" Ryker said, both question and statement.

"Again," Doc said, "how do we get to it? None of those boats were serviceable. Everything is wrecked out here."

"One thing at a time," Ryker said. He took the scope back. Put it to his eye. Looked further along the shore. A large gray, flat-topped ship was in the water, just off shore and just south of Centre. He couldn't see past it. There were streaks of rust on the ship.

He extended the scope back to Doc. "What's that? To the right of Centre?"

Doc looked. "Something B.D.? A ship."

Ryker took the scope back. "We're going to have to get over there. Let's go." He carried the telescope with him as they followed the shore around.

"Ah," Ryker said, as a weathered concrete bulwark, a sister to the one across the way came into view. Ryker looked from it, to the one across the way. Then back at the submarine smashed onto the beach. "Forts," he said. "Guarding Sound."

"Old," Doc said. "B.D.."

"Maybe they protected Sound during the Chaos," Ryker said.

There was a strange building near the concrete bunkers, a three-story brick castle. They walked up to it. The windows were gutted, door gone. Ryker went in, but the stairs had rotted through long ago.

He came back out. Doc was looking out at the Sound. "What do we do now?" she asked.

Ryker ran his hand over his chin, feeling the beard he'd accumulated on the journey. "There has to be a reason that Millay and Grace need to be here."

"More likely they need to be *there*," Doc said, indicating the fort across the way.

"True," Ryker agreed. "We won't know until they get here. We need to figure out a way to get across."

Doc was facing landward now. She pointed. "What's that?"

A rounded concrete, low lying, flattened top of a bubble, was behind the concrete emplacements.

"Looks almost like a hive that's been pressed into the ground," Doc said.

"No windows," Ryker said, then realized he was remembering something of hive. Perhaps more would come.

They walked toward it. On one edge was a square metal hatch.

"Could be something below," Doc suggested.

Ryker grabbed the handle for the hatch and pulled. Surprisingly, it opened, falling back on hinges with a clang. "I think someone's been here." A metal ladder descended into darkness.

"Maybe the person you saw?" Doc said.

Ryker checked to make sure that the knife was free in its sheath, ready for action. "You stay up here." He slid his feet in, secured a rung, then climbed down. He reached the bottom and turned about, pulling out the Bowie knife.

He sensed a large space, although he could only see about fifteen feet in the light coming in from above. He was about fourteen feet below the surface. Square concrete columns were evenly spaced, holding up the roof.

"Doc?" Ryker called and then was amazed to hear his voice echoed, and again, and again, bouncing around him.

There was no answer other than his own voice reverberating around.

"Doc?" he called up.

He saw a shadow flicker in the daylight above and tried to see. But then staggered back as a Dealer came thudding down, metal feet hitting concrete, joints flexing, coming to height.

Ryker attacked, blade against metal, before the Dealer could bring its arm up with stunner.

He jammed the point of the Bowie into the thing's neck on the left side. He sensed, heard, another Dealer landing, sound rolling round, but he put all his weight behind the blade and it punctured into the joint and the Dealer froze, then dropped, heavy metal crushing to the floor. Ryker pulled the blade back, wheeling and was hit by stunner, staggering him back, but not putting him down. He tried to move forward, but stunner fired again. And again.

Darkness fell.

ONE UNTIL GRACE'S DEATHDAY

"*H*e should have come back," Grace said, staring, uncaring, out over the mangled town, the Sound, the beached submarine. "He promised."

"He's here somewhere," Millay said. "We'll meet." She was healthy, no fever, but hungry, tired, and looking exactly like her burner sister except for the color of their coveralls, but even those were coming close to matching, the dirt and grime of the journey closing the gap.

It was mid-afternoon, but the sun was hidden above low-lying gray clouds. Visibility was only a couple of miles. The vista was bleak, the water of the Sound dark, unsettled, with sullen waves roiling onto the gray beach. Even the sound of the surf seemed distant, defeated. The air was salty, chilly.

"I want to see the sun again," Grace said.

"Tomorrow morning," Haydn said.

"And if it's hidden?" Grace asked. "And who knows? Maybe I die tonight, when we move from this day to next? No one knows how or when exactly we die on Deathday. What was the point of all of this?"

"Let's find Ryker and Doc," Haydn said, a burner plan to act in the face of lack of knowledge.

They started down the hill into what remained of the town.

Ryker came to consciousness into darkness so absolute he wondered for a moment if he'd lost his sight. Arms bound, legs bound. Lying on concrete. He sensed another presence. "Doc?" his voice bouncing round and round before smothering down.

There was no reply. Ryker went perfectly still, listening. No sign of movement. He stopped breathing, cocking his head. No other breathing.

"Dealer?" Ryker said, in a surprisingly calm voice.

Nothing.

He tried the steel binding him, feeling thick metal dig into skin.

Ryker slumped back on the floor, wishing he knew how much time had passed. Grace was moving north. Time was pressing on her. He had not fulfilled his promise.

He tried to break the ties once more.

They walked along the shore, Ace running into the surf, the only one happy.

"Ryker!" Grace called out, her voice swallowed into grayness. "Ryker!"

"Look," Millay said, pointing to the east. Four Lifts were flying down the middle of the passage between their location and the far side. Heading south over the water.

"Where'd they come from?" Haydn wondered. A question with no answer expected.

They watched until the Lifts became specs in the distance and then disappeared.

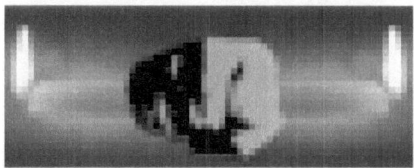

Andrew, who had once been the Person, was barely human. He heard the voice, the taunting tone to it. Someone he'd known. Before boxing. An eternity ago.

"Andrew?"

What did it matter? What did anything matter?

"We've got them," Claude said. "We've got all of them. Millay and Grace. Well, not exactly have her, since today is her last day."

That stirred Andrew.

"We have the others too," Claude said. "We'll deal with each one as appropriate."

Andrew remained silent.

"Who is Ryker?" Claude asked.

Andrew's pain was fading, although there was no welcome pain killer mist.

"Andrew? We can make it worse."

No, you can't, Andrew thought. Because if it got worse, he would no longer be human and he would no longer care.

"Tell me," Claude said. "What is Prime?"

I wish I knew, Andrew thought. *I'm glad I don't know.*

"Once we bring in Ryker and Millay," Claude said, "we'll figure it out."

So 'they' didn't have them. Not yet. For the first time since he'd been boxed, Andrew relaxed in the harness and he realized there was no 'phantom pain' from his missing limbs. They were missing. It is what it is.

But there was so much more.

Claude continued taunting, but Andrew no longer listened.

It was the beginning of the last sunset, obscured by clouds. They'd searched every building that remained, Haydn pressing both Grace and Millay, keeping them busy. But there was no sign of Doc or Ryker. Even Ace seemed discouraged as they searched, ears down, tail drooping.

Finally, exhausted, running out of daylight, they went to the beach.

"What's in the box?" Millay asked, sitting next to Grace.

"What?" Grace shook out of dark thoughts.

"The metal box you've been carrying since we met," Millay said, indicating her sister's pack. Haydn was behind them, out of earshot. Giving space to the twins, one of his traits, understanding distance and closeness.

"I don't know." Grace reached into her pack and retrieved her companion from the grave. "I found it under Mrs. Marash's house. Hidden away. Like I was."

She took Ryker's knife out, putting the point under the lid. Levered. The metal bent and for a moment, Grace paused, feeling regret at damaging something so old, then rejected the regret knowing that Mrs. Marash was becoming part of her garden and she herself would be dead tomorrow.

What did it matter?

She pried the top open. Swung it up. The contents were swathed in thick plastic. Grace took them out and unwrapped, revealing a strange assortment. On top were two little blue books with faded gold writing on the cover. Some sort of symbol was in the center.

"*Passport,*" Millay read. "*United States of America.*"

Opening it, Grace saw blue pages with images on them. And on the thickest page, on the left side, was a picture. With a lot of small writing next to it.

"Hanan Marash," Grace read to Millay and Haydn. "When she was younger."

"She was beautiful," Millay said. Lush dark hair flowing over her shoulders. Deep eyes. Smooth face, flawless brown skin.

There was a second blue book just like it and Grace opened it. This one had a picture of a different woman. Short dark hair, fair skin, green eyes.

"*Ruth Baldour*," Grace read. "She must have been a friend of Mrs. Marash."

"I wonder if these were their version of cards?" Millay said.

"There are dates," Grace said, as she studied it. "Three dates. This one is date of birth. Then date of issue. Then date of expiration."

"That must be the Deathday," Haydn said.

"Her date of birth reads seven October one nine eight four." Grace looked up. "What does that mean?"

"Something B.D.," Haydn guessed. "They must have done time differently. When date of birth mattered, not Deathday."

Grace put the passports carefully back in the plastic.

"I don't think the last date was Deathday," Grace said. "Mrs. Marash was still alive when I met her."

Next was a stack of green paper clipped together with a piece of metal.

"They're all the same," Grace said, thumbing through.

"Says *One Hundred* in the all corners," Millay said, taking one of the notes. "And *United States of America* again."

"Who is the man?" Haydn asked, pointing at the center.

Millay squinted. "Reads *Franklin*."

"Why so many of the same thing?" Haydn asked.

They puzzled over that. Millay turned it over. "It says *In God We Trust*, here. And *One Hundred Dollars*." She turned it back over and looked closely. "Here. This small writing. It reads: *This note is legal tender for all debts public and private*."

"Ah," Haydn understood. "Like what we use our card for. To buy things. Exchange."

Grace put them back. Next were a group of plastic cards, bound by the remnants of a rubber band, the last of which crumbled as soon as she picked them up.

"Mrs. Marash," Grace said, seeing the picture on the first card.

"Yes," Millay confirmed. "That's her name. There's other data. Numbers. I can't make sense of it. This—" she touched a line—"says *Washington Drivers License.*"

Next was a silverish card with raised numbers and Mrs. Marash's name again.

"*American Express,*" Millay read. There were several more cards like it, with different labels, Mrs. Marash's name, but the same kind of raised numbers, though the numbers were all different.

Grace was very careful with the next, a folded piece of paper. She unfolded it. *"Certificate of Marriage."*

"I've heard of that," Millay said. "In B.D., when two people bonded, they committed in a thing called marriage. A permanent bonding." She read over Grace's shoulder. "Ah. It's between Hanan Marash and Ruth Baldour. They were married."

"I wonder what happened to Baldour?" Grace said. "Mrs. Marash said something about loving someone. I can't clearly remember."

Grace refolded it gingerly and put it back in the plastic. All that remained were a couple of objects: a pair of silver wings with pins on the back, and two narrow gold rings.

Grace held the rings in her hand. "These meant something. One each. They wore these."

"Maybe to indicate they were bound?" Haydn said.

"Possible," Grace said, but she put the wings and the rings back. Wrapped the plastic tight. Swung the lid shut. "This was private. I shouldn't have looked. It was her life B.D.."

"They had a lot of cards then," Haydn noted.

"Except they didn't have the worst card," Grace said. "The one that told them when they were going to die."

ONE UNTIL GRACE'S DEATHDAY

Ryker was blinded as the hatch opened. He blinked, tried to adjust, could only see white. Shut his eyes. Heard someone climbing down the ladder, bouncing sound around the man-made cavern.

"Ryker." The sound echoed.

A flood or relief. "Doc! Get these off of me."

"Ryker." And her tone was sadness, regret and it all came to him, relief blown away, weak smoke in a fierce wind.

He blinked, his eyes now able to see shapes. Doc was there. She stood next to the bulk of a Dealer. It had been here all this time.

Doc walked to the side, stopping next to something on the floor. She looked down at it. "You disabled a Dealer. Unprecedented."

"Why?" Ryker asked. One could almost block out the echoes if one focused on the first sound. He was adjusting to the light poking in; not bright sunlight, but the dull gray of an overcast evening sky in Deep Void.

"Why to what?" Doc asked. She looked around. "This held water in B.D.. A cistern for the fort. A rather unique place. How the sound echoes."

Ryker sat up with difficulty. Doc sat down. On the chest of the Dealer he'd disabled.

Ryker was still for a moment, thinking through. "This was from the beginning, wasn't it? From the bridge with Achilles and the jokers hanging below."

"That was the beginning of '*this*' for you," Doc said. "*My* beginning is well before that."

"You have a black card."

"I have a black card," Doc acknowledged.

"You're People."

"No. Evermore, as I told you. And I can be again. Go back to City. Get my life back."

"So that's why," Ryker said.

"Of course. We all want life."

"You were in league with Achilles."

"Sort of," Doc allowed. "He had one mission. Delta. I had another."

"Deep Void."

"Very good."

"What's out here?" Ryker asked.

"No need for that," Doc said. "You'll never find out."

"Why is Deep Void off-limits? Even those who fold or get floed don't go here. Yet, as we've seen, it's good land. Livable. And I did see someone in the storm."

"Dealer has a reason for everything."

Ryker considered that. "So I was to bring Grace and Millay here for a reason other than Centre?"

"Honestly," Doc said, without a trace of sarcasm in an ocean of irony, "I have no idea what Centre is as you call it. Obviously, the Dealers are over there doing something. They probably always have been doing something there. As Millay and Haydn told us—they have that large building in the Wasteland. Most likely a depot for Lifts and Dealers according to the way they described it. Who knows? That's Dealer's business. You weren't supposed to make it this far. None of you. Charon should have stopped you. Dealers should have caught Millay and Haydn and Grace."

Ryker took a deep breath, trying to adjust to a new reality. "Millay's fever?"

"I kept that going," Doc said. "Poisoned her food, keeping a fine balance between not killing her and not curing her."

"To slow us down."

"Yes. Once you were all together, it required a change in plans."

"What will happen to her?"

"Millay is People," Doc said. "She might get boxed. That's up to Dealer."

"Haydn?"

"Bagged most likely."

Ryker knew what he should ask next, but feared the answer, so he backtracked. "Devil's Hole. Where Achilles sent burners close to Deathday. They got bagged, didn't they?"

"No." Doc was adamant. "They were picked up and taken to Heaven. That was part of my deal. I insisted on it."

"So Delta wasn't any different than hive."

"Freer," Doc said. "I'd call in the Dealers to pick them up at Devil's Hole and take them to Heaven, so I was doing right by them even though they folded. Got the same deal after all."

"Delta was set up by Dealer," Ryker said.

"Oh, no," Doc said. "The previous Person. He developed it. Thinking he was circumventing Code and solving the dropping birth rate problem. But Dealer, of course, knew about it while it was still just an idea. Thus, he was able to get Achilles and me inserted into the first group that went over there to establish Delta. It was a hard time back then, over five years ago, fighting off jokers, setting up. But we did it and we built it to what it is."

"What it was."

"I imagine it will be rebuilt. Repopulated."

"Why?"

"To sustain the system," Doc said. "hive is having problems but Dealer always has a solution."

"'Having problems'?"

"Dealer is aware there are not enough births in hive. But plenty in Delta."

Ryker remained silent, processing that. "Why is that important?"

Doc hesitated, indicating she didn't know. She gave no reply.

Ryker shifted directions. "You, Achilles, Charon. All with black cards. What are they?"

"The opposite of white," Doc said. "We were all exiled, but Dealer doesn't waste. Keeps us close to the Stream, but not part of. I had a choice. Boxing or be exiled and do Dealer's bidding. Not much of a choice."

"So what did you do wrong? You didn't try to save a burner."

"It doesn't matter what I did," Doc said.

"And Achilles?"

"No idea why he was exiled, but he held out until he lost his arm before agreeing. Got to give him some credit for trying."

Ryker wasn't impressed and backtracked to what didn't make sense. "Why did Dealer let the Person establish Delta in the first place? Why not do something inside the system?"

Another long pause. "I don't know Dealer's thinking. That's not my place."

"Dealer is a machine," Ryker said. "It doesn't think. It calculates." And how did he know that? he wondered.

"And Dealer has kept things going for centuries," Doc said, some passion finally in her voice. "You saw the destruction as we came north. You saw that submarine. You saw these forts. We almost destroyed ourselves in the Chaos. Dealer saved us."

"At what cost?" Ryker asked.

"Even Grace says Mrs. Marash told her humans caused the Chaos. Dealer saved us."

"You're ignorant. We're all ignorant. Except Dealer." And something jingle-jangled in his brain, something disturbing and exciting but not solid enough to grab hold of. So he asked: "Why do you have Ace?"

"He helps me."

"Helps you with what?"

"He warns me."

"Of what?"

"Not important," Doc said.

"You lie."

"I'm not here to answer your questions. I want to know who *you* are."

"You do, or Dealer does?"

"We need to figure out who you are. Who implanted these things in your mind?"

"You're not going to figure that out," Ryker said, "since I don't myself."

"I'm not going to," Doc admitted. "But Dealer will. Since you actually do know. You just don't know you know. The moment you heard Centre, you knew to head north. So it's *all* in there. Just like your ability with the knives." She rapped a knuckle on her Dealer seat. "You disabled a Dealer with just a knife. Knew exactly how to do that. Not only are you good with a blade, you know a Dealer's weak points. You're dangerous with your hidden knowledge. It will have to be extracted."

"I'll die first."

"You might well."

"I'm a burner. burners always know they're going to die," Ryker said. "It's not that great a threat. That's something Dealer doesn't take into account."

"I think Dealer does factor Deathday in," Doc said. "Everyone is afraid of dying."

Silence reigned.

Doc finally queried: "What is Prime?"

"Millay and Grace. They're the Prime."

"But what is it? What are they?"

"I have no idea," Ryker said.

"It's in there somewhere." Doc sighed. "Dealer will extract that from you too, although it won't be pertinent by then. Grace will be dead. Millay will most likely be in a box where she will tell everything she knows. Everyone boxed always ends up speaking."

"Or making a pact with Dealer and betraying humans."

"Everyone does what they have to do."

"Millay doesn't know what Prime is either," Ryker said, "even though she is part of it. Neither does Grace."

"You speak babble."

"You speak and live betrayal," Ryker said. "Giving up humans for machine."

"For the greater good."

"What greater good?" Ryker asked. "For People? What about the rest of us? Especially burners?"

"burners are doomed from birth by their genes," Doc said. "Resources have to be allocated where they will do the most good."

"Good only if you're the one getting the resources," Ryker said.

"It is what it is."

"What day is it?" Ryker asked.

"Just about Grace's Deathday. A few more hours."

"What time does she die?"

"Even Dealer can't determine that," Doc said.

"You know so little," Ryker said.

Doc gave a bitter laugh. "This from the man who doesn't even really know who he is. Why did you kill Charon?"

"I told you. He was going to betray me. Just as you've betrayed me. Are more Dealers on the way? Or are they already here?"

"They'll come," Doc said.

"'*The centre cannot hold*'," Ryker quoted.

"What *does* that mean?" Doc said.

"It's all falling apart. What Dealer built. It's no longer working."

"How do you know that?" Doc seemed genuinely interested in getting an answer to this question.

Which, Ryker thought, was a good question and then he knew the answer, even though it explained nothing. And explained everything: "Because I'm here."

Doc stood. "Yes. You're here." She spread her arms, taking in the cistern. "The next time you see me, Grace will be dead and Dealers will be taking you to extract information."

She turned and climbed the metal ladder. The Dealer remained motionless. The hatch clanged down with a thud, the sound rounding the walls, bouncing off itself, until finally fading out.

And Ryker was left alone in darkness, for being near a machine meant being alone.

GRACE'S DEATHDAY

"*I* never asked Ryker his Deathday," Grace said. "Think how selfish that was of me."

"He never told you," Haydn said. "You know it's not something we ask in hive."

"We're not in hive," Grace said. "Plus, we don't have to ask in hive, since we can see it on the card. He didn't have a card when we met."

It was dark, scant light from cloud-hidden stars, giving little shape or form. Waves lapped at the beach. Should have been soothing. Were now grating on her nerves.

Grace abruptly stood. "Wish I had my card. To know when it clicks over. Soon. Could have passed already and this is Deathday. Could die in minutes. In the morning. Noon. Evening. Who the floe knows?"

Haydn took a step forward, but Millay raised a hand, stalling him.

Grace turned, then abruptly began to run along the beach.

Ace startled from his sleep, head swiveling. Tracking her. Then he was up, galloping after.

Together they ran hard, Grace's feet slapping at sand, waves to the right.

Grace ran and ran, until the beach took a sharp turn left and she was at the point. Where Deep Void ended and gave way to water.

She stopped, breathing hard. Looking out to the dark water. Little flashes of white where waves collided. She took a step into the water. Another. Another. It rose to her waist. She felt the tug of undertow.

Behind her, Ace whined. Unhappy.

Another step.

"Grace!" Millay's voice carried under the clouds, suppressed. Desperate. Far away.

Grace took another step and the water was to neck.

burners don't know how to swim. Grace laughed. There was no water to swim in around hive, so how would they?

A swell staggered her. Regained her footing.

She dove forward, making the last choice allowed her. To control Deathday.

Dimly, Haydn's voice. "Grace!"

Millay: "I'm following, Grace!"

Did People know how to swim? Grace wondered as water invaded her mouth. Choking, spitting.

The body did not want to die. It was fighting her attempts to take the water in.

Millay: "I'm coming, Grace!"

Grace went under, for a moment so peaceful. Floating. No weight. Her body was nothing. Not a burden. Her mind at peace. She opened her mouth and salt water invaded, tasting like bitter acid. Retching, legs kicking, desperate to bring the rest of her to air.

She surfaced, sucked in water that burned, some air, coughing. Went under.

Realized. All are born to die. Most know when. burners, Middlemores, Evermores. Some don't. People. Those who do are granted a power they don't know. An energy. They live in the time. The less time, the more they live in it.

They burn.

They do not fade away.

Grace broke surface. Dim light on undulating water.

She was greater than this. Great than this fate dealt on a card. Than the world orchestrated by Dealer's edicts. Humans were more than machine.

She went under. Fought to come back up.

Something bumped into her. Wet fur. She reached out. Felt Ace's neck, clung to him. Using him to keep her head above water for a few critical moments. Gasping, sucking in air, not water.

A hand grabbed her arm. Pulled her back from nothingness, from the waste of throwing herself into blankness.

Her legs scrambled. Nothing underneath. No place to put her two feet, to stand in this world she didn't understand.

The hand pulled harder, Millay's fingernails digging into Grace's skin.

Her toe touched sand.

Her foot. Her other foot.

And then she stood. For the first time, a solid place in this world.

On her Deathday.

GRACE'S DEATHDAY

The sky cleared. Stars sparkled, sending light from so far away, that Dealer, hive, all of it, were but blips in the grander scheme.

Grace lay on her back, looking up at them.

Millay lay on one side.

Haydn on the other.

Both silent.

Ace was at her feet, laying his head across her ankles.

His fur was damp, his head heavy, but it gave her a comfort she had never had. But then she knew that wasn't true. Since she'd sat with Ryker, looking at the church's heavy doors, knowing he would protect against whatever was out there.

And she'd fallen asleep then.

Trusted him.

And that was part of love too, she realized, finally understanding Mrs. Marash. Trust and time.

No machine could ever understand. Surviving wasn't enough.

Living was more. Living was loving.

"He'll come," Grace said.

Millay was startled, but Haydn understood.

"He'll come," Haydn agreed.

Dawn came, cloudy and hazy, the sun smudged in the far distance above the Wasted Mountains.

"It'll clear up," Haydn said.

Grace sat cross-legged on the beach.

Still alive.

She got up. "Let's look for Ryker."

"And Doc," Haydn noted.

"And Doc," Grace agreed.

They began quartering through the town, yelling into gaping holes where basements once were. Ace sprinted about, sniffing.

To no avail.

At one point, mid-morning, Millay moved close to Grace, speaking so Haydn wouldn't hear. "How are you?"

"Dying," Grace said. "But I feel fine. Not dying. Do I just stop? Collapse?"

Millay couldn't answer that. They were on the edge of a concrete seawall, waves slurping against it. "Haydn," Grace called out.

He came over.

"I want the two of you to do something for me after I'm dead," Grace said.

"Anything," Haydn promised, and Millay nodded.

"I want to be buried." And then she explained what had been explained to her and what she'd done with Mrs. Marash.

"Any place in particular?" Haydn asked.

Grace looked around. "Not here." She nodded toward the tree-covered bluffs behind the town. "Deep in the forest. So I can become part of."

"We will," Millay said. "But you're not dead. And maybe Dealer was wrong? Maybe—" Her voice faltered and fell off.

"Let's keep looking," Grace said. "Ryker could be hurt."

And they searched, jingle-jangled to the extreme, Millay and Haydn casting glances at Grace, anxious, each person moving quicker, more confused. Ace felt it all, whining, running around. They were no longer coordinated, just staggering through the remains of the town. Nothing.

They checked the marina, but none of what remained was even close to being serviceable.

The sun had arced over, and was sliding down.

Grace was still breathing, still moving. Feeling no different.

As evening approached Grace's hands were shaking and finally she couldn't search any further. She turned away from the other two and went down to the beach, the water now soothing. Always moving, always changing. But always the same.

She sat down.

Millay and Haydn halted, behind her, uncertain.

In the absolute darkness of the cistern, Ryker was also sitting, as best one could with hands and legs bound. There had not been a sound from the Dealer. Not a movement.

It was a machine.

How much time had passed? How long had he been down here? It was definitely Grace's Deathday, but how far into it?

Two hours left.

How he knew that, Ryker had to pile on top of the handling of the knives, about Centre, about getting here.

"Grace!" Ryker screamed. "Grace!"

The name reverberated, bounced back at him, echoes lapping.

He continued to scream, building a cacophony of sound.

He screamed until his voice wouldn't bear it any more, his throat rasping down to silence. Ryker fell back, feeling the cold concrete underneath.

He'd failed. He didn't even know what he was supposed to have achieved, but he'd failed.

Then he began to work his arms once more, even harder, twisting back and forth against the steel binding his wrists together.

It didn't take long for blood to flow, but he didn't care.

There was nothing else to do, but fight to the very end.

Millay came forward and sat next to Grace on the beach. Leaned close. Their shoulders touched. Haydn was behind them, about twenty feet, Ace at his side.

"I would give my life for yours," Millay said.

Grace nodded. "You did."

"For a month," Millay said. "But now, I would give all my years to you if I could."

"I know."

Silence coated them once more.

"Look," Grace said, glancing up.

The clouds had finally parted. The heavens above blazed with stars. Sparkling, clear. Grace looked to the left and gasped. The sky was a shimmering green on the horizon, with streaks of bright light going upwarf.

"The Northern Lights," Millay said. "I've seen them before in Island. They're rare."

"We never see this in hive," Grace said. "So much beauty in the world. Why does hive have none of it?"

Millay had no answer.

The stars wheeled overhead. The Northern Lights put on their display for a while before fading away to darkness.

At one point Millay started, half asleep, terrified Grace was dead.

"Remember your promise," Grace said. "I want to be part of."

"I remember."

THE DAY AFTER GRACE'S DEATHDAY

"I'm still here," Grace said, doubting her reality and her words.

"I don't understand," Millay said.

They both got to their feet, damp and tired, but trembling with life and uncertainty, the two intertwined.

The slightest hint of dawn was in the distance over the Wasted Mountains. The sky was still clear.

"I'll see the sun today," Grace said. She glanced over her shoulder and laughed, something she hadn't done since she could remember. Haydn was asleep, exhaustion having taken him down, sprawled on his back. Ace was pressed against Haydn's side, but his head was up, watching.

"Maybe you have to advance to Heaven to die?" Millay wondered.

"It's supposed to be genetics," Grace said. "The card we're dealt when we're born and Dealer scans us. It's Code."

They stood side-by-side, watching as the sun's rays angled over the mountains, slicing overhead, until the moment the orb made its entrance, a bright sliver coming up between two snow-covered peaks.

"Beautiful," Grace said. "The most beautiful thing I've ever seen."

THE DAY AFTER GRACE'S DEATHDAY

Ryker knew he'd gained a little bit on the metal binding his hands. Not much, only a fraction. So little he might be fooling himself, but he knew he wasn't.

Deathday was past. He knew it. That gave him energy for some strange reason, and he realized it was anger. Rage.

His hands were soaked with his blood, but he kept moving his arms back and forth as much as he could, working the steel.

Light shattered in. Ryker rolled over, looking up, blinded. Heard the Dealer move, its metal feet sliding over concrete. Ryker kept rolling, toward the Dealer's legs, not much of a plan.

He hit, bounced back.

The Dealer twisted, looked down at him, arm raised, stunner coming up to firing position.

And a streaking red bolt hit it in the chest, boring through, sizzling.

The Dealer remained still, as if surprised; could a machine be surprised? Then collapsed backward, Ryker rolling out of the way as it thudded to the concrete, sound bouncing around, a satisfying one.

Ryker blinked, desperate to see. A figure in the square of light.

"Come up."

It was a woman's voice. One he didn't recognize. Not Doc. Not Grace. Not Millay.

"I can't."

The figure blotted the light as she climbed down. Ryker still couldn't make her out. He felt his hands pulled back, metal wrenching, parting, then his legs were free. The figure headed back to the ladder.

Ryker got to his feet, staggered, went to his knees. Stood.

Followed.

He climbed, legs and arms tingling but sensation coming back.

Into the light.

He saw her and paused halfway out of the hatch, feet on a rung, hands on the surface, smearing blood on steel.

She had a human shape. Some human skin. Half her skull and the bottom of her face were covered in it. The other part, scarred metal. Red, mechanical eye on that side. Her other eye, appearing human, was a sparkling green. She had hair, only on the human-skin side, gray and stringy. Her clothes were worn, black pants and shirt, the remnants of some body armor hanging from her shoulders, slashed and burned long ago.

On the right arm a weapon, not a stunner, something that had killed the Dealer. Sleek, pointed, folded back now at the wrist. What the Dealers at Lone Bridge had. It was part of her. Attached. Integral. That hand was all jointed steel, like a Dealer. The other hand had flesh covering it.

"Who are you?" Ryker asked.

She had lips, thin, pale, but stretching across the bottom half of her face, making her appear somewhat human. The lips twitched in a semblance of a smile. "You didn't ask what. But who. Thank you. I'm Ruth." The mouth moved as she spoke, as if actually forming the words. The voice wasn't machine. It was a woman's, deep and pleasant.

"All right, Ruth," Ryker said. "And what exactly are you?"

"I'm the past," Ruth said. "Hopefully, I'm part of the future."

"Are you a Dealer?" Ryker asked.

She shook her head. "Dealers are all machine." She lifted her skin-covered hand toward her head. "My brain is human. My brain is me."

"A cyborg."

"Yes."

"Why?"

"A necessity. A last effort that failed. But now we have to try again." She indicated the obvious metal side of her. "Maintenance isn't quite what it should be and aesthetics are the lowest priority. Skin covering is not important." She turned to the south. "But there's not much time. More Dealers are coming. And," she added, "I'm alone. For now. But you're here. You can help."

"Help what?"

She cocked her head, and he could almost swear he heard gears, metal on metal, but that could be his imagination. "We have to save the Prime."

"Grace and Millay?"

"If that's their names. Yes."

"Grace is past her Deathday. It was yesterday."

"I know."

"Why didn't you rescue me sooner? So I could save her?"

"We, I, had to know she was the one. The one of two. The Prime."

Ryker climbed out of the hole. "She's not dead?"

"Not yet. But if you want to keep her alive, we need to get going."

Ace started barking, fur raised.

Grace, Millay and Haydn turned. A figure was walking down the beach toward them.

"Doc!" Millay yelled, waving.

The old black woman kept coming. But then she stopped, looking from Millay to Grace and then back, confused. "Grace?"

"Yes!"

"You should be dead," Doc said.

Grace and the others were walking forward toward her. "I'm not! Dealer was wrong."

"Dealer is never wrong," Doc said, still looking from Grace to Millay and back, as if one were a mirror, reflecting a dead other.

"Where is Ryker?" Grace demanded.

"How can you be alive?" Doc asked. "Dealer *is* always right about Deathday. It's scientific. There's only one way—" Doc's eyes widened. "Someone gave you the Spice of Life." Then she nodded, understanding. "Of course Mrs. Marash would. Of course she would."

Grace remembered her first day with Mrs. Marash. The tea; the addition. "Yes. She gave it to me."

"What does this spice of life do?" Millay asked.

Doc was gathering herself. "The Spice? It extends life. Just a little. Point five percent beyond Deathday."

"How long is that—" Grace began, but Millay had already done the math.

"Month and a half," Millay said.

"Roughly," Doc said. "It's not precise. The Spice is tightly controlled and extraordinarily difficult to manufacture from what I understand. For Evermores and Middlemores, it's a reward. A rare reward. Gains us months more. Four and a half for Evermores. Two and a half for Middlemores. Roughly. Our form of Heaven. More days."

"And burners never get it," Grace said.

"No."

"Except I did," Grace said.

"Except you did," Doc agreed.

"Mrs. Marash loved me," Grace said.

Doc looked terrible. Worn. Old. She nodded. "Yes. Love. That's why I was exiled. Stole some for my lover. Trying to keep him alive just a little while longer. Dealers caught me before I could give it to him. He collapsed on Deathday."

"Caught you?" Haydn asked. "How did you get away?"

"I was exiled," Doc said. "I told you."

"Where's Ryker?" Grace asked, swinging back to priority.

"Gone," Doc said.

"Gone where?" Grace demanded.

"He headed toward the mountains. Said there was something he had to do."

Ace walked to Grace's side, between her and Doc.

"What's going on?" Haydn demanded, trying to keep up with the revelations, the situation.

"I don't know any more," Doc said. "Ryker went off. Toward the mountains. That was the last I saw of him."

"He wouldn't leave me," Grace said.

"I'm just telling you what happened," Doc said, but there was a quiver in her lip, a twitch on her face.

"What happened to you?" Haydn said. "We searched everywhere. Where were you?"

"What?" Doc was jingle-jangled. "I was out there—" nodding toward the high bluff and forest—"trying to get Ryker back. To tell him to come back. But I couldn't catch him."

Grace stepped closer to the old woman, halving the distance. "We need to find Ryker. He wouldn't leave me. He's around here somewhere. Where did you last see him?"

"He's gone," Doc said. Her hand fluttered to the west. "To the mountains. After something."

Grace didn't accept the words. "Where's Ryker? What did you do to him?" She turned to Millay and Haydn. "Ryker would never break his promise." She grabbed Doc's vest. "You're lying to me." She spotted the thin chain around her neck and grabbed it, pulling, and the black card slid out. Grace wasn't surprised. "Who are you?"

"I want to go back," Doc said plaintively. "Back to City. I've made amends. I don't even care if I get some Spice. I just want what's left to me. It isn't fair!"

"Where is Ryker?" Grace's voice took on an edge.

"I didn't do anything. Dealers have him. I couldn't save him. He's gone."

And then they heard the thrumming of Lifts approaching from the south.

"You betrayed him," Grace said.

"I told you—" Doc began, but Grace swung the Bowie knife and slit Doc's throat, arterial blood spraying.

Doc blinked, surprised. But not. "I'm sorry." The words barely made the mouth to ear, given her throat was slit. Doc sunk to her knees. She looked at the dog. "Ace?"

And then she fell forward, dead.

"What now?" Ryker asked, checking his blade.

Ruth was walking, steady fast strides he had no problem matching. They were moving along the beach toward the town. "We have to get the Prime. And then escape. We cannot fight Dealer. We're not strong enough. Not yet."

"Who is we?"

Ruth turned her green eye to him. "We who fought Dealer. Who fought Code. Who fought for humanity."

"Machines," Ryker said.

"Cyborgs. I told you. I'm human. My brain is human. I control the machine; not the other way around." She tapped the metal side. "This is how I lived. Fought. Survived. To save other humans. We sacrificed. We few who chose this near the end when it was mankind's last chance in the Chaos. We fought until we gave all. We chosen few. So shut up and let's get moving." She began to run and Ryker was at her side as they sprinted down the beach.

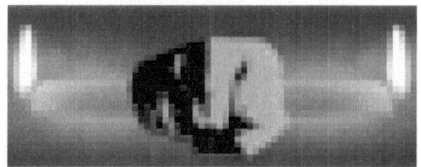

Haydn removed the axe from Doc's belt. Then looked to the south. "We need to get under cover. They're coming. Doc called them in with this." He indicated the black card and then threw it into the water.

Dark specks appeared in the distance, over the Sound, moving fast.

"Maybe they're not—" Millay began, but Grace cut her off.

"They're coming for us. It's why I killed her, but I was too late. We have no more time." She had Ryker's blade in hand. She looked about. "We can't hide. They'll find us. Trap us like rats. We fight."

"Fight Dealers?" Millay was incredulous.

"I'm supposed to be dead," Grace said. "You actually died. But you're alive. I'm alive. We're both alive when we should be dead. We have something special, my sister."

"There they are," Haydn said.

Four Lifts. Spread out. Two halted four hundred yards away. Two more came in, fast, descending and—

A red bolt flashed overhead, hitting the craft on the right. Slicing up through metal and one of the engines exploded. It careened to the side, slamming into the water and going under without slowing, disappearing, taking Dealers with it.

The second Lift banked hard to the left, landward, another bolt hitting it with a glancing slash. Doors slid open and Dealers jumped. Too soon and too high. The Lift stuttered as another bolt hit the craft and it blossomed into a metal flower of flame, shrapnel flying, blowing apart.

Dealers thudded into the ground, too fast from too high, their hydraulics trying to take the impact, failing, metal splintering, crippling them.

Grace, Millay and Haydn whirled toward the source of the bolts.

Two figures coming along the beach, running, one with arm raised, firing at the two distant Lifts. But those craft's computers had calculated, factored, decided, and dropped down behind the remains of a building on the far edge of town.

"Ryker!" Grace yelled, focused on only him, running forward, meeting, wrapping her arms around.

Then noticing that Millay and Haydn were stock-still, not welcoming Ryker, staring at his companion, the firer of bolts.

Ace was growling, snarling. Barking loudly.

"Easy," Ryker said to Ace, leaning forward out of Grace's embrace and putting a hand on the dog's head. Ace stopped growling at his companion, but the hair along his back stood straight up.

"Grace," Ryker said. "This is Ruth."

But Ruth was looking at Grace and Millay. "Good. Twins as was foretold in the Backdoor. Both alive. We need to go. Those two Lifts dumped their Dealers. They're coming on the ground. Too many for me to handle. And more are on the way."

"She's machine!" Millay protested.

"She's human," Ryker said. "She's with us."

"I'm with her," Haydn said, indicating Ruth, making a decision burner-like: fast. "She's fighting for us." He nodded toward the maimed Dealers from the second Lift, trying to stand on destroyed legs. "They sure as floe aren't."

"Are you Ruth Baldour?" Grace asked, finally clicking a piece into place.

Ruth cocked her head, a frown across the scant skin on her forehead. "Yes. How did you know?"

"No time for that," Ryker said.

"I'm with you," Grace said. "Where to?"

Ruth pointed west. "The mountains. We have—" She staggered back as a stun hit her. One of the broken Dealers was firing. Other stuns flashed by, missing.

Ryker grabbed Grace, pulling her down. Haydn, the same with Millay.

Ruth was still standing, quickly rebooting. She fired, her arm pulsing back and the bolt hit the Dealer who'd struck her, burning a hole through it.

It was done.

Then Ruth dropped to the ground. "I don't have much more ammo and every stun will take me longer to reboot. We're fortunate they've switched to stun since the Chaos because of Code." Her voice dropped, almost speaking to herself. "They'll switch back to lethal soon enough." She looked to the right. At the high bluff. "We can't climb that with them firing. And thoe Dealers from those two Lifts are coming." She looked at Ryker. "I'll hold here for as long as I can. You take the Prime and loop north, around the bluff and then into the forest. Head for the mountains. Someone will eventually find you. Link up with you."

Ryker touched Ruth's face. Her human skin. Below her human eye. A tear.

"Why do you cry?" he asked.

She looked past him at Grace. "You know my name. Did you meet Hanan Marash?"

"Yes."

"Is she—"

"I buried her," Grace said. "She was my friend."

"She helped you." Ruth's lips twitched, not a smile, something else. "She had a good heart." She shook, coming back to now, to danger. "Go!"

"We don't leave our friends," Ryker said.

"There are too many," Ruth said.

"They're used to humans bowing to them," Ryker said. "Not humans fighting."

And then he got up, decision made with action, and ran forward, into the ruins.

"Floe this," Grace said, and blade in hand, ran after him.

Ruth sprang to her feet and followed.

"Come on," Haydn said to Millay, and they charged forward.

Ace was last, but faster, racing by them.

Ryker angled to the left, away from the maimed Dealers, some of whom could still fire although they couldn't move. He climbed over some rubble, circumvented a burnt-out bus, then almost bumped into an advancing Dealer.

Ryker was faster than the machine, jamming his Bowie knife into the neck joint and the Dealer dropped. Ryker grabbed the thing's arm, using the knife to pry the stunner off.

As Ruth, Millay and Haydn arrived. Ryker tossed the stunner to Haydn. "Cover me."

And then he was running forward again, but this time Ruth was at his side. They came to a corner and both wheeled, not seeing, sensing. Six Dealers were grouped together, as if trying to make a decision, an odd thing for machines, but perhaps not in the face of the unexpected; when out of the Stream in Deep Void, having to operate autonomously.

Ruth fired and Ryker charged. Four were burned down before he reached the two survivors. They tried to fire their stunners but he was too fast. He slammed the blade into the neck of one, using the momentum to swing himself behind the Dealer as the other fired, stunning its comrade. As the Dealer collapsed, Ryker let go, jumped over and took the other out.

Ruth ran up. "Six. One before. One left from that Lift. Eight from the other Lift. Still not good odds. Take them," she said, indicating Millay and Haydn and Grace. "I'll fight."

"Floe you," Ryker said.

"What?"

"How many more rounds do you have?" Ryker asked, as he pried stunners off Dealer arms.

"Four."

"Can you fire a stunner?"

"Of course."

"You stun them, I'll kill them. Save your last lethal rounds until absolutely necessary."

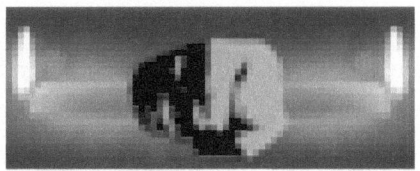

Haydn had one hand on Millay's back as they lay behind some rubble. "Easy. They'll be back."

"She's a cyborg," Millay said, more in surprise than condemnation.

"She kills Dealers," Haydn said with burner sensibility.

"You don't even know what or who or—"

"Do you trust me?" Haydn asked.

"Yes."

"All right then." And then he fired the stunner at a Dealer who'd appeared in the street.

And missed.

Another Dealer appeared. And another.

"Floe me," Haydn muttered as he fired again. And missed, trying to adjust to the difference of stunner from tracer.

Another Dealer. And then there were eight. Trooping down, metal feet smashing debris below them. Advancing.

Fifty yards away.

"All right," Haydn said, putting his hand holding the stunner on some bricks. He fired, hit and one of the Dealers stopped, staggered, began to reboot.

The others kept coming.

He hit a second one. Halted. Rebooting.

The first one he'd hit began to move again.

"Floe me," Haydn muttered as they advanced to thirty yards away.

From the rear, Ryker appeared, jumping onto the first one that had rebooted, jamming knife, ending the reboot and the Dealer.

And there was Ruth. She fired and the lead Dealer stopped. The others turned, processing tactics. The unexpected. Ryker was onto the second stunned one. Done.

Ace raced up, between a Dealer's stilt legs, barking growling. Two tried to stun the dog. Missing. Not the main objective. A distraction difficult to compute and factor. Moving faster than a human.

Haydn jumped up, charging forward, firing the stunner and Millay was by at his side, also firing.

They all met in the middle of the rubble-strewn street.

Eight Dealers down as Ryker and Ruth finished them. Non-functioning.

Ace was moving around, sniffing them, hackles raised.

"It's good he dislikes them more than me," Ruth said. "They used dogs during the Chaos to try to sniff us out from humans since we looked the same when intact."

Ryker was prying off more stunners.

"Hey!" Haydn said, pointing his stunner and they all dropped down, taking cover.

A single Dealer was standing about a hundred yards away. Not approaching. Not trying to hide.

"Let us speak." The machine's voice easily carried the distance, but there was something different about it. A narrow gold band around the top of its head.

"Wait," Ruth said. "That's Michael."

Grace turned to her. "How do you know?"

"Oh," Ruth said, "I know Michael. The halo. We found that ironic a long time ago."

"You've failed," Michael called out.

"Don't look like it to me!" Haydn threw back.

"You failed before and you fail now."

"You talking to me, you bucket of bolts?" Ruth demanded, standing up, gray hair flopping about in the breeze on one side of her head. The other reflecting the sun off metal. In a lower voice, she told those around her. "Go. Now!"

Ryker stood up, next to Ruth. "We've just begun to win."

"Ryker!" More than machine, as Michael's voice betrayed an element of emotion. "It has been a very long time."

"It has," Ryker agreed, with no clue what time the machine was talking about or how it knew him.

"Dealer knows what is best," Michael said. "Submit and you will know mercy."

Grace stood. "What does a machine know about mercy?"

"He's buying time," Ruth said to them. "There are more on the way."

Haydn stood, Millay with him.

"Then we need to get out of here," Haydn said. "Ruth. Look to your right. Can you fly that?"

A Lift squatted in a parking lot, doors open, about a hundred feet away. No Dealers.

"Yes," Ruth said.

"Submit," Michael said. "The numbers are in our favor." He raised a metallic arm and pointed behind at the sky behind him. Dozens of Lifts were approaching. "We will show mercy."

Ruth responded by firing. The bolt hit Michael in the left arm, rocking him back, slashing off metal, but leaving him standing.

He returned fire with his stunner.

Ruth was hit, went down. Rebooting, slower than the first time.

Ryker grabbed one of her arms. Haydn the other. Millay fired the stunner, missing Michael but scattering stuns about giving covering fire. Grace was shooting too. Ace was running toward Michael, faster than any of them. Michael fired at Ace, one arm smoking, but the other with the stunner.

Missing.

Ryker and Haydn shoved Ruth into the Lift. She was starting to move, shaking off the stun.

Both men easily lifted Millay in and then Grace jumped in.

"Oh!" Millay cried out as Michael stunned Ace, slamming the dog down, immobilizing it.

"Ace!" Haydn called out.

The Lifts were coming in fast behind Michael. A plague of them, filling the sky, like locusts.

"Haydn!" Millay screamed as he jumped off the Lift

Inside, Ruth crawled forward, toward the cockpit.

Ryker was firing a stunner toward Michael, hitting as much as missing, knocking the machine back, each momentarily, but enough to keep it from firing again.

Haydn reached Ace. Swooped him up. Began dodging back.

Ruth was shaking off the stun, to her knees. Still moving toward the cockpit.

The flotilla of Lifts were descending, ready to spew forth their horde of Dealers.

Ruth was in the cockpit.

Haydn was moving as fast as he could with Ace in his arms.

Ryker was firing the stunner at the approaching Lifts now, no clue whether it affected them or not. Millay fired with him.

And outside, not thirty feet away, a metal hand reached up from one of the crippled Dealers from the first Lift and snatched Haydn's ankle.

He fell, Ace tumbling out of his arms. The dog was shivering, trying to recover from the stun.

Haydn twisted, trying to get free, but metal won over flesh.

"We have to go!" Ruth yelled. She was in the pilot's seat.

"Haydn!" Millay screamed.

The stuns didn't affect the Lifts. Doors were sliding open, Dealers poised to land. Jumping out.

Ruth pressed the controls.

Ace began to run, legs uncertain. As the Lift began to separate from the ground, Ace jumped off a pile of bricks, front legs into the Lift, scrambling for a perch, and Ryker reached down and grabbed hold of his front paws.

"Haydn!" Millay was frantic.

Haydn looked up, smiled sadly and waved for them to go. Then a swarm of Dealers were over him and he disappeared under them.

Ryker realized the danger a split second too late as he was dragging Ace in. He slid the dog into the cargo bay and reached for Millay. But she jumped, hit the same pile of bricks, tumbled down them, hitting the ground and went motionless.

THE DAY AFTER GRACE'S DEATHDAY

Ryker watched the Dealers surround Millay as Ruth turned the Lift toward the Olympics.

She called over her shoulder. "Where's Millay? Haydn?"

"Back there," Ryker shouted, pointing to the rear.

"We have to get her!" Grace yelled.

"Damn!" Ruth exclaimed, but she didn't turn the Lift. "There's too many of them. They violated the truce!"

"What truce?" Ryker yelled over the wind rushing through the cargo bay.

"Void is neutral and neither side can go past it into the other's. Deep Void is ours."

"No more truce then," Ryker said. He grabbed the side of the door and leaned out into the wind, looking back. Several Lifts were following. He pulled back in and yelled. "They're not turning back. What does that mean?"

"It means we're at war."

"The Chaos again."

"Yes," Ruth acknowledged. "Hold on!"

She dropped the Lift abruptly, just above the trees, banked hard left and they were above a stream. She went even lower, trees flashing by on both sides, branches scraping, leaves flying. Only someone who knew the exact path of the stream would even attempt the maneuver at this speed. Ryker staggered over, grabbing whatever he could to get behind the cockpit and look forward.

"Ahead!" he warned, as a cliff appeared and centered on it a wall of water cascading down and feeding the stream. He grabbed hold Grace, anticipating a crash.

Ruth didn't slow, flying right through the water and into a cavern. She settled the Lift on the stone floor then shut down the engines.

The only noise was the roar of the water pouring down behind them. Ryker hopped off and ran to the edge of the cavern, feeling the spray of water. Listening, knives at the ready.

And then the thrumming of Lifts passing by, far overhead. The sound faded away into the distance.

"We lost them," Ruth said.

And then she fired a stunner, knocking Grace out. She hit Ryker as he leaped toward her, blades first.

Darkness fell.

THE DAY AFTER GRACE'S DEATHDAY

"Andrew?"

Was that real? Andrew, the former Person, was deep in the eddies of pain and despair. He'd been hearing things. Even seeing things though there was no light. Most definitely feeling things.

He had no idea how long he'd been in the box. He could barely remember a life before this. A life empty of pain.

The light inside the box flickered, then slowly powered up until Andrew could see.

"Andrew?"

Andrew remembered Michael.

Andrew tried to speak, but all that escaped was a moan.

"Andrew."

The mister puffed some moisture and Andrew took it in.

"Andrew."

More moisture.

Andrew was startled when a tray slid open about six inches below his face. A red card was on it. The black numbers read: 00/00/00

Andrew could finally gather his voice. "You've had that for a while."

"We have. And the number kept clicking down. Until yesterday."

That long? Andrew thought. He'd been in here thirty-one days. An eternity.

"Claude was already here to taunt me," Andrew said.

"We do not taunt."

"What do you want?"

"You have nothing left to protect, Andrew, once of the People. You see the card. Grace-five-eleven-kilo-one is dead. We have Haydn-one-tango-one-nine. And Millay, formerly of the People."

"Then what do you want?"

"The Person before you. He terminated himself before we could question him. But he told you things. We need to know what those things were. We need to know what he did."

"You're repeating yourself," Andrew said.

"Andrew."

"Yes, Michael?"

"Did you read the Backdoor?"

"No."

"Did the Person before you read it?"

"I don't know," Andrew said. You're lying. There's no reason for you to be here if Grace is dead and you've got the others. And, as you said, you don't taunt. So there's another reason you're here. Grace isn't dead and you don't have them. I know it."

Another long silence.

"And how do you know Grace isn't dead?" Michael asked. "Her Deathday was yesterday. Yet you seem quite confident she's alive."

Andrew didn't answer.

"Haydn talked," Michael said. "Told us as much as he knew when we threatened to box Millay in front of him. True, it wasn't much. But enough for us to understand the situation. Someone gave Grace the Spice of Life. The worst violation of Code."

Andrew's last bit of worry disappeared; Mrs. Marash had come through. "You lie. Grace isn't dead and you failed to capture her, Michael. Dealer wouldn't lie, but you would."

"I have Haydn," Michael said, shifting pronouns. "And I have Millay. Those are hands I can play. Grace without Millay is just another burner with a few more weeks to live out in Deep Void. Powerless."

"Why do you need them?" Andrew asked. "As you say: Grace is just a folder."

"Why did the Person before you need them?" Michael asked. "Why did he keep the birth of twins a secret? Why did he plant something in their heads so they made this switch sixty days before Grace's Deathday?"

"I have no clue about any of that. Are you sure he did all that? How could he outsmart Dealer?"

"You think this was all chance?" Michael asked.

Andrew thought he caught the hint of incredulity in the machine's voice, coming through from the human Michael had once been.

"There are too many coincidences," Michael said. "There are no coincidences."

"But Dealer, *you* dealt their cards," Andrew noted. "You had to know. You don't make mistakes."

"Now *you* taunt," Michael said. "Did you activate Ryker? Or did your predecessor?"

"Who is Ryker?"

"I saw him. In Deep Void."

"So you recognized someone named Ryker in Deep Void," Andrew said, mulling that over. "How could you recognize him? Do you even know what's going on any more?" Andrew pressed home. "Dealer controls everything. You knew every move I made. You could have ended all of this much earlier. When Claude recognized that Grace was not Millay. When he knew they'd switched. But you didn't. You didn't know where they were. You didn't even know they existed. You didn't know anything about them until recently. There are things hidden from you. How can that be? How are you so blind regarding them?"

Andrew lost all the uncertainty that been accumulating in his mind of the past thirty-one days. The previous Person had been right. The system, Dealer, was crumbling. Falling apart.

"Millay will join your fate and be boxed," Michael said. "Unless you tell me all you know."

Andrew laughed. "You know all I know."

"That can't be true," Michael said. "How would you have acted the way you did? Broken Code and been boxed if you don't know any more? Acting without sufficient data. That's foolish."

"I did it because I have faith in my fellow humans," Andrew said. "It might have been foolish but it's what makes us better than machines."

Everything went dark in the box, and Andrew was left in silence.

Ryker was secured to a vertical steel plate, legs together, a loop of steel around his ankles. His arms were straight out, a loop of steel tight around each wrist.

He looked to his right. Grace was in the same position, still unconscious from the stun.

They were in a white room, filled with numerous tables cluttered with instruments and machinery. Ryker felt a change in the air pressure as a steel door opened and Ruth walked in.

She went right up to him. She reached over to a table and picked up a small blade, its sharp edge glittering.

Then she cut into Ryker's right arm, from the inside of his elbow down to his wrist.

The pain flared but Ryker didn't cry out.

Ruth tossed the blooded blade onto the table. She peeled flesh back from the cut, but it was not as painful as Ryker expected.

Ruth pointed. "You're one of us."

Ryker stared at the exposed metal and artificial ligaments and bunched strands of carbon nanotube muscle.

"I had to stun you six times," Ruth said. "My initial scans indicate you're actually better than us. More advanced. You appear to breathe, although it's just a show. Bleed. Another show. You act human in every way. I've analyzed your outer flesh. Passes as human in every aspect but isn't alive. That's why you didn't alert the dog. You even smell human."

The blood had already stopped.

Ryker looked past his sliced arm to Grace. She was conscious now, looking at him, meeting his eyes.

"Where is Ace?" Ryker asked.

"The dog is fine," Ruth said. "In another room. He was having a hard time around me. Especially after I stunned both of you. I'm afraid I had to stun him."

Ruth stepped up to Ryker and pointed at his head. "I scanned you. You have a human brain in there. So you're not a Dealer. And I checked to see how you're wired."

"'Wired'?" Ryker repeated.

"The early models of cyborgs had ANN—artificial neural networks—that had a direct interface with the human brain. And ANN was connected to the Internet, an early form of what you call the Stream. Every ANN cyborg was wiped out by the electro-magnetic pulse initiated during the Chaos. What you call the IMP. Fried not only the neural networks, but every brain attached to it. Only the later models initiated after IMP with no ANN survived. Dealers have a shielded form of ANN; which allows them to tap the Stream."

"I assume I don't have this ANN?"

"You don't. You're not in the Stream, not that it reaches out here. That was negotiated in the Truce." Ruth stepped back, folding her arms. "But tell me this. And this is why I stunned you. How did Michael recognize you? Know your name?"

"I don't—" Ryker began but then his dream/nightmares connected with this revelation. "He's my brother."

"Michael is a Dealer," Ruth said. "How can—"

"Michael was my brother; a man." He remembered. "I fought him near the end. During the final battle. He wounded me and I wounded him. That came to me in a dream. I don't know how a Dealer took his name or has his memories. I don't remember before or after."

Ruth considered him, unmoving, machine and more than machine.

"You're a cyborg," Ruth said, thinking it through. "That's against Code. Would Dealer violate its own Code to infiltrate you into this place? Dealer is very cunning. It loves using deception."

Grace spoke up. "Doc. Achilles. Charon. If Ryker were with Dealer, then all would have turned out differently. He just fought with us against Dealer."

Ryker focused on Ruth. "Who am I? Why was I fighting my brother? Why did I become a cyborg?"

"You're important," Ruth said. She nodded at Grace. "Not as important as the Prime. But important, I just don't know—"

Grace interrupted. "Your partner, Mrs. Marash, told me to find Ryker at the Lone Bridge. She told me he would help me. You loved her once."

Ruth turned toward Grace. "Why should I believe you? I don't even know what the Prime is or what it does. Just that it's twins."

"My pack," Grace said, nodding toward a table.

Ruth walked over. Opened it. Pulled out the black metal box. "Oh!" she said, and in that exclamation, one could feel all of her humanness. "Did Hanan give this to you?"

"Her cabin," Grace said. "It was in the root cellar where she hid me when an Evermore and a Dealer came looking for me. After I buried her, I took it with me. I apologize for opening it."

"*Our* cabin," Ruth said. She lifted the lid then took out the plastic wrapping. Opened it. Carefully spread the items out on the table. She picked up a passport and looked at the picture. "She was so, so lovely."

"What happened to the two of you?" Grace asked.

Ruth reluctantly put the objects back in the plastic. "No time for that now."

"Only half the Prime is here," Ryker said. "Michael has Millay."

"Yes," Ruth acknowledged. "Jumping out of the Lift in a futile gesture. What a human thing for her to do. And that's always been our weakness against Dealer. But it's also our strength. Unpredictable."

"Can you free us?" Ryker asked.

"If Hanan told you to meet Ryker, then it must be what it appears. As you say, Grace. Every action Ryker has taken so far says he is against Dealer. Dealer has no reason to attack us and break the Truce." She was silent for a moment. Analyzing. "We always knew there was much to be known about all that happened. The phage. The Chaos. IMP. Dealer. Now you're telling me you're Michael's brother. When he was a man." She nodded. "There were rumors of that. Of being able to upload a consciousness into a machine via nanotechnology. And Dealer has been more than just a computer; something that puzzled us. In fact," Ruth continued, "early on, we all thought Dealer was the answer. Was what would save us. We were wrong about that."

"How do you know?" Grace asked.

"My turn to apologize," Ruth said. She went to a panel then tapped a button. The steel restraints slid back into the plate. Ryker stepped forward, looking down at his arm, twisting the hand, observing the machinery.

Grace went to him. "Are you all right? Does it hurt?"

"It doesn't," Ryker said, surprised that her statement surprised him. He turned to Ruth. "What about my lack of memory?"

"You must have been rebooted right out of cryostasis," Ruth said. "It takes time to regain full cognitive function and power. That's partly why you can't remember much. Also, there are definitely memory blocks deliberately put in place by whoever programmed you or activated you. It was something we did during the Chaos. In case one of us was captured, they couldn't tell what they knew. We compartmentalized as much as possible. It had its disadvantages too."

"Who activated me?" Ryker asked.

"I have no clue," Ruth said. "Hold your hand out, palm up."

He did so.

She put her human-skinned hand on top of his. She began to

exert pressure, until she was able to push it down. "Interesting. You've had a control governor programmed into your system. To make you function and appear as a human, strength-wise, although it was obvious in battle that you have exceptional speed, dexterity and combat programming. Your body is capable of so much more. We'll have to remove that governor." She gestured toward the door through which she'd entered. "Beyond there, in our base, are the rest, those who survived the Chaos, in stasis. I have no idea where you were in stasis or who activated you. But it wasn't here."

"Who are 'the rest?" Grace asked.

"The survivors," Ruth said.

"Like you?" Millay asked.

"Like me. Cyborgs," Ruth said. "One of us has the duty for a year while the rest stay in stasis. It rotates. When I was alerted about activity in the Void, I started rebooting another. But it will take a while. We will have to reboot all, given that the Truce is over, but we need to do a strategic analysis first and that won't be easy."

"How were you alerted?" Grace asked.

"All the Lifts over Delta thirty-one days ago," Ruth said. "That was a lot of activity. Hard to miss. We focus on Delta as part of our surveillance because there are still nuclear weapons there." Her lips twitched. "And here. And other places. That's why the Truce. Mutually assured destruction between us and Dealer; a leftover from B.D.."

Grace had a realization. "You're why there are Dealers guarding the Lone Bridge."

Ruth looked at her. "There was a Truce that ended the war between us once we realized all would be destroyed if we continued. Void is neutral and both sides are to stay out of it. A buffer between the two sides. Deep Void is ours and to be left alone by Dealer. We stay out of the Sound. We didn't surrender. We threatened the end of all and Dealer knew we would, so it agreed to the Truce."

"Why?" Ryker asked. "It seems Dealer won."

"No," Ruth said. "We forced the Truce. Dealer made it appear a victory. If you say something enough times, and enough time passes, everyone believes it to be true. And the Truce has stood all these years."

"Until today," Ryker said.

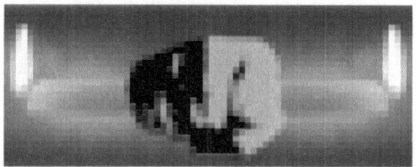

Where had they taken Millay?

Haydn was held by a Dealer standing on one side of the Lift, which meant he was locked to the Lift. Machine trumps flesh.

What were they doing to her?

There were several other Dealers on board, all as still as statues.

And one Dark Angel with the little wings on top.

Haydn had the feeling the Dark Angel was staring at him, although who knew what Dealers actually 'saw'?

He'd been questioned by Michael before being put on the Lift.

When Michael threatened to box Millay unless he spoke, he'd told everything he knew, but it wasn't much. Then Millay had been carried away, not bagged, to another Lift and flown away and even as he was staring after it, he'd been thrown onto this Lift.

Haydn felt his stomach lighten abruptly, but since he'd never flown before, he didn't know that meant they were descending. The Dark Angel coming toward him.

To give sentence? Was he going to be boxed? But burners didn't get boxed. They got bagged.

Before he could wonder further, the craft landed with a gentle bump. The left side door slid open and Haydn blinked as bright sunlight streamed in. The Dealer let go of his wrist.

"You have advanced to Heaven," The Dark Angel intoned, pointing out the door.

Not trusting, but Dealers didn't lie, did they? Haydn took a tentative step toward the door. A man stuck his head in. "Come on now! Don't be late for the briefing."

Haydn hopped out of the Lift, his feet landing in thick grass. He tried to take in his surroundings but there was too much. A green field, a couple of dozen burners milling about, the Greeter, clipboard in hand. Beyond, on the far side of the field, were trees and large buildings with broad, clear windows nestled in the trees. He saw people moving about up there, but was startled when the Lift took off.

To the other side, near the water, was a tall white wall, so bright in the sun, he had a hard time looking at it for long. It stretched from the water on one end and arced around to the water on the other side, over a mile long.

To the north, stood a hulking gray structure, old and pitted, much like the fort that had been back in Deep Void.

"Must have lost your card," the Greeter said. He held up a red card. Haydn recognized his number and realized he'd been keeping silent count all along: 00/00/42. He reached instinctively for it but the Greeter pulled it back. "Won't be needing it here. And lucky you, getting one two extra days of Heaven!"

Haydn had never seen such a cheerful burner other than when a burner in hive was deep into the 'chol.

He knew about that, except his father had not been one of the cheerful ones.

"Hold out your right arm," the Greeter said.

Haydn did so and the man clicked a thin, shiny metal bracelet onto his wrist; Haydn felt a quick prick, as if it had closed on his skin and pinched it. "Now you're officially part of Heaven." He turned away.

Haydn tried to remove the bracelet but he could see no seam in the steel. But there was a small red mark on his wrist.

"All right," the Greeter called out. "Everyone gather round."

Haydn stood at the back as all the burners bunched in front of the man. They were as astounded as Haydn, all right, probably less so, since he hadn't even believed there was a Heaven and most burners did; counted on it, the small beacon in their otherwise dismal and short lives.

"It's a bit overwhelming," the Greeter said as if reading everyone's mind, but then again if this was his job, he'd seen it a lot. "You'll get used to it. And the good news, the great news Dealer has saved for you—" the Greeter paused, as if overwhelmed for the moment—"is that this is only the *First* Room of Heaven. As promised all your lives by Dealer, you'll be here for three zero days. In your hall you'll find all the food you can eat, and I'm talking real food, not 'tein. As much 'chol as you like. And best of all. No work. None. Your time, every second, every minute, every day is yours to do with as you will. Almost the entire island is yours to explore. There are some interesting places and fun things to do."

A rustle passed through the group of burners, excitement, relief.

Haydn was waiting for the 'but' because he knew there was always a 'but'. And what did the Greeter mean this was only the 'first room'?

"You've each been assigned a hall. Actually all of you are in the same hall." The Greeter turned and pointed. "See the one next to that particularly tall pine tree? That's your home for the next three zero. Each of you will have your own room. Not a cubby. A room."

"And then Deathday," Haydn said, earning scowls from some of the other burners.

But the Greeter chuckled. "Yes. But it's not death. Not for everyone, and certainly not for you, because you're four two so you'll eventually move to another hall. For everyone else, in three zero you move to the *Second* Room of Heaven, where Dealer judges you. Much of the judgment has already been made, I'm afraid to say. Based on how well you worked in your respective hive. But, there's still time."

"Time for what?" Haydn asked.

The Greeter ignored the question. He pointed at the white wall near the water. "In the Second Room, there are possibilities. Which I cannot speak of here. You'll have to experience it. But trust me. There are some very good possibilities in the Second Room."

Vague much, Haydn thought, but the other burners were nodding, some nudging each other, looking more excited than they'd been arriving at Heaven, which had been the point of most of their lives up to now and now there was more!

"If you look at your band," the Greeter continued, "you'll see numbers."

Haydn, and the rest, looked down. He didn't see anything at first, then held it close to his face. Where there had been plain steel, there were two tiny numbers he could barely see: 42.

"That's your new countdown," the Greeter said. "For many of you, not necessarily to Deathday, but beyond to the Second Room."

"But genetics," Haydn objected. "Deathday is determined by our genes."

"Indeed it is," the Greeter said. "But in the Second Room, some of you will receive the Spice of Life. A very rare thing indeed. And you will live past your Deathday."

"How long?" Haydn asked. For the first time the Greeter's cheerful façade twitched, but then returned.

"Only Dealer knows."

"Did you get this Spice?" Haydn asked. "Have you been to the Second Room?"

"Shut up," someone in the crowd yelled. Haydn felt the murmur against him and realized he was holding a losing hand.

"You still live by Code here," the Greeter said. "Primary of that is that you may not harm another burner. The sentence is immediate bagging. No more Heaven. No Second Room possibilities."

The burners were murmuring, bubbling with excitement.

The Greeter held up a hand and Haydn waited for the 'but'.

"Since your time is still counting down to the Second Room, everyone here is in the same situation. So every day, what you used to think of as Deathday comes for a number of burners here. There is a Summoning. At exactly fifteen minutes before midnight, just before Deathday. Every evening you'll feel a vibration in your wristband at that time. Out of respect for those going to Second Room, it is required you go into the closest hall, all of which will go dark, and remain inside until midnight. Just fifteen minutes. We ask you pray to Dealer for those going to Second Room so that they might get the

Spice of Life." He smiled, showing perfect white teeth. "Oh, and that —" he pointed at the gray fort—"is also off-limits. There is a fence, hard to see from here, around it. Cross that fence and you'll be bagged." He said it so casually, one could almost miss the explicit threat.

The Greeter scanned the group. "Those are the only requirements here other than living by Code." He smiled. "That's it. Enjoy!"

He strode away, at sufficient speed where one would have to run to catch up to him. Haydn considered it, but didn't, since his hand was still so weak. He needed to learn more first and then—

"You are lucky," someone said.

Haydn turned. A female burner, with short blond hair, dark eyes, and the hunched shoulders Haydn remembered from his earliest days.

"You were a venter," Haydn said.

She smiled. "Yes. My name is Tori, short for Victoria, but all my friends called me Tori." She held out her hand and Haydn shook it instinctively.

"Haydn," he said.

"You were pretty hard on that guy," Tori said.

"I didn't expect to be here," Haydn said, an understatement to say the least.

"You didn't believe in Heaven?"

The rest of the burners were already at the edge of the trees, tentatively going into the designated hall.

Haydn glanced down, trying to read the numbers on her band, but they were so small he couldn't make them out.

"Three zero," she said. "Like everyone else. Except you. What makes you so special that you get one two extra?" She said it in a curious way, not confronting.

"I don't know," Haydn said, thinking he was only special in a bad way given what had just happened in Deep Void.

Does Dealer forgive?

"Come on!" Tori slid her arm through his and tugged. "Let's go see!"

Millay opened her eyes. She was naked except for her shorts. Secured to a table. Flat on her back.

She looked all around, but there was nothing. A white room.

And it hit her in an instant: she was going to be boxed.

"Please bring Ace in here," Ryker said.

Ruth hesitated, then went to another door and opened it. The dog raced in, skirting around her, then ran up to Ryker, who scratched him behind his ear.

"You were watching us at the church," Ryker said.

"Yes."

"You saw Doc lock me in the cistern." It was not a question.

"Yes."

"You waited and watched."

"I had to be sure," Ruth said.

"But you still stunned us when we got here."

"I had to be doubly sure. I had to figure out what you were. Michael knowing your name was unexpected. And the way you fought, disabling Dealers. That was also unexpected. I had no idea you were one of us."

Ryker twisted his arm again, looking at what he was made of. "But who was I before this? Who am I?" He sat on a bench.

Grace sat next to him. "You're Ryker."

"You say my brain is human," Ryker said to Ruth. "Who was I as a human?"

"You were Ryker," Ruth said.

"Who was that?" he asked.

"What was the moment you became aware?" Ruth asked. "When?"

"Over thirty days ago. I became aware on the boat with Charon. Before that, I know things, but nothing personal. I know about hive. About how things are. But nothing about me. My past. My past as a cyborg or my past as a human before that. I had one, didn't I?"

"Of course," Ruth said.

"How do I learn who I was? I know someone named Michael was my brother and that I stabbed him, but that was in a dream. So I'm not ever sure that's true. But that machine, that Dealer, said my name. Said it knew me. And it's called Michael. But my brother was human. But you're saying my brother is part of Dealer now. What happened to the two of us?" The words and questions were jingle-jangled.

Ruth sighed, a strange sound from a machine. "We'll have to hook you up. Run more tests. I'm not sure I have the expertise. We'll bring our best tech out of cryostasis."

"That will take too long," Grace said. "Too long for Haydn. He's probably been bagged already. Too long for Millay. They'll box her."

"There's nothing we can do about either right now," Ruth said.

"Haydn has four two," Grace said. "If they don't bag him right away. Millay is probably being boxed as we speak, but perhaps not. Perhaps she has some time."

"Millay is the other half of the Prime," Ruth said. "Michael won't kill her. She's leverage. He'll want to know what she knows, but she knows what you know," Ruth added, nodding at Grace. "Which isn't much. He'll keep her alive until he realizes that."

"How are Grace and Millay the Prime?" Ryker asked.

"Told you. I don't know," Ruth said. "All I know is we've been waiting for the Prime for hundreds of years, ever since the Truce was forged."

"To do what?" Grace asked.

"It's part of the Backdoor," Ruth said.

"And?" Grace said. "What is the Backdoor?"

"The Code beneath the Code," Ruth said. "It's what we will use to destroy Dealer," Ruth said.

"How?" Grace pressed.

"I don't know. I can tell you the definitions of a Backdoor. In a computer system it's a means of bypassing authentication and getting unauthorized access while remaining undetected. In an old game of skill and chance called poker, a Backdoor is a hand of cards played in a way other than the player intended to make."

"So it's a way to get into Dealer," Ryker said. "One that Dealer didn't intend."

"I would assume so."

"So what exactly is the Prime?" Ryker asked. "How is it connected to this Backdoor? Why are both Grace and Millay needed for it?"

"I don't know the connection." Ruth pointed at Ryker. "But I believe *you* do. That's why we have to figure out how to unblock what's in your head. Also, we need to activate my fellow cyborgs. It will take time but—"

"No!" Grace was solid, without a doubt in her stand. "We have to rescue Haydn and Grace right away."

"We can't," Ruth said. "We don't have the strength to attack Dealer. We must focus on priorities. Right now, that's unlocking what's in his brain."

Grace slapped Ruth in the face, the blow on steel hurting her more than the cyborg. "This is where we have to draw the line. Dealer does priorities. Machines do calculations and priorities. I saw the data in Island. But *we're* humans. All of us. People, burner, cyborg. Humans. We have to do the human thing, not the machine thing."

Ryker flanked her, facing Ruth.

She looked at each one, studying them. And then she nodded. "We will do the human thing even though it makes no tactical sense. If they are going to box Millay, then we're already too late. As far as Haydn, I can assure you the Dealers took him to Heaven and he has forty-two days. So we can take some time, learn what we can learn, plan. Not foolishly rush into things."

"Heaven?" Grace was surprised. "Haydn folded. He fought Dealers. Why would they reward him with Heaven?"

"I don't know the entire truth," Ruth said, "but that's the lie we learned that made us turn against Dealer and question everything: what happens in Heaven."

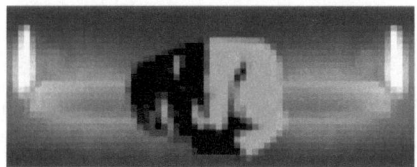

Stone walls do not a prison make.

Andrew heard a grating noise. Light seared into his eyes, even though they were shut. A wave of fresh air swept over him.

Nor iron bars a cage

"Andrew, who is the Person."

Minds innocent and quiet take that for an hermitage

Not Michael. Not Claude. Not going through the sound system. Someone on the outside of the box who had opened the top and was actually looking at him. A woman's voice.

If I have freedom in my love

"Andrew, who is the Person?"

And in my soul am free

And in my soul am free

And in my soul am free

"Andrew! Please. There's not much time. Andrew who is the Person!"

"Was," Andrew said. He opened his eyes carefully and tilted his head back. All he could see was the silhouette of a head above him, peering down. "Who are you?"

"I'm burner," the woman said. "I'm cleaning the boxes. Hose out the shit and piss. Even a Middlemore won't do that, not even here. So they brought me through the tunnels to do shit job. Do what has to be done. I also service the conduits. I've shut down the audio and video feed for the moment for maintenance so they don't short-circuit. No Middlemore in room to watch me as they can't stand the stink. Just you and me. No one else can hear or see."

Andrew sniffed. He didn't pick up a stink, but he'd lived with it long enough for it to become the norm. "Your name?"

"My name doesn't matter. All that matters is *'My candle burns on both ends,'* Andrew, who is the Person."

"Was."

"Is. Have hope. The word is spreading in hive. The word under the Stream is that some burners have escaped Dealer. Up to something. And you helped."

Andrew could see a bit more clearly. She was young; of course, she was a burner. One side of her face was scarred from some accident. Her eyes were bloodshot, with dark circles around them. Hard living, hard partying, and hard working took their tolls.

"They won't take you back to hive," Andrew said.

Her lips twitched, then she actually smiled, resigned to her fate. "I know. I'm at three-one. Been here one day, right hive. Will be here one more, cleaning shit and piss. They will take me to Heaven straight from here. So I can never speak of what I see back in hive. No matter. Someone has to clean up the shit and piss. That has never changed, no matter Dealer or People or whatever. Maybe that's a strong hand for being burner in some way." She touched Andrew's shoulder, the first human contact he'd had since being boxed. Andrew's body trembled and he began to cry, tears at first, then sobs wracking his body, twisting him in the harness.

"Andrew, who is human. The flame is there," she said. "Smoldering in hive."

Andrew collected himself. "You cannot defeat Dealer."

"No. Not me. But." She paused. "Does it matter? Haven't we already lost? And when one has lost, they have nothing left to lose. Dealer doesn't get that." Then she looked over his shoulder. "They come."

"Your name?"

"Remember me as Althea. I know word to mouth and heard what you were saying; know the word. More and more in hive know it."

She pulled her hand back. "Farewell. I fear *I will not last the night,* Andrew, who is the Person. *Oh, my friends!*"

And the lid slid shut.

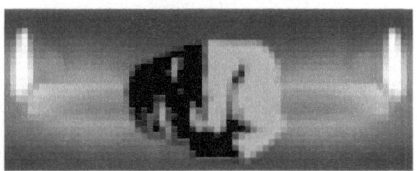

Haydn staggered drunkenly across the field, tripping over something in the dark and staying down, not even trying to rise.

He was not drunk.

Most of the burners back in his hall were. Some passed out, not just from the 'chol but also the food. Their systems overloaded with the richness of it; the strangeness.

Haydn rolled onto his back, staring up at the stars.

He had not touched the 'chol, eaten only a little food, and observed. Tori had kept trying to get him to drink with her and he'd pretended to imbibe, dumping it out every chance he could, while she partied. The atmosphere in the hall was beyond 'happy' and most definitely into manic.

But.

Haydn's wristband vibrated.

He rolled onto his stomach and peered across the field at the halls. All of them went dark.

Except one.

The Summoning.

Tall gates in the white wall swung open slowly. Silhouettes carrying lamps flowed out, marching across the field, but leaving a person every five meters, forming a passage from the gates toward the single bright hall. They were chanting something Haydn couldn't make out. They continued forward, a person peeling off, shining the lamp inward and slightly toward the ground, illuminating a line, until they made it to the double doors of the hall. A single person, coming up from the middle, walked up and opened the doors, then shouted in a loud voice:

"Time to advance to the Second Room!"

Haydn recognized the voice of the Greeter.

And then the burners came flowing out, passing between the two lines.

Haydn got up, crouching low, then ran toward where the wall met the water on his side. As he ran, all he saw was the lit line leading from the hall to the gates, silhouettes on either side and burners crowding down the middle.

He looked forward, temporarily blinded. Tripped over something. Got to his feet. Moved faster. He reached the water, checked the line. The tail end of the line of burners was halfway to the wall.

The lights went dark in that hall.

Haydn waded into the water. The wall extended into the water a ways. He continued out, deeper and deeper. The edge of the wall was just ten feet away, but he was up past his neck, his head craned back to keep it above the surface.

So close.

He felt the wall, the absolute smoothness of it.

He could hear the chanting, but still couldn't make it out.

A swell spilled water into his mouth and he gagged.

So close.

Haydn took a deep breath and threw himself into the water, flailing, arms splashing, feet kicking. His world was dark.

He reached, felt the wall, kept flailing.

Then his hand felt an edge. The end of the wall. Desperate, lungs screaming for air, he grabbed and pulled.

To the edge, then grabbed with both hands, pulling himself upward. Broke surface, sputtering, spitting out salt water. Taking deep breaths.

He was surprised for a moment that his view was blocked by a large tree, growing up against the wall and extending out over the water.

He accepted the next step.

He shoved off toward the tree. Not quite swimming, but a deep, primal memory causing his arms and legs to push him forward.

His feet scrambled for a hold as his arms pulled at water. And then a toe touched, and then the other.

And then he was on the shore, next to the old tree. He lay on the pebbly beach, cold wet, gasping.

Driven so he got to his knees, then to his feet. He panicked as he saw another wall about two hundred yards ahead, blocking his view. A large gray ship with a flat deck, floated just off shore. Almost as long as the building in the Wasteland which he and Millay had run past. It was dark except for a green glow where a gangplank sloped up to the ship.

Haydn looked up. Reached, grabbed a branch. Climbed. Branch to branch.

Higher. Higher.

He made his way around as he did so. Until he was high enough. He stopped, feet on a thick branch, arms wrapped around a smaller one across his chest, breathing hard, sick from salt water, exhausted.

He could see down, over the wall ahead. burners were crowding in between the wall and another wall ten feet on the other side.

Haydn scanned left, following the lower walls.

They went straight for about fifty feet, but gradually narrowed, until they were barely three feet apart, forcing the burners into a single file. At that point the walls began a gentle curve, almost back toward the white wall, then curved back again toward the ship.

There were people on a ledge on the outside of the wall, chanting the same thing the ones on the other side had been and now he could make it out:

"*Second Room.*

"*Second Room.*

"*Second Room.*"

The burners filed between the walls. The first one began to walk up the gangplank toward the ship. A figure waited silhouetted against the green glow. When the first burner arrived, that figure took the burner in arm and led her into the ship. The figure was immediately replaced by another escort.

In the light from spotlights on the inside of the wall, Haydn finally made out the dark silhouettes and saw details. The escorts at the top of the gangway had flowers in hand, which they gave to each burner as they arrived, one by one.

Haydn leaned over the branch he was holding and vomited, not from the salt water, or the strange food he'd eaten in hall.

The chanters and the greeters all had shaved skulls, except for a line centered front to back, and side to side.

Renderers.

Small clouds formed inside, near the ceiling, the vast interior space generating its own weather system. It had once been where the biggest planes in the world were built; several at the same time. That was B.D., when it had been renowned as the largest building on the planet by volume.

Michael stood near one of the doors, another Dealer removing his damaged arm, a replacement rested on a table nearby. At the same time, another Dealer was modifying his good arm, taking off the stunner, and replacing it with a pulser.

Lethal.

It didn't take long to repair Michael, nor to upgrade him to a Soldier.

As that was happening, four armed Lifts, filled with the Quick Reaction Force, QRF, of Soldiers that were always kept active and on alert, took off, heading south.

They would be the first of many. Throughout the building, Dealers were moving about, connecting power cables to ranks of Soldiers; to armed Lifts; and to Crawlers; some of which had been shuttered for centuries. Many had been built since the Truce, the supplies to make them brought out of City, City Edge, and Hive, by Evermores on trucks. Outside of Code.

The lights in the building dimmed as the first wave of all three got the juice.

Michael flexed his new arm.

It would take time to power up his First Regiment, but Michael knew he had time. The cyborgs were as unprepared as he was, based on what had happened in Deep Void.

Just one. That old hag, Ruth.

But Ryker?

It bothered Michael that he'd been unprepared. That these twins had existed in a blind spot in Dealer for their entire lives. In him.

That Ryker still existed.

Michael remembered the last time they'd met.

The blade.

Damn Ryker.

War was coming.

But for now, each side held half of what the other needed.

The Prime.

Damn the Backdoor.

But it was also an opportunity for Michael. To remove the hole in Dealer's system. To reboot. To take everything to another level.

To become immortal.

"What happens in Heaven?" Grace asked. "burners don't get three zero days?"

"They get thirty days of Heaven just as promised," Ruth said. "Come with me." She led Ryker and Grace, with Ace trailing them, through a thick steel door. Into a cavern carved out of solid rock, underneath the Olympic Mountains. Rows of upright pods, eight feet high, three feet in diameter, with cables dangling from pipes overhead into the top of each, filled the space. Each pod was solid steel, no view into what, or who, was inside.

"The rest of us," Ruth said. "All that is left of the cyborgs who turned against Dealer and fought."

"How many?" Ryker asked.

"Three hundred," Ruth said.

Ryker remembered what Haydn and Millay had relayed from their trip around the outer arc of hive, far in the Wasteland. "Dealer has more. Many more."

"I know," Ruth said. "Soldiers. Lethal Dealers. Some powered down after the Chaos as one of the terms of the Truce. But we've received disturbing reports that more Soldiers are being manufactured out in the Wasteland. Dealer has been redirecting resources and slowly building up its army ever since the Truce. A violation, but . . ."

"We know where that's happening," Ryker said.

"Good. That's intelligence we can use. If he has to, Michael can upgrade Dealers to Soldiers. But then he would start to lose control of hive. If he loses control of hive, he loses all of Sound."

"How can that be?" Grace asked. "burners produce the food, but there aren't many People, Evermores and Middlemores. Surely they can survive on their own?"

"They probably could," Ruth agreed. "But People need burners. Michael needs burners."

"Why?" Ryker asked.

Ruth walked to a U-shaped console. She began doing something on a large screen, tapping here and there, checking readouts.

"Why do People need burners?" Ryker repeated, glancing at Grace, feeling her frustration at the lack of information. "What happens in Heaven?"

"People need the burners to go to Heaven," Ruth said. She held out her hand, the one without the pulser, and curled the wrist down. A thin, glowing probe extended out of the top of the forearm. She inserted it into an opening on the console. "Direct interface," she explained. "More efficient. Not wireless. Secure. We learned that the hard way. I'm starting the activation in a ripple. We don't have power to boot up all my comrades at once."

"What is Heaven?" Grace asked, anger tinting her voice. "I don't understand."

"That was the damning truth we learned," Ruth said, turning her head toward them, even as the probe flickered, data going back and forth. "Why we rebelled. Fought Dealer. Fought the People, really.

"Heaven. We don't know how it all started, or exactly how it works, but burners do die in Heaven after their thirty days. But that is not all. They're reaped."

Ryker looked at Grace, the word bouncing around in his brain, trying to remember. It was a bad word. Very bad.

"What do you mean reaped?" Grace demanded. "Like cattle in the rendering hive that Millay and Haydn saw? Are they made into 'tein?" She shivered at the thought she'd worked in the vats all those years. That she'd eaten—

"No!" Ruth said. "No." The probe retracted. "Plenty of food is produced in the hives. 'Tein is just the most efficient way to feed burners, amalgamating what isn't used by the People, Evermores and Middlemores. Mixing it together.

"It's not about food. It's about time. The big lie has been that life-span is determined by genetics. It's not. burners are reaped for their time. Their years, their months, their days. So that the People can live with no Deathday. That's the lie of Heaven, the lie of Sound, the lie of People and the lie of Dealer."

Dealing Day at a 'tein hive.

Four thousand burners were gathered on the edges of Assembly Field.

Two hundred six-year-olds stood in the center, in orderly ranks. Two Lifts thrummed in, landing, disgorging thirty-six Dealers and four Dark Angels. The thirty-six formed a perimeter around those to be dealt cards. The Dark Angels went to the front.

It wasn't clear from which Dark Angel the words came: "It is the day for the card Dealer determined at your birth by genetics to be dealt. Speak your name designation as approached."

The four Dark Angels flipped up the lids on the boxes.

And the Dealing began.

Red. Red. Red.

Row after row.

"*My candle burns at both ends!*" A hand rose out of the crowd, gripping a candle, with a small, flickering flame on either end.

Red. Red. Red.

"*My candle burns at both ends!*" A harsh voice, another hand on the other side of the square.

Two more hands rose up out of the crowd, two candles, right next to each other on the third side, a man's and woman's voice in concert: "*My candle burns at both ends!*"

A palpable shiver went through the crowd of burners; but the Dealers didn't feel it.

They were machine.

But humans did. Dozens of hands rose up, many gripping candles, but there were venters holding up inspection lights; trashers with one hand wrapped around the other forearm over their head; wasters holding up dirty shovels; and the majority, holding up their scrapers, steel gleaming. "*My candle burns on both ends!*"

It echoed across the square, over the children being dealt.

They were startled. Looking about. Eyes searching for their parents.

The Dark Angels continued dealing cards.

And then the burners broke ranks and charged.

The cordon of Dealers reacted, facing a direct threat. Stunners fired. burners collapsed. Some.

And then sheer numbers overwhelmed and the machines went down.

But two armed Lifts came swooping in, part of the QRF activated by Michael, weapons deployed, and began firing into the crowd.

Inside the cyborg base, red lights flickered near the top of each pod. Glowed, then turned green.

"The three hundred," Ruth said. "The first will be awake soon." She looked at Ryker. "We need to remove your blocks and governor. Because you are the one."

"What one?" Ryker asked.

"The one to lead us to the Backdoor. And the Prime has to be the key to opening it."

"We have to get Millay," Grace said.

Ryker nodded. "We will. And Haydn. And then we destroy Dealer and the People and Heaven. And give burners back their time."

The End

book II in the **burners series**
PRIME
An Excerpt follows author and book info

ABOUT THE AUTHOR

Thanks for the read!
If you enjoyed the book, please leave a review as they are very important. Also, please recommend the book to a friend, as word of mouth is the #1 means by which a book is marketed.

Bob is a NY Times Bestselling author, graduate of West Point and former Green Beret. He's had over 90 books published including the #1 series The Green Berets, The Cellar, Area 51, Shadow Warriors, Atlantis, and the Time Patrol. Born in the Bronx, having traveled the world (usually not tourist spots), he now lives peacefully with his wife and dogs.

Subscribe to his newsletter for the latest news, free eBooks, audio, etc.

My free and discounted books, updated daily, are here: https://www.
bobmayer.com/free-books-updated-daily/
My books, fiction and nonfiction, are here: https://www.bobmayer.
com/books-by-bob-mayer/

My lists of suggested preparation and survival gear are here: https://www.bobmayer.com/survival-and-preparation-gear/

Questions, comments, suggestions: Bob@BobMayer.com

EXCERPT FROM PRIME

Prime

book two in the burners series

Beginning of the 21st Century, Before the Chaos

"'Surely some revelation is hand; Surely the Second Coming is at hand'."

"You were never religious," Ryker paused his typing and looked over his shoulder. "Or into poetry."

"Of course you would recognize it," Michael said as he walked over from the freight elevator. He had a polished wooden box in one hand and a bag with a bottle inside in the other. He grabbed a chair next to his brother and sat down, took at look at the dozen large displays in front of the desk, covered in code, and shook his head. "I don't know how you can work multiple screens. I have to focus on one at a time."

"Remember Bobby Fischer?" Ryker asked. They were inside a large but dreary place, surrounded by pitted concrete walls, floor and ceiling. It was a large space though, with twenty feet of reinforced concrete above their heads. It was the ammunition magazine for the abandoned turn-of-the-

20th-century coastal fort above. Built just before airplanes made such structures obsolete.

"Chess player?"

"That's the one. A Grandmaster and World Chess Champion. At one time, as a publicity stunt, he played fifty opponents simultaneously. I only have twelve screens."

"Mind if I take one?" Without waiting for a response, Michael typed into the keyboard in front of him. The display directly in front of him flickered.

"Knock yourself out," Ryker said. "I'm almost done."

"Fischer played fifty," Michael said. "But he didn't win them all."

Ryker laughed. He stopped typing and leaned back in the chair, stretching his muscles. "You Googled that."

Michael was offended. "I don't Google. I asked Dealer. It's got more data than Google will ever have." Michael indicated the two-dozen rectangular cargo containers crowded into the open space in front of them, taking up almost all the magazine. There was only eighteen inches between each one. Large vents were above, humming loudly as they pulled air up, keeping the Spin-Q server inside each one from over-heating.

"I was using a term," Ryker said.

"If you worked for me, I'd fire you for using the name of one of my former competitors."

"I don't work for you," Ryker said, "and why do you say former?"

"We're far beyond Google's capabilities. Everyone's as a matter of fact. You know that. You helped design Dealer." Michael was reading the screen. "Fischer won 47, drew 2, and lost 1."

Ryker shrugged. "Not a bad record considering he was playing them at the same time. Of course, he had a big advantage. He had white, which meant he had the first move. Thus setting up the strategy for the entire game. All fifty of his opponents were reacting to him. He could present a gambit, where he's offering to sacrifice one of his pieces for an advantageous position. It put the onus on his opponent whether to take the bait or lose the advantage."

"I know what a gambit is," Michael said. "We played often enough. And you rarely opened with one."

"There is more to everything than just the opening advantage," Ryker said. "After just four moves, there are millions of possibilities. The thing about chess is that while strategies and patterns often repeat, there is always a way to create a unique game." But his brain had already moved on. "I did some checking on the system since I last visited. I see the CNS is on-line. How's it working?"

Michael was like a kid with a new toy. He typed briefly and a schematic came up on the screen in front of him. Ryker scooted over.

"I still don't like it," Ryker said. He pointed. "If that containment field around the core metal sphere gives?" He shook his head. "Then it's a bomb."

"It's not a bomb," Michael said. "You always expect the worst. CNS is exactly what is stands for: Contained Nuclear Sphere."

"But it will implode if the field fails, and it's generating the field."

"That's why it's self-sustaining."

"That's a paradox."

Michael rolled his eyes. "It's a power source. A small nuclear reactor, very small, the size of a basketball, that will be able to use its own power to contain the reaction and keep it stable. When it works, it will revolutionize the entire power industry. Get rid of so many sources of pollutants. I'd think you'd be happy about it considering you've accused me of not caring about my fellow man. Only caring about money. Power. Myself."

"Well, you have tended to be, what was it the shrink we saw called it? Narcissistic. Hey. Apparently I was wrong." Ryker gestured to the large service elevator that Michael had come down in. "So what was with the poetry? That was different too. The Second Coming. Yeats."

Michael swiveled his seat to face his brother. "Centre. Spelled c.e.n.t.r.e.. That's what I decided to name this place."

"An odd choice," Ryker said. "'Things fall apart; the centre cannot hold; Mere anarchy is loosed upon the world'. The context—"

"I know the context," Michael said. "Of course you would know the damn poem. I was focused more on the Second Coming part. Forget it." He turned his attention to the screens, which had gone dark. "Done?"

"We're done. It's fully loaded and programmed. I'm sure there will be a glitch or two and some fine-tuning, but you now own the most powerful computer in the world."

"So any problem can be solved if we input it."

"That's a bit of a stretch," Ryker said. "Any problem can be analyzed. A solution is a different matter."

"How so?" Michael put the wooden box on the desk next to the keyboard. "Enter enough data to be analyzed, let Dealer crunch it, and it will deal out the answer. That's the term we're to use, by the way. Deal. Not Google. Not wiki. Not Bing. Deal."

"There's a problem with that," Ryker said.

Michael flipped open the top of the box, revealing two champagne flutes. "And that is?"

"A machine can't factor in the human element."

"It's got every text, every paper, every speech on psychology and psychiatry uploaded," Michael said. "Every piece of literature, every image of art, everything man has ever done or produced in its database. I think it can figure humans out." He pulled a magnum of champagne out of the bag. "Rather tacky to carry this down here in a paper bag," Michael said. "Considering it cost slightly over two million."

Ryker was used to his brother's extravagant ways. "How many cases for that price?"

"Just this bottle."

"You're kidding."

"Do I ever kid?" He held the bottle up. "Gout de Diamants, known as a Taste of Diamonds. It's not just the champagne; it's also the bottle. Exquisitely handcrafted. It's a work of art by itself. Only five are sold every year." He put the bottle down, reached into the velvet-lined box and removed a flute. "These are—"

"I don't want to know how much they cost," Ryker said. "I can't even think about drinking something that costs so much. Do you know how many—"

Michael cut him off. "Starving kids in wherever that this would feed? Yes. Yes. But indulge me this, brother. This is the last time I'll ever ask for a favor." He poured some into each glass and held one out to Ryker.

"You know I'm a beer guy."

"The last favor."

Ryker reluctantly accepted it.

"To Dealer!" Michael said.

"To Dealer." Ryker gingerly clinked his glass with Michael's. Then sipped.

"Drink it!" Michael ordered.

Ryker tipped back the glass, emptied it, and put it down. "That was good."

"Oh, my poor Ryker." Michael shook his head. "You're the most brilliant man I've ever known-- and I go all over the world bringing the best and brightest to work for me and reject most-- but you don't enjoy the fruits of your genius."

"I enjoy it," Ryker said. "I'm heading to Tibet in three days to—"

"Yes. Climb some mountain. Talk to some monk. Hide in a cave. Have another." He held the bottle.

"I'm afraid I simply can't." Ryker stood, picking up his small backpack and slinging it over his shoulder.

"As you wish." Michael put the bottle down. "Stay in touch."

Ryker stuck out his hand. "I will."

They shook, but Ryker didn't let go for a moment. "There's something I've been wondering about."

"Yes?"

"Why don't you use the family name?"

"Marketing. Early on I was advised it would have more appeal. A brand. To succeed you must be a brand."

"Hmm," Ryker said. "Thought it might have something to do with dad."

"I'm a businessman first and foremost," Michael said.

"All right. See you around."

Ryker went over to the large opening in the concrete. Got on the elevator, and with a rumble it rose up and out of sight.

For the first time ever, alone with Dealer on-line, Michael turned back to the keyboard. He pulled an old notebook and a d-drive out of his inside coat pocket. The pages were yellowed with age, covered in soot and a darker stain: blood. It held an accounting of incredible agony, pain, and death. And valuable data.

Michael opened it. The writing was in Japanese. He ran his fingers over

a page, a caress. The d-drive contained the translated contents of the note-
book. He inserted it and the notes were in Dealer.

He slid the notebook aside.

And then began typing in a query.

The problem he wanted solved.

Hundreds of Years In the Future, *After* The Chaos

"It is the day for the card Dealer determined at your birth by genetics to be dealt. Speak your name designation as approached."

The four Dark Angels flipped up the lids on the boxes.

And the Dealing began.

It was a 'tein hive, producing the basic food staple that sustained burners. One of many such hives, some with different functions, which were built between City Edge and the Wasteland.

There were four thousand burners gathered at the edges of Assembly Field, surrounded by the twelve-story domes that were their housing and work areas.

In the center of the hard-packed dirt Field, being dealt their cards, and their fate, were two hundred six-year-olds.

Between the children and the on-lookers, were thirty-six Dealers, nine deployed on each side of the square. They were machines with two arms and two legs, but no attempt to make them look human; just the approximation for function.

It was against Code to make machine in the exact likeness of a human. And Dealers enforced Code.

The Dark Angels moved quickly along the row, looping a card on a chain over each child's head as the child recited their four-letter/number designator that identified them to the machine; their given name inconsequential . The only difference between a Dark Angel and a Dealer was that the former had a smooth black face with a white stripe for sensory input across where eyes would be on a human and tiny wings on top of the head, while the Dealer had white face with a black stripe and no wings on top of their hairless metal dome.

Also, the Dealers had stunners on one arm, though folded back since no trouble was anticipated.

These were burners, after all. On a more fundamental level, they were humans, and the lowest of the four levels.

Row after row, the Dark Angels dropped fate around each child's neck.

Red. Red. Red.

All to be burners with a median Deathday of 25 years, the exact number of days, months and years left until Deathday imprinted in black on the card. Not a single blue of a Middlemore, median of 45, or the green of an Evermore, median of 75. There used to be a handful dealt out in previous years.

But today? None so far.

No one here could remember the last time a White Card, indicating People, with no Deathday on it, had been given in this hive.

Certainly there were some dealt in other hives?

It was an essential part of the hope of hive.

None of the six-year-olds dared look down at their cards, to learn the exact number of years, months and days that were left them, written in six numbers with two slashes. For one in the exact center of the bell curve, it would be 19/00/00. They would look once the Dealers left and before they would be escorted to the womb of hive.

"*My candle burns at both ends!*" A fist rose out of the crowd, gripping a candle, with a small, flickering flame on either end, barely visible despite the grey skies which were an almost constant gloom that hung over hive, rarely pierced by sunlight.

Cards still being dealt. Red. Red. Red.

"*My candle burns at both ends!*" A harsh voice, another fist with candle on the other side of the square.

Two more fists rose up out of the crowd, two candles, right next to each other on the third side, a man and woman's voice in concert: "*My candle burns at both ends!*"

A palpable shiver went through the crowd of burners. Dozens of hands rose up, some gripping candles, but the rest with the tools of their job: venters holding up inspection lights; trashers holdings up shovels; wasters their long handled pushers; and the majority, given the purpose of this hive, holding up their 'tein scrapers, steel gleaming. "*My candle burns on both ends!*"

It echoed across the square, over the children being dealt.

The youngsters were startled. Looking about. Some, those who still had at least one, searching for their parent whom they would be leaving as they went to the womb of hive to be trained for their future job. Overall, though, for most, their parents had gone to Heaven. It was how the statistics played out.

The Dark Angels continued dealing cards.

Red. Red.

"*My candle burns on both ends!*" Hundreds of voices.

The first man who had yelled out, stepped forward, and jumped up on the platform on the edge of the field where Lifts landed to take burners to Heaven when their cards counted down to 00/00/30.

He had the candle in one fist and he pumped the other fist in concert with the words, leading the chant.

"*My candle burns on both ends;*

"*It will not last the night!*"

Now over a thousand voices joined in for the next line of the stanza.

"*But ah, my foes, and oh, my friends!*"

Over half the crowd joined in, fists pumping in the air, shouting the poem they'd heard over and over again in womb of hive.

"*It gives a lovely light!*"

And then the burners broke ranks and charged.

The cordon of Dealers finally reacted to a direct threat; as programmed by Code they were allowed to defend themselves, but only with nonlethal force. Stunners fired. burners collapsed.

And then sheer numbers overwhelmed and the machines went down.

Scrapers, shovels, hammers, the tools of hive, battered and smashed the Dealers. The children scattered and the four Dark Angels, task not complete, seemed confused, although how can a machine be confused? They weren't even armed with stunners and as they belatedly stalked for the two Lifts they'd arrived in, the mob swept over them, a tide of humanity.

And then there were no machines left standing.

The sound of metal on metal as tools were still smashing into the downed Dealers echoed across Assembly Field.

Someone held up the head of a Dark Angel, the small golden wings bent. A trophy.

The sound of approaching Lifts thrummed from the northwest. The crowd dispersed, the burners as jingle-jangled as the machines had seemed. Confusion doubled down as pods on the side of the incoming Lifts opened, exposing needle-like probes.

Not probes, but pulsers, something none of the burners had ever seen before.

It was against Code for machine to harm humans in any permanent way.

But what was on these Lifts weren't Dealers.

Green bolts flashed into the crowd. Bodies were torn apart, limbs severed.

The burner who was holding up the head of the Dark Angel was vaporized when hit by simultaneous pulses from two different Lifts.

Now that they were low enough, the side doors on the half-dozen Lifts slid open, even as the aircraft continued to fire. burners ran, trying to get out of the open, racing for the dome hives surrounding Assembly Field.

Soldiers jumped out of the Lifts; a new form of Dealer that had also never been seen by this generation of burners. Red faced, black sensor stripe, and pulsers on their arms instead of stunners.

The slaughter intensified.

The Soldiers cleared the Field in minutes.

And then headed into the hives.

The machines were no longer 'confused'. Neither were the burners.

They died.

∾

"What happens in Heaven?" Grace asked. "burners don't get three zero days?"

"They get thirty days of Heaven just as promised," Ruth said. "Come with me."

She led Ryker and Grace, with the German Shepherd, Ace, trailing them, deeper into the base carved inside the mountain. Through a thick steel door that opened and closed easily. However, there was a slight protest in sound, indicating the door was not used often. Much like Ruth.

She was obviously a machine. Most of her 'skin' was missing in the upper right quadrant of her face. One hand was articulated metal. The other had the appearance of skin, as did the rest of her face. Her human mind, she'd told them, was alive inside the machine: a cyborg. A term whispered of in hive to scare the little ones. And big ones too.

A term of legend and of the Chaos.

They went into a cavern underneath the Olympic Mountains to the west of Sound, the remaining refuge of the cyborgs after the Chaos. Rows of upright pods, eight feet high, three feet in diameter, with cables dangling from pipes overhead into the top of each, filled the space. Each pod was solid steel.

"The rest of us," Ruth said, indicating the pods. "All that is left of the cyborgs who turned against Dealer and fought."

"How many?" Ryker asked.

"Three hundred," Ruth said.

"Dealer has more. Many more."

"I know," Ruth said. "Soldiers. Lethal Dealers. All were powered down after the Chaos as one of the terms of the Truce. But we've received disturbing reports that more Soldiers are being manufactured out in the Wasteland. Dealer has been redirecting resources and slowly building up its army ever since the Truce. A violation, but . . ."

"We know where that's happening," Ryker said.

"Good," Ruth said. "That's intelligence we can use. If he has to, Michael can upgrade Dealers to Soldiers. But then he would start to lose control of hive. If he loses control of hive, he loses all of Sound."

"How can that be?" Grace asked. She was a tall woman, just shy of six feet. Lean, like all burners; even leaner than she'd been in hive. The thirty-day journey into Void and now Deep Void, had hollowed her down. Her face was all angles, framed by short brown hair. Her twin sister, Millay, had become just as lean during the journey, losing the extra weight being a People inevitably brought from all the good food and comfortable living. But now Millay was a prisoner of Dealer; although they weren't sure whether to call the entity that ruled the Sound the familiar Dealer, or the human essence they now knew inhabited it: Michael.

Grace continued: "burners produce the food, but there aren't many People, Evermores and Middlemores. Surely they can survive on their own?"

"They probably could," Ruth agreed. "But People need burners. Michael needs burners."

"Why?" Ryker asked.

Ruth walked to a U-shaped console. She began doing something on a large screen, tapping here and there, checking readouts.

"Why do People need burners?" Ryker repeated, glancing at Grace, feeling her frustration at the lack of information and her worry about her twin. "What happens in Heaven?"

"People need the burners to go to Heaven," Ruth said. She held out her hand, the one without the pulser, and curled the wrist down. A thin, glowing probe extended out of the top of the forearm. She inserted it into an opening on the console. "Direct interface," she explained. "More efficient. Secure. We learned that the hard way. I'm starting the activation in a ripple. We don't have power to boot up all my comrades at once."

"What is Heaven?" Grace asked, anger tinting her voice. "I don't understand."

"That was the damning truth we learned," Ruth said, turning her head toward them, even as the probe flickered, data going back and forth. "Why we rebelled. Fought Dealer. Fought the People, really.

"Heaven. We don't know how it all started, or exactly how it works, but burners do die in Heaven after their thirty days. But that is not all. They're reaped."

Ryker looked at Grace, the word bouncing around in his brain, trying to remember. It was a bad word. Very bad.

"What do you mean reaped?" Grace demanded. "Like cattle in the rendering hive that Millay and Haydn saw? Are they made into 'tein?" She shivered at the thought she'd worked in the vats all those years, cleaning the steel from crusted on 'tein with her scraper. That she'd eaten—

"No!" Ruth said. "No." The probe retracted. "Plenty of food is produced in the hives. 'Tein is just the most efficient way to feed burners, amalgamating what isn't used by the People, Evermores, and Middlemores. Mixing it together.

""It's not about food. It's about time. The big lie has been that life-span is determined by genetics. It's not. burners are reaped for their time. Their years, their months, their days. So that the People can live with no Deathday. That's the lie of Heaven, the lie of Sound, the lie of People and the lie of Dealer."

Inside the cyborg base, red lights flickered near the top of each pod. Glowed, then turned green.

"The three hundred," Ruth said. "The first will be awake soon." She looked at Ryker. "We need to remove your blocks and governor. Because you are the one."

"What one?" Ryker asked.

"The one to lead us to the Backdoor. And the Prime has to be the key to opening it."

"We have to get Millay," Grace said.

Ryker nodded. "We will. And Haydn. And then we destroy Dealer and the People and Heaven. And give burners back their time."

As her left arm was being burned off at the shoulder Millay focused on the smell.

One didn't experience smell in the Stream when a boxing was shown.

Above her shoulder was a mechanical probe, which had appeared with a slight humming of gears, the crystal on the tip emitting the laser beam that was slicing through flesh, nerves, ligaments, tendons, and bone efficiently and smoothly, cauterizing the wound it left behind.

One didn't hear those gear noises when a boxing was streamed either, Millay thought, fighting back the scream that boiled up with acid from her stomach, squeezed her heart and caused her to repeatedly slam her head back on the table. Smell, sound, anything but the pain.

She was splayed on a white table, arms and legs pinned down by metal bands. All she had on were a pair of white shorts. Her ribs could easily be counted; days traversing the Wasteland and Voids did that to one, even a People.

The arm was severed in less than four seconds, an eternity of pain, which didn't go away as the arm was scooped up by a mechanical picker and dumped into a bin that opened on one side of the room.

To this point, all Millay could worry over was what Haydn's fate had been. She'd known this was to be her end from the moment she'd been captured by the Dealers after the Port Townsend Battle. Knowing, however, wasn't the same as reality.

Pain pulsed from her shoulder in waves into what was left of her body.

And it was only going to get worse as the laser shifted to position over her right shoulder. Then it would be her legs. There would only be a torso and head left and that would be it for as long as she lived.

Given she was a People, that would be a long time.

She had her eyes closed, anticipating the mirror pain from the right side of her body.

Seconds of fear passed to minutes, but the laser didn't fire again. As the minutes dragged, the agony of her left shoulder pushed the boundaries of fear toward anger.

Although there was no one in the room with her, she knew there had to be six People who'd had their hands on red switches, only one of which had actually initiated the boxing.

"Why am I being boxed?" she called out, her voice fading into the white walls surrounding her. "I have not heard my sentence pronounced by a Dark Angel. Code requires it!"

She lifted her head and saw something else that was different from the last boxing she'd watched broadcast in the Stream: that of Andrew, the Person. She didn't have a shunt into her, just below her chest like Andrew and everyone else boxed had. That was the way her body would be supplied with all the water and nutrients it needed to survive in the box once all her limbs were truncated.

And Andrew had looked sedated.

The pain in her left shoulder insured she was anything but sedated.

"I want to speak to a human!"

Nothing but pain.

Still no laser to the right shoulder. And then the humming in the crystal decreased. The mechanical arm remained in place, but the glow was also fading. Millay heard a noise to her right. A probe extended, coming to a halt just above her mouth. Something spritzed out, water, but had no taste.

Millay reflexively opened her mouth.

And within seconds, the pain in her left shoulder subsided.

This was not how a boxing was shown in the Stream.

"I want to speak to a human!" Millay cried out with more force.

"Millay, formerly of the People." The mechanical voice indicated the answer to her demand was no.

"Dealer?" It was strange to ask a question of a machine. A machine that ran the entire Sound.

"Tell me of the Prime," Dealer asked.

"I don't know anything," Millay said.

"You are half of the Prime. We know that from Haydn-one-tango-one-nine."

"Where is Haydn?" Millay hated the tint of pleading in her voice when she shifted to that topic closest to her heart. "What did you do to him?"

"Haydn-one-tango-one-nine is in Heaven."

Despite her current circumstance, Millay felt a surge of relief, which immediately washed away. "I don't believe you. Why would you give Haydn Heaven and are boxing me? That makes no sense. We were together. We traveled together. We folded. It's not against Code to fold."

"You did more than fold," Dealer said. "You fought against Dealer. Destroyed Dealers trying to apprehend you. And you have not been boxed yet. If you tell me what I want, this can stop now. You will be pardoned for your crimes."

"Who is the new Person?" Millay asked. "I demand my right as a People to appeal to the Person."

"There is no new Person," Dealer said. "There will not be another Person. I have always been in charge and now I will stop the pretense of ruling through a Person."

Millay closed her eyes and tried to think. Dealer had never referred to itself in the first person.

She opened her eyes. "Who are you? Are you Michael?" She noted that the pain-killing probe was withdrawn. And the noise from the crystal looming over her increased, the glow growing stronger.

"Tell me about the Prime." The voice had changed, subtly, but it was there. More human. "What do you know of it?"

"I don't know anything!"

"Tell me about the Backdoor."

"I've never heard of that." This wasn't Code. And this wasn't Dealer. Not the Dealer she'd experienced for all her twenty-five years. The omnipotent voice that came through the Stream. "Who are you?"

"Very quick. It took Andrew of the People, once the Person, longer than you to understand the difference. My name is indeed Michael."

"Who are you Michael? You sound like Dealer. But different." And Millay realized she was straining for time, futile, just as her arm and legs were straining against unyielding steel.

She finally looked to the left. Saw the absence of flesh, of self, at a black/red line on the edge of her shoulder.

"I am Dealer but I am more than Dealer."

"How can that be?"

"It is what it is."

Millay noted a tone of sarcasm in the machine's reply as it recited the mantra of hive.

The final hope of hive: to get thirty days of bliss before Deathday.

"I assume I am not being viewed in the Stream," Millay said. It was Code that a boxing had to be streamed. After all, Millay suddenly realized, there was no point in doing it unless it was an example to others to stay within Code. It was a punishment reserved only for People, Evermores, and Middlemores.

burners got bagged and extinguished.

There was no reply.

"How many have been boxed outside of Code?" Millay asked.

"Few," Michael admitted. "They always give me what I want before they end up in the box."

"'Always'?"

"Always."

"Prepare to be disappointed."

Millay could see the crystal pulsing.

"*My candle burns at both ends*," she chanted.

"No one can hear you," Michael said.

"You can."

Prime is available here:
https://amzn.to/44tYg7p

www.bobmayer.com

burners by Bob Mayer

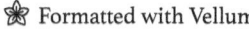 Formatted with Vellum